RUZNIEL

Book Two
The End of the Universe

Daniel Nanavati

artwork
Jennika Bastian

Ruzniel Book 2
Footsteps Press First Edition
Americana and PT Serif

Typeset by Drupath Hutingali

ISBN 978-1-908867-75-9

Any Resemblance to real Magicians, Ruzniel and Magical Folk is entirely on purpose and taken from the original translation of the Laws of Magic. The words of the poems spoken by Rimfelder are here republished with permission as are the excerpts from the Book of Derivations which is one of my most precious possessions. The descriptions of the äis and onäis were taken from the only copy of the plans for Trecrogo in existence in any universe.
How did I come to see it, you may wonder?
That, also, is another story ...

Synopsis

In 'The Laws of Magic', we sat with the Sangyma as they discussed the coming end of the universe and the final battle with Crilodach. We learned that Crilodach was the first living being, a fact that had made It selfish, cruel and unconquerable.

We met Midrak Earthshaker, Lilah's brother, and the Ruzniel Tobia. We discovered how they both embodied the spirits of two great Sangyma, Fulminar and Tegriel.

We adventured with Lilah as she saved Midrak's life fighting the mind-twisting Lazab, and as she aided the Arvernat in what she thought was their final battle before their world was destroyed by Crilodach's armies.

We walked with the clone of the last human being, Demeter and his teacher Chloe, until they found the magnificent fortress Trecrogo. Here they met with the bear Copret. We watched as they fought the huge army arraigned against them.

We travelled with the poet Rimfelder as he set out on a quest across Xibalba to find the magic in his words, free the dragon brothers and uncover one of the precious Sagitæ.

We learned that the Sagitæ are three jewels known to have survived the Big Crunch and the Big Bang. Crilodach seeks them hoping they hold the secret to It survival and so eternal life.

We read about the Laws of Magic as written by Filvani and we found out that there are particles of magic all over the universe and that every atom must be part of a living being before the universe can come to an end.

We saw Opiar die and joined Lilah's ambush against Crilodach's armada in which she and Tethval were wounded. We found the Sangyma Gertis hiding in the labyrinth Hagôn with an army of heroes long thought lost.

Finally we met Mojolo magically saved to spend her last two days of life fighting on Trecrogo with the gift of the living hair given her by the Sangyma, Sanjava...

Chapters

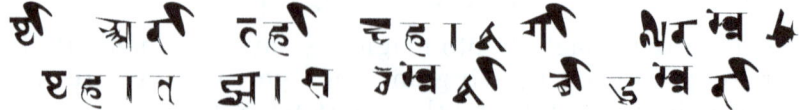

The Beginning of Prophecy

Ruzniel have to get used to astonishing changes. The often distressing variety of surroundings that naturally flow from living and working with magicians would perplex the unprepared. Craziness, of course, exists amongst all living beings but the confusion generated around the complex lives of magicians is extreme.

This craziness is so varied Ruzniel have to study three years to understand a tenth of what they are up against. One moment one thing that may or may not threaten your life, another moment another thing so completely different you would be forgiven for thinking you had a whole new life. That is, if your first thought was not whether or not this new event was also life threatening. Most of us have never planet-hopped like magical folk, plummeting pell-mell through the Ossendark, getting sucked back in time by the Upala, or rubbing shoulders with strange, weird sounding animals (though some of us do.) Going from one planet to another is quite fun the first time, but I wonder what you would think after four hundred or so times. That would get to us all after a while. All the muddy feet, torn clothes, sand in ears, muscle aching, eye tiring, back aching, sore throat, ripped nail times make you just want things to stop for a few hours so you can sleep, think, eat and simply calm down. When you are with a Sangyma, with Zaqui round the corner and an eternity of fighting hanging in the balance, you will not get a choice to do any of the normal things of life, and you are certainly not offered time to pack.

Lessons in Planetology are considered amongst the most important in the academies on Ruz. You must not show any shock. You must keep a level head. You must always be ready for danger. Along with the practicals on the best way to get sand out of your ears while running, mud out of your shoes while jumping and how to make flatbread which keeps for weeks, can be put into a mud free, inside pocket and tastes

1

delicious in all weather conditions. Magicians are not surprised that keeping clean and cooking are two important classes in the academies, but this fact astonishes everyone else.

Tobia, whose memory had fully returned, had done this training. She was not shocked by where she was or what had happened. Especially as they had been in Hâgon, then Damkina, without being touched by It, which was truly astonishing. She had dusted the table in Its lair which would never be on anyone's list of the one hundred things you want to do before you die. However, for all her training, she did feel some astonishment because she was experiencing one thing no Ruzniel had ever experienced before.

What shook her was seeing Tegriel large as life, standing a little way away from her. Well not exactly seeing. Her eyes were still blind but she saw him inside her head quite clearly although he was no longer a part of her. Just as she had as a cockroach, her ability to sense the world around her had stayed with her in the journey through the Upala. All the grass, trees and plants were arranged in her head in colour. She could have run through them with ease. The sun above them, the clouds, the fact they were on the edge of a plain, were all perfectly visualized without her eyes.

She felt let down for more than a few moments by this new sensation. She had not been blind that long but she had become very used to Tegriel's voice in her head and in her way, she had felt safe with his being a part of her. Now she felt she had lost something. Her delight in knowing he was alive was mixed with a touch of melancholy at realizing he could take off without her at any moment.

She took in her surroundings very quickly to try to take her mind off this separation. She was sitting up feeling the air, as cold as ice, sweeping down the unusually high mountains which were recently covered with snow. A snow which had now almost gone leaving the rocks peppered with lichen and odd scratches of names and dates left by passing animals. Despite the cold air she sensed the warm sunlight on her skin. A bright, yet lonely, sun. She saw in her head the blue sky woven with clouds high above her. The air was pure. Cleaner than she ever remembered any air being before. Filling her lungs and lifting her spirits at the same time. As she moved for the first time, she felt aches in her muscles from the exertions of the past few days. Even her

2

bones ached. She had failed to realize how much she had been bruised in her travels and by the knocks and bumps she had sustained as a cockroach. Her shoulders sported two huge bruises from where she had bounced off Midrak's back onto the floor entering Crilodach's lair.

She stood up. Usually when Ruzniel travel like this they are always standing when they arrive but she was sitting. She assumed that had something to do with the fact that Tegriel's spirit had separated from her. Powerful magic can knock you off your feet. She was about to say something to him when the fears that had riven her mind for the past days vanished in the instant she heard a bird singing. She knew this species; a bright red, long tailed spring visitor. In her time the red–feathered Latchet only lived on Ruz. For an instant she thought she might see her father again and she was filled with pleasure at the silly idea. So much so that the emptiness in her stomach vanished and she was overcome with a feeling that all things have their place and everything happens for a reason, and after all they had endured she was somewhere beautiful. Home. A home though, she knew, long before her father was even born.

A few feet away Tegriel slowly gathered the magical essence that was his, to harden in the sunlight like a butterfly's wings drying after struggling out of the chrysalis. Clothing himself in the fibres of the plants around him while his skin and hair shone and the sun remade his eyes and fingernails. The long, green tunic and close fitting neck–scarf of blue. The short–stemmed, strong grass that made an excellent hat. Smooth mosses wrapping his fingers in gloves. The inner fibres of sedges stitching everything together. He brushed back the brown hair from his eyes and ears and stood for a few moments in thought. She saw all the grandeur of the Sangyma her father had painted. She quickly visualized he looked the same despite being far in his own past. Time–travel through the Upala did not change one's age. What she did not understand yet was she had witnessed Tegriel's birth. That in a magical way she was partly his mother. That everything that was to be was because she had been alive just before Zaqui. In his Book of Derivations Filvani writes,

The Individual Is Dependent Upon Every Other Individual That Has Ever Lived

Tegriel's feelings were different from Tobia's. Being part

of her had been a necessity that had saved his life and brought him here, but had also limited his powers. He did not like to see people in danger when he could not help them. He eased his shoulders back and swayed his head in slow circles as if getting used to having muscles again. He was worried, too, about how their allies were all doing in the future they had just left, in the final battle he would not join, and what was going to happen to them in that incredible struggle. But though he worried he knew his path was to meet Fulminar for the first time (as far as Fulminar would know), to meet and know thousands he would come to love because he loved them already. In many ways his path was the strangest of all that the Sangyma had to follow. To prepare the ground for endless battles, yet never to know if what he did ensured Lilah succeeded or failed at Zaqui. He had no magic to help him pull back that veil. That was why he told Filvani the most important of all things is knowledge, because the one thing he wanted to know, the one thing that could give a roundness to his life and satisfaction to his endless toil, he would never know nor find anyone who could tell him. Tobia heard him mumbling under his breath, got up and moved towards him.

"Are you alright?" she asked, brushing back her hair.

"Perfectly," he told her, not immediately looking down at her face.

"Was our separation meant to happen?"

"Yes. Only one Ruzniel can pass through the bejal to the past at a time. We had to make sure not many people would use the Upala so we limited the bejal's power."

"Why only one?"

"If I could not keep tabs on everyone who ever used this unique magic, they could inadvertently upset my work. I had to be within a Ruzniel to get here and letting my body pass away was not from defeat as It thought but from necessity. Fusion with another is a little trick Crilodach has never known."

"You knew we'd be coming here from that day when you saw me with my father," she said.

"How could I have failed to recognize my greatest companion? I knew you would be there. I had taken a keen interest in your family from the beginning, tracing your bloodlines with great care. I would not allow any of them to be companions to preserve their lives for this very reason."

"Did you need the Ruzniel you chose that day or was the whole Choosing a charade?"

"I took him to a friend and as far as I know he had great success, as do we if I manage to keep us on the same path."

"So far I've accomplished very little."

"You are important to the cosmos in ways you cannot imagine."

"Are you being serious with me?"

"You do not believe me?"

"I'm always where the action is but not because I planned to be. I spent all my time with Midrak following his lead. I was easily overrun by the enemy sitting with Lilah."

"Few geniuses have ever felt their genius. They are simply as they are, and you are simply Tobia, a Ruzniel who is not simple at all. We who know you, can judge your worth far better than you can. Trust me. Great things await. Great things."

"I'd trust you more if you didn't keep so much to yourself."

"Force of habit Tobia. I have had to be very careful about what I say and to whom, all my life. I cannot stop being cautious after such a long time. Perhaps there have been times I could have trusted people more but I have to try to make sure things are as they were. Otherwise I could be responsible for unknown consequences."

"You have to be watchful of absolutely everything?" she asked.

"Everything."

"That's an extremely hard way to live."

"Not compared to others who struggle against It," he told her. "I do know that with everything I will do, inspire and ask of our comrades, we get to within a day of Zaqui without It possessing a Sagitæ. That is a towering achievement."

"We Ruzniel are pretty much all or nothing people," she smiled back at him. "But I can't even begin to imagine how much knowledge is in your head."

"I knew everything up to the point in Damkina when we left. I knew my magic in this universe looped from the end to the beginning. All I knew that linked them was you. The constant fear I have is that our enemies could work out what I did, and change things."

"The stories of you being the greatest of the Sangyma are true."

"A necessary part of my aura and not at all true," he

argued. "We all serve the laws of magic in one way or another and no single Sangyma is more important than any other."

"We never met after that day in the academy. Weren't you taking a chance? What if Crilodach had heard of your strange behaviour in having a six year old chosen."

"It has no spies on Ruz. We did not need to meet for a while. I knew you as a blind Ruzniel and you were very much sighted. I secreted part of my magical being in your eyes that only became known to you when the attack by Crilodach's armies left you blind. That triggered my magic in you. My body had been dead quite a while by then."

"I'm more than happy for you to have made use of me, but couldn't you have stopped It blinding me?"

"Do you think I should have?"

"A friend would do that for a friend."

"You sound angry."

"Well you knew, yet made no move to prevent them blinding me. You didn't even warn me."

"And of course a Sangyma would have."

"I think so."

"And if I did not would that suggest something to you?"

"I ... suppose so."

"And that something might be?"

"That there is a greater purpose to my being blind than to my being sighted."

"The mind of a Ruzniel is very strong Tobia, you are a race that never yields. If my magical self was ever to be able to talk to you I needed you to look inward. Seek me out. Your blindness fully released me and because we were able to talk, I was able to guide you. I have always trusted your clear, inner sight."

"I can see you in my mind."

"That is the residue of my being within you. That sight will be invaluable to you in the times ahead. Talking about time," he changed the subject, "we have no more than an hour."

"Where are we going?"

"To see Kalevala. A friend of mine. Though he does not know he is a friend of mine yet or, for that matter, how long you two will know each other."

"The first spellmaker?"

"The very same."

"You have brought me back to a time of myths and

legends."

"You are part of those myths and will be a legend."

"How strange you must feel to know everything that'll happen."

"If what I know about our future is to be of any value to us, I must make sure nothing changes. The smallest sequence out of place and everything may change, then all the knowledge I have of what will be, will become utterly useless. Limiting the use of the Upala is just one of many things I have to do. In a strange way It did not understand, Crilodach's taking the Upala and keeping her locked up helped me. I could never have kept track if there had been thousands of Ruzniel going back into their past to alter events at their choosing. No one would brave Crilodach's lair just for a chance to go back who knows when, to do who knows what."

"How come I've no memory of this happening if this is my life too?"

"Because to you, your life is still going forwards. My life has gone back to ground I have already covered. I was born in the moment we arrived here but you were born far in the future."

"Tegriel, the Sangyma with no parents. Who came from nowhere to fight Crilodach. That is why there are so many myths about your father and mother."

"Not exactly from nowhere but you must never speak of how we got here. Never. Not even to those you will love. One whisper and Crilodach will destroy the Upala or kill the cockroach army and change everything. It must remain in the dark with only Its guesses and surmises. Crilodach is dangerous enough when It suspects something, but when It knows for sure, It is unstoppable."

"I won't say anything, I promise."

"Feel free to make something up. If I remember rightly one of those myths about my parents came from you."

"Why didn't you tell me all this before? Prepare me at least. I'm walking the universe before my ancestors were born. Just plain weird."

"You may have acted differently if I had said anything. Knowing the future can give one hubris. Make you want to change something, save someone, alter events. Always with the best intentions of course, but we have to stay the course. I have to be loyal to what I remember and keep everyone on their path."

"Doesn't Crilodach know anything about this at all?" she asked, running to keep up.

"The bejals are magical. You cannot hide great magic from It. That is why It stole the Upala, but when It thought It had killed many Sangyma including me It thought It had changed things anyway. It didn't realize I was still living, in you. You saved my life. As you were meant to do. Now It knows, of course, that some Sangyma live on and It knows how we have managed to but with Zaqui only a day away Crilodach is too late to change anything. That was very important to accomplish. In fact making sure Crilodach does not have a chance to alter matters is our greatest achievement — next to defeating It."

"You did all the work on that one," she observed.

"Tobia, believe me, I could not have achieved anything without you. You have enabled our fight to begin. What is more you still have a great deal to do and a great task ahead."

She was bursting to know what that task might be.

"Is It here yet?" she asked.

"Nothing is too far away from Crilodach. It is stretching out Its claws amongst the emerging worlds. The first peoples are gathering to decide how to deal with the menace they feel. As yet they do not know enough about It to know how to fight It but that knowledge will come."

"From us."

"We appear at the right moment. The Upala knew just when to send me. Somehow the Upala and the Sagitæ are connected. I never tried to find out how because there are some things that I, too, do not need to know but I have never solved the mystery of why Crilodach appeared at this exact time. The universe is already old, planets have formed, but only now does It decide to reveal Its existence. Its nature is such that It should have fallen on the first beings to evolve without hesitation."

"Some say the Sagitæ prevented Crilodach from interfering in the worlds for a long time."

"That is one explanation."

"I wonder why Crilodach didn't use the Upala, a perfect weapon for a creature like It. It would never have been defeated. It would have known we were here and be waiting for us."

"It probably gave some serious thought to trying."

"What do you think stopped It?" she asked.

"Can you imagine me coming back from later in time and meeting me?" She laughed as he said this and almost tripped over,

"That would be novel and somewhat confusing. I bet you'd both have a good chat and then go and play a joke on Fulminar."

"You see I came back as the essence of myself and found I am able to create my body. Crilodach could never do that. It would never limit Its essence enough to go into another being. It was the first being to taste life. Coming back It would not be unique. It would find Itself here. What would happen if Crilodach met Crilodach?"

"It has always been ruled by the belief Its the most powerful creature in the universe. It wouldn't tolerate another. They would fight."

"Exactly. Crilodach might well have wanted to use the Upala, but It is no fool. Even if my some incalculable magic It entered a Ruzniel, It knows It would face the one enemy against which It would be powerless. Itself. And if It developed any weapons or magic It could use to overpower Its past self, It would know we would sense that same magic. It would have given us a weapon against It. No, the Upala is one bejal Crilodach, who existed before the Upala was made, was prevented from ever using by Its own twisted nature."

"How do you know the Upala never existed before It?"

"Because I know who made the bejal work and she is a rare creature," he told her, stretching his arms.

"Who?" she asked, intrigued

"Hiesia. You are going to meet her soon. Right now though, I must get to Bofindle."

"I am going to meet Hiesia too. Is there anyone I won't meet?" Tegriel smiled,

"Don't ever act in front of any of these people as if you know anything about them you should not. They are very quick on the uptake. The skill in our existence is not giving credence to any of the accurate guesses our allies will make about us."

"I only know the stories."

"Many aspects of which are true."

They walked on. Tobia feeling the depression of the past days, of not having her memory and seeing the city fall and Midrak almost die, fall away from her. She wished the others could feel as she did right now. Filled with energy. Looking forward to the next hour. Enjoying the day. She shivered at what they must be facing. Tegriel knew what she was thinking. He too was worried. But then he always would be.

"Do you now how the Upala works?" she asked.

"The Upala recreates herself every twenty–minutes, or every hour depending upon what part of the universe you are in. Each existence is shed like a snake shedding a skin, only the Upala sheds the images within time and time keeps them perfect as if caught in amber. So the Upala is attached to every one of her previous forms. As the Ossendark can go from place to place so she takes you from time to time. The very first of the Upala has already been created. All we need to do is to make sure only Ruzniel ever make use of the bejal by spells I can cast."

"What if you don't manage to?"

"Crilodach would make sure the Upala was never created if It could. It knows the value of being able to travel in time."

"But that would mean ..."

"We could not do what we are doing," he said.

"But that would mean ..."

"We lose before we even begin."

"Hurry up then!"

"I am," he told her, "you are the one dawdling."

"I'm not dawdling. I've smaller legs than you."

They made more haste. Tobia's heart was beating with excitement as she realized all the time she suddenly had to live.

"I am still surprised Crilodach left the Upala in Damkina," said Tegriel, "of all the bejals to take with It, I would have thought that one would have been high on Its list."

"It made a huge mistake," she said.

"It did," he agreed.

"Which is unlike It," she said, uncomfortably.

"You think It left the Upala for a purpose?" he asked.

"I don't know. There doesn't seem much It could do after all, you came back and now no one can use the Upala again before Zaqui."

"Changing the smallest thing could upset the whole of history. Crilodach could throw in one difference and the whole enterprise of the Sangyma would hang in the balance."

"Why does that worry you now? Is something different?"

"There was one small difference in Damkina. A ring in the dust where something had been placed."

"Do you know what a ring could mean?"

"Crilodach is not the type to admit It ever made a mistake that needs changing. It just tries something else. Until we turn the tide in the first battles ahead and secure allies to fight It, we will not know for sure I am on the same path as I was before. We are safe for a while until Its present self knows we are here." She scrambled to keep up and said,

"Will you tell them all about Crilodach straightaway?"

"Eventually you will. You and your son."

"My son."

She sounded astonished. She did not even have a boyfriend and had not had any thoughts about having a family. Something that upset her mother because she would have liked lots of grandchildren. Now Tobia would have a child and her mother would never know. Her mother's grandchildren were born before her mother. Time was amazing and not a little mad. She suddenly thought she must have spent her childhood living amongst her own descendants.

"Tobia, not always the strongest person, or the wisest, makes the biggest difference. Just the ordinary person who is there at the time. You are here and you will love and you will bear a child."

"Why tell me that of all things?"

"In the hopes your curiosity will be satisfied enough to get you to stop asking questions."

"I'm sorry but a few moments ago I was in Damkina, I've been blinded, seen Ruz wiped off the face of the cosmos, left thousands to die and travelled back in time. I'm bursting with questions."

"You have a lot to do before you start a family. We have to meet Kalevala, find Bofindle and get to Ruz."

"We're on Ruz already," she said.

"Ah the red-feathered Latchet, yes I heard him singing too. But no Tobia we are not on Ruz. That little fellow and a few of his kind will be put onto Ruz when they join us on a journey in the Ossendark in the future. When messengers will be needed and friends will be abundant. Right now Ruz does not even exist. The Ruzniel themselves do not yet exist. You are the first."

Tobia was taken aback by that revelation. She thought for a long time and then she remembered the nursery rhymes and myths. The first of the Ruzniel, a blind woman with inner sight. A strong willed, magical being who designed the first city and taught the Ruzniel to be magicians' companions. They say she and Tegriel were brother and sister in some stories. In others that she had wings. That woman, that amazing woman half real, half myth, the woman in the oldest stories and a character in every Ruzniel nursery, the founding mother of the great Ruzniel academies, the woman she had heard about as a toddler, would be her. She was a story from the birth of her people. She lost her footing in her amazement and tumbled over some lilies and pebbles and stood up immediately brushing herself down.

"I'm alright," she said, self-consciously.

When he had said she had a crucial role to play he had not been joking. They hurried along the pathways Tegriel knew, walking high above a mountain lake that shone clear blue in the daylight. Speckled with huge, white rocks. She looked up at his back as they proceeded in single file and asked,

"Where are we if this isn't Ruz?"

"This place will become Damkina. We have come back in time, but we have not changed the place."

"But this place is so beautiful," she shivered.

"For now."

"How long do we have to be here?"

"We have to go to where Bofindle was found. Then to a new planet where the first Sangyma council was held. The more myths I can wrap around my own birth and yours the less Crilodach will suspect. After all, It knows the Universe gave birth to It so It will acknowledge another might be born the same way."

"I miss the others you know," she said. "Here we are, driving forward with our lives and they haven't a day left to live."

"Midrak has his own work to do. Gertis and the others all have things to do if we are to win. Rimfelder, too, I assume, will play his part. Our work right now is to prepare the million, million seemingly random events that will give our friends and allies their chance to be born."

"We'll never go back and see what happens will we?"

"No."

"But Tegriel we've done so much, so many will lose their lives, not to know what happens is like ... is like being blind."

"Who's to say if we are blind or not, or if we succeed or not? We are but two in a myriad of beings who will all play their part. My work is on every planet, amongst thousands of different peoples. Finding them, telling them a little of what may be in a thousand different guises. Never telling them too much. Just a hint. Telling someone a woman will rise with six toes who will lead them to victory at a time of great sadness; or foretelling the coming of great storms that will wash away their enemies; how wood will defeat iron when the stars are aligned in just such a fashion; how the hidden will be revealed; how champions will arise whose names begin with R or P; telling some people their worlds were made when dragons died and parts of their body fell to the ground so that they will honour dragons and when a dragon appears they will not kill him. So ensuring the dragon is free to fight on their side and die for them. To save a city by leaving the whisper of a name on a mountain side; the scent of a hidden treasure in sacred texts that will destroy an enemy stronghold; instilling the longing to be on another world inside the minds of those who need to travel from their doomed planets; the idea that people do not die but can be reborn in other species so that people will learn the language of animals and together they will become a strong phalanx against Crilodach; to leave Its name in dark places and make people fear It before they ever meet Its generals; to start crusades and end them; to be a god on one planet and a demon on another; to scare people to do one thing, and help people in love to do another. To create civilizations and later mourn as they fall. To watch as those rise who will be Its lieutenants so that knowing what they do, I can be at crucial places at crucial times and focus Its venom upon me. Making It think the Sangyma know Its plans because they are magical, and not because I have already lived through the events. I will prophecy in every place, and many times prophecy nothing that will actually happen."

"Why would you do that?"

"Because knowing the enemy, if I were always accurate in my predictions It would not just suspect something like this had happened, It would know and know how. That is why we must be careful, swear some people to secrecy and leave the legends foretelling of things to come in the hands of small numbers of people. Select groups. They will not be believed. They will be hounded, sometimes they will be revered. Foremost amongst whom will be the Sangyma whose names will reverberate throughout the universe. Although there will be many others. Wanderers, outcasts no one takes seriously. But eventually, for many of them, their time will come."

"And for those whose time never comes because the prophecy was false?"

"They will have fought Crilodach in their own way. You saw in Its lair how even cockroaches have their time and place. Those insects are there because Gertis created them. Some of them waited there because I told them they would be in the dark. Without that knowledge they may have all fallen into despair and died. One person living a lie may be a potent weapon because they confuse the enemy. And if the enemy believes them to be telling the truth when It tortures them, they become even more powerful. Deceit, as well as honour, gives victory."

"How do you choose those you mislead?" she asked him, skirting a large boulder in their path and happily picking a blue flower nestling underneath, which smelled of the sea. They had left the lake behind. The open, unfarmed land ahead of them spread out like a green ocean covered in colourful flower–heads.

"That is the saddest part of my existence. For those people, too, I know by name. I have to meet them again, see them again, know they will suffer again. For everyone else in the universe life only moves forwards, but not for me. I have to have the strength to bear their sorrow and mine again."

"That must hurt."

"In a way I am glad that there will be pain in my losing my body. At least that makes me feel that I suffer as others have. I have ever regretted the loss of friends. Try as I might, explain as I might, I am never at peace with my decisions. If I could have found a power to defeat Crilodach in one go I would have. If Filvani were ever to tell me he thought we could create a magic strong enough to imprison Crilodach forever, I would build the prison with my own two hands. But there is no such power. We thought the Sagitæ might be powerful enough but I have never been able to bring all three together any more than Crilodach."

"If confusing It is the best we can do then that will have to suffice. I'd still prefer to kill It but so would most Ruzniel."

"Confusing It is all important because It cannot be

14

subdued by any weapon. The challenge is always to out think It. Stay ahead of It. The Upala is our greatest gift because she gives us foreknowledge through me."

"Is that why you never told anyone of this before; because you think no one has the willpower to handle such knowledge wisely?"

"Neither your mind nor anyone's else's would trip you up, but your heart will. You would try to change things for the better," he explained.

"I suppose that's true," she conceded.

"To be honest with you, for all I have said about keeping things secret, there was one who knew. One I told. And I will tell her again. Oh how I long to meet Yu-Te."

"Who's she?"

"She will be my only love Tobia. You will not meet her nor will anyone but the Sangyma ever know she exists."

"Now I'm worried about you even more."

"Why so?"

"Your memories are precious. Who is here to make sure you're kept safe?"

"I managed to take care of myself pretty well last time, even after I was dead."

She laughed at that. He stopped walking and looked around,

"Now let me get my bearings. If I remember rightly we need to head westwards. There is a path which starts between the pillar and the ... ah over there. Be careful the drop is sheer."

"Did I slip last time?"

"No."

"Then why warn me?"

"Because I did last time. You were wise enough to listen."

"I feel awkward with you knowing everything I'll do."

"I always have. What has changed?" She thought for a moment and then added,

"I didn't know you knew everything, I just thought you were wise."

"I am wise."

"And crafty."

"Every magician has his craft."

"If Midrak were here he'd point out that's not always a good thing."

"You got fond of him even after so short a time."

"A Ruzniel and their magician seem to others to be two different beings from two different species but actually we function more like one whole being."

"Sentiments that are as yet, unknown in this time."

"Just as well I remember them as I'll be writing some of them. Wouldn't my tutors be surprised to know that. I wonder where they all are now. Do you know what happened to Ruz in the future?"

"Ruz's fate is tied up with another story and another piece of magic Crilodach should never get wind of. I know … " he put up his hand as she opened her mouth, "you would never tell but you must know no more on that subject."

"You know the way my tutors spoke of you, I think some of them suspected something like this."

"Gertis may well tell Midrak what is happening to you. He knows."

"Gertis knows?"

"All the Sangyma knew I had a special knowledge. None of them ever asked me how but I am sure they made educated guesses. If they had questions, they kept them to themselves. Sometimes knowing means knowing how to be silent. They are famed for keeping their own counsel."

"I'd just like to know how this all ends, and how our friends die."

"You will have new friends here, my dear Tobia, and you are about to find out how everything begins."

"I haven't fully come to terms with that has happened to us."

"I understand. Midrak is your magician after all, and I cannot soften the pain of your parting. I cannot soften any pain." He grew wistful for a second and then pulled himself together and warned,

"Watch your step here. We go right here. Ah! Here we are. The cave. The steps in here are slippery so be careful. If all goes well in the coming weeks we will give It, Its first taste of defeat. After that It will retrench, plan deeper and longer. It will make this Its centre of operations after the first battles when It comes looking for me to find out who I am. Once here It realizes It needs somewhere to plan and to gather armies to Itself. See that planet close by? It will use that as Its training camp Ghirzanben. Come, let us see if the Ossendark is in place yet."

"Wait a moment," she asked, "if you know It will use this

place can't we leave something here? Something It doesn't know about?"

"Such as?"

"A listening device ... or a hidden bomb to blow the planet to pieces."

"It mines the whole planet Tobia. It builds Hâgon, the labyrinth that goes deep into the planet's heart. And It will be here a long time. Anything left It would find. Then It would ask Itself, who put that there and why. If It thinks we knew It would use this planet as Its base, It would naturally ask how we were able to second-guess It so accurately. Anything we could leave here would actually alert It to our secret."

"We can't plant anything at all?"

"Nothing at all."

Tegriel moved his hands in wide circles as he spoke so much, Tobia thought his arms were getting longer. Then they were travelling again. She could almost touch the sides of the Ossendark, the sparkling hit the back of her eyes and her scalp felt heavy with the warmth. Then Tegriel let go her hand. She stood in valley surrounded by mountains. The valley was verdant, filled with rhododendrons and tall flowering trees. In the branches animals danced around and small, blue-breasted birds, called Sunpeppers, wove hasty flight paths to avoid their sudden arrival. Multi-coloured parrots called out in the distance in languages she understood. Languages that Ruzniel had not used in centuries but they said they were the languages of races of animals long gone from the universe.

"We are on the other side of the planet. We have talked far too much. Kalevala!" cried our Tegriel. "Kal ... ev ... ala."

"Kalevala. First amongst the spellmakers, greatest of dogs and wisest amongst the magicians who lived before the Sangyma. We have come back to the beginning and how." She shook her head in wonder as she whispered to herself.

"Firstly, we must go with Kalevala and dig out Bofindle. Then we must make sure Hiesia has the Upala and eventually we can begin a long journey to commence gathering forces to fight against Crilodach."

"How long is eventually?"

"Tobia so many questions. You haven't stopped since we arrived."

"Well, you're saying things that tantalize me! Just when

there is something really interesting to reveal, you clam up and say nothing more."

"I know something of what we did before Tobia, but who knows this time you may choose differently. I may forget something. It may find us. Who can say? Kal ... ev ... ala!"

"Well if you can't, apparently no one else can that's for sure."

"I remember this feeling of yours lasted a long time." Then he corrected himself, "Lasts a long time."

"Enough. I don't want to know anything unless I ask."

"Fair enough."

"And I don't want to know what I asked or decided before, unless I ask," she added.

"Fair enough."

"Don't mention any names unless I ask."

"Anything else?"

"No."

"Then you must agree that I won't always answer you when you do ask me. Ah, Kalevala. At last."

Kalevala came loping out of the trees wondering who was calling him. He was a huge dog, much taller than Tobia, with white and brown legs and a heavy, black nose set on either side by large, brown eyes. He sniffed the air and slowed to a walk as he saw them both. He had not recognized the voice but for the most part Kalevala was good natured and had not yet learned to be cautious about people who called to him. A few years later and several scars would make him far more cautious. He sniffed. He sensed the magic within the two smiling people walking towards him.

Tegriel with arms extended like a man meeting an old friend he was overjoyed to see, walked up to Kalevala who did not know who he was and wondered what all the affection was about.

"Welcome stranger," Kalevala greeted him.

"I am not as strange as you think," replied Tegriel.

"Really?" Kalevala sniffed him. "I don't recognize your smell or that of your companion. I can see you've come from far away. You've dressed yourself in the flowers of the high mountains of the far country."

"That nose never fails you," smiled Tegriel."

"You're from the future," Kalevala added.

"And you always could smell time on a person."

"You know me from our future?" he asked Tegriel.

"I do. We are great friends there."

"How far into the future?"

"We will be friends all our lives."

Kalevala looked into the Sangyma's genial eyes and saw a depth of sorrow as deep as space itself. He shook his head and his long ears flapped,

"You will live longer than I," he said.

"I will," agreed Tegriel.

"This gives you a lot of sadness."

"Immense but for the fact that I know I will see you again."

"There's definitely something unworldish about you."

"And yet I was born here. On your very mountains."

"Impossible if you'd been born here I'd have known."

"Not if I was born but a few moments ago."

"Are you telling me you were never a baby?" asked the dog. Tobia was glad someone else was asking the questions.

"Never."

Kalevala sniffed Tegriel's hand and walked around them both letting his fur flick into Tobia's face.

"Definitely unworldish," he repeated. "But not harmful."

"We are here to help you with your problem," said Tegriel.

"And what problem would that be?"

"Crilodach."

Kalevala flicked both ears back and forward. The very end of his tail flicked once. He walked around them shaking his body and sniffing the air, lowering and raising his head as he thought. He sat down on his haunches, his tongue slightly hanging out. He was bemused by these people. Tobia knew how he was feeling. Then he got up and lapped at the water in the pool by their feet.

"Do you have a name?" he asked.

"Tegriel, and this is Tobia."

"Do you have a purpose?"

"Only to help you."

"With Crilodach?" observed the dog.

"Yes."

"How?"

"By showing you how to use the weapon your nose has found underground."

Kalevala dipped his front feet into the pool and looked across the water. The reflections rippled with the surface as he lapped.

"When did I find this weapon?" he asked them.

"If I recall you told me just yesterday, or maybe the day before. Something has been calling to you and in that calling you felt you heard a name. A simple name that filled you with strength. Bofindle."

"Well, well, well. You certainly do know me."

"We have come from far in the future my old friend to help you with the enemy you sense is on the way, whose name you know, whose immense power you can smell. There is less to fear than you think but much to do. I could explain on the way."

"There's never less to fear than I think," replied Kalevala. "But explanations are always welcome."

"We must plan for Crilodach's arrival," said Tegriel.

"That makes sense to me. This Bofindle will help us?"

"Bofindle will need a champion. The first of five spellmakers who will wield the bejal until a woman spellmaker makes Bofindle her weapon of choice at the end of this universe."

Already, thought Tobia, he was laying down the prophecies and ideas in those he knew would make the best use of them.

"A very useful weapon," said Kalevala.

"Come along," said Tegriel, knowing the way to go without being shown. "Bofindle is far more than useful. The bejal will turn the tide against our enemies on several occasions."

"Then how come Crilodach isn't already here digging the bejal up?" asked Kalevala.

"It would if It could. It does not know Bofindle exists yet. It will find out only when It is attacked!" replied Tegriel.

"They say on the news that swims in the Ossendark that It rose like a behemoth taking up a whole ocean and turning the waters black. Giving no quarter It tears worlds to pieces. It is driven by a madness none can stop. It reasons with no one. It seems to only want to destroy."

"That is just the form It takes to instil fear in people. Crilodach is just a man. Though there will be very few who, after this first battle, will never see It as anything but a behemoth."

"I would prefer to fight this being in Its true form," said Kalevala.

"You my friend, you will fight It many times for you are the first of the champions who will wield Bofindle."

He marched past Kalevala in mid-thought and Tobia raced after him. Time was running out. Kalevala dipped his head into the pool to wash his face and then followed them. Friends were always good to have but he found being told they were friends before he had decided they were was taking good sense for granted, something only Tegriel would ever do. That said from what he had heard of Crilodach he might have expected something like this. The creature was powerful and deadly and normal people were not able to stand against It. He caught up with Tobia whom he could see was blind but walked without difficulty and without sniffing her way with her nose.

"Your friend tells me to follow him and off he goes. Is he always this abrupt?" Kalevala asked her.

"I tend to just agree with him," she told Kalevala, "in the long run that saves me a lot of headaches. Magicians can be very confusing and the Sangyma even more so."

"Sangyma, is that some special magician?"

"Oh there will be few indeed who do not know about the Sangyma in times to come. In fact wherever Crilodach is, they will be. They are Its greatest enemies."

"You say the name as if you've lived with It for a long time. I heard this name whispered but a few days ago. Have you met this Crilodach in either of Its forms?"

"Personally no but I've heard of Its work and met Its armies recently. Its a fierce creature and not someone you'd want to meet at any time."

As she said this Tobia surprised herself. For she vividly understood she too knew something about the future. She knew she would have to be as careful as Tegriel about speaking of Ruz, Midrak and Lilah, or of the battle with Tethval and his people and even the cockroaches in the labyrinth. As she thought of that she got a small indication of the huge responsibility that lay on Tegriel's shoulders. The fate of the whole universe was in his hands. One wrong word in one mis-spoken moment, and all could be changed and in that change all could be lost.

"You know," she said wisely, "you should keep all this talk of the future and stuff to yourself."

"I'm not given to gossip," confided the dog.

"All the same, keep this all a secret between the three of us. If It got wind of who Tegriel is and how he got here, It would try to change things. That could spell disaster."

"You know of It and you live? Yet you are not mighty in magic. Is It truly that dangerous?"

"I was saved by others, as you're being saved now by Tegriel."

"Can It be defeated?"

"Its armies can."

"That is good to know," growled Kalevala.

"One of Its armies blinded me."

"Yet you see."

"Tegriel has given me an inner sight. We are separate in body but not in spirit."

Kalevala was impressed by her. He wagged his tail and lifted his head. He was feeling the dread of Crilodach less and less as he learned from his new friends.

"I've been told Crilodach intends to crush all life," he told her.

"It will also take over whole planets and use the inhabitants as soldiers."

"Fearsome yet predictable," cursed Kalevala, "another tyrant."

"The tyrant of tyrants. We try to give It the kind of victories It craves to limit Its activities."

"I begin to understand. A creature that cannot be killed, has to be controlled."

"If you want, that's as good a description as any," she said.

"And this Tegriel comes to us with the knowledge to control It?"

"He saves many," she told him.

"Well I'm sure ... ." He was cut short in mid sentence.

Tegriel was making his way straight to Bofindle thinking everything was as before. For all his caution there was an air of excitement in his step. There were a few things he was glad to be going to do again. A few people he was glad to be going to meet again. Maybe he could carve out the time to spend longer with those he loved; an extra evening, maybe even a whole day more. Kalevala was loping along behind him talking to Tobia just as he remembered them doing. He had time to meet Hiesia and make sure she knew what the Upala would achieve. Once that was done the urgency of his situation would be passed and they could go forward with the preparations to meet Crilodach, and a little while later Its first army. He thrilled as he recalled the gathering of those people and animals who fought the first battles. Faces that were, to him, as bright as stars.

Tobia in her way was getting happier too, because she was

secure in the knowledge she was going to live for a while, something she had not been sure about the past days. She was also sure that she would see Ruz again and many of the things she missed would be hers to enjoy every day. You might even say she was feeling a touch of happiness.

Then there came a roaring sound. A trumpeting like a huge gale that this age, this world had never heard before. A trumpeting that was new to Kalevala and Tegriel. Nothing should be new to Tegriel. A shock wave of sound that bounced off the ground, emptied the pools of water and silenced the birds and every living thing around them, stripped leaves from trees and turned clouds into solid ice that came crashing down to the ground, exploding into shards and crystals forming a dense, icy fog that rolled over the ground towards them, preceded by a cold that chilled their bones and curled their toes. A screeching, roaring sound. A screeching and roaring of Tegriel's name.

"What's that?" she asked Tegriel.

The Sangyma looked up and listened and said words she never thought she would ever hear him say after all they had spoken about since arriving,

"I do not know."

The Summons

Yaltha was in a bad mood. She had been in a bad mood all night and she was not going to get any better. So great was her vexation, the heat building up in her quarters was melting the gold-threaded wallpaper. Everyone knew she was in a foul mood. The air pressure changed all over the palace because of her anger, hearts sank, and serfs moved very slowly, dreading her temper tantrum which invariably turned to violence. When she was like this she was likely to stab someone in the eye or cut off their nose just to make herself feel better.

Dalved's usual, firm footfall was far more careful as he walked the familiar, long hallways of the palace towards her chambers. The smell of her anger on the air was cordite and coal, acid and rotting flesh. A smell that made serfs' stomachs tighten and want to vomit. Some days her anger was so intense their eyes watered. No one in the palace envied Dalved, who had been sold into service as a boy, on these days. He alone was allowed to stand in her presence. Although 'allowed' is a strange description. No one wanted to stand in her presence but Dalved could not refuse. A slavery that had led to many whippings. Today he had to go and disturb her without being summoned. On a bad mood day. He feared for his life.

The palace was old. Older than Yaltha or her sister, Freyom. They said this dark, dread palace had once belonged to a beautiful woman whose mother had died in childbirth giving birth to her brother. She always blamed him for her mother's death and planned his death over many years, finally murdering him in his bed by smothering him with two fine, silk pillows. She was burned for her crime by her step-mother who in turn, on the same day, was stabbed by her daughter's husband. From that day on, the palace had a sinister feel. A cold, creeping, caustic feel that went well with Yaltha's and Freyom's bad moods. The story was not true of course but people have a need for stories to explain why times are hard. Good mood days were rare and for both of them to have a good mood on the same day was cause for celebration.

Everyone else in the palace was enslaved to work for them. They whispered to each other that the palace felt like they imagined a tomb might feel to those who are buried alive. They whispered because to speak was to be heard. To be heard was to be punished. For all of them their slavery was an early death. All of them taken from the lives they had known, from places where there was a day-time and a night-time and from where they had families, to die in servitude to the terrible sisters in the sprawling palace where no one could hide and from which, no one left alive.

Some mumbled behind his back that Dalved had privileges, but no one else would have dared do what he did. They all admitted he never pushed them around. He never threatened anyone. A lesser man would have used his position to make others do his bidding, to make them suffer when he was in a bad mood, but Dalved never did. The women serfs thought him a lonely figure, always by himself since his wife had died. No children. But Dalved had a reason for keeping his distance, he knew the others were much safer not being close to him, for he had a secret that could get them all killed.

On these bad-mood days the long, echoing corridors he walked down seemed even more stretched out and unhappy than usual. The blacked out windows peered down at him mocking him and his thin, taut body with skin that seemed barely enough to cover his bones. As he passed them he always had the feeling they left something on his shoulder. Like an eye that was not an eye, but just as watchful. Added to which he seemed to hear voices coming from them, inside his head. Dalved the serf, Dalved the weakling, Dalved the lonely, Dalved the dying. Dalved who had a secret. A wicked secret. A secret that could get him killed. The dread windows were like lines of judges passing down their sentence wrapped in thick black cloth so you could not see the pleasure in their eyes as they luxuriated in their power. To walk down these hallways was an act of bravery.

His sallow face, never having been allowed to sit in the sun since birth, was pock marked with old spots and one or two scars where she had bitten him when they were children. When she had been a child. He did not think he had ever been a child or rather that he had never been allowed to be a child. He had tried to forget so much about his early life that he could no longer recall anything that happened to him before he had met his doomed wife.

As the only person allowed into Yaltha's personal living rooms he knew things no one else knew. He had learned quickly to be silent. Show no surprise. He had had to fight not to go sour and withered like the sisters. Not to let their temperament influence him. He did not wholly succeed. Dalved had forgotten how to smile. He never wanted to remind Yaltha he had thoughts in case she ripped out his tongue just to make sure he never spoke about her behind her back. He never dared, for even though no one else spoke to her unless she spoke to them, she found out things. Finding out was her specialty. She could repeat whole conversations whispered between two serfs in the darkest place, in the quietest hour when she was supposed to have been asleep. If she ever really slept. He had come to doubt the sisters could do anything so normal. Dalved had become an expert in staying quiet.

The rota and duty rosters had become part of his life before he even knew how to walk. The words in his head were all taken from etiquette created by the builder who had given the palace to the sisters. How strange he must have been. To have created the dominion of this dynasty. Epochs ago. Giving so much power to envy, malice and anger. Where was he now? Did he know what he had done? Did he know if there had ever been a sun you could live under? Not like the sun now. A fierce and bright sun the stories said. A sun to be feared. A sun that withered a man on his bone, dried up his eyes in his head and cracked his fingernails, stifled the cry in his throat and burned all his skin to dust before he had time to properly die. A sun everyone feared.

Where was the sun now? Still out there. Someone had once told him they thought there were millions of suns in a huge space outside. He had laughed. 'People believe anything when they are desperate,' he thought. When he had dared to voice his thoughts. He did not think out loud anymore. He just reacted with a nod. He had become a breathing automaton. That was all that kept him alive. He had had a counterpart. A serf who was the personal manservant to Freyom. He had not been careful. Dalved did not know exactly what he had done. Dropped something over Freyom, spoken when he should have been silent, argued when he had no right to. He disappeared. His rooms were emptied.

All his clothing vanished as if he had never existed. Soon Dalved even forgot his face along with his name. Remembering all those who had gone would have been a waste of energy. Did he really die a long time ago, when they were children? He did not remember. Did he want to remember? Remembering bad things was not healthy. Remembering dried his lips so Dalved left them as shadows in his mind.

She noticed people remembering. He could not afford to let her notice things. He had never let on he had a secret. Especially not to her. Not to anyone. He kept his tongue from wagging and so kept his life.

There was that sun outside beating down on the blacked-out windows and closed, iron doors and still the palace was chill. Dark. Noisy. Well over a million people lived inside the walls looking after one family. A family of two. Two wicked and strong half-women. Was a million enough? He did not know. There had been fewer once. They were allowed to breed but few people had children. Somehow this was not a place for childhood. Instinctively everyone knew children would grow up here to be 'different', and then there was always the terror in their hearts; that the sisters would take an interest in the child. There were stories of course. There always are. Of the children the sisters had taken under their wing. Of what had happened to them. He shivered. He turned a corner and the guards stood smartly to attention. He had never asked them to but the guards knew who he was and decided amongst themselves to salute when he passed. As if he could protect them. As if salutes meant anything. He did not like their deference but he did not tell them to stop. Not to want to be saluted would look odd. He noticed one of them was new but said nothing. You could not have friends if you were Dalved. You could not have friends if you were a serf.

There were many who were still brought here of course. Many of them did not last long. They bleated on about sunshine. Really, he thought, who needed to talk about the sunshine if talking was going to get you killed. Better to live in the dark and live. Live somehow. Live a little while. He did not have much use for disappearing. He did not have any use for death. Although he knew his life was not much use to him, something inside him held on. He knew the sisters had many uses for death though; they used other people's deaths as a weapon. He saw how potent fear was at keeping serfs down. Fear. Fear of someone else. Fear of oneself and what one becomes. Fear of speaking. Fear of knowing and not knowing. Fear of being betrayed. A life of wicked confusion fed by the sisters, watered by the serfs. A palace of selfishness. But then, all palaces are selfish. Vingura would have told Dalved they could not be otherwise but Dalved had never heard of Vingura.

The ones who did survive the first month complained about being bowed down with protocol. No thinking outside of the rules was permitted. What better way to assure compliance than to deprive people of the words in which to express ideas outside the rules. There were words for service, for cleaning and doing, for polishing and bowing but some of the words the new comers used were useless here. So they were forgotten. So they all thought. But inside some heads the great invention of people, imagination, had made doors a password for doors to rooms in the palace, and doors to ideas in the mind. Silver was not just tableware but light. Stone was hard but walls of the mind were to be broken down. Feet walked the corridors but they also travelled the byways of the mind. Eyes could be stopped from seeing but the mind was not blind. Bowing was subservience but also hid hatred by hiding facial expressions. Cooking was also cleansing, obeying was just being careful for one's life. Ideas. Ideas that had been taught to Dalved by many of those brought here from outside. He spoke to them. Knowing they would be dead soon he let them talk openly to him. They told him 'things'. They gave him ideas. Ideas that could get him killed. He had a whole other palace in his head. A palace that was his secret. Not the secret that could get him killed but dangerous enough, nonetheless. He had always been so careful. So perfectly a serf. He wondered when he had started to be this way. Inside himself he had become another man than the personal manservant. Inside, in his imagination, sometimes just before he fell asleep, he was not even a man. In these dreams he saw faces of people he had never met and they were laughing. These dreams were not of the palace.

He was now standing at the bottom of the stairs leading to her apartments. One last look at his clothes and he walked up.

Ideas. Knowledge. Both had changed him. All because one day he had looked. When Yaltha had been resting. She forgot he was in the room. For that blissful moment when he was behind her as she lay down. Near the heavy curtain. He had seen the curtain move. At first he was scared but the breeze caught his hand and felt cool. Enticing. And as the curtains moved he had let his hand slide behind them and the air moved on his tired skin. Warmth touched his ageing fingers. Not the oven warmth of the kitchens, or the sweaty warmth of the palace fires, but a cooling warmth. An invigorating warmth. A warmth he had not known before.

And he had put his head behind that enticing curtain and looked.

The light blinded him.

The light did not kill him.

The light did not dry him up or whither him.

The light seared his heart. They had been lied to. A lie to shut them all up inside the palace. To keep them ignorant. The sun was beautiful. Knowing that could get him killed.

He came to Yaltha's door. The apartments which were the centre of his servitude and yet which had released him. The rooms where the curtains could be moved. Where he had come to know the sunshine through so much bitterness. The room reeked of Yaltha but this was the place where he was closest to the only warmth he had ever known, the place which filled him with longing. He both longed for and feared being in these rooms. Without her there they would be perfect rooms. He could pull down that curtain and stare outside and never move.

Tucking the green cloak, which was his mark of office, behind him, he took the blue and red bangle from his pocket that Qolcrift had brought, touched the door, kissed the panelling, and then knocked with his left hand knuckles four times. She knew his different knocks. When he was scared more than usual, when he had brought her news or just a meal. She knew how he smelled in the mornings and how he smelled in the evenings. She knew when he was tired and when he was annoyed. She always knew. She remembered when they had been children together. She even knew his secret. But that pleased her in her crafty way and she did not kill him. Her sister would have killed him if she had known but Yaltha never told her. She did not keep him alive out of mercy. She liked showing him off to Freyom. Prodding her sister with all the things she missed, having killed her own personal servant. Their father refused her another.

Yaltha held Dalved's life over her sister as a medal she wore that Freyom could not have. Rivalry between the sisters kept Dalved alive.

The door opened and, taking three steps in, he knelt on the ground his eyes one inch in front of his hands which were pressed onto the marble with his fingers splayed out. The others always thought this subservience was because the sisters wanted to make sure he did not have any concealed weapons in his hands but Dalved knew weapons would have been useless. He knew every so often Yaltha liked stepping on his fingers almost to snapping them.

"What?" she demanded.

"I bring a message," he said.

He waited. This was the worst part. The waiting. When she was in a good mood waiting was easier for she responded quickly. But when she was in bad mood she might make him stay like this for hours. Even hit him. He was deeply scarred all over his body from her thrashings. She had beaten him so much his body shut down when she hit him now. She knew that. She knew he did not feel pain the way he had when they were young. That was why she beat him less. Now she beat him only to have him remember she could.

"I thought I'd do without your ugly face today," she said. "No! Don't move. Don't squirm. What's the message?"

"A summons."

"A summons?" Yaltha was livid, "Who dares summon me?"

"There's only one who would."

There was a long pause. Ice had come between them. He heard her breathing like a bull about to charge. She spoke slowly, her voice dripping with threat,

"Come."

He straightened his back, stood like a man cornered and came to the large chair in which she sat. Her long fingers held the arms of the chair tightly, and her dull, blue eyes looked ahead of her as if they were trying to peer out of the darkened window to see the sun he was supposed to never have seen. He kissed her hand gently feeling the steel fingernails, his lips dry on her hard skin. He offered her the bangle. She took the message from him. Sliding the bangle onto her wrist where another she never took off always sparkled. They touched and fused. Shone. Communicated Crilodach's orders to her. Her eyes flashed. Something like a smile crossed her mouth. Dalved waited. Her face went white. Drained of all blood. Her fingers curled into clenched fists. Something had changed in her. Something new had happened. She was not looking at him. She stood up and paced the floor. She pulled back the curtains and the sunshine flooded the whole room. He put his arm up to his eyes and half turned away.

"Not running away. Not terrified to be withered by the sunlight." she scoffed.

"I trust my mistress to do nothing that would harm her servant," he blurted out, but he knew she knew.

"Trust. That's the one thing you lost long ago. Why aren't you afraid?"

"Because I'm with you."

"Pitiable animal. You think I don't know? You know the sunlight won't hurt you." She hit him across his head. He fell to the ground coughing,

"When did you look?" she demanded to know.

"Never, not ever. Just now. You ... made me."

"Liar!"

She raised her hand. He felt the blow in the air without seeing her movements. He felt her anger. He silently awaited death. The blow never landed.

"You'll pay for your lies by accompanying us. Call my sister."

"When?" he choked,

"Immediately."

"Where?"

"To the great tower."

Dalved got up from the floor bowing repeatedly, and went to kiss her fingers. She slapped his mouth with the back of her hand and broke his lip. He tasted his own, sweet blood. She was agitated but that was not his doing. She had never pulled back the curtains before. He was surprised. Amazed. Scared. He left the room. But all he could see was bright light. Everywhere he looked the sunshine in his eyes lit up the darkness. He went to her sister's part of the palace. His long strides urgent and quick. Since the death of his counterpart he was the only one to take messages between the sisters. Freyom was a long way away but somehow the sunshine came with him.

Freyom was different in some ways to Yaltha. Freyom was less of a schemer. She had the same temper though and she showed anger more often. Dalved knew the sisters hated each other. They hated the way they were cooped up in the palace with their serfs. They had done everything to amuse themselves at their serfs' expense and they had grown bored. They, too, felt they were in prison. Locked away for some purpose he did not know. Today he was going to find out. He was going to find out there was a whole universe of secrets.

His cloak allowed him to pass the guards on each floor without questions. Allowed him to pass the serfs on each corridor who would have stopped anyone else. Some knew him by sight but no one expressed any pleasantries here. No one asked how they each were, no one smiled. He came to the stairs that led to Freyom's chambers hot and panting. He found another door exactly like Yaltha's in all respects but his knock had to be different. For here he was only a visitor. He had to wait. A voice asked what he wanted. He gave Yaltha's message. Freyom told him to go without opening her door. He left.

He hurried to his room and gratefully closed the door behind him. He wept. He never wept. What were her words? He was to go with them. As a form of punishment. Where? When? His fear was intense. His hands shook. He sensed his death was near at hand. He was filled with that strange betwixt–and–between feeling. Although he hated the palace, this was all he knew and he feared leaving for the unknown even if the unknown included that sweet, warm sunshine. So he wept until his lungs ached. Wondering where all the tears came from. He was not just weeping for what had happened, but for everything that had happened since his birth. For every day and for every hour. For his wife. He wept until he had no more tears but his body still cried until his chest ached and his head hurt and he felt he was dying of grief.

Then the palace waited. News swept the hallways that the sisters were meeting in the great tower. Cleaning and cooking slowed down, eyes looked into eyes, shadows changed, ripples of whispers rolled around the rooms and halls as one million people held their breath. No one knew what was happening. Dalved had said nothing. He could not be found. Was he dead? No one knocked on his door to ask. Going into someone else's room was forbidden.

Freyom swept out of her room and almost ran to the tower. Yaltha walked more slowly. The message had been sent to her because she had a personal servant. She would let her sister wait an hour before joining her. She liked Freyom waiting for her. On the other hand she could not be more than an hour for the summons was from Crilodach.

The two sisters met in the high tower. No one knew what was being said. Gossip channels from the sisters to everyone else were limited in the palace. Dalved rubbed his wrist continuously wondering what the band had said. What terrible message had been contained in his duty of the day? Qolcrift had told him nothing. He rubbed his tired eyes and drank what passed for water in the palace. He wanted to sleep but could not. Instead he waited. Wrapped in his green cloak. Wrapped in his thoughts. He closed his eyes. He felt the sunshine on his tired skin in his memory. What a glorious second that had been. He would have let her whip him to death just so he did not have to move from that spot. Why did he still cling to protocol? All he wanted was to bathe in the sunlight. Life was not that important. He wanted to go back. He wanted to stand outside.

The sisters came down from their tower after a few hours and Dalved was summoned to the main hall. There he met with the chiefs of the militia and the main supplier of armour for the palace guards. Never had so many been summoned at once. Everyone was sweating. Trembling. The sisters sat next to each other with stony faces, their long fingers flashing with rubies.

"We're going to war," announced Freyom.

"War!" gasped the serfs.

The generals were astounded. They had never gone to war. They had always thought they were there to protect the sisters. They practised combat in the armouries that stretched for miles in the basements. They had never been outside in all their lives. The idea struck them as absurd. Who was the enemy? Where was the battle? How much did they need in supplies? Would their armour protect them against the dangers of the sunshine?

"The orders," said Yaltha, stemming any argument, "are that the Sangyma have to be destroyed."

Dalved's heart felt a pang. He knew the history. The great wars and great battles but he had never liked the sound or feel of Crilodach. He knew all about power. A few who came here as prisoners had been great and mighty rulers. They all looked ordinary when they were in chains. He had no

The Great Tower

desire to have power himself, so Crilodach's endless promises meant nothing to him. He did feel the smart for revenge every so often but, when he did, he always heard a voice telling him he was better than that. That revenge was not justice. He knew Crilodach promised much and gave little. It found many who looked to It as a mighty magician. Dalved hated Its name.

Dalved had never liked the fact Crilodach had given the sisters this palace. That It had put them in charge. In every story he ever heard there was always a sliver of a thought in the back of his mind that Crilodach, more than any other, profited most when It gave gifts. Without ever having met It, Dalved had an instinctive horror of some of the things the sisters plotted and planned and if they reflected Crilodach's power and teachings ... well Dalved wanted none of them. His new ideas had built houses outside in the open air. Had made water run in rivers which fed pools and irrigated crops, as some of the prisoners had described to him before the life was crushed out of them. In his mind he climbed mountains with them and saw gardens grow. He knew what 'colourful' meant. Now, he despised the sisters' stories and their calculated promises. He had pulled down this palace with all the thousands of rooms many times in his imagination and he had rebuilt them nearer to his heart's desire. But those were dreams.

Though he had never met any of them either, and though in the stories they were depicted as slow, dull, weak and spiteful, he rather liked the sound of the Sangyma. They went wherever they wanted, whenever they wanted. They were always there when Crilodach was there and they were always ready to fight It. That said something to Dalved. That said Crilodach needed fighting. There were so many stories there must have been a lot of fighting. He liked the fact that the sisters were scared of the Sangyma. He felt good knowing there were beings around who were stronger than the sisters. He would have enjoyed seeing the sisters bowing at someone's feet. They should be taught how that felt.

"So Dalved," smiled his mistress, "you'll be going on those travels you've longed for, only you'll be going to fight and die."

"Whatever you desire," he replied, bowing.

"I desire to bathe. I don't want to start the war dirty."

She got up and left the hall taking Dalved with her. He

alone was allowed to touch her skin. Her sister stayed to talk through with the generals mobilizing the palace militia. She would not tell them where they were going. They would not have believed her. They all knew Crilodach had prepared this palace in great secrecy. That no one knew of the existence of the sisters and that was why everyone was held prisoner who came here. Crilodach's way of keeping his daughters, born through Its twisted magic, entertained while they waited for Its summons. The generals did not know Crilodach hatched this plan. Nor did they know that the sisters were Its daughters and were central to Its scheme. Nor did they know that they were about to embark on a battle that was going to achieve what everyone thought impossible. They were going to change history. Nor did they know they were all going to die without raising a hand in anger. Like all things that are just plans, when the time comes to enact them people do things you never expect, and despite Its teachings even the sisters were going to do things It only half guessed.

Yaltha's skin was hard, like her heart. The spine, arched with barbs which folded when clothed, had been bequeathed them both by their father. Dalved was under oath never to reveal they were more than other people and he knew if he ever spoke of what he knew, the whole palace would be put to death. The sisters would simply get new serfs. Their secret meant more to them than any number of lives. The secret that they were part beast. He kept silent but in his head he had killed them a hundred times. In his head he had given rousing speeches to the militia and marched down these hallways to end their reign. And now he could talk because they were all leaving, could tell them all about the sunshine and the sisters' spines, he seriously wondered if the serfs would care. Now they knew the sisters were taking them away from the narrow existence they had endured all their lives, they would be far more interested in getting out.

So what if they were half beast, he had a chance to see the stars. He would follow anyone just to see those stars. For now Dalved knew there was sunshine he also knew there was night and he knew there must be stars, just as he had been told. He had seen sunshine, he longed to see stars.

As the militia prepared with noisy precision, the sisters met to put on their war clothes. The light but protective bodices, leg and arm armour and the helmets that showed only their eyes but allowed them to bite.

"I was beginning to think we'd never get to wear 'em," Yaltha commented, tying on her under clothes.

"Sister-mine you always did worry too much," remarked Freyom.

"And you never had doubts?"

"Never one."

"I did," admitted Yaltha.

"I count that as disrespecting our father. No doubt you count that as a wisdom."

"No more than you would, if you ever thought anything more than what father wants you to think," argued Yaltha.

"I'm content with his decisions. He gave us life."

"Oh please, you're scared of him."

"You're not?"

"We're wise to be scared of father. You're unwise to be grateful."

"You always did vie with father too much," scolded Freyom. "You take everything as a challenge. Why can't you just do as father wants for once instead of belly-aching."

"Belly-aching is no more than being smart. You act like father's slave, not Its daughter."

"And you act like Its enemy not his daughter!" snapped back Freyom.

Yaltha bridled at that and snatched up her sword with the point at Freyom's neck but Freyom was not slow when fighting. Her sword had been unsheathed on her chair all the while and even as she felt the point of her sister's sword on her throat her own was pressing into Yaltha's unprotected rib.

"You've been practicing," Yaltha noted.

"With you as my sister that's the smart play," said Freyom.

Yaltha lowered her sword and flung the weapon onto the chair, Freyom did the same. The two swords chimed briefly as they hit each other.

"I'm not father's enemy," said Yaltha.

"And I'm not father's slave," said Freyom.

The two sisters looked at each other. They were stuck with each other. Without the slightest bit of love for the other, each had to work with the other because their father had ordered them to. They gained no comfort from the other's existence. These two sisters had never sat down and braided each other's hair, or talked about old boyfriends or the things they most wanted to do in life. In their way, they knew they had been prisoners in this palace. True, they were the prisoners with the most privileges, but they were prisoners nonetheless. Now, at last, they were to be free but even in their freedom they had to do their father's bidding. And though they longed to fight, Yaltha disliked being told what to do as much as their serfs.

"We must hurry and dress before Damkina is destroyed," Yaltha told her,

"Sister-mine I told you, you worry too much. Do you think our father has left anything to chance? We'll get there. We'll find the Upala waiting."

"I want to make sure," said Yaltha.

"I'm sure you do."

"What's that supposed to mean?"

"You don't want father to be angry with you, you've seen what he does when he is," said Freyom.

"You saw what he did to our mothers."

"They were useless after they had breast-fed us, what else was he to do?"

"He'd do the same to us."

"Oh, Yaltha you talk big but you're as scared of him as me." Freyom stretched out her arm and picked up her body armour. "Come. Lock me into this, I want to feel more power."

Yaltha moved like a cat and slid the armour over her sister's head lacing up the back. The metal shone and bent round to fit her form as she moved, anticipating her smallest movements. After a few moments Freyom's skin meshed with the metal and from the breastplate, spikes slid out and the spikes in her spine strengthened, slid out and laced themselves around her armour. She breathed in. The armour moved with her lungs, more like a second skin.

"I feel magnificent," she said. "Try yours."

Freyom picked up Yaltha's armour with one strong hand and slung the breastplate over her sister's head. Yaltha felt the metal clasp to her, mould to her and become part of her. She felt no additional weight from the metal at all. Yaltha picked up a sword from the chair and struck her sister. The sword rang out. Freyom shot her a fierce glance,

"Never do that again!"

"You'll feel a lot more of them before we're through with the Sangyma," Yaltha told her.

"Their tricks don't scare me."

"They're more than tricks," warned Yaltha.

"You doubt us."

"I don't underestimate them."

"You think they're that powerful?"

"By nature I'm wary of everything."

"What is there to doubt?"

"There's always room for doubt."

"I don't believe that, not where father is concerned," said Freyom.

"Really? You trust father's power so much?"

"I do."

"Do you think any of our serfs have ever seen the sun?" asked Yaltha.

"Not the ones born here."

"Are you sure?"

"Certain."

"I think one has."

"You've proof of that?"

"I know."

Freyom arched her shoulders in her armour, and sneering she said,

"Then my sword should do some work before we go."

"No he'll have his uses still," said Yaltha.

"No? Oh, Dalved. You're always protecting that little git. You should've gutted him years ago the way I did mine."

"Why do you assume I mean him?"

"He's the only one you'd stay your hand for. You always had a sentimental streak in you. I found watching mine vomit up blood a lot more satisfying than having him bow and scape to me all day."

"Dalved's been very useful," said Yaltha.

"You'd as much cause to bite his head off as I did mine and you never did. I don't regret killing mine, apart from the fact you've rubbed Dalved in my face ever since as if he were some bloody trophy."

"I'm not so quick to anger as you. He's proven useful and will do so again."

"Don't leave me alone with him."

"Whatever is to happen to him, I'll decide."

"Does that make you feel good?"

"I feel good about having power over all their lives, yes," Yaltha said.

"I'm beginning to wonder how close you two have become, you protect him too much."

"What a revolting thought. The man has the skin of an animal. But I still say he has his uses."

"Oh these creatures have limited uses sister-mine. Personally I'd leave them all here to die in the palace when we leave."

"Don't you remember father telling us to keep clear heads? To make sure we got to where we're going?"

"He said our task would be dangerous. I remember you saying you didn't care about any dangers."

"I don't."

"Even so I can't see letting Dalved live is wise. If the others have to die so should he. How long have you known he's seen sunshine?"

"A few hours," Yaltha lied, "I pulled the curtains back when I received the summons. He didn't scuttle for cover. He knew the truth."

"Only a few hours? I understand then. Nonetheless, you should've killed him on the spot."

"You only say that because father would've," said Yaltha.

"There's no room for hesitation where we're going sister-mine. The fault here is with you not our father."

"Me? When have I ever let any of these snivelling creatures live? I've killed them for plain fun," Yaltha pointed out.

"You haven't killed any lately."

"I was bored with them. They all bleed the same way. This war has come none to soon for me."

"I'll show no hesitation. I've longed for this fight."

"We've daggers too. Father thinks of everything," said Yaltha peering at the blades.

"They're not ordinary daggers. Remember what Frin-Ghirzan taught to us. The swords will work with our arms and these daggers will protect our backs," said Freyom, taking hers.

"Of course I remember. I remember the hours of backbreaking exercises and training we went through. Do you remember that sour-puss Rataplan? Did you ever manage to disarm him?"

"Not by myself," remembered Freyom.

"No, that's why there's two of us. Father wouldn't have bothered with two children if one could've accomplished the task."

"You think we're expendable."

"I know we're expendable, but if we achieve our aim ..." said her sister.

"What? You're thinking something?"

"Think! We'll be in a universe that's all ours. Nothing to stay our hands."

"Except father."

"A father who doesn't know we exist," said Yaltha.

"I wouldn't assume that. I don't trust father to have given us all the powers we'd need to defeat It. We've got just enough to take on Tegriel. Father ain't stupid," said Freyom, moving around in her armour making sure everything fitted.

"Then maybe we can go looking for the additional powers we'll need when we get there."

"Our task is to kill Tegriel."

"And we should just carry out orders without any questions?"

"You can't seriously believe you'd get away with going against father."

"I never suggested we should or would. I'm just saying we don't have to just carry out the task we've been trained for without scouting around first. See what's what. The newness; the possibilities, for us. Think! Not a palace but whole worlds for us to use. Everything fresh. No one knowing who we are or where we came from. We could be brilliant empresses."

"And how'd you think we'd pull that off?"

"We could talk to Tegriel," said Yaltha.

"You're insane!"

"Why?"

"Surprise is our most valued ally. He isn't expecting us. We could just take him out and you want to have dinner with him."

"I don't want to lose the chance of all that power and knowledge. He knows all that has happened, that's his life. All things to come, ponder that one. He knows our father's weaknesses. He knows magic we've never heard of and he doesn't know who we are. We could pretend to be his allies and learn from him. Drain him of every moment of what will be the future for our own benefit," said Yaltha, her voice animated and excited.

"He's a Sangyma, sister–mine, we'd never fool him. Our powers of mind reading would never work on him."

"Maybe not all the time but if we could fool him long

enough ... ."

"And what would we do with all this knowledge he'll so kindly give us?"

"Knowledge is power. Who knows what we'd do."

"I doubt you'd share your powers with me."

"You're the only one in the universe I'd share with," said Yaltha.

"You frighten me," Freyom told her.

"No, you don't fear me. Our father fills you with doubts and fears. You can clearly see I'm speaking the truth. We've a chance here greater than we've been told and you're too scared to join me."

"Our father knows we'd think of this plot," said Freyom.

"And what could father do about us? We'll be in the distant past. Father can't reach us there."

"He's not to be toyed with Yaltha."

"Oh please, he treats us like mere toys. What are we to It? Daughters? We're mere pawns in Its greater game. If we fail we simply vanish from the board and It goes on with other players. We probably have two brothers somewhere even now preparing to cut off our heads if we fail."

"We were born to be key fighters and winners in this war," Freyom argued.

"Open your eyes. You'll begin to see things differently when we get out of this stuffy, forsaken palace."

"Betrayal's a big step. Tegriel would never trust us. All we have is each other and our orders. Father doesn't trust us much and you'll destroy even that little," warned Freyom.

"I'm sure It doesn't. Father knows we love Its presents. It knows we love power. Father's never shared a tenth of Its power with us."

"We have to do as It says. Its sent the summons. We're going back."

"Just be open to the possibilities when we get there. Everything is achievable," insisted Yaltha.

Her sister nodded, putting a dagger in her sister's hand,

"Yes, everything's achievable."

"And Tegriel will know a lot more about father than we do."

"Yes, he would." Her eyes flashed. "But would he know enough. He's never defeated father in all these millenniums. How could he help us do so?" asked Freyom.

"In all these millenniums he never had us with him. Father

never used the Upala himself, can you think why not?"

"Because if It did It would go back to a time where It would be facing Itself. The only enemy Father can't defeat," said Freyom.

"Exactly."

"I see what your getting at. Maybe that part of us which is from It holds the key to defeating It."

"Maybe."

"And Tegriel is the one who can help us unlock our potential."

"Maybe."

Freyom put her hand on her sister's shoulder and replied,

"And when we do, we kill Tegriel and our father, is that your idea?"

"We kill everyone we want to," replied Yaltha.

Freyom rattled her spines. Her sister had a point. She was also mad. She was going to have to watch her carefully. If she achieved what she was suggesting she would never share her hard–won kingdom. That, Freyom thought, was why she kept Dalved by her side. He was to kill Freyom at the appropriate time from behind. She could see the plot in her mind. The hours she would have trained Dalved secretly in her rooms, to know just the right part of the body to hit to wound her enough to allow Yaltha to finish her off. Freyom looked at her sister's dagger and scabbard. Her eyes narrowed even more.

Even as she decided not to trust Yaltha as far as she could throw her, she saw the brilliance in the plan. They could be so much more than just Crilodach's doting daughters. So much more than Its lackeys. So much more than brainwashed robots.

Dalved knocked on the door and came in with a drink for the sisters in tall, thin glasses. He was not shocked to see them armoured and armed, but his eyes betrayed feelings of anticipation for the first time. Luckily the sisters were thinking of greater things than their palace at that moment and they did not notice the momentary look of loathing that crossed Dalved's face. They drank down the glasses and threw them into the corner of the room. The glass shattered into fragments that scattered across the floor never to be swept away.

"Leave 'em," ordered Yaltha, as Dalved moved towards the mess, "you don't need to clean up. Come."

The sisters pulled back the heavy curtains to the room and the sunlight poured in making Dalved shield his face from the glare. But he did not run away. That warmth on his body gave him yet more energy that seemed to bless his skin with comfort, and soothe his blood until the ice in his heart melted away.

"You're right sister–mine," said Freyom. "He's not afraid."

She slapped him on the back taking the wind out of his lungs. Making him cough,

"But there'll be times ahead when you'll have a great deal to fear little man. Believe me. Where you're going fear will be your breakfast, dinner and tea."

"Sister," smiled Yaltha thinking she had convinced Freyom of the rightness of their betrayal, "stop attacking my serf."

She took pills from a secret compartment in her rings and swallowed them, letting them and the drink course into her blood stream

Freyom laughed and pushed him onto the balcony outside the palace. He shivered for a second at her touch, even in the warmth. His eyes drank in the view, the sky, the clouds, the trees and distant mountains. He looked at the dirty grey of the palace stone as, for the first time, he saw the palace walls from the outside. An impressive and massive mistake amidst the beauty of the world around them. He looked across, down and up. Gauging from the distances where other rooms were in the palace in a second. And all the time he kept one eye on the sisters. He was amazed at how big the world was and the idea that there were millions of worlds like this filled him with awe but most of all he felt the warm air and breathed in like a man who wanted to get drunk for the first time in his life. At that moment Dalved would not have cared if they had thrown him off the balcony, but would have spread out his arms and delighted in his few seconds of flight and the feeling of the wind in the ears, before hitting the ground.

Below him vast doors opened up in the empty courtyard and the generals walked out a few paces like nervous rabbits. The sisters called forth the Ossendark which swirled in the courtyard, drank in their militia as fast as the men could run. Thousands. Hundreds of thousands. The palace emptied. A revolution was happening and no one was given the time to comment or think.

The sisters with Dalved firmly between them entered their

own Ossendark that opened above the courtyard a step away from the balcony, and everything that Dalved had ever known vanished from his life. All the years gone in the instant into nothing more than memory. He would never see the palace again. None of them would. The moment the sisters left, the entire place crumbled to dust along with all the families left behind. Then the fields and mountains crumbled and soon the whole world was a funnel of dust stretching out like a whirlwind spiralling into the darkness. Vanishing towards Zaqui. No longer sustained by Crilodach's spells.

The sisters stood like metal statues at his side. He had worked for them all his life but his days had been a picnic beside what he was going to go through. All those hundreds of stories he had been told unfolded before him in an endless torrent of places, names and peoples. And yet, if he could have been honest at that moment, travelling in a mind–numbing fear, he would have said that the sensation of moving without walking was thrilling. Speeding across the universe without raising a single muscle. Without being tired. Without any effort. He knew he should already be dead a hundred times, he knew that his being alive meant something not just to him, though he could never have guessed exactly what. For with all the stories he had heard he could never have imagined he was one such story. He was just Dalved the serf. Dalved who never had a secret. Dalved the quiet. He thought he knew everything about himself, but he was the most important story of all.

The Ossendark streaked across the sky appearing like a shooting star to the cockroaches scrambling onto the last of the Rounds. Appearing to Gertis and Midrak who wondered who they could be. Slicing through the darkness announcing to all and sundry that the travellers cared not for secrecy. The sisters arrived at what was left of Damkina before their militia. They did not wait. Crilodach's denuded and riven planet was not their true destination. Its lair primed to explode by Fulminar as Its armada moved out to attack Trecrogo, was nothing more than a way–station.

The sisters in their new armour, ran through Damkina swords in one hand, their daggers in another in case they met with any enemies. The hilts of their swords shone, the walls flashed with the light bouncing off their blades as they ran, flickering over the uneven surface as if the walls were telling a story. Their half–monster natures clearly visible for all to see in the shadows. This was why blotting out the sunshine was so important back in the palace, so as to hide the true nature of the sisters, because shadows never lie.

Dalved tried to keep up. A great shout went up behind them as the generals and their militia began to arrive. Freyom was not too sure who they were trying to impress with all their shouting, and Yaltha thought they were probably grateful to have arrived anywhere. Their generals set up sentries and sent down support platoons at a run, to guard the sisters. As they all ran down the corridors the spider's webs were broken by their hurrying feet and unseen spells ran like currents through the warren of cockroach tunnels. Meshing and splitting off until the whole area below and around them hummed. A countdown. Yaltha and Freyom heard the hum.

"Didn't you teach those idiots to watch their feet?" complained Yaltha.

"I only ever taught them how to kill," replied her sister.

"Good thing we're not planning to take any of them with us." She looked at Dalved. "Yes little Dalved, you're the only one to survive and you won't live much longer unless you keep up."

The Upala was glowing as the sisters ran into the large room. Yaltha nodded to her sister and Freyom opened the bejal up with a touch. Tegriel had told many people the Upala would only work for one person at a time and that person had to be a Ruzniel. Crilodach had spent a long time finding out who the right Ruzniel might be. The clues were far from certain but It assumed whomever they were, Tegriel would keep them close. Not one to leave anything to chance once It knew what the Upala could do It tested It. Sending the satellite which landed on Tethval's world and became a tyrant from deep in the past into a future unimagined by the machine's designers. When It knew It had succeeded It knew It could send Its daughters from their time into the distant past.

Yaltha and Freyom were not Its only daughters, Yaltha had been right. It had sired many others from many different species. Only when It finally knew who was most likely to be going back, when It was sure these daughters were the right choice, did It send Its summons. Part Ruzniel, they had the best chance of getting through. Crilodach never told them how they were sired. The sisters never asked him. It had broken the spell limiting the passage to only one but in so doing the Upala would be destroyed. The modification It had introduced into Hiesia's original design really made the bejal a one–use only device. The sisters did not care. They listened to Its instructions with half an ear. They just wanted action.

The presence of their father was in every crack of Its lair, but even on the threshold of the meaning for their existence Freyom saw the cockroach trails in the dust. She wondered what the insects had been doing in here in such large numbers.

"You see them too," observed Yaltha.

"What do you make of them sister–mine?"

"We don't have any time to pursue them this place is going to blow in a few seconds."

Yaltha took out the small box her father had given them from her side and attached the mechanism to the Upala which fitted like a glove. The box started to break the magic code and follow the pattern of Tobia's journey.

"Well?" asked Freyom.

"A Ruzniel has gone back in the past hour."

"So father was right. What about Tegriel?"

"Only the Ruzniel."

"Then where's Tegriel?" said Freyom.

"How do I know?" asked Yaltha.

"Let me look at that thing." Freyom peered at the device and pointed,

"Look at that. The surge in magical power. That's no Ruzniel."

"Only a Ruzniel passed through," insisted Yaltha.

"Not according to this unless the Ruzniel was a Sangyma."

"That would be a first. Maybe the Sangyma was dressed up like a Ruzniel?"

"That wouldn't fool the Upala," argued Freyom.

"Then what did he do?" asked Yaltha.

"Not what sister, who. Tegriel was part of the Ruzniel."

"What?"

"Amazing ... and very clever," said Freyom.

"They can do that?"

"Why not? Father's pretended to be a beast most of Its life."

"Inside, father is a beast."

"Come on let's go."

Crilodach's device in destroying the Upala ensured Its daughters could not return. That was no sacrifice. It did not want Its daughters returning, It only wanted them to fulfill their duty and kill Tegriel. It did not know they would take Dalved with them. It did not even know who Dalved was. So of course, It could not factor in anything Dalved might or might not do to Its plans. Though It, like Its daughters, was so dismissive of Dalved's kind of people, a peaceful, suspicious race that had emerged only in the last few million years, that, had It known, It probably would not have taken any notice. Which is the kind of thing the Sangyma liked. Crilodach always underestimated everyone else.

It had created Freyom and Yaltha and others to be just powerful enough to give them a chance against a Sangyma and yet manageable if they turned against It. Freyom's and Yaltha's mothers did not live through the birthing. Sired through spells that bound them to It because Crilodach could not breed naturally. They had been breast fed by wet nurses. The women they thought their mothers were strangers. Then It had had them trained. Taught. Indoctrinated with Its belief in Itself. Since they were half Its blood they did not take that long. They relished who they were and what they could do. Crilodach only asked for brief reports on their progress. It had given the palace to them when they were ready, to wait. Wait for their time. They were going to take the war to Tegriel. Crilodach knew Tegriel had a special knowledge because he had lived through history despite Tegriel's attempts to disguise the fact. Now It would change all that. Even as It ranged Its armada against Trecrogo It was secretly satisfied that Its plans were going well. Events would change decisively in Its favour. It, too, had seen the Ossendark arcing through space towards Damkina. So did the deep laid plans of Crilodach and the Sangyma meet each other, for nothing was exactly as either planned.

Freyom, Dalved and Yaltha vanished as the Upala sent them back towards an unsuspecting Tegriel and Tobia. The spells in their armour protected Dalved. As the Upala began to disintegrate at the mass of people being ferried back in time, the timing of Fulminar's booby-trap ran out. The first men from the militia they had left behind began to follow them into the lair, just as the walls blew in and then the whole place exploded in a chain reaction taking all of their troops in a series of huge explosions that turned the remains of Damkina into dust. The sisters no more thought of them than if they had been killing a fly. Crilodach did not look back as It knew Damkina was gone and It did not care who was left there. Gertis looked though. For he had misgivings.

Fulminar did not remind Gertis of the first line Filvani ever wrote in the Book of Derivations, which whilst not governing the others, nonetheless always gives pause for thought, *'There Is A First Time For Everything'*

The times Fulminar had wished Damkina did not exist. Now Crilodach's world was gone. Everything was still hanging in the balance across the whole of time.

Malevolent beings never feel lost no matter where they find themselves. Benevolence can quickly feel disorientated in new surroundings. This is because Crilodach's creatures do not want to learn where they are, or what the people there do, or how they speak or what they believe; they just want to rule, plunder or kill. When you want to know, when you are curious, the new, the unusual, make a deep impact on your mind and trying to find out all the answers leaves you confused for a while.

Freyom and Yaltha arrived into the past without so much as a gasp of surprise. The fact that many stars had not yet been created did not go unnoticed. Besides that they were unmoved by the experience. All they wanted to do was find Tegriel.

Freyom stood on a section of hard ground, looking across a lake and sniffed the air, her armour glinting in the moonlight. Yaltha looked up at the sky and then far into the distance with her keen eyes.

"I can almost smell them," she said.

"This place already stinks of Sangyma," said Freyom.

"Father told us about this place. Tegriel's land. Samphin, meaning 'lost home' in some language of his. Stand up Dalved."

"He's here," sniffed Freyom

"He and another animal. Kalevala," said Yaltha.

"Ah, the dog. I hate clever animals."

"You're a clever animal," laughed Yaltha.

"I'm far more than an animal."

"Kalevala's known for his intellect more than his fighting skills."

"I'm known for my sword arm," said Freyom, wanting to have the first go.

"Move yourself Dalved. We've a lot to do."

He was looking at the open space around them, confused and bemused. The journey had been so fast he barely had time to take a breath. He wished he had brought warmer clothes with him. In his bliss at feeling the sun he forgot about the cold. Most of him was still locked in the palace, slowly becoming aware that he was free but not yet free of the sisters. Yet the hope that he would be was growing inside him. The feeling that they were going to meet a Sangyma had a powerful effect upon him. He wanted to hurt the sisters. To take advantage. To betray them. He was finding his courage, something that had not existed in the palace.

"I wouldn't have minded bringing the militia," spat Freyom, "I've never been in a really big, enjoyable battle."

"You'll get your battle," promised Yaltha.

"We lose our generals and keep Dalved. Pointless. He's like a virus you can't shake off," cursed Freyom.

"Just because you don't have your manservant don't belittle mine."

"Maybe here I'll find a new servant."

"Use your sword wisely and your mind well, and you'll have a whole universe of slaves. Come."

Dalved, with a surprise that awed him, found himself glad the militia had not arrived. He hoped that meant their enemies were cleverer than the sisters assumed. Just because he knew some of the militia by sight and many by name, did not excuse them from being killers under the sisters' command. He did not know the sisters had let them all die because they had no intention of allowing their serfs to enjoy free-run of the palace for so much as a second.

The sisters marched with little fear of being seen. No one knew of their existence. Yaltha thought she could pretend to be anyone she wanted depending only upon whom they met. When they fought, they were sure they could overcome any opposition.

The last of the night around them flowed seamlessly into the other half of the world and the fresh daylight flowed onto their backs. Dawn saw them closing in on Tegriel, like dogs on the scent, from the opposite direction to the one he was taking.

Crilodach's understanding that Tegriel went back to meet Kalevala was a brilliant deduction. It had sought for years from prisoners to know what was taught about Tegriel's birth. Knowing that he was the only Sangyma who had no parents was a major clue. Then It had found out Tegriel had just appeared with Kalevala, from a story told by Kalevala to his close friend and Sangyma, Padrex. He in turn had mentioned this not only to other Sangyma, who said 'so what?' but also to Sewalt, who betrayed them all when he joined Rataplan before a battle on the rain soaked island of Uriedi. Sewalt told Rataplan. Sewalt's words rang true. That rankled It. It remembered that first fight. It had been taken by surprise. Things had been going so well. After It had gained Its freedom, It found out that there were other beings in the universe. It had found them. Discovering they were mere toys It had set about destroying them. Crilodach never conceived for a moment that there could be any power in the universe that could stop or hinder Its desires. And yet there was Tegriel, suddenly. Kalevala, a spellmaker and Bofindle a weapon It could not control. How was all that possible? Sewalt's story fitted the facts. And when It knew about the Upala It put the last pieces of the puzzle together. It kept the bejal in Its lair because like Tegriel, It feared anyone using It to upset Its plans. No matter where Tegriel started from, he ended up with Kalevala and It made sure Its daughters would be where Kalevala was to be found. It set a trap It hoped would change the course of Sangyma history.

The sun grew warm and Dalved's sickly skin, unused to being in the sun for anything but a few seconds, began to blister, as did his feet because he had no strong boots. Were they right after all, was the sunshine going to kill him? As long as the palace halls had been in existence and as often as he had had to traipse down them, he had never walked this far. All day they marched until the ravine between the mountains appeared. Freyom stopped them and sniffed the air. Dalved felt his legs going from under him but he was too scared to show weakness.

"What d'you think?" Yaltha asked.

"The mountains could snap shut on us," Freyom warned her.

"Dalved you go through the ravine. Freyom left or right?"

"Left."

"I'll go over the mountains to the right flank."

"But I could be killed," complained Dalved.

"Follow your orders," spat Yaltha.

She snapped her fingers and the three of them divided up. Dalved swallowed and looked at the ravine the way a fly looks at an oncoming spider-web that's too late to avoid. He went in, his eyes looking up, around and ahead all the time with fear feeding his naturally furtive nature. He had a sense of foreboding the whole way, alarmed at every bush and every twist as he picked out his pathway. Outcrops might conceal a soldier, or worse a fierce animal. At each step he took he thought about trying to run away but he knew the sisters would find him in seconds. He could not see them but even here, alone and afraid, he felt their eyes on him. He thought about crawling under a rock and hiding, but they would find him. In his imagination he had dreamed that once outside the palace he would be free of their power but he had been wrong. He could never free himself from them. He knew that now. The walk was a long and slow one. When he saw the end of the ravine he was more than delighted. He lived again. His feet picked up and he almost ran to the exit seeing the countryside open up to him like a flower opening up to greet the sunshine. More trees were growing this side and in the far distance he could see a sea glinting in the twilight. The view was beautiful.

Yaltha was waiting tapping her armour with her finger in impatience. Dalved did not ask how she had managed to beat him despite having to cover more ground and go over a mountain. Although his only experience of the sisters had been in the palace nothing they could do surprised him. He hurried over still feeling prickles of fear on his back as he left the ravine behind.

"See anything?" she asked him.

"Was I supposed to be looking?"

"By my father's claw you're useless. If I wasn't used to your face I'd tear your eyes out."

"A light," said Dalved, looking to the north grateful to be able to change the subject.

"Freyom's arrived." She raised her hand. "On the run, forward!"

She shouted as if Dalved had been the whole militia. The sisters ran like horses, though fully laden with weapons, they raced across the ground which reverberated with the power of their tread. The sisters seemed to grow as they ran. Dalved felt he was in the middle of a forest not just stuck between the two of them. How did they do this. How did they make him feel so much fear? Had they not divided up at the ravine. Did that not mean they were wary of their enemies? They were wearing armour. Did that not mean they could be wounded? But no matter how he tried to persuade himself otherwise, his dread of them was too deep to escape.

"No ambushes," said Freyom.

"We're not expected just as father told us."

But even as the sisters turned their heads towards their goal, others were listening. Kalevala was closely joined to Samphin. He knew every part of this world; felt every change; felt the presence of others. When magical folk move the atoms around them communicate the movement to every other atom. As the sisters ran and walked Kalevala felt this world move in time to them. Until Freyom screamed out Tegriel's name much to Yaltha's annoyance because now she knew he would fight and she had wanted to talk first. She silently cursed her father for making her such a stupid sister. But Freyom had done some thinking of her own. Knowing Yaltha would betray her she had decided to let Tegriel know they were there and hoped in any fight Yaltha would fall at Tegriel's hand, freeing her from any responsibility for her sister's death, then Freyom would put her sister's plan into action and rule alone.

"Three beings," noted Kalevala, feeling them through his fur after the loudest scream they had ever heard.

"Who are they?" Tobia asked.

"I don't know but they're bent on murder," replied Kalevala, breathing in. "The two in armour give off a scent much as I would have expected this Crilodach to smell. I don't know what they're doing here."

"Can we fight them?" Tobia asked.

"These three yes, but right now we don't know if there's more coming, and more importantly we don't know who they are. If they're part of a larger force we need to find out their plans."

"They seek nothing less than my murder," said Tegriel, looking at the approaching sisters in the distance."

"Are you certain?" Tobia asked.

"Yes. Kalevala we must run from here," Tegriel told them.

"I understand," said Kalevala.

"Well I don't. We need to stop them before they change everything," Tobia argued.

"Crilodach must have found out. When I saw the message bracelet impression in the dust I thought something had changed. I do not know how but It has. This is not something that happened before. What does that say to you?" asked Tegriel.

"That someone has been waiting for us," replied Tobia.

"Not here," said Kalevala, "they appeared just after you did. In the same manner."

"The Upala. They were at Damkina. They must have been sent to kill us with all the knowledge of tactics and weapons this time has yet to see."

"Three to kill you? That's never enough. Where are the others?" she asked.

"Who knows. Maybe they had a whole army. Maybe Midrak and the others are dead. Maybe not. Kalevala, we must divide our forces. Hide yourself."

"Hide myself," grumbled Kalevala.

"They will follow us and you will have a chance to escape whilst they track me. This land must survive to become Damkina so that the events that flow from Crilodach's being here, mature. Bofindle must be brought forth and you must survive, do you understand."

"Not a word," replied the dog, "but if they've come from Crilodach then It knows about you being here. It worked out how you defeated It many times by knowing what was going to happen. It won't have sent back anyone who isn't powerful enough to stop you. But these two aren't. Not as far as I can gauge."

"He'd not have risked sending back anyone who'd fail. Something must be blocking your senses."

"Maybe their armour. I've never smelled metal like that before but I still don't see they have the power. But go, I'll be here when you get back."

"Can you evade them?" Tobia asked, worried.

"I have my ways," Kalevala said to her. He licked her hand. "Have no fears little one."

Kalevala bounded out of sight. Tegriel gripping Tobia tightly by the arm, ran forward even as Freyom roared again. Taking dust from her hand, she scattered them into the air and the particles from all sides came together to point the way Tegriel had taken.

"After them," Freyom shouted, running into an opening in the trees.

Yaltha followed her, the thirst for a fight pumping her veins with hatred so hard she was finding thinking straight difficult. Dalved hung back for a second and then went to follow only to be thrown sideways by a heavy attack from the left. He tried to turn but his body was held tightly and his right arm was held against his chest like a vice. He hit with his left fist against what held him and he felt fur. Lots of fur. He shivered.

The sisters disappeared. Ahead of them Tegriel had opened the Ossendark and dived through. They quickly followed him and as the Ossendark closed Dalved was finally free of them. All struggle went out of him. He felt he could die a happy man. He felt himself dropped on the ground. He quickly turned and pulled himself backwards with his hands and feet and stared into two, angry eyes peering over his shaking knees.

"You hit like a falling leaf from an autumn tree," Kalevala told him, "and for an assassin you're unarmed, not very threatening."

"I'm not much of a threat and I'm no assassin," agreed Dalved, "But Freyom and Yaltha are more than enough for anyone."

"Are those the two who followed my friends?"

"Are you friends with Tegriel?" said Dalved in awe.

"Yes."

"Was that him?"

"Yes."

"Then yes they mean him harm. You should warn him."

"I think he knows."

"They have magical powers."

"You and I should have a talk," suggested Kalevala.

"Why don't you just kill me?"

"I don't just kill people," replied Kalevala. "Least of all confused, harmless ones. Stand up."

Dalved stood up and a very thin, weak spectacle he looked next to Kalevala. The two of them looked each other up and down and Kalevala nodded.

"I think you could help me," he said.

"Glad to," replied Dalved, "until they get back. Then they'll kill and eat you and I'll be back where I belong."

"You belong to them?"

"All my life."

"A serf," said Kalevala, with understanding.

"With many others, in a palace."

"Must be hard to be a serf."

"Hateful," agreed Dalved.

"So you've no regard or love for them?"

"None. I loathe the sisters with all my heart," Dalved assured him.

"You can help me protect the Upala."

"The what?"

"A bejal of great worth."

"A what?"

"Did they teach you nothing in this palace?"

"Only what a serf needs to know."

"Well you can help me protect things that need protecting."

"From who?"

"Those sisters."

"I ... I would like to but if they found out they would torture us terribly."

"Tell me, have you ever thought about doing something they didn't like?"

"Always. Every day," Dalved said.

"But you've never done anything?"

"Once, by accident," admitted Dalved.

"Why only once?"

"I was always scared. I've seen what they do to people when they're angry. That isn't something I'd want to go through."

"I'll fight beside you," promised Kalevala.

"Really?" Dalved asked with genuine surprise.

Kalevala and

Dalved

"Yes."

"We wouldn't last ten minutes against them but wouldn't that be a great ten minutes."

❖

"Tegriiiiieeeeeel." Freyom's shriek from within the Ossendark was just as powerful.

"This way," Tegriel told Tobia smartly.

"Did Crilodach send them?" she asked him, her heart thumping.

"Who else would even know we are here? It obviously

found some way to use the Upala. It has had enough time for the study ... here, in here, go on."

Tobia was swept down and along as if she were on a slide at a fair, rolling this way and that, diving low and rising high but unlike other rides this one never slowed.

"It probably knows more about the Upala than I do," said Tegriel.

"Why don't we fight?" she asked.

"We will Tobia but right now I need to know who they are. Everything is at stake. We cannot leave Samphin without answers or without them. I do not like Kalevala being alone. I should have stayed with him."

"And risked everything."

"Everything is already at risk. In here now ... jump!"

"Tegriiiiieeeeeel."

Tobia's felt the hairs on her head rise at the sound. He took her hand. They jumped out of the Ossendark onto a small platform. The same one Lilah would use for her attack on Crilodach's army. The äis Tegriel created to escape Freyom and Yaltha in the first battle.

"There now, a quiet a moment," he whispered.

They held their breath and as the seconds passed his grip on her hand lessened until he let go.

"We are safe for a while," he told her. "Kalevala and I did not know what power they had but we could see the little man in-between them was not armed. Probably a servant. We hatched a plan telepathically. Hopefully he is talking to him right now."

"Why didn't I hear the plan?"

"I am sorry Tobia, in the heat of the moment I just told Kalevala what I thought. He understood the immediate danger and the implications of what we both knew had happened. My first thought has to be to protect the future. Until we know the extent of their power I need to play things close to my chest."

"Implications such as?" she asked, catching the ice in his voice.

"We must kill whoever they are."

"Not imprison them?" she asked.

"They know everything Crilodach has told them; that could be every war, every enemy It has which means every ally we have yet to make. These people could change history every second they remain alive. If they had been wiser they would not have revealed themselves to me and just gone about their work. Their eagerness may have given us a chance to salvage the situation."

"But you would have found them out sooner or later. You are the one person ... the only person who would know them for what they are."

"I am not infallible."

"They have to kill you as much as you have to kill them."

"If I die Tobia, the future is in your hands," said Tegriel.

"You won't die."

"No? We have an enemy we do not know on our backs who knows what I am going to do, who I am going to see. Every day will become a trap for me. Even I do not know how many traps I can survive. I know this for sure, many of those to come with me have no chance at all and would die before they even knew there was a war to fight. This way ... "

"Shh. I hear something," she warned.

"Hold my coat."

"Why?"

"Just hold my coat."

She did as she was told and with his hands free Tegriel clapped them. The Ossendark trembled and several parts quaked and closed down but Yaltha and Freyom were too fast for him and escaped his first attack.

"They feel like Crilodach and yet not quite so," said Tegriel to Tobia.

Inside the Ossendark Yaltha held out her hands and her armour moved growing a bow. Plucking out an eyebrow which changed into an arrow she shot out in the direction the magic had come from that had tried to trap them. Even as Tegriel stood with Tobia the arrow flew out of the Ossendark and narrowly missed them, burning up in empty space. He was amazed. Nothing could do that from within the Ossendark except one thing. His eyes shone in understanding.

"It has daughters."

"How do you know."

"Their knowledge. Its plans. That is why It took the Upala. Unsure of when I would make my journey back. It worked out how I knew so much and managed to defeat It so many times. It must have seen through my ploys of prophecy for what they were, real knowledge."

"How would It have known."

"Intelligence Tobia. Prophecy in a people who do not know about the whole universe may seem mystical but to a being that sees the whole story It saw the places where prophecy was used. It listened to what the prophecy said and It knew. It knew. Despite my attempts at concealment, but how did they use the Upala only the Ruzniel ... oh, that must be why!" He thumped his fist into the palm of his other hand realising that Crilodach had used Ruzniel prisoners as mothers.

"Tegriiiiieeeeeel," shrieked Freyom, knowing he was close enough to hear them though she couldn't quite place him yet.

Tegriel gave Tobia a push forward and said,

"How long can you hold your breath?"

"As long as I need to."

"Good."

Tegriel twisted round and sat up and from his hands dropped two white round objects no bigger than tennis balls. They stuck to the sides of the Ossendark and then as they flew down the tunnels he let another two go. The explosions blotted out everything and suddenly they were floating in the void. Distant and quiet. Tegriel wrapped her in his left arm and then breathed out very slowly.

His breath broke into the emptiness and grew. Expanded. Before a minute had passed her feet touched something solid and the solid became bigger. Broadening out in all directions. She felt wrapped in warmth as an atmosphere was created on the äis. Thankfully, she breathed in.

"You found a place to land?"

"No I created a small haven for the time being. We could not use any of the places the Ossendark goes, those creatures would have followed us immediately. They have no knowledge of the äis, and we are too small to be easily found. For now we are safe. But only for now. They are part Ruzniel Tobia. That is how they managed to use the Upala."

"But no Ruzniel would ever ..."

"Not willingly but Crilodach always made a point of not killing everyone It captured. It used them for Its experiments. What did they suffer to give birth to those two creatures crate from Its ill spells.

"What shall we do now?"

"I must get back to Kalevala and change some of what I had planned to do."

"They'll be waiting," she guessed.

"I only hope they do not also know what you are going to do," he muttered.

"The sooner we kill those two creatures the better."

"I wish the bears were close," he said.

"Would they help us?"

"Without a moment's hesitation but their time is not yet."

"Can you use Bofindle."

"Spellmakers are the only ones who can use Bofindle. I must find a way to defeat these sisters. I wonder how much else It knows or guesses."

"Do you think It will use the Upala again even if we defeat them, to send more people back?"

"Remind me to ask Hiesia to make sure if ever more than one person uses the Upala at a time the bejal will blow up. That way It won't have the chance to do this again. It must have tried to create Its own Upala but It does not possess the Tree of Life from which the opals grew. We are in for a tough time now. Everything has changed."

Prisoner

Copret stretched out his thick arms, eased back his huge shoulders and rolled his neck. He growled deeply. The bones in his aching neck clicked the way they always did just before a fight, relieving some of the tension in his spine. There was no loose skin on his body, his muscles rippled through the fur. His claws shone. His back was straight. His eyes watchful. His feet were firmly planted on the warm stones of the fortress. His wound was little more than irksome.

For all his strength and courage he did not like war. Had Crilodach and Its hordes not existed he would never have fought anyone, nor learned the arts of hand-to-hand combat, nor how to handle any of seventy different weapons the bears had perfected. Fierce and proud as he was, he loved all things that lived because they lived. Like all bears his respect for life ran deep. So many were the battles he had had to fight, he had come to believe war was inescapable. Only in his long talks with Tegriel had he learned never to lose his love of peace even as he planned his battles. Not always an easy thing to do.

Fighting Crilodach carried a massive cost.

His loathing of his enemies had grown over the years. Grown as he had seen the atrocities they committed. Grown as he had had to deal with them claw-to-claw, as he interrogated the few prisoners he had taken. Grown with every friend he had buried, with every world he had seen fall, with every tired muscle and dirty face he had held watch beside, on long cold nights when all seemed lost. When day after day and perilous hour after hour the smell of war machines never left him. When he was so caked in dirt and blood he looked as if he was wearing a flat, hardy coat with threadbare edges where tufts of his fur were still recognizable. His life had not left him with any compassion for them. Yet he tried. He always tried. He tried to see things from the perspective of the foot soldier bred to kill. He tried to get into Rataplan's mind and discovered he had long ago forgotten where and to whom he had been born. He tried to forgive the cousins in the name of their dragon fathers. Everything around Crilodach became a part of It, how could they possibly escape and think for themselves. And yet how they seemed to enjoy themselves and their killing. How they sneered and provoked him. Did that all come from Crilodach? If the universe could create a Crilodach surely the same universe could infest worlds with Its willing, deadly followers? Of all people only the bears had never given anyone to Crilodach's armies. They had a saying they taught to their young, 'if every bear was dead except you, how much of our thoughts, art and culture would be preserved in your being?' Every bear cub grew up to embody everything noble in their people. The bears who had been prisoners in Damkina, and their daring escape, was subject to legend and endless story–telling as was their leader, Hiesia, who defied Crilodach and lived. Who had stolen back the Sagitæ It had taken, and hidden the gem so deep It would never know how to search, let alone where to look.

Around Copret they waited for news from the ambush. The Arvernat, who had known little more of life than slavery and war, talked, if at all, in low tones Copret could barely hear. Their language was unknown to him, but he liked the sounds their words made. None of them was as tall as Copret but all of them were his equal in strength. He was fascinated by their eyes, by their calmness, by their kindred spirit. He was mildly surprised that a machine could have manufactured such a noble race and decided there was more to their creation than ever the machine had known.

They milled around their defensive positions, some staying close to each other for a few moments as if taking their leave of friends, and then moving back, their thoughts roaming idly. Remembering people they had already lost. Hoping for small victories such as living to see the last of all hours, cleaning their weapons or taking a seat on the parapet and softly singing some songs they had been taught by their mothers when Crilodach had not existed for them. Nodding to anyone who walked past. Showing respect to their allies. Feeling the kinship of all those who stood upon the fortress on the last of all days, at the end of the war, at the moment of truth when finally they understood that self–knowledge gave greater power than all other knowledge.

Some Arvernat were pointing to specific areas, moving

around to get the lines of sight organized just as they had agreed with Tethval, to be in place by the time he either returned or Crilodach attacked, whichever came first. Copret noted how the weapons given them suited them well. He marvelled yet again at how the Sangyma laid their plans with such precision. Though Tegriel being inside Tobia and seeing the Arvernat through her, and being in close contact with Bofindle, would have explained to him how Trecrogo came to be. If he had thought he needed an answer. Anything was possible with them. The Sangyma learned the art of understanding the hearts of their allies before they learned anything else. Learning how they thought. Learning what made them fight. Learning what made them surrender. This knowledge fed into all the plans the Sangyma made. The strategies they used, the thinking they had done in choosing the final few who would populate Trecrogo. Most importantly they knew the bejals were their own masters and the power to dictate their comings–and–goings was not given to just any magician. Without magic, they taught, the universe could not function. Most magicians thought they created magic but the Sangyma always believed spells already existed, they merely discovered them. As proof of this they pointed to the fact that once a spellmaker had created a new spell all the Sangyma could recreate the same spell. As if a new piece of magic had locked into place in their minds.

Copret rubbed his paws together and held them over his face imbibing their warmth through his fur and shutting out the stars for a few seconds whilst he gave way to the long, deep bear thoughts that traverse infinity and hold the seconds at bay. He saw in his mind his enemies, recalling for the thousandth time their fighting techniques. He ran down the preparations and went over what he had told Demeter. He had to make sure he had left out nothing. He lowered his hands and looked into the distance. Roughly in the direction he thought Lilah, Tethval and the others might be fighting. He waited. He looked for bright flashes, strained to hear roars or shouts, even lifted his paws to try to feel any onrush of the armada. Everything was ominously quiet.

They knew of course. They had fought on worlds before with rock beneath their feet. They had fought on seas with ships, they had fought in tornadoes, on fire and across ice.

There was always a quiet moment.

They had always known today's quiet would be unique.

That to fight in space, upon Trecrogo would be a new experience. This silence was vast. If the exploding stars made any sounds they did not reach their ears. Instead they listened to their own blood pumping through their necks into their heads. A sound without harmony. A discordant though rhythmic music clad with skin.

Copret curled his feet feeling the comforting stone of the fortress. The clinks of metal filled the air from thousands of weapons. The stones beneath his feet hummed with energy. All those generations of planning were nearing the crisis. Before long he would know, if he lived, the answer to so many doubts he had had about Zaqui. The faces of many bears were in his mind. Every one of whom had contributed to this moment. All were long gone. If they were with him in spirit he could not be defeated this day, but that was 'if', for even the dead might fear to appear before Crilodach.

"I can almost hear the ambush. Smell the closeness of the foe. My fur tingles," he told Mojolo, having walked over to her as he checked the defences.

She stood next to him, her hair in control, her eyes looking from him into the distance from where, she supposed, the enemy would come. A darkness deeper than endless dreams stretched out around them. The only colour in the whole place emanated from Trecrogo as the last stars gave out their lament of weak, white light. The lack of light made them all look like shadows except where Demeter's intense aura caught them. Then Copret shone like copper, the Arvernat glittered like green marble, Chloe's bow shone silver and blue, Mojolo's hair shimmered like a rainbow of light bouncing off rippling water. Somewhere in that darkness Tethval, Lilah and the others were fighting and dying.

Lilah was Lilah. Light or darkness made no difference to how she looked. She had an inner light more potent than a sun. Sparkling in the inner tears she shed for all those It had killed and tortured. Above her head Bofindle would be slowly rotating, moving with her, ready for a surprise attack. Then she would leap into the midst of the enemy. Eyes blazing. Her arms beating them all back. Giving Crilodach a sense that this could be the moment It failed. By her side Tethval and over a hundred Arvernat leaping like a green tide washing everything away. Copret imagined from Trecrogo how the ambush must look. His own muscles tensed as he thought of the flow of the brief but violent fight.

Mojolo peered into the darkness seeing absolutely nothing. She had watched the ever faster disappearance of the stars. Light meant life and light was vanishing. The growing emptiness became a torment, as if the stars, as they vanished, took with them parts of the defenders' hearts. She also felt the warm stones of Trecrogo beneath her thin, light shoes which Demeter had given to her. The stones were the only reassuring thing she could touch. She wanted to hold onto Copret's furry arm and share his strength but she was too respectful of him and too scared. In her world bears had been animals people feared, locked up, made to dance or be torn to pieces by wild dogs. She had never treated one as an equal let alone a superior until she had fought with them. Then she had been thrown into a new world and the only reason she accepted anything that was happening now was because of Sanjava. The great adventures they had had. She had made the choice to be here for herself, long ago. She took strength from his memory and his gift to her.

"How close are they?" she asked.

"In all my life the enemy has only ever been a heartbeat away," he told her.

"Which means?"

"Closer than you would suspect. They'll be here soon enough don't wish them upon yourself. The waiting is always the worst part of battle. I wish we didn't have to wait, lets be doing and be done, but sometimes, as I was told by a very wise magician once, victory is conceived in the waiting and then born in the fighting."

"Really?" she said, "he must have taught Sanjava. He said the same thing."

"Tegriel also said every battle is carried on with weapons, but the greatest weapon you have is your mind. You must keep a clear head. Control your fears and you'll have more control over events."

She thought for a moment and asked,

"How does he explain the mind may be a weapon?"

"You have no other weapons without your mind. Even Bofindle is useless without a mind for a guide. In fact Bofindle's strength flows from the mind of the spellmakers. Only their minds are strong and inventive enough to understand the heart in the weapon."

"Still you need both, mind and weapons," she pointed out.

"Some people do. Some people only need their minds."

"If there are minds stronger than Bofindle I wish they were here."

"But they are."

"They are?" she was surprised.

"Yes."

She looked around with deeper curiosity and stopped herself muttering,

"Great."

"What?"

"Now you've got me fidgeting, wondering just who these people are who're fighting with me."

"You see them well enough," said Copret.

"But I don't know them well enough." She did a short dance with her feet. "Just keeping awake," she said as Copret looked at her quizzically, "I don't like waiting any more than you."

"Waiting's very difficult," agreed the bear. "If something's got to happen, the sooner the better so I know how things turn out. This not knowing bothers me. The uncertainty and the fear that ..." he stopped.

"Yes?"

"I might fail. Not be strong enough, quick enough, fierce enough. That all the effort'll come to nothing. That we might've forgotten something or be taken by surprise by a spell too great to overcome."

"Well I doubt that last one. You know what's coming. All I can tell you is that I see nothing but I seem to hear something now that my hair is tingling."

"What do you hear?" he asked her, eagerly.

"My hair is resonating to a sound my ears cannot quite catch. A soft kind of song."

"Really?" His paws curled into fists. "That's a residue of your time with Sanjava. Interesting."

"Because?"

"Sanjava once told me his hair knew more than he did. Like when rain was coming a day before any rains fell. Or knew when he met a stranger if that person were a friend or an enemy. Like a watchdog, his hair knew when enemies were close and saved him from ambushes on many occasions. He said he believed his hair was a gift that linked him to the Sagitæ, but he was never sure. Filvani failed to find any mention of living hair anywhere. The Sangyma are not people who tend to believe in things without some evidence, but he was sure his hair lived in a realm beyond the one he could see. As if communicating through his nervous system with the universe. Guiding him. He trusted his hair. By giving you the magic of his hair he gave you his greatest gift."

"A pity he had to die," she mourned, remembering well the times Sanjava talked about his magic to her.

"In you he lives," Copret assured her.

"They told me about Midrak having a Sangyma fuse with him. If Sanjava was inside my head he'd talk to me."

"Are you sure?"

"If that's the way Fulminar works in Midrak why not for me? People used to hear voices in my world and we locked them up. Now I'm in the middle of nowhere facing certain death and I actually wish I had a voice in my head. How weird is that?"

"You've awakened to a changed universe," said Copret.

"I can usually take change but this makes me feel really uncomfortable."

"Your hair?"

"No. The sound. As if my scalp were continually being strummed by a not very good guitar player."

"Crilodach does that to people. It gives us all the creeps. This time, travelling with It, will be Its strongest ever army. Rataplan. The dragon cousins. The burning Grafiers will be shot across the top of us, on fire and trying to grasp at us as they burn up in their effort to burn us to ashes with them. Demeter should be able to handle most of them. The Stagetes, Brujans and Midrats are the ones the watch. The first come out of rock before you know they are there and crush you to powder, the second will burrow below our foundations, they are excellent sappers. The third can blow you to pieces with a touch of their fingers. They move swiftly, can change their tactics in half a second, and come at you from all sides, lying in wait for you, sneaking up on you from cover. I've even seen one lying under a dead comrade waiting to kill whomever comes to pick up the body."

"Frin-Ghirzan has been busy in his training camps since the days when I fought Zibanda."

In ages past, near to Crilodach's world, a planet had the

misfortune to rise that was rich in minerals and just warm enough to hold intelligent species that could adapt to their surroundings, carrying their heat with them in the form of the food they ate, adapting their bodies to all climates and terrains. Tegriel had pointed to this world for Tobia.

They were not sophisticated thinkers. Crilodach learned how to rule other life with this species when It broke out of Hâgon and built Damkina and then reached out to grasp this world. Before they ever found their own pathway through the evolution of life, Crilodach began to use their world as a place to train Its finest soldiers. Ghirzanben, the name of the planet, became a name synonymous with fighting, war and soldiery. No more than a vast barracks. Here creatures of all kinds went to train in all kinds of terrains. The harshest mountains, the coldest ice, the hottest deserts, the darkest seas. They did not train for weeks or months. They trained for generations. They lived and died in the terrains they trained to fight upon. Different kinds of soldiers for different kinds of places. All of them specialists. All of them adapting their natural body types and abilities to kill at a moment's notice. Crilodach's forces held many specialist troops whose abilities shone forth only when they were called upon to fight. When not at war they were disruptive and lazy so their training never stopped. The weak died. The strong bred ever stronger soldiers.

Crilodach did not stop at attack training. It also had very well trained spies who were secreted in places right across the universe. Some went to empty but habitable worlds just to wait and watch in case something happened; in case some enemy came there to rest or some magician mistakenly thought themselves safe and could take refuge on an empty world. People began to say Crilodach could see them all, that it was omnipresent, but actually It had millions of eyes watching for It. Watching everything that It knew to watch. The greatest web of spies ever to have existed. These spies had to be special. To keep discipline in a vast army ruled over by Rataplan is one thing, but for an individual to live amongst another race for years and not be seduced away from Crilodach's service is quite another. Special they were for It had manipulated their brains. Everything they heard and saw It heard and saw at the same time. That is why they were never caught, they never had to send messages. They were like cameras that were never turned off.

It spied on Its own troops, getting information of what was being said, when and by whom. If the spies lived for a year amongst Its own troops, It knew they were good. If they were discovered the angry troops usually killed them. To those who survived It gave a gift, It extended their lives. One of Its spies had lived for over five hundred years, many of those amongst whom he lived for that time were not so fortunate.

Crilodach had trained interrogation specialists who learned their craft by getting into the minds of those the spies exposed in the army. Crilodach was fond of Its interrogators. Their commander, Frin-Ghirzan carried the name of the world with him because, as the armada said, he knew everything that went on and everything that was going to go on. He was a feared individual. They said he was part worm because he could regrow bits of his body and part fish for he had scales and small, yellow eyes. Frin-Ghirzan was indifferent to what people thought of him. Rataplan had given him many worlds to investigate and Frin-Ghirzan loved nothing better than learning about worlds the hard way, through the screams of those who tried to resist him. His talent lay not in killing but torturing. Many said he was a more fearful enemy than Rataplan, for Rataplan was a soldier and once he had defeated an enemy he moved on. Frin-Ghirzan was not just a soldier. He was something of a philosopher. Picking away at the mind, exploiting anything that might be a weakness. Once you were in his power you always saw him night and day in your brain. He imprinted himself on your subconscious. He drained you dry as if you had been a well from which he thirsted to drink. He was a desert, sucking in every juice of existence so that he could continue his own selfish life. Like a black hole he was unable to let anything be free once captured. His character and Crilodach's wishes, were in perfect harmony.

From the worlds that fell to Its armies Frin-Ghirzan often found species capable of some extraordinary feats which he would communicate to Crilodach and soon babies from those worlds found their way to the training camps on Ghirzanben and the watchful eyes of the trainer in command, Frin-Ghirzan himself.

There was no planet, no place, no part of the universe in to which Crilodach could not send an army trained to fight in the prevailing conditions. Men who could go without water for weeks, others who could swim for miles under water, yet others whose bodies healed fast even from deep wounds ... and more. So strong were Its armies that sometimes watching them fight was more like watching a steamroller move inexorably forward, than a battle. Everything was a weapon, every moment a cause, nothing stopped them but the Sangyma. The magic they possessed could stop Crilodach's armada and was much feared by the armada for as Lilah had told Tethval, to win against Its army, Bofindle had destroyed his world. Truly a Pyrrhic victory but nonetheless proof of immense might. That was not even a hundredth of what the bejal was capable. Bofindle had brought Crilodach to Its knees as long ago, when they first met, the bejal had buried Crilodach beneath Samphin.

Everyone knew about Ghirzanben who knew anything about Crilodach. Once a warrior from a proud race of birds had allowed himself to be taken deliberately so he could see the world for himself and bring back news of what went on there. Five years later they found his body on a battlefield. He had died a loyal soldier of Crilodach's. After that the Sangyma never let anyone try to go to Ghirzanben again.

So the Sangyma had to create their own places as outposts against Crilodach's armies, their own safe havens, and ring them with spells. Some hidden like Earth where the bears built Trecrogo, some so strong like Ruz Crilodach would have had to attack them in person and that was something It never did. Besides which Ruz was useful to It, for Ruz was watched and It knew when magicians visited, and managed to follow some of the Sangyma for a while after they left. But even Its greatest spies always lost them after a few days. Still in those few days the Sangyma were always attacked and they knew why. Ruz was a weak spot in their defences although well defended. Ruz was like a beacon, and every time the beacon flashed Crilodach looked. So they made the planet a stronger player, and used Its spying to put It off their scent whenever they could.

Crilodach had always had a maxim that It would be seen as mightier if It never actually went to battle. If It could vanquish others from afar, enemies would understand that Its power was awesome. It knew this was true because Its spies told It of the stories and myths that were growing up around Its name because no one ever saw It. The imagination of weaker races amused It greatly, yet none of them came half close enough to either Its real power or Its real intent. Crilodach liked the fear It instilled. Fear helped It to create more power than any of Its generals. The power to defeat an enemy without a fight, for those that feared It most feared to go to war against It.

Many were the myths around Ghirzanben. The planet's darkness, purpose and militias. The Brujans were trained on Ghirzanben. Men and women with soft fur on their backs and metal plates attached to their chests that went up to and over their shoulders during a campaign. Each plate was individually made. Most of the battalions in Its army had excellent craftsmen who made their armour and weapons with great pride. They had to make sure the weapons had the greatest strength and yet were easy to clean as Rataplan liked his men to look impressive in the field of battle.

The Grafiers were the only ones not to wear any armour as their lightness in the air was crucial and since they were sure to die, armour was considered a waste of resources. Crilodach never minded such things, but Rataplan spent his life with other species and he knew how to make the most formidable use of great numbers. How to make his men shine like fire and instil terror in the enemy before a life had been lost. To make the siege engines glitter so the enemy could not take their eyes off them. By making his men take a pride in what they did he made them care, for they cared for nothing else. When they were not at war they had games and endless tests to see who could make the best weapons, the best armour, dismantle the engines and put them back together the fastest. He rarely let them sit still longer than the time taken to eat a quick meal.

The Brujans had huge hands and their powerful pincers were long which meant they were able to dig at frightening speeds. They had been known to bore through a whole mountain from one side to the other in less than a day on Ghirzanben. Long, thin tunnels in which they had to crawl on their steel–hard bellies. The heat from their bodies solidifying the earth and stone as they passed so they never needed to shore them up. They said iron could melt on the skin of a Brujan sapper when they were working. But then many things were said of Crilodach's armies. For this siege the Brujans would not rely on their pincers but use huge drills, for thousands of men would funnel down the tunnels they made. For this siege was unlike any other.

When seers in sadness said Crilodach feared nothing. When the evening fires were high. When story–tellers told of how everyone surrendered to It and memories of childhood stories came back as the stars twinkled in the skies and everyone felt cold, a soft voice would say,

"Except the Sangyma."

In the darkest moments when all hope has been lost, many other things were said of the Sangyma. The people they saved, the magic they wielded, the prophecies that had come true. And for a brief second those assembled would feel lighter, and happier and nod once or twice before sleeping. People who had never seen the Sangyma still felt reassured by the mention of their names and the telling of their battles against It. Peoples needed their magic to exist in the face of Crilodach's brutality. That much had not changed since Mojolo first became Sanjava's finest pupil. Since she had stepped outside her own life and into one she had never suspected existed. Much else had changed while she had slept. She had not heard of some of the creatures Copret had warned them would be coming. She was interested.

"Can the Stagetes come out of the stonework of Trecrogo?"

"No," said the bear.

"Well, there isn't much more stone around," she said, confidently, "and what are the Brujans going to burrow through?"

"Crilodach will create a battlefield upon which will stand Its forces," explained Copret, "They'll not leave a spare inch visible, and they'll stretch around you on every side. You'll see nothing else. When they start even the space above will be clouded with the enemy. All that abundance of life taught to bring death, crammed into such a tight space, will face us with the most violent battle we have ever had to fight. If the space were any bigger It would be able to swamp us but in these last hours Trecrogo is the higher ground."

"I have faced Its hordes before. I bear Its wounds even now."

"That's just some of Its specialized troops. Its infantry are just as skilled. Well armed. I sometimes wonder if they are more dangerous unarmed. They fight with everything they have. Crilodach kills anyone who comes home in defeat. Except Its generals. Those It scars with Its claws if they lose to remind them of their failure, but the infantry It wipes out. Every one of Its soldiers knows they must win or die fighting. Beings faced with no choice but to fight with every fibre in their bodies, never stop fighting."

"Zibanda fought hard. I never bested him in the three battles in which we faced each other. If this Rataplan is a worthy successor I know exactly what he'll be like."

"I've seen Its infantrymen cut in half still trying to slice at the feet of their enemies from the ground with their last ounce of strength. I've caught them alive before now. Had them in prison. They don't break. You can see the darkness in their eyes. No matter how often you wash them the smell never goes. Their armour is never taken off, but becomes part of their skin. When they're almost full grown they're given a slight size too small and their skin pushes into the inner fibres. Remove the armour and you'd rip their skin away."

"Do we have the advantage up here?" she asked, patting the crenelated stones.

"We're in a strong position, but we mustn't be complacent. This will be the finest, most intelligent enemy we could ever face," said Copret.

"You don't sound downhearted about our chances for all that."

"I'm not. No one told us to kill them all. That we could never do, but hold them off. I think we've as good a chance as any. Especially since Sanjava made sure you were here. That was an unexpected master–stroke."

"I'm not sure I'm worthy of that much confidence."

"I've heard the stories about you. Your adventures with Sanjava were every young bear's dream and in those days you didn't even have Sanjava's gift."

"I am not so expert as Sanjava with this hair."

"His hair will fight without your direction."

"I hope so."

"Other Sangyma have done the same thing, and that fills me with hope. As I heard of them dying one by one over the years I became less certain of our cause and more despondent. Even with Lilah growing stronger everyday I feared our prospects were hopeless. She told me Fulminar and Tegriel are still in the fight. Now I begin to see a deeper purpose and some of Trecrogo's design makes more sense to me."

"Is hope a weapon strong enough to defeat It?" she asked him.

"Hope is the first of all weapons. Hope is your hands. Without hope you wouldn't stand before an enemy, you'd never hold onto any bejal. Hope is your eyes without which you'd be blind. When you looked you'd not see friends but lose your inner sight and with that would go any chance of victory. Hope is your voice without which you'd cease to make sense, you wouldn't talk to your friends or speak of home or even remember what you were fighting for. Hope is your heart that pumps the blood around your body no matter how numerous the enemy becomes, how weary you get, how far you've gone or how far you've yet to go. Hope's your best friend who picks you up when you fall in the dark, mends you when you hurt and cherishes your life with every passing second. Hope stands by you, stands above you, beside you, below you and behind you morning and night."

"You know," she said, impressed by Copret who embodied all she knew of the greatness of the bears, "the last thing I remember happened before you were born, yet I'm standing next to you as if I've known you all my life."

"Maybe you have. You just didn't realize until now," smiled Copret.

"Oh come now don't try to tell me we met in some other life."

"Other life? Is that what your people believed?"

"Some, yes," Mojolo said.

"Mine believed that bears learned to talk because they met a Ruzniel many ages ago, lost in the mists of time. A Ruzniel who was on a quest. Three bears helped her. Hiesia was one of them but she never returned. When the other two came back, they had language. How they learned we're never told. But our language is unlike all other languages in history because we've never changed a word. Perfect then and perfect now. We've had words for things long before we ever met with them. Because we had the words we knew these things existed in the first place. The names of the bears who first met new peoples and realized who they were, are all listed in our great books. Many say the language is proof there is a higher power of magic working amongst the bears. Who's to know. Ebiric is the most brilliant language though and serves as a bedrock to our civilization. Mojolo does not translate well. But you're a woman, a warrior, an ally, a beacon carrying the magic of Sanjava. We've words for all those things."

"Is that the Hiesia I know?"

"You know Hiesia?"

"I fought beside a bear called Hiesia once, in Ghirzanben. Freeing her family from Crilodach's vile experiments."

"Hiesia was a white bear with a purple streak down her back. She was a mystic."

"That's her."

"There is a story that, once, she found a child cold and alone so she took the fur off her back and wrapped her up to keep her warm all night and thus saved her life. Then in the morning she put her fur back on but the ice had made a home in her flesh and from that day forward she was changed. They say her claws could tell the future and her eyes could draw out the smallest, wicked thought. That somehow the ice had given her knowledge of all things cold and since most of the universe is cold she had more knowledge than any bear before or after her."

"The girl's name was Vemadi."

"You know the story?"

"I was there. I didn't know she told the future after that."

"They say she could read scratches made in talik wood, the hardest wood known. And she must have had strong claws I can tell you because I can't make much of a scratch in talik. A black wood with golden veins. Rare on our world. Rare in the universe. But then we bears have a penchant for rare things. She was the most successful mystic we have ever had. No one knows what became of her, not even her two last companions. Not even the Ruzniel they met. I asked Fulminar once if he knew anything about her and he shook his head. But I noticed even as he denied knowing, there was a slight smile on his lips."

"You think he knew something don't you?" she asked.

"Probably," replied Copret, "but I was not to be told."

"Did he ever tell you?"

"I never asked again."

"I would have."

"If he'd wanted me to know he'd have told me. If he never told me I wasn't meant to know. Maybe because my knowing was dangerous for her or for me, maybe for another reason."

"She was a strong fighter for sure. There are not many who could lead a fight against Frin-Ghirzan and escape."

"Did you get to know her well?"

"We were with each other for months. And again right

Hiesia's skin saves a child

before the battle in which I almost lost all the days of my life."

"You are the first I have ever met who knew her."

"Knew her and loved her. But she never trusted me with her secret."

"She had many."

"After her escape from Ghirzanben she was changed. Something happened but I never knew what before."

"Stories. Fables, myths, sagas. I've heard a great many of them in my time. I'm a descendant of hers."

"So you've tried to find her."

"What makes you think that?" he asked.

"You're that kind of bear. Even if she wasn't a relative but more so because she is."

"I've tried too many things. If bears love what's rare you're looking at the bear who above all things loves what's hidden. I want to know why a secret is secret. I've a feeling she did too. Probably that's what killed her."

"You can't be sure she was killed."

"Well, no I can't, but after her escape her trail vanishes but neither Crilodach nor any of Its hoard ever boasted about her death. If they had killed her they would have. There were just no clues as to what happened. And stories about her spread across the ages, far longer than any bear has ever lived. So whatever happened to her was strange. I wonder sometimes if she decided to disappear. If there was something important she had to do and one day she might reappear surprising us all."

"After her escape we went to Ruz. I had to wait for Sanjava. She seemed uncomfortable at times. Always rubbing her fur. I thought her saving the child had something to do with that but I was never sure. After that we lost touch. She just vanished as you say. I also liked to disappear before I met Sanjava. That's why I loved sailing. I'd go off and not be bothered by anyone. As things turned out I vanished from my entire planet."

"But until you met Sanjava you always went back."

"Sure, but I never really wanted to. That last time with Sanjava I disappeared from my family as thoroughly as your Hiesia. More so. They forgot I had ever existed. But I wasn't sad about leaving, in fact I was glad."

"My point exactly, you found your purpose and you've a purpose here. Who knows she may come back yet. With her talik wood predictions and all knowing eyes. Who knows but her work was with the Sangyma and is important to us here, now. What will happen, will happen. I count only on the allies I can see, as well as the intricate plans of the Sangyma. Now I count on you also."

"Me. Sanjava saved my backside three times. Fighting was never my strong point."

"You have good sense and a clear head. Prophecy and legend have ended. Tegriel told me once, in the last two days there'd be no more prophecy. Indeed the sayings and legends of all peoples have nothing to say about this time. We're in the day of silence. We'll not leave behind a record of what happens here. Only we'll know for sure and then only one or two of us may ever know the whole story."

She gazed across the embattled parapet watching the Arvernat standing, waiting. Chloe was taking up her station on the far side from where Mojolo was standing. Everyone sensed the armada was closing in on them.

"What else do you believe in besides the Sangyma?" she asked him.

"I take the universe for what she is, a magical, strange place filled with a knowledge of her own. Greater than me and you, even greater than Crilodach. The cosmos created the Sagitæ, and who knows truly what secrets they hide. If I believe in anything, I believe in the Sagitæ, the Sangyma and Trecrogo. That's all I've ever known. I've played amongst the stars with the Sangyma and travelled half the known worlds and everything always comes down to the same thing, the present moment. Here. You and me. Demeter and Chloe. Lilah and Tethval. The Arvernat. All the others out there coming here to fight and die. Lives converging. I've looked for a reason but as far as I can tell trying to find answers is as easy as casting spells whilst balancing on springs. You use your hands to create a spell, you fall, you stay upright and use your arms to balance, you cannot make a spell. Choices. Our lives are all about choices in the chaos of events."

"Perhaps we're all part of a cosmic magic," she thought out loud.

"Or part of nothing at all. Magic is all about balance. How are we to know? How are we to learn? Now the time has come when we can learn no more. Memories are only portraits of nature's face painted by untrained artists. They teach us everything and then take everything away from us in an instant. We think ourselves important but the universe holds everything, she is the most important thing. We're not worth as much as a passing second."

"That's a cold idea for anything living."

"The truth is never cold," argued Copret, "You wish to live again. Be different, be proud or angry, male or female, good or bad you don't really know; what you wish is just to live again. For this all to happen again but in a different mix. That too is cold. In a way, colder than indifference because you're saying you want people to go on suffering, go on being part of wars and battles, go on and on and never cease from the treadmill. At least I believe there's a chance this all ends."

"I didn't mean that," she said.

"Of course you didn't."

"Sometimes a little suffering isn't harmful. We need to have something to struggle with to make us strong. To better ourselves."

"And where is this little suffering? Who's to say what is little and what's not? Who's to suffer and who not and to what degree? They say, in the darkest stories, the three Ruzniel who never came back, have been tortured by Crilodach past death. Can you imagine that? Would you want that to happen again?"

"Of course not but what use is there in your universe for any of us?"

"We choose a side and we fight everyday we live. What other use is there?"

"But that is so ... meaningless."

"You think so? How do you come to make a choice? When you saw Sanjava fighting how did you decide what was going on? What was in you that said you even needed to make a choice?"

"I don't know. By accident. Even Sanjava didn't know why I saw everything."

"There you're wrong. There are no accidents in the universe. They may seem like guesses to you, but they're not. What seems like chance to you isn't. From the very first, every spell has led to a specific outcome. Unthinking matter reacts with everything, but thinking matter doesn't. Thinking matter can make a choice. The energy within you can make a choice. But don't suppose choices come free of consequences. I told you the mind is the greatest weapon of all. We live with our minds and our minds are connected. The choices we make, they come to us from the birth of all things. From the energy and the magic of seeming chaos are the billion pathways by which energy moves from one atom to another. What seems to us a guess, a chance decision, a surprise choice is in fact part of a huge matrix. A flow of minds into the magic of ideas. Every choice we make is a parry, a thrust or a cut in the great war of minds. Life, you see, is the key to unlocking the secret of why time exists."

"I don't understand you," she complained.

"Ah, but you do. The closeness you feel to the people here. People you've never met. You feel their purpose in your bones. You know you're in the right place even if you're scared and unsure. After all, you've had a very amazing experience. Your race is not supposed to live as long as you. You've been touched by a Sangyma. You didn't run screaming from your room when you met the Arvernat, you didn't attack them. You knew. Those years you spent with Sanjava prepared you. I would go so far as to say from the moment you saw Sanjava fighting, you were being prepared for these hours here with us."

"I suppose there's something in what you say. My life has been unusual."

"The magic you've been through is nothing more than an extension of yourself. You believed you'd live again and Sanjava has brought you to a place no one else in your world has ever known. You represent your people here. As I do mine. As Lilah does the Ifari, Demeter the human race, as the Arvernat represent all those who've been oppressed by Crilodach's armies and Chloe all children. Look around you. Tell me this was all chance, nothing more than a reaction against Crilodach. Can you not see that all the things done and not done by all peoples have led to this? Here we stand. Tell me that what we do makes no sense to you at all."

"I understand the reasons, really I do. You're all so powerful. You're all so well trained, well armed. I am amazed. I'm sorry to have woken too late to have been part of the preparations."

"This siege will be our greatest victory."

"This place was built to take more than a siege."

"You know about that?" he asked her.

"Sanjava told me."

But before she could go on with the last conversation Copret would ever have, which Mojolo was enjoying, they were interrupted.

"I think our newest warrior would prefer us to have all gone out with Tethval and Lilah and met the enemy face to face," said Demeter, floating over.

He had been slowly going round the parapet all the time Mojolo and Copret were speaking, making sure everyone was in place. Giving confidence by his translucent appearance. The light that surrounded him shone without blinding anyone. The shadows of all who stood upon Trecrogo swayed and rotated as he moved across the parapet. The light from Demeter and the Arvernat shone out in all directions giving the fortress the look of a city on a night of the Blitz.

"I'd always prefer to attack," she responded, "than to be standing here waiting for It to arrive. For one thing we can't leave easily once we're surrounded."

"We don't intend to leave," replied Copret.

"We don't have a fall back position?" she asked.

"This is the fall back position," replied Copret.

"Don't frighten her with your talk," Demeter scolded him, "besides I'm almost able to leave, Trecrogo can send me anywhere. I can stretch out my sight. I can see Zaqui from here."

"I don't scare that easily," said Mojolo.

"This fortress embodies the accumulated power of the bears. Taken from a hundred thousand worlds," Copret said with pride, "Every piece of stone is independent yet joined. Every atom has been placed in an exactly perfect position. The bonds between the atoms are as strong as the universe can make them. Around and through them flows an energy that's the very mother of magic. The Onäis built into the parapet are based on the famous äis of the Sangyma. But even this is not enough to stop Crilodach for long. If we time things badly and give It a free hour before the end It could still win."

"And capture the Sagitæ," said Demeter.

"Sanjava never knew if the Sagitæ could survive Zaqui. Have you ever found out?" she asked.

"No one knows for sure. A good deal of what we do say about them is inferred from the experiences of the precious few who have been close to them," said Demeter, with his new found, obvious authority.

"That's true of Crilodach too, but we know all about It," replied Mojolo.

"The Sagitæ have always been hidden. Their exact nature secret," said Copret, "Crilodach hid away in Damkina but always made Its intentions known. Its character has been easy to read through Its armies and generals. We assume the Sagitæ are Its opposite."

"You're not sure," she said.

"Tegriel was sure," said Demeter.

"The only thing I know for certain is the nature of the Sangyma and the nature of Crilodach," said Copret.

"Is that enough?" she asked.

"Enough to bring us to war," noted Copret.

Seeing them talking Chloe began to feel a little alone. She walked over to them.

"I wonder how Lilah, Tethval and the others are getting on?" she said, doing some finger stretching so she could handle the bow faster.

Her quiver was fuller now as more arrows had been found for her. The first armoury was almost empty. All over the parapet stashes of arms had been laid against the walls so the defenders could fight on the run if the enemy got over the battlements, and Copret had assured them that for all the fortress' strength, Trecrogo was made to be invaded. None of them questioned the plan. They were to fight as if they would rather die than let a single enemy past the walls but Crilodach had to be lured into the fortress somehow. Demeter knew how. He now knew the reason there was one, single window in the chart room on the far side of the fortress. They had to make Crilodach enter. They had to make It eager to destroy them. The best way to do that was to pose a huge obstacle to Its armada. To slow them down, wrong-foot them and play to Crilodach's growing impatience, fuelled by Lilah and Tethval's costly ambush. As Zaqui drew near Crilodach was showing signs of desperation. It had allowed Damkina to fall. It had left Its lair to lead the armada. They were filling It with doubts.

Demeter had been looking into the distance, when Chloe came up. Listening. His face betrayed nothing for the long minutes he had been aware of the fight going on against Crilodach's army, but now he answered Mojolo, and all of their unspoken questions, by saying,

"They're falling back. Tethval has taken on Crilodach. One-on-one. He's insanely brave."

"Is he dead?" asked Copret.

"No, the attempt didn't last long. Crilodach hates being touched. It unnerves It. It fears another's touch. I don't know why but I sense Its fear covering It like water cascading over Its head. Saving Tethval has wounded Lilah. Her golden necklet is broken. Fifteen Arvernat are left standing. The armada stalled for a moment. Rataplan was not expecting such a bold affray. He missed Lilah by a second. They are looking in all directions waiting for more of us, not believing so few would attack alone."

"Now Lilah's wounded," complained Mojolo.

"Time is a two-edged weapon Mojolo. Against and also for us." Copret eased back his shoulders again.

"It fell!" cried out Demeter. They all looked at the boy whose eyes shone with excitement, "It fell onto Its knees. Bofindle brought It down." Then he added with deep depression, "Its up again."

"Enough exercising for me," commanded Copret, "Listen to me. All of you." His voice carried to everyone's ears and they all turned to listen to him for a moment,

"The enemy is here. There'll be ten thousand of them to each one of you ready to tear you to pieces so remain in position on the parapet. Do not find yourself alone. Our strength is the fortress and each other. Don't be fooled by any enemy you face who's not armed. These creatures are dangerous. They will tear at you with their teeth and fingernails. They've no mercy, show none to them. Don't fight to wound, fight to kill. Keep your focus. If you're disarmed and still alive, find new weapons immediately. You all know where the caches are stacked around us. Make use of them. The enemy cannot wield them. Our weapons will tire and blunt as the fight goes on and your arms will grow weary, new weapons will fill you with renewed energy. Stand ready. Stand firm. Stand together."

He looked at all their faces, their eyes steady and their mouths set with determination. He had seen many soldiers. He had been with many men and women giving their all.

"I'm proud you're with me at this time," he told them. "This is our final battle. I've no doubt you'll give your all." He turned to Demeter. "There are a few things I want to check. Keep an eye out for Lilah and the others. When they finally come It'll be close on their heels and I want them back on Trecrogo before It catches them."

"Time for part two of the plan," said Demeter, as Copret went off to make a last quick tour of their defensive lines.

"I'm sorry we could not talk more about Hiesia," said Copret to Mojolo.

"I'm sorry we could not talk about many things," she replied.

❖

Demeter was lifted upwards by Trecrogo. Looking far out towards the ambush, seeing Lilah fighting off hordes of Crilodach's soldiers with the remaining Arvernat, as Tethval raised himself up and hacked at anything that came close, he sent out a shock wave that swept through the Rounds in the armada like a tsunami. Titling the Rounds on which Its army stood, throwing many onto their backs, grabbing wildly at anyone or anything close by, certain they were being sent spinning again. The force of the move caused a second moment of uncertainty to sweep through a large section of the armada. The army hesitated, looking to Crilodach to stop the assault. Those holding the siege engines fast had to strain to stop them slipping off and falling onto their own troops or into the void of space. There were many screaming orders, many more loud shouts, but above them all Crilodach roared out to quieten the armada and settled the Rounds with a flick of Its claw, looking avidly for Lilah.

It was in no mood for tricks. It guessed Lilah's manœuvre had been designed to check Its strength. It had felt the power of Bofindle. It grimaced. Where had Bofindle come from? What power had created such a weapon that had, long ago, once before brought It to Its knees? Its mind, not slow to ideas or plots, suddenly had an idea It had never had before. Not in all the ages of Its life, nor in all the trials and tests of the Sangyma, nor in all Its own plots and plans.

Suddenly It wondered if It, too, had been created.

Not merely by the universe but by something that thought. Something that could design purpose. But then anger and darkness took over and It dismissed the notion. It wanted blood. It wanted to grind Trecrogo into dust. It wanted the Sagitæ. It wanted their lives. It craved victory.

Lilah did not know what It was thinking but she knew It

hesitated as the armada momentarily stopped. In that instant Lilah with the wounded gathered close to her, swirled Bofindle over her head and they were propelled back towards Trecrogo on the broken Onäis as if by a storm, so fast they had to hold onto each other for support. Everything seemed to be rushing along with them. Only Lilah was fixed and immovable. But however fast they raced, the sound of the armada did not leave them. Their ears rang with the roar of the enemy close at their backs. Even as they arrived right behind them, like a rainstorm you can see crossing over the ground streaming towards you turning all colours darker; even as they jumped onto the parapet and turned to prepare again for battle barely taking in the deployment of their friends, the armada arrived like some legendary, ferocious beast with millions of heads. Ravenous for victory, unperturbed by the ambush or the apparent might of so few, they shouted with one voice. An armada dedicated to their master, regardless. Ignorant of exactly what Zaqui was or how their sacrifice was irrevocably their fate. They were part and parcel of the clash of weapons, the roar of war, the march, the parade, the kill.

They had been told the stars were in Crilodach's power. That It was destroying them one by one. This was the war to end all wars. Final victory. They had been worked up into a frenzy. The encroaching darkness did not display the death of the universe to them, but, rather, Crilodach's immense power. Stars vanishing were not a call to mourn but a cry of supremacy. Their own eyes showed them the certainty of their master's power.

They saw the stars vanishing.

It had left Damkina, Its home throughout the ages.

They still lived as everything else died.

Their enemies skulked behind fortress walls.

They were utterly incapable of seeing anything but what It wanted them to see. Fear of Crilodach propelled them just as much as their sense of purpose, which was, in fact, Its sense of purpose. Crilodach's lies were all they knew. Their willingness to die blinded them to this truth. They thundered towards Trecrogo gorged to bursting on Its promises.

Crilodach, that general of mighty wars in unnumbered places, thought at last It had a great conquest ahead of It. So the Sangyma had managed to keep alive some of their magic. So not everything It thought dead was dead. Here they were, holed up in a fortress. It sensed them. It lusted for the Sagitæ that must be there. At last Its enemies were penned in one place. It had the greatest armada ever assembled. It did not have to speak, Its own feelings were so powerful everyone in Its armada felt them; this was their time, this was their calling, this was their rightful place. They all roared. But roars do not win battles. The defenders did not shift in fear from foot to foot. The Arvernat had already faced this implacable enemy and come through. They were prepared.

The Rounds, upon which stood Its infantrymen and specialist fighters, began to mesh as a whole again. All around Trecrogo they came back together, like a jigsaw-puzzle sliding into place. Juddering as they came to a halt. The men on each Round giving out a huge cry as their comrades joined with them into battalions, becoming part of the besieging terrain. The ground did not reshape into an oval world but formed perfectly to fit the outside of Trecrogo. So had the Sangyma achieved two things; Crilodach had come to them to a part of space of their choosing, and the size of Its armada had been judged accurately as the size of a substantial part of Its world. Only those who had studied Crilodach's every character trait could have planned such a strategy with such accuracy. Only a bear like Hiesia could have volunteered to go to Its lair and gather the necessary information, then fight her way out. Less than half in the armada had ever seen such a massive fortress and those that had from their first battle and could still use their eyes, could see no end of Trecrogo as they looked left and right. They also saw they surrounded this immense fortress. So advanced was Crilodach in their minds that only Rataplan realized that the top of Trecrogo was now almost the height of all that was left of the universe. Had the universe stretched further the Rounds would have fallen onto the fortress, not settled all around. He did not wonder about that for more than a second. He did not have the time.

The Rounds reared up close to the walls of the fortress, a flood of rock and soil not quite daring to touch the magical stone. A tide sweeping all the way round the walls, growing as deep as Trecrogo was high. The landmass menaced the defenders. Sections rose higher than others and upon these stood men marshaling metal onagers. The odd spear or arrow and even rock was thrown at the defenders by over eager soldiers anxious to be fighting. Soldiers shook angry fists and shouted, challenging anyone to jump down and fight. Slowly, as the Rounds grew upwards, the defenders began to be able to make out the grimaces on the faces of the foe and pick out the different helmets of squad leaders, engineers, and the host of specialized battalions Frin-Ghirzan had spent his life training. But under strict orders from Copret the defenders held their places. They looked. They heard. They waited. No response came from the fortress.

The thoughts that usually go through the minds of men about to fight did not go through their minds. On the parapet the defenders knew that each of them was the last of their people. There were no homes to miss, no friends to return to, no stories to be told, no eyes to witness this last day. Copret and Lilah knew this to be one of their defining strengths. Few though they were, because they were the last of all, they too, just like Crilodach's armada, would never stop fighting. They would meet determination with determination. Force with force. Tirelessness with tirelessness. For these men and women there was nothing else. Zaqui was close and they had to make sure Crilodach died. They did not fight out of fear of retribution from their commanders. They did not fight for a promise of eternal life. They stood for what they had all stood for in their separate ways all their lives; liberty.

Tracks appeared between the lines of Its battalions upon which the siege engines were set to run. Along these they threatened to run straight at the walls with their cargo of men and armaments. Throwing huge boulders at Trecrogo was not going to be good enough but upon these engines the Grafiers were preparing to be thrown high into the air, pouring their own flaming bodies down onto the embattled parapet. Upon others the Midrats formed into lines ready to give their lives for a moment's chance to touch any of the defenders and blow them to pieces. Mojolo looked. Her hair was quiet. Other engines, in different places along the battle lines, started to dig into the ground with large, silent drills that sliced through the rock like butter. Without being directed, like some animals on the hunt sniffing out prey, they manœuvred themselves to create tunnels pointing in straight lines towards the fortress. Behind them came the

Brujans. Steel clad, thick skinned men and women with their strong, long pincers. Just as Copret had described them. More like worms than people. Another of Its creations who always looked as if they were in as much pain as they inflicted. Unlike many of those in the armada they knew what they were up against. They could talk to stone. They had trained to face all kinds of stone and they knew this fortress was different. They felt the power of Trecrogo just as Crilodach did. How could they not, for just as the others were looking at the defenders and not looking at the fortress, in their dark tunnels they were looking for the fortress and could not see the defenders. The Brujans followed their drills into the ground where the heat and dust stuck to the metal plates around their bodies. Lost in the darkness they grunted their way forward while above their heads they heard the dull thump of their comrades manoeuvering across the mud soaked land. The grinding of wheels on tracks, the shouting, the clamour for blood. The heated atmosphere heavy with war. The battle that had really started for them at their birth, had begun to end.

The defenders looked on as the growing world hugged to within an inch of Trecrogo; until the Rounds surrounded the whole fortress, until the last Round was in place. Still the armada moved upon the terrain as waves of men moved in unison. The odd flaming arrow shot across the spectacle showering light across the armada like a flare, revealing a huge array of weapons, engines and once, set where It was directly facing Copret, Crilodach Itself which, for all Its size, seemed dwarfed by the size of Its own armada.

Upon two thick legs, Its claws clearly visible, Its eyes watchful, Its face ribboned with layers of extra skin, Its thick arms bent at the elbows, Its mouth slightly open showing rows of incisor teeth. Copret looked at It. Into It. Through Its magic he saw the real Crilodach. There was no animal here, no predator of men's flesh, but a being filled with anger. In love with dread. Hidden deep within the facade that Crilodach had created for Itself, was the man, in every way the opposite of Tegriel. His hair was white and cropped short, his arms were set on thin shoulders, his tight lips almost masking the fact he had a mouth at all. His burning blue eyes glaring out of a long–chinned, sallow face. This was the great enemy.

The high walls that had taken Chloe and Demeter a day

to scale, were vanishing beneath a rising tide of stone, rock and soil. From all sides the Rounds eclipsed their view as ever more men and ever more siege engines locked into place until their eyes were dizzy with watching them and their ears rang with the clamour. Demeter blocked out much of the noise to give them respite. Still none of them moved from their positions. Mojolo stood with her hair loose and still, the lariat in her hand. Her thoughts were of other times. Older faces. Rataplan saw her standing apart from the others and a lesser general would have concentrated his forces against her. But a lesser general would not have realized that for the defenders to have allowed her to be alone like this meant she was not only strong, but dangerous to his men. He eyed her hair. He knew.

Discipline began to be imposed in this huge armada. Ranks and battalions became visible. The lieutenants under Rataplan took up their places, clear for all to see. Their prominence was a way of telling their men they were not scared of the defenders of the fortress even as the names of those very defenders were whispered amongst the army. Many had seen Copret before but there was a whisper that a human was there. No one had seen a human before. The stories of humans, even amongst Crilodach's forces, were many. A race that seemed to epitomize the war between the Sangyma and Crilodach, though they did not come in touch with Crilodach until they were ancient. As if they had been overlooked by Crilodach on their small, blue planet. But they made up for lost time. Butchery was their way of life. As many would join Crilodach as would fight against It. The humans were a race that could never make up their minds but each one worked against all the others. Irascible and independent they could never be trusted though they were magnificent in battle. To them all wars were civil wars for unlike almost every other race in the universe, human beings were always to be found on every side.

The armada also knew that the bejal Bofindle was here. They had seen the staff make Crilodach stagger to Its knees. They now knew a spellmaker was alive and of all their enemies, she was the strongest. For never once, in all the ages they had assembled, had Crilodach's armada defeated any of the five spellmakers. Even the thought of them made the armada wary. They had seen the green men with lights in their eyes, each one with the strength of ten men. How many of them were there? One had touched Crilodach and lived. This fortress was huge and imposing. Large enough to hold millions. Its armada knew they were facing mighty foes. So they looked at their commanders and saw Ferveiss sharpening his teeth, saw Jurveiss sneering in contempt, saw Rataplan steady and unforgiving. Saw Frin-Ghirzan ordering men into position. What were Arvernat and spellmakers to them, asked the whispers. Less than nothing, came the replies.

So they stood emblazoned, and in their midst stood Crilodach. Its reason their voice. Its idea their aim. Its strength their confidence. These were not ordinary warriors, each one was part of Crilodach's greater self. Fired into existence by Its own thoughts. The work of thousands of corps, clear and defined. The orders known before they were given, the training they had all gone through with Frin-Ghirzan showed as they mustered together in disciplined perfection. Higher and higher the Rounds encroached on Trecrogo's defences until the combatants were almost on a par, almost in danger of being face to face with each other. For one second Chloe even thought the Rounds would swallow them up and they would be caught in Crilodach's trap, not the other way round.

Copret gritted his teeth. Beneath them, where the others could never have seen, there was a small mark on the fortress walls. Only one bear knew where to look because he had set the mark there. A solitary line. A line that he had drawn with a single claw, to show him where Crilodach's Rounds might reach. A point based on their careful calculations of the structure and size of Damkina. Information that had been gained at a high cost. This mark was based on the idea that breaking up Its planet was one of the things Crilodach could do if It wanted to transport Its army to a free–floating Trecrogo. Trecrogo's entire dimensions were drawn from those calculations. Once It knew a direct assault on the Earth upon which Trecrogo was built could not succeed, It destroyed that planet as the bears had foreseen. But It had not known the true nature of Earth. They had saved the magic. They had grown Trecrogo's roots in Losek soil and the magic was potent.

Copret didn't congratulate himself on having gauged his enemy's mind. He just watched. Tense. Much of the battle plan they would pursue depended upon his being more than close. They had to have gauged the height to the inch. The Rounds slowed just before the line. The ground stopped rising as the mark was reached. Then, with a last effort the Rounds settled and the line disappeared, just hidden by the forces arrayed against the defenders. Copret breathed in and growled. Those who advised him had been knowing and wise. The enemy would not overrun the parapet immediately. A fact that was not lost on Crilodach. The defenders had a chance to do what Trecrogo had been built to do.

The light from Demeter and the Arvernat shone out across the enemy soldiers catching metal and eyes, casting long shadows from the siege engines across the heads of the armada. Shadows that themselves almost came alive with their twisted shapes, catching all the shaded colours of the enemy helmets as they crept up the walls of the fortress and even fell across the parapet. Until Demeter let Trecrogo shine with a deep light from within the stones, that turned the dark shadows to nothingness, and bathed the forward rows of the armada so clearly the light showed every movement of the enemy, every face and every weapon. The breath of the armada came out like steam and formed a mist around the bottom of the siege engines, giving them an almost ghostly appearance.

Until needed, Lilah had shrouded the window to blend with the stone. She would know when to make this single window visible. Enticing. Unmissable.

Crilodach had set the armada at all points facing the fortress leaving not a single avenue of escape. It stood upright, a huge presence above Its army, incapable of being moved. Crilodach's soldiers could see It from wherever they were even those on the other sides of Trecrogo, by some form of magic that bent Its image around objects. Even the Brujans beneath the ground only saw Crilodach before their eyes as if It had etched Itself onto their eyeballs and burned Its image onto their brains. Appearing to be everywhere at once was one of Its special skills. Its eyes seemed to be looking at all of them at the same time. And every one of Its armada felt those eyes burning into them. Judging them. Urging them on. Damning their mistakes. Cursing them to die for It.

The defenders felt those same eyes. In their own different ways. To Copret they burned with an anger equal to his own and as long lasting. An anger hammered into his brain on the anvil of his own actions. An anger swimming in blood and muscle that pumped through the hearts of the bear nation. An anger that at this moment became a life-force, became reason and purpose, became his stubborn future. There were a great many to avenge in these final hours.

To Mojolo the eyes seemed so deep she could drown in them, feel lost and never want to be found but for the fact that they were cold. Deathly cold. Sucking at her own eyes as if It were trying to pluck them out. Drawing her toward them with such intensity she needed to concentrate just to stand up straight and not be thrown forward onto the stones. Like an incessant urge welling up inside her dragging her away from the others. If she had seen those eyes by herself Crilodach would have had her begging It for mercy without ever raising a claw. Her hair held her safe. Crilodach had no power over Sanjava's gift.

To Demeter they were lit with all the colours of the rainbow and every colour said something negative. How to give up, how to see his weakness, how to feel betrayed, how to know he would lose. Nothing was spoken, just felt. And he gave back the light of Trecrogo, warning Crilodach with equal intensity that this was Its end. That It stood no chance, that the defenders would grind Its armada and all the armies It sent against them, to dust. To Crilodach this was a novel experience. To be warned. Its anger increased.

To Chloe they were grey and stood in judgment of her. Questioning all she thought she knew. Questioning why she had brought Demeter here to die, why she had believed her teacher Wei K'un, why she had taken up a bow and learned to kill. Asking her how she could think, for a single second, that a young girl had any chance against this armada. Willing her to try to run and find out what had happened to her people. They made her shiver despite herself.

Deep under the ground of the Rounds the cockroach army felt those eyes but they did not fix on the insects. Cockroaches were too much a part of the mud and soil, too much a part of the ground to be noticed. Cockroaches were their own shadows, in possession of no special magic, being simply designed to creep and crawl and hide behind the stones of Damkina. It gave them no thought.

The Arvernat saw those eyes each in their own way. Testing their emotions to the limit without seeking their loyalty. Crilodach was far too subtle for that. They did not suggest that the Arvernat should lay down their arms, or stop fighting a battle they could not win. No, Crilodach's eyes made them think, forcing them to fight their resolve before Its armada had struck so much as a single blow. Forced them to struggle to just stand there. Forced them to grasp their weapons more tightly for fear they would slip to the stone from the lifeless hands that had surrendered to inevitable defeat.

So Its eyes were reflective of all their personalities. Always It had used Its eyes to make others cower and grovel, but here It used them to make the defenders uncertain of their power, a little off balance.

Copret's eyes spoke to It as an equal, as an old adversary. And in Copret's anger Crilodach was reminded not of the millions It had ordered killed, enslaved or tortured. It was reminded that Copret was still alive. That was a failure. And It marvelled at the strength of them all. Crilodach, the butcher of endless wars, the commander of bloodthirsty hordes, discovered It was matched by those who were not themselves Sangyma. That added to Its anger. To think life had evolved so far as to challenge It. To think that a human child could hold the secret to defeating It. Of all the races the very one It had thought least significant, more of a burden to the Sangyma than of use to It.

It did not judge enemies by their number but by their brilliance. Many a time It had won Its battles with force and overpowering strength but only against those who relied wholly upon their own power and strength in arms. It had learned the Sangyma rarely relied upon magic alone. It had learned how crafty and secretive the Sangyma had been. They preferred traps and stratagems, lures and retreats. It was wrong in Its interpretation of why they did this. It believed this was because they did not want to have individuals die and nations exterminated, whereas It would kill whole galaxies if It could gain one tiny victory by doing so, or imprison one enemy to question, or harm one Sangyma. And whilst Tegriel might have argued and told It to Its face that his strategies had little to do with saving lives, It would not have listened. Crilodach had never been a good listener.

Copret hoped Crilodach's inability to let go one piece of Its overall power and control would be Its undoing. It crowned Itself king. The bears had gauged their enemy exactly after their millenniums of watching It. Learning from the many, many battles they had fought and the many they had avoided. Copret felt this was a sign that their strategy was well judged. Not that he looked for signs. In his people's long trek towards the civilizing of their minds, signs were the first thing they had held in utmost suspicion. Even Tegriel's prophecies were frowned upon at first until they discerned a deeper mystery behind them. Hiesia told them not to ignore his prophecies. Not even the one that said Lilah would stand upon Trecrogo, for even though no one knew for sure, they knew Hiesia's character. She was too strong to be lied to but none of the bears ever knew her secret. Not even her own family whom she had rescued from the dungeons on Ghirzanben.

He saw Chloe shake herself awake tearing her eyes away from Crilodach's glare, lowering her bow, taking an arrow in her hand and placing the feathers against the string. The child, thought Copret as he watched, has already chosen her first target. He could not say if making a warrior of a twelve year old were a good or a sad thing. All he could do was wonder how this war could ever have been otherwise.

As Its men made their first sorties to test the defenders, the Arvernat supported each other with alacrity and skill. Its eyes searched the parapet. It was looking for Lilah. Her useless ambush amused It now It was standing again. It had taken blood from her. That felt good. But It still felt the touch of the foul, green man whose eyes shone and It saw many more such on the parapet. It did not know this species well. They were few. It had old scores to settle which would be settled this day. Plans flooded Its mind. Battalions moved in Its imagination. Enemies fell like a harvest. But most of all It wanted to smell Lilah's blood again. Spellmakers were not a race. It had never been able to control their births and more than once had cause to curse the way they were able to create new magic. In Its deeper thoughts It believed this was all to do with the Sagitæ but It had no proof. Even now, as It looked with unyielding devotion to Its greater aim, It wanted answers to questions It had never had answered. What would Its eternal life mean to It if It did not also know everything?

"Rataplan," It growled. Its general heard It in his head as he had moved to the other side of the battleground.

"Yes?"

"Concentrate the 34th battalion against Demeter. Press

him hard. Engage the 55ᵗʰ and 43ʳᵈ if you need to, he's part of the core power of the fortress."

"One human boy?" questioned Rataplan.

"All the magic in the species is in him."

Rataplan signalled and three battalions lined up near to where Demeter stood. From the fortress they looked like a stream flowing through the body of the armada as heads slid past stationary soldiers and made their way to their positions. Others gave way to let them pass. They moved seamlessly round the engines that could not yet be moved. Their discipline was not lost on the defenders against whom they were being drawn up.

It had made sure some of Its best men were concentrated against Demeter. Although this was the first time Mojolo had ever seen Crilodach It knew her. It had sensed the Sangyma but could not see one. This puzzled Crilodach until It saw her, but then Its eyes narrowed as It looked at her hair. How many of the 'dead' Sangyma, It wondered again, were alive in one form or another? More than anything else that had happened to It, the sight of their magic still thriving in the universe angered It. Tegriel's deep cunning. That hair could be almost as great a weapon as Bofindle. It looked to the emptiness of space around the fortress. Where, It wondered, where was Lilah? It vaguely sensed another Sangyma was close. But It could not place where. As It was not looking at the cockroaches Gertis would take Its Brujans by surprise and It would not sense Fulminar until the final moments of the battle.

Rataplan signalled the Grafiers and all along the front-line, they climbed onto the engines and set themselves besides the fires ready to be thrown high into the air like burning arrows to land on the parapet amongst the defenders, attempting to burn to ash anything they touched. They did not scream nor beg but waited their turns as long lines of them took to the dark sky turning everything within sight red and white. Their skill was to burn but not to die until they had chosen an enemy and directed their flight to embrace their target.

Its eyes scanned the parapet several more times. It did not understand where Lilah was and why she was not here. It was certain she had retreated to this place. Certain she had arrived. Was she away getting reinforcements? Where would they come from? Rataplan had told It how the Arvernat had appeared. So what? It also had a few tricks no on had seen before.

"Rataplan," It growled again.

"Yes."

"Split the 164th into four watches send them out on the outer Rounds to scan for reinforcements."

"Already done."

"You used the 164th?"

"They're the ones with the best eyes," said the general.

"How close are the Brujans?"

"They will be at the walls before the last Grafier falls."

Copret, It thought, would know many of Its tactics but Lilah was the one to fear. It thought about Demeter. They had been clever to choose a child. An adult would have more readily been seduced by It to betray their comrades. A child was more naturally honest. Susceptible to noble thought. When It saw Chloe standing close to the boy It rightly guessed she, too, was part of Demeter's determination to do the right thing and not simply another warrior. Its enemies always relied upon emotional ties to make them strong. It was not tied to anything or anyone and that is what made It stronger. It knew how It was going to pursue this battle. Just by seeing them arrayed along the parapet It knew. It actually elated, a feeling induced by Its own arrogance.

"Rataplan," It growled a third time.

"Yes."

"Where are those Midrats?"

"With Jurveiss," the general told It.

"Bring them to bear on the girl. Her name is Chloe."

"The one with the bow."

"The one with the bow. Use the 3rd and 59th, 14th and 86th to take her first attacks with her arrows to enable the Midrats to get close."

"She can hold off four battalions?"

"Her bow could hold off half the armada. Send the order."

Rataplan gave the orders but he was beginning to wonder at the might and magic of those they faced. A fortress they could not destroy, children who could do more in a fight than he could ever achieve, a weapon that in the right hands could bring Crilodach to Its knees. He felt no elation. But then Rataplan's self-belief had evaporated as he held the dead body of his first child in his arms. After that he just did as he was told with a burning heart.

Crilodach's anger was greatest at this moment. The creature that had touched It was still alive, hiding away somewhere with Lilah. Why had Tethval not been afraid of It? What were these Arvernat made of that made them fearless? It could have done with a few battalions of them in Its armada. Why had Frin-Ghirzan never asked for beings such as these? How could a mere machine It had sent into the past design such men? The thought crossed Its mind that they had not been created just by the machine, that somehow Sangyma plots lay in their evolution. Spells within spells. Again the idea spread across Its brain that It was not as free as It thought It was, that somehow It was being used. It roared. These were not Its thoughts. Trecrogo was playing with It.

Though It could take Its anger out on Tethval's comrades, the feeling of pleasure would not be the same as ripping Tethval to pieces. When It had been touched by Tethval It had felt all Tethval's life. It wasn't memories but a rush of feelings. Feelings Crilodach had never felt before. The feelings of a lower form of life from Itself, without Its power. To be enslaved. To be in love. To be hurt. To despair. To want to be free. Crilodach hated feeling these things. Once before It had had to endure deep feelings. Long ago when another had touched It. Such feelings of loneliness. Of darkness. No pleasure just an horizon of sameness. Serfdom. But Tethval's time would come. He would not escape. None of them would escape.

Rataplan moved to be with his forces on the left flank. Jurveiss took the right flank and his cousin Ferveiss was behind them with the Brujans busily following the drills towards the walls, weighed down with weapons and equipment for when they breached the fortress and clashed with the enemy. Their mouths salivated at the thought of the slaughter. Other commanders waited in reserve to be called. Each with vast detachments of troops. Dotted around the army were yet more smaller groups of a few hundred soldiers who were to take advantage of any situation as they saw fit: a sudden charge at the right moment, a timely reinforcement, a feigned retreat, all were possible. Their eyes fixed on the fortress, waiting for the commands that would come from Rataplan or Crilodach. Any command would reach any man, from wherever the commanders were fighting, in a second. The trouble for them was Demeter and

Copret would see the command coming, hear with an inner voice. No secret code or whisper would elude them. They both knew what all the commands meant in whatever language they were given. Crilodach was too self-assured to have changed them just for this battle.

Never had Crilodach's men besieged a fortress that had not fallen. They were hardy, strong, well equipped and never gave up. Their enemies always needed more supplies, or rest, or sunshine, or water. Crilodach's commanders all trained their men to need nothing more than someone to fight. They were never short of supplies for Crilodach had no need of supply lines. What Its men needed It created for them. But here was a magic made to match Its own and they had less than one day, less than one short day, to break the walls down. As they were about to learn, they had never seen this before.

In the past the Sangyma had tried to avoid sieges. Sieges cost lives. They forced people into dangerous situations. Yet It sensed they had wanted this fight. They had brought Its armada here. This was a holding position. Crilodach weighed the possibilities. Chief amongst them was the fact It could not see Lilah.

It did not think that the Sangyma had avoided sieges in order to blind It at this time. In order to make It believe the situation was not going their way, make It believe the battle had some advantage to It. It thought It had them cornered and there was Its mistake. Lilah's invisibility at this crucial time put Crilodach off the scent. It did not see Trecrogo as a trap but an opportunity. Its keen senses were dulled just enough for the anger to overwhelm the questions in Its mind.

Ordinarily It could have walked into a fortress but Trecrogo was protected by spells It had come across before. Spells It now realized had been used to test Its army in the past. Although they had never been used on Crilodach Itself, Crilodach was not greater than the laws of magic. It knew Trecrogo was using those very spells which were most harmful to It. Light and time were very powerful adversaries. Crilodach knew in the back of Its mind that Trecrogo had been long in the planning but even this place could not end Its life. It needed a crack in the walls to overcome these spells. One single crack and It could get inside. Confident, It raised Its claw and from the voices of every one of Its men came the same words,

"Your Blood Is Our Right," screamed in the magical language Tatlit, which meant everyone on the parapet heard the scream in their own language.

The walls of Trecrogo were too strong to reverberate with the force of the sound but the armour the defenders wore, their swords and bows, tingled as the shout was repeated time and time over. The final frenzy of the enemy had begun. The enthusiastic attacks of the few, the first eager Grafiers who had launched themselves too early looking for glory but burned to dust whilst still in the air, would soon become the horde of fireballs clustered like meteors, along with forests of arrows and the bodies, endless bodies of the enemy.

Rataplan was waiting for the expectant armada to be fully drawn up before giving the go ahead to attack. The battalions moved with amazing speed. Copret, although he never took his eyes off Crilodach, saw everything else with his wide vision. He communicated what he thought the troop formations meant with Demeter. Demeter drew closer to Chloe. Mojolo calmly stood with her hair unfurled. Their first repulse of the enemy's first attack must be total and complete. The armada must feel the true power they were up against. The Arvernat played their eyes over the closest troops in the armada. As yet they had been told to keep the light merely for seeing, and not to use the magic given to them by Bofindle. At that moment the armada were more wary of the Arvernat than the other way round. Greedy to kill they may have been but they already knew these men came out of Bofindle. The weapon that hurt Crilodach. Throughout the armada, fuelled by the determination of Crilodach to rule their minds, thoughts ran that were being fed to them by Demeter. Until many in the armada were not sure what was true or false, what was possible or impossible. They did not even know if they could win. Crilodach felt these thoughts and blocked them. Demeter was trying to use Its own tricks against Its armada. It roared.

Below the defenders, as if the world created around them were groaning, they heard the first heavy thumps as the drilling siege–engines began closing in on the walls, with eager Brujans in thick clusters behind them longing to make holes in the stones and scrape out their enemies from within the fortress, like scraping out the heart of a fruit with a spoon. For many in Crilodach's armada, enemy formations were like a food to be ripped open and digested. Others saw themselves as cleansing the universe of the unclean powers that would stand against Crilodach, and by killing them they made the universe a safer place. Yet others, the majority of the armada, felt that by doing Crilodach's bidding they were protecting their own lives. All were no more than bullies loving the feeling of power they had over others.

Chloe held her first arrow securely between her fingers with her bow raised waiting for something to happen. Scared to be the first to shoot and not wanting to be the last. Her lips were tight shut as she peered along the arrow wondering if a shot to Crilodach would achieve anything. But she had been told the arrows would not pierce It. She moved her gaze towards a siege engine and stared hard to make sure she saw as many of the armada as she could at one time. Her eyes were wide with the horrific wonder of the armada surrounding them. She could make out individual faces. She could almost feel their steaming breath coming across the parapet like a stench-filled, noisy, fetid breeze. She imagined she could see some of them mouthing her name and then to her astonishment she saw some of them were. She moved the bow to a mass of men drawn up in front of her. They were looking right at her. Thousands of eyes. The 34th battalion. Then she felt Demeter move closer to her.

"You don't have to worry about me." She was irked to be fretted over at a time like this.

"They're all here," Copret whispered to her.

"Who?"

"Crilodach's commanders. Soldiers I've fought before. Ferveiss, Jurveiss, Frin-Ghirzan and Rataplan. Jurveiss has his battalions drawn up on our left. Ferveiss is stationed behind the Brujans who are tunnelling towards us. Rataplan has drawn up several battalions in front of you, including the infamous 34th. They'll come for you Chloe, beware their colours but the real enemy are the Midrats behind them."

"The lieutenants want revenge for the death of their cousin Arnveiss," warned Demeter

"I'll give them what I gave him." Copret reached out and leant his heavy paw gently upon her back. "Don't leave yourself with no arrows, keep one back at all times," he ordered.

"Understood."

"Things'll happen very quickly," he emphasized,

"sometimes so fast we can barely think. Keep on your toes."
Chloe did not take her eyes off the enemy as she replied,

"Look at my belt."

"Why?" asked the bear.

"The other side."

He did so and there slipped under her belt, was a single
arrow kept out of the quiver to ensure that, if in the heat of
battle she found no arrows in her quiver, one would still
remain to her. Copret approved.

"Remember an important strength is to look out for each
other," he said to them all.

She eased her hand off the arrow and looked into his eyes
as he added,

"Never underestimate your own worth Chloe. In a battle
we all become different people."

The signal went up from Crilodach as the drills hit the
walls. Rataplan sent his men forward. So slight, more like a
casual wave, the signal was barely noticeable but the
general's men were anxious. Enthusiastic. They moved
before his command had ended. Their very movement
forwards felt like a wave. A huge thump on the ground. The
long tunnels beneath shook and the Brujans spat out soil
that fell onto their faces. They breathed in for a second. If
the tunnel roofs broke they would have to dig their way out.
They held.

Chloe swiftly brought the arrow up to her eye and aimed
again and even as the first battalion moved towards her,
their rush died after three steps as the single arrow swept
through them. A roar came from Copret that could be heard
over the massed ranks of the armada. Some Arvernat moved
to protect Chloe's position and Demeter sent out a bolt that
seared straight though a siege engine leaving the machine
burning, like a firework shooting off into the darkness until
the sparks were as harmless as freckles on a face.

Ferveiss and Jurveiss moved their troops quickly. All the
defenders' oppressive, tense feelings vanished in a second.
All worries were brushed aside by fighters on both sides.
Battle is about movement, reflexes and effort. The parapet
became the focus of a titanic struggle born in selfishness
and nurtured in arrogance. Surrounded and outnumbered,
the defenders took to the fight like ducks to water.

Gertis' antennae quivered along with the throng of cockroaches around him as their bodies were thrown this way and that when the Rounds collided outside the fortress. They felt Ferveiss move his armada above their heads. Felt the battalions take up their positions, saw the rocks compress with the weight of the siege engines. They twitched excitedly as they understood how close they were to Trecrogo. He and the other cockroaches signalled to each other beneath the crowded battlefield. Gertis thought they could do the most damage to the armada by following the Brujans. So they had dug and crawled. Finding the tunnels, they came up behind the Brujans from the moment the sappers started digging. Watching them as they moved into place behind the massive drill engines, pressing against each other like termites under bark, they were so many. As each underground tunnel grew, unseen by the Brujans, still unfelt by Crilodach, the army of cockroaches crawled along ceilings and walls until they were in every tunnel. Bathed in the smell of the Brujans and the heat of the drills that was so intense the ground above steamed, they hanged above the heads of the enemy clinging onto compressed clumps of stone and clumps of soil, hot from the drilling. The insect army waited. They could not remain as cockroaches if they were to fight. Their time was close.

Inside their small bodies the minds of the people and animals they had once been were thinking. Hoping to inflict the greatest damage on the enemy. To make a difference after all the generations of making no difference. For all the years in which Crilodach thought them dead. Irrelevant. Dealt with. Throughout the cockroach army a feeling arose that for the first time, war was worthwhile. These heroes of a hundred worlds who had never wanted to fight, who fought because they were attacked, had been broken and stripped by Crilodach, had been imprisoned by It and hardened to pain by Its labyrinth, had watched all they loved die at Its hands. These heroes had been remade. No longer merely men or merely insects or merely animals, they were a fighting force. Many of them did not even think of victory, they just wanted a chance to kill the Brujans. Gertis had always told them never to lose their belief in life but the ways of Hâgon are cruel. Not always breaking a person's mind, but always breaking their hearts.

Their intent made Gertis both glad and sad. Glad that they would match the instincts of the Brujans and not be taken by surprise, sad because he recalled many of their lives. He had talked to them all over the years. He knew who they had once been and though he knew they would fight for the Sangyma, fight for what he thought was right, he could no longer describe them or himself as noble. Here, in these hot sapper tunnels, there was the very smell of blood lust coming from every creature. No one was unaltered by the bitterness in their fate.

All their antennae twitched in unison. They had discussed tactics many times in the past but even he had not grasped how much their daily lives had been practice runs for this battle. How they had been strengthened in the dark as they worked their way around the labyrinth. Meeting. Sleeping. Eating. How in learning to be cockroaches they had developed skills great enough to take on Crilodach's Brujans. They had never said as much but they had all accepted that he had saved their lives for a reason. That their apparent degradation in being turned into insects, in having to hide behind walls, crawl in the dirt, eat sparingly, would end and they would be themselves again; yet not wholly themselves. They had become that different self that is the passion and dedication of the soldier. Disciplined. Stoical. Resolute. Comrades. In the moment of transformation the surprise and strength of their assault would be an unstoppable onslaught of pure revenge.

Quickly. Without much discussion they had followed the enemy to a great and important battle. They had felt Lilah like a whirlwind get close enough to make Crilodach buckle. They knew Tethval had touched Crilodach without thinking of his own safety. Fabulous powers were unleashed against their enemy. Their hearts were full. Their allies were mighty.

Gertis whispered softly to the soil. His own cockroach feet folded at the ends around balls of clay and mud. His wings buzzed softly in their casings. His spell of Bolaine, a spell of remaking that can also be used to call seeds to grow into flowers, fed into the ancient soil tarnished with the crimes of Crilodach. A soil thirsting for a sense of justice. A soil that had quietly witnessed everything. A soil that longed to be bright, clean and fresh. Unafraid. Unashamed. Moving in time to the steps of living creatures that loved the sunshine. Orbiting to the hours of a long day and night.

Passing through space untouched by the claws of those with cosmic delusions. The soil longed to be Samphin again and grasped at Gertis' spell like an artist reaching for the paints that will create a masterpiece. Suddenly awake. Deeply inspired. Overcome by the passion within.

The spell drained out of Gertis into the cracks and crevices of the ground, and spread out across the planet. Touched with water-magic the spell flowed through the millions of cracks in the ground, around stones, boulders and minerals. There was no resistance at any point. This was a spell that was wanted.

In tunnel after tunnel the spell touched the waiting army of cockroaches hanging above, beside and around the Brujans until the cockroaches, watching with their insect eyes and feeling with their antennae, began to change. As the spell touched them, memory and hope became fact and action. The past became the present. The lost became the found. Claws, paws, wings and hands grew from insect feet. Antennae changed to ears, mouths formed teeth. Faces changed. Voices were found. Small and tall, thin and strong the enemies of Crilodach who had been brave enough to confront Its armies and lost, came back for one last battle. Came back in the sapper tunnels which were forcing their way towards the fortress walls crammed with another kind of insect; the parasitical Brujans. Came back as if from the dead, from another time, from a million places. Everyone had a name. Everyone had had a family. Everyone had had a purpose. But whether they had started life as carpenters, thinkers, lawyers, cubs, fledglings or doctors here they were one thing and one thing only ... vengeance.

Propelled from the sides of the tunnels, growing from the floor of the tunnels, behind, and in the midst of the Brujans, they fell upon their enemies with awful suddenness. Hands reaching out from the past, from the victims of the crimes Crilodach had committed across the ages, they fell like the insects they had been to fight as the men and animals they had returned to being.

In those tunnels old hatreds and old enmities were born once more as the cockroaches became an army and they fought the Brujans in the heat and the dark. Brujans who had been there when their worlds fell, when their lives were shattered. Brujans who represented to them everything they hated most and everything they wanted to destroy. The enemy that tunnelled from below. The enemy that ate children alive. The enemy that knew nothing of love.

Crilodach felt the spell. Saw the veins rippling across the ground, snaking into crevices in the soil. It roared.

Demeter, standing as he had stood like a sentinel since first taking on the power of Trecrogo, knew what was happening and heard all their names in his head. He heard their voices mingling with the noise of the drilling engines and the hisses of the Brujans. He felt their presence as if they had been a flock of birds stretching from one end of Trecrogo to the other, their wings flapping in unison as they migrated. Though he did not know them personally the names conjured up for him places and worlds long extinct. They spoke of pride that crippled, greed that destroyed and races lost to their own egos believing they were the only races in the Universe. They spoke of old alliances, and even older friendships, between strangers. They spoke of workers, philosophers and artists, of the weak and the courageous. He saw visions in his head of lost worlds, unknown animals and even his own Earth. The home he had never known. Born again for him in the minds of the human beings now fighting their last battle. Human beings whom no-one but Gertis had known were still alive. The humans who had always trusted the Sangyma and had fought at their side. The few who had stayed hidden in Hâgon.

Crilodach roared.

The fighters in the tunnels, from all the millions who had lived in all their worlds, were the few who saw through greed, pride and ignorance. The few who had looked to their skies and wondered. Thought about what could be, and what made sense should be. They became champions to those who knew them. To the Sangyma, dragons and the bears. To the Ruzniel and their allies. One by one these champions had been defeated and sent to Hâgon. In this dark, neither old ranks nor titles were important. Time was not important. Purpose and life had become one and the same thing. But still their names sang out to those with the power to hear them like Demeter.

Manfray who came close to touching Crilodach, in the Great Satuphen War in which the bears won their proudest battle. So fast on his feet when Rataplan had brought him and thrown him on the floor before It, thinking him too weak to stand, he had leapt at Crilodach's throat. No sooner had he jumped at It then he found himself in the Labyrinth. No more than a moment but the attempt upon Crilodach, however absurd, had shocked Rataplan. His error of judgment flashed in Crilodach's eyes every time he stood before It or looked at the deep scar on his shoulder made by Crilodach's left claw for his failure.

Leoprin the wolf, who had found out Crilodach had sired two daughters and sought to warn the Sangyma but was stopped by Rataplan and hauled off to serve as entertainment. Whipped until he bled, blinded with his teeth broken, he was sent to die. Gertis had healed him. At first he asked why he had bothered and in that small, smiling, heartfelt way he had, the Sangyma had replied that helping was no bother at all. Now Leoprin's eyes were clear. His teeth sharp as knives.

Voltia, last of the women of Radine who had travelled a hundred worlds seeking knowledge of Crilodach and Its hordes and been instrumental in the defeat of Its army when the leader of a world fell in love with her and put his forces under her command. Respected by Tegriel she was betrayed and imprisoned by those she had helped. She watched her love being blinded and then mauled by a beast she had never seen before, flaying his skin until all the blood in him lay in the dust and dirt. Crilodach had even thought of her as a mother for Its children but when she learned what It intended she drove a knife into her stomach and bleeding It had sent her to the labyrinth to die. Gertis spent a year healing her before she could walk.

Peäron, a small almost insignificant magician who boasted one day that he knew where a Sagitæ was kept and for his boast, had been imprisoned. He had seen the last of those first Ruzniel prisoners and talked to her, learning from her the true nature of Crilodach before being thrown into Hâgon and becoming a cockroach.

Elvandon, the small tree–dwelling monkey with his prehensile tail, who was born with eight fingers which he had been told was a sign of greatness. He had tried to protect his people from Ferveiss and paid the price beyond prices. He had watched as half his race were decimated by Crilodach's army because he had crawled into the enemy camp and spied upon them as they talked, learning of the experiments they wanted to perform on his people. Ferveiss had brought him to Crilodach who liked to see new species but dismissed him as of no use to Its army.

Demeter knew all their names now and all their histories as they changed back into their true selves. He also knew they only had their wits and bare hands, claws and paws. He sent the fierce army in the tunnels beneath them weapons of fire, ice and stone. From the depths of Trecrogo where many strange weapons had lain waiting, he sent them gloves that turned ordinary hands into hammers, helmets that gave the wearers clear sight in the dark, spears that burned with liquid flames without being consumed, boots that could fly and strange guns that would slice the drills into pieces. Weapons that appeared in their hand, on their heads and feet even as they became their true selves, and in that way with magical folk, they did not even stop to wonder how they had come to them. So as the army grew to be what they had once been, their hands felt the touch of magic and they were able to see the Brujans clearly. They found they had weapons allied to their will; they found the ability to take on the Brujans and kill them face–to–face not as desperate groups of failed heroes, but as a deadly army. The Brujans were taken by surprise. Without retreat. The enemy everywhere at once. This had never happened before.

Crilodach roared.

Deep below them all, deeper than the tunnels, the roots of Trecrogo began to dig into the Rounds. Dig upwards. Seeking out the enemy. Roots that let out a strange perfume onto the battlefield. A deep, lasting perfume that made the ground sweeter. Crilodach felt the roots and roared. It stamped Its feet in anger. The strategies of the enemy ran deep but Its strategy ran deeper. Even as the roots made their way upwards It threw Its forces against the fortress with more vigour. Insistent that It and It alone would be victorious.

The new army below made the ground beneath Its feet warmer. Again Crilodach roared. So many of Its enemies were still alive. With every life It felt the hand of the Sangyma trying to strangle It. There were no retreats. They all faced one enemy none of them could defeat. Fighting them both, an ally of neither side. Time fought against everybody.

Crilodach's army was driven forward now by the pressure of numbers. Aware that the stones could kill them, those in the front screamed as they were pushed against the fortress but their screams were lost in the shouts from the living behind them. In other places the living of the armada would have used the dead to step upon but this time Demeter burned the bodies to ash, leaving room for more to be consumed. An ash that blew upwards like billowing clouds but fell back onto the armada not the defenders. Stuffing up their noses, and making them cough so violently they dropped to their knees to catch their breath. In this way did Demeter show the armada the strength in his silence.

The defenders saw the smoke from the fires rise in front of them in continuous thin, black wisps. The first of the Grafiers, who had been hurled without command in one's and twos by over eager catapults, now came in long phalanxes raining down with screams that were part death agony and part relish. Demeter protected all of the defenders individually, so any fires that fell on the parapet burned and anything that came close to them bounced off an unseen shield. Even so, some of the Arvernat raised their swords in a reflex action, to defend themselves against the Grafiers as they fell onto them. They were glad to see them bounce out of the way and fall to their own deaths. A few fell outside the parapet and onto their own men. The Arvernat pointed to the smoke and waved their weapons in defiance.

"Lay down your weapons and you'll die quickly," shouted Rataplan, with the unnaturally loud voice he always used in battle.

"If you want these weapons so much," called back Copret without taking his eyes off Crilodach, "come get them."

Even now, seeing the assault that would soon become the flood beginning slowly, deep down, Crilodach wondered what Its daughters were doing. How they had fared in finding Tegriel. Whether this battle was as meant originally or had happened because of their work. It looked and looked, but It could not discern any hand other than Its own and Its enemies. It cursed time for drawing such a veil over actions. It wondered if It should not have taken the immense risk and gone back Itself. It knew Freyom and Yaltha well. Yaltha was not to be trusted. What if she had formed an alliance in the past with others? What if she was, even now, creeping up on Its army? Waiting for some disaster to befall It. Ready to kill her own father. Could they have made a weapon that could do that? It looked at Copret. For a moment It wondered if these thoughts were being given It by the bear, but then

It dismissed that idea. Copret did not have the power. These thoughts had no meaning. It roared again. Nothing could stop It. There was a Sagitæ here. It could smell the jewel. Right under Its nose. How It longed to hold one again. Come what may this would be Its finest hour.

In the tunnels the cockroaches were still changing even as the first of them engaged the Brujans with bone–shaking strikes, some of which bounced off the metal plates of the sappers. They had spent generations in Hâgon. Seeing their number swell with every recruit Gertis could persuade to remain alive. At first he had just changed them into cockroaches and explained afterwards but then he had begun to ask them. Always given them a choice. Most had agreed and been saved before Gâmor blew and flayed them alive, but some were so heartbroken and sad they barely heard his words. They looked at the dark walls of the dank Pângil. They could not get out of their heads the sight of Crilodach and Its armies or their loss of friends. They longed for the green fields they knew, the open spaces they had been brought up in, the mountains and seas that were their birthrights, so they curled up and waited for death. Gertis did not offer them life, they thought, he offered them the chance to never forget and they wanted to forget. They died longing for home. Only those who put home into the back of their minds, and learned to live in pain, survived. A trick known to all prisoners. They found some reason in living. Getting through each hour and not planning for the next. They drew their stories on the walls. They slept uneasily in their individual chambers. Their one source of joy was to save yet more victims, to listen to Its plans and to wait until they could strike a blow for the Sangyma.

Watching those who refused his help die, had been hard for Gertis but when he had changed them without asking a few of them had gone mad, crawling up to Damkina, trying to get to Crilodach. Fortunately a cockroach that is mad and one that is normal were much the same. Although listening to the dying screams of those who refused to become cockroaches, even before Gâmor ripped them to pieces, was difficult, they were safer doing nothing. Anything else risked discovery. Afterwards they would sorrowfully go to pick up pieces of their bodies. The cockroaches that were real insects ate the remains. No one blamed them for they were only doing what cockroaches do.

If any of them had thought of taking on Crilodach with any dream of victory, or fullness of heart, they had been metamorphosed by the labyrinth. The cockroach army was as hardened as the Arvernat. They did not flinch at the new blood being shed. They did not fear the touch of metal. They did not worry for their lives. More importantly still, as the weapons from Trecrogo manifested themselves, they felt complete. They did not hesitate. Here was a chance to be defined by one last act of bravery and determination. To do some of what they failed to do before as individuals. To take the chance to carve out a slice of Crilodach's arrogance, even if they would never be remembered.

They fell amongst the Brujans with glee but the Brujans fought their new enemy. They, too, wanted blood. They, too, knew the dark well. They, too, were hardened to pain through lives lived in the shadow of Crilodach.

The first clashes of weapons, hand to hand, body to body, sent shock waves down the tunnels. The Brujans crawled along the sides of the tunnels and along the top and dropped down into this enemy just as this enemy did to them. In the mêlée enemies were tightly packed. Soon Manfray found himself fighting a Brujan with two more pressing their backs into his as they fought others behind him. He reached his hand back and grabbed one of them by the neck, kicking at his opponent who was trying to stab at him without being able to raise his arm. Lifting a dagger became a hard thing to do. The tunnels became a heaving, pushing mass of enemies struggling for advantage. Strangling became the main weapon. Teeth more useful than blades.

In this mass Leoprin used his agility to bite and tear at legs, taking down Brujans to rip out their throats as they were crushed by the feet of the grappling fighters. No one looked at who they were standing on. They could smell each other, spit in each others' eyes, shout and call each other names, but actually killing each other was hard.

Elvandon jumped up grabbing Brujans off the tunnel walls and slicing into them with the two swords he had been given and slipping so swiftly one to another the Brujans could not bring him down. He danced over heads using shoulders to launch himself upward as if the enemy were a sprung dance floor.

Peäron used his power to push groups of Brujans against the drilling engine in his tunnel hoping to make them fall

111

beneath the grinding drills against which others had them pinned down, shooting at the engine to break the mechanism. All across the tunnels the drills were being slowed and broken. The incessant drilling was grinding to halt. Voltia, indifferent to her own safety, scratched and tore at her enemy. In the momentary space that opened up as one slipped to the ground she sliced off the heads of others close to her. So fast were her ams she killed eighty before Brujans overpowered her and ripped her to pieces.

Rataplan had directed over two hundred tunnels to be dug, as if he wanted to rip Trecrogo out of the ground rather than just make a breech in the defensive walls. Other battalions were ready at the entrances to the tunnels to launch their assault the moment a breach was made. Battalions that shone brightly in the fires that swept the battlefield made by the Grafiers burning to their deaths in fruitless, continuous attacks. The drills ploughed through the soil and rock. The drills were fast. The engines waiting to enter the tunnels were even more magnificent. Red and black, each one containing hundreds of men, they had been made in one entire piece. Atom by atom using the same technique that made Trecrogo, to make them impregnable. Their wheels were tracked and from every inch of them heavily poisoned spikes protruded. They could turn like a worm, rear up like a snake, prowl like a tiger or swim like a shark. These engines had their own energy sources and would have as easily rolled over the Brujans as the enemy, so they had to be kept back until the Brujans were ready. Even then, none of the Brujans wanted to be near them when they swept through the tunnels.

Through this very size, in his huge purposes, Rataplan lost the battle for the sapper tunnels. If they had been narrow, no more than one Brujan high as all the others had been, no army could have taken them but as they were so large there was room for a second army to gain a foothold. The moment the cockroach army attacked, the strategy of the Brujan phalanxes faltered. With the huge engines waiting to enter the tunnels Gertis and his army slowly crushed the Brujan hordes and as the spaces between the enemies widened the fighting became even more fierce. They fought amidst the bodies of the dead. Weapons flashed as they clashed with defiant intensity, as if the fighters were trying to recreate all the stars that had vanished from the universe. For crucial minutes Rataplan did not know what was happening and for crucial minutes the training of Frin-Ghirzan dissolved in a growing fear amongst the Brujans that they were losing.

From the Onäis, Tethval and his remaining men from the ambush, appeared and jumped onto the parapet as Stagetes were thrown onto the merlons. Hacking through them as they fell, some of his men even jumped from one to another to kill two at the same time. The Arvernat on the parapet shouted in unison at the sight of Tethval. Lilah had kept them hidden. Waiting. Watching. Seeing everything.

The tactic of Arvernat protecting Arvernat was a powerful strategy. The Arvernat swords swirled like great wheels and flew from hand to hand slicing through heads and arms. Like a swift and brutal ballet the blades rotated through the air being caught by other Arvernat and aimed at yet more Stagetes who came perilously close to making a successful breach. As their numbers swelled on the right flank with Demeter still active in destroying the Grafiers and levelling siege engines that came without end to within inches of the parapet, Lilah appeared from the broken Onäis. Another tranche of Grafiers were loosed but Lilah raised her hand and they exploded in mid air. Crilodach roared when It saw her. It smelled the Sagitæ she held. That was what It had waited for and she knew now It would come for her.

This assault was not going to be straightforward, Rataplan gauged the defenders had an answer for every weapon he could bring to bear against them. His tactic of penetration, to harry them at all points with different men, to keep them thinly spread out along the parapet to keep them on their toes, was his best option. If nothing else there would come a moment when Crilodach would lose patience and engage them directly. A moment he both wanted and feared.

"Did you bring the Jalrin dust?" Lilah shouted to Copret.

Copret felt in his belt and handed her the pouch he had had there since arriving, gathering which had made him late in getting to Trecrogo. She poured the red dust into her hands and went to the battlements blowing the red powder across the armada. A dust Copret had collected with such delicacy from the sacred rocks of an ancient planet on the other side of the universe. When there had been another side. Lilah ran around the parapet blowing more of the dust on every side.

113

The Jalrin dust dissipated in the artificial wind made by the breath of the armada. Crilodach sniffed the air trying to figure out what this dust was. It felt nothing because Lilah had not yet cast the new spell that would make the dust something special.

"The spellmaker plans something," It sneered.

"Do I change the attack plan?" asked Rataplan, who always looked to Crilodach to advise him about spells.

"No, let her do what she will do. I can't run out of men to fight. Her time is coming. She cannot escape."

The first wounded Brujans crawled out of the tunnels to the terreplein set behind them and managed to get word of what was happening.

"The enemy is in the tunnels," Rataplan warned. "They're gaining ground and destroying the drills."Crilodach cursed, "Then send in the support troops. Wipe out the vermin below. Don't bother me with your details." Its eyes flashed. The Sagitæ was all It wanted to think about.

Rataplan waved on more men. Along with more engines that rolled forward as his armada tried to scale the defensive walls to keep the defenders busy. He sent in the 97th reserve battalion to see what was going on in the nearest tunnels. Rataplan always had an excellent idea of how long any of his men took to carry out a specific task. A skill that came with knowing them well and training with them for years. Like many a good general he felt, as well as fought, the battle. He could discern how a battle was going by the sound of the shouts on the battlefield. The raucous glee of exuberance that could turn to a strained yell of retreat. The passionate bellows that could turn to the screams of fear. The eagerness with which orders were carried out or the twisted appeal from a subordinate who had lost any clue of what to do next. This mayhem of slaughter was as much an emotional experience as a military one.

Mojolo longed to sail again. She did not see the blood spattered on her face. She could feel the wind in her hair, made from the storm of shouts of the attacking armada. She could almost feel her feet tensing at the strength of the boat bouncing through the waves and her fingers gripping the ropes squeezing the moisture that glittered on her nails. As she thought of the sea, the ground beneath Rataplan's army bubbled up and turned to mud. Where a soldier could have run a few seconds before they were up to their ankles in clay, sticking to them like glue. Even in the tunnels below, water dripped from the roofs mixing with the sweat of the fighters until, when one slipped, five more slipped with them. None of them loosened their death grip on the other. They drowned in the mud still grasping each others' throats.

The heavy engines sank into the mud as the rails they moved along buckled, and gave way beneath them. In front of the fortress hundreds began to prop up the tracks to keep them level enough for the siege engines to move upon. Some men were up to their thighs in thick mud. The water in the Rounds was heeding Mojolo's instinctive call and soon most of the front line troops were bogged down in the clay. The whole frontal assault was faltering just as the Brujans assault was faltering. Rataplan raised his arms and the winged 7th, 305th and 64th battalions flew down upon the parapet from the starless dark just above them. Battalions that had been hidden from the defenders. Barely higher than the heads of the defenders. Crilodach roared. It, too, could hide fighters away.

Then Lilah created a spell, to make the red dust that covered much of the armada, into flameless fire. The dust which had landed on skin and armour immediately burned blue. The victims screamed in pain and ripped off their hair, their clothes and cut off their limbs to escape being engulfed in the burning. Line upon line of men fell down, rolling in the mud hoping to put out the fire but nothing worked. Every man touched by a grain of dust burned to death. Rataplan ground his teeth in anger. The fine dust had been spread by his own men's breath and movements. The very actions of attack had made her spell more effective. He raised his claws above his head and over the flames more men marched heedless of the men they marched over and Crilodach with a blink, gave them all silver shoes that floated over the mud and could not burn.

"They redeploy like locusts," Copret shouted, heaving three over the side and back onto the ground.

"Crilodach only has two strategies, never give up, fight on all fronts," shouted back Lilah.

"Effective," cried Chloe, waiting for her arrows to return.

"So is Trecrogo," Demeter said.

"Demeter look to the Arvernat," warned the bear.

Demeter heeded Copret's warning. The Arvernat were fighting Midrats and other kinds of men in such huge numbers that they all felt they needed three hands. They were being herded away from the parapet by long spears wielded by the 81st, 54th, 43rd, 19th and 107th. Demeter raised a finger and sliced through them all in one shot, like a samurai sword through wheat. Their spears fell uselessly to the stone floor. Then more men from more battalions mounted on the siege engines, jumped down onto the stones of the parapet drawing other weapons from their intricate armour. Their feet protected by the silver shoes sparked but the men did not burn to ash. Secure on the parapet they rushed at the Arvernat. They had their enemy. They had breached the fortress.

That was when they learned for the first time in their many years service to Crilodach that It did not know everything. That Its spies had not been everywhere. The Arvernat, armed by Trecrogo, protected at their rear by Demeter, were not like a few hundred men. They were like thousands. Their eyes blazed a blinding light that pushed the armada back to the edge of the parapet as if the light had been solid. Holding the spears of the attackers with one hand they would cut through their bodies with their swords. Attackers who got close enough to bite the Arvernat found their skin broke their teeth. The attackers were hurled down to the mud and fire, their roars of victory stifled in their throats. Rataplan heard them. Felt them. He spat a curse. Crilodach roared. The wall of light on the parapet vanished and a line of green stood along the stones. The Arvernat did not roar or wave their weapons at the enemy. They immediately went back to their positions. Rataplan wondered who these disciplined men were. Crilodach just itched to get that Sagitæ.

Rataplan had hoped some of the Brujans would have signalled a break through by now. He had hoped the 97th reinforcements would be back from the tunnel closest to him to bring word of the assault. But there was no sign of success. From some of the tunnels shocked men from Gertis' army crawled wounded and half blind, some still locked in battle with Brujans. Crilodach's men fell on them. They were not taking prisoners. From other tunnels a few Brujans ran screaming in terror at what they had faced, unable to overcome the attackers. The men Rataplan had in reserve ready to launch strikes through the tunnels, were now ordered into them right across the battlefield. Every tunnel was entered. Rataplan gave the order for them to cut down the fleeing Brujans too. He would not accept cowardice this day. If the entire army perished and only he and Crilodach survived, as long as Trecrogo lay in ashes, they would have won.

"I want to know what's going on in the tunnels," Rataplan snapped.

"I can tell you that," replied Frin-Ghirzan, his eyes smarting from the Jalrin dust he was fighting with his own magic, "I warned you there were hidden enemies in our ranks."

"I've no traitors here," argued the general.

"None that you would recognize," replied Frin-Ghirzan.

"Show them to me." ordered Rataplan.

Frin-Ghirzan showed Rataplan a cockroach in his open hand.

"Is that supposed to mean something?" asked the general, smashing his clawed hand against his hip.

"Your unseen enemy," Frin–Girzan replied.

He threw the cockroach to the ground and the spell from Gertis seeped into the insect body and immediately there appeared a tall, well built man with long flowing black hair. He jumped up only to be struck down by Rataplan, his head rolling into the tunnel at the general's feet. Everything became clear. Except where the insects had come from.

"Someone will pay for this," shouted Rataplan.

"But not you," smiled Frin-Ghirzan.

Rataplan took out his dagger and with both claws armed jumped into the nearest sapper tunnel. Running down the dark, messy tunnel dripping with water from the ceiling as Mojolo's spells worked above, he could smell the enemy. So many smells. He cursed. Near the end he saw many creatures breaking the drill to pieces. Brujans lay dead with their enemies, his reinforcements lay dead and with the victors he saw Gertis. He knew him.

"You," he screamed, running at the Sangyma without hesitation.

"You," replied Gertis, holding out a long spear against the charge.

The spear broke on Rataplan's armour and before those around him had time to protect him, Rataplan cut off Gertis' head. From his body there seemed to come a brief sigh and then the Sangyma vanished. Around them the air filled with the smell of a sweet perfume which seeped upwards, swirled across the battlefield and up the walls of the fortress. Lilah felt the loss and caught her chest. She knew she could not take many more deaths of friends without going mad. This being the final hours meant more than victory, this was also the end of her pain for which she craved. The end to ever deciding again who lived and who died. Demeter, filled with the knowledge of Trecrogo, knew what had happened and faltered for a second. The winged battalions fell onto the shoulders of the Arvernat and before he could move them ten Arvernat lay dead. They quickly rallied and Chloe loosed several arrows that followed the enemy as they tried to duck and dive out of their way but found her arrows were unavoidable.

"Are you alright?" Demeter asked Lilah, as he crushed more of the offensive armada.

"Never take your eyes off the enemy," she ordered firmly, and beneath her breath she whispered, "farewell old friend."

Ropes like steel were flung at the Arvernat and the Midrats pulled their enemies to their deaths. Some Arvernat, overcome with the passion in battle, jumped onto the siege engines and fought their way down, dying in the midst of their enemies.

Inside the tunnel, alone and outnumbered, Rataplan fought his enemies. They circled around him. Like predators looking at the tastiest morsel. Two men slashed at him with their swords whilst a woman took long swipes at his head from behind him. He ducked her blows and with the swiftest moves killed one man and the woman, and dug his dagger deep into the neck of the third man. Their bodies fell at his feet. Others followed and he fought them with his back against the tunnel wall until his men arrived. As they took the heat off their general he looked around at the mess. The drill was useless now. This tunnel was lost. He spat and wiped his nose and mouth which were covered in the blood of his enemies. He needed to know the situation in every tunnel to report to Crilodach. He turned to leave and saw Gertis' head.

"For this. You gave your life for this. Why for this? This futile nothing."

He stopped shouting. Knowing he would get no answer. But somehow he knew Gertis would have smiled, even laughed saying,

"Rataplan, we are all just part of the picture painting Crilodach's defeat."

As he left the water broke the tunnel walls and whilst the Brujan dead were sucked into the soil, Gertis and his army were washed clean of their blood and sweat and floated until the roots of Trecrogo broke through and carried them away, with a respect for the fallen few have equalled.

Gertis' death was an answer to every question Rataplan could ever have asked him. For the Sangyma had always worked so that every death and any suffering, inspired by fighting Crilodach, should have a purpose. This had always been the only meaning they could offer those who faced insurmountable odds. A meaning beyond what is seen, even beyond what is known. Sometimes Gertis was unsure if there was a greater meaning to dying, but he was always sure there was a purpose to his life and he shared that purpose with those who worked with him. With everyone in the cockroach army. From the moment he had been summoned to join the Sangyma he had known he would die young. He had survived to the very day of Zaqui. He had brought a great army to a great fight. He had kept friends alive against the odds, in the most difficult and dangerous of places. Tegriel would have been more than proud of him. But he would never have said as much, for pride in how a friend lives and dies was not to be taken. They were friends. That meant everything to them both because Crilodach had no friends, only servants. Because Rataplan had no friends, only orders. Because Frin-Ghirzan had no friends, only enemies. That is one of the most important differences between them and the Sangyma.

Rataplan's keen eyes looked at every spot his feet touched and he bent down near the entrance to a tunnel. He touched a small, translucent fibre on the end of his claw. He nodded his head. The wing of a cockroach. Frin-Ghirzan had been telling him the truth. How many thousands of them could there be if every tunnel was infected. Everything was on the line in this battle. He could expect every trick to be used. Well, he had a few of his own. He raced out of the tunnel into the deepening mud and hastened to Crilodach's side.

"Well?" snapped Crilodach, his voice unmistakable and clear in the roar of war.

"That tunnel is lost we'll have to see which ones are left. Gertis was alive," Rataplan said, emphasizing the 'was'.

"He couldn't have been in them all," cursed Crilodach.

"He wasn't. He had an army. From Hâgon. The cockroaches Frin-Ghirzan showed me were your enemies in disguise. I'm not sure he didn't know before." Frin-Ghirzan slid over and hissed,

"Don't blame me for your failings."

"When did you know?" demanded Rataplan.

"One of my people saw them running into the Rounds as we left. I caught one. I didn't think they were leaving for their own safety but I had no real way of knowing they were Sangyma spies until they were in the tunnels."

"Why didn't you tell me?" Rataplan shouted.

"I told you to expect anything. I didn't think you had any interest in insects," replied Frin-Ghirzan.

"I do when they're an army that kills Brujans and destroys our drills."

"They became an army. Gertis changed them. Didn't you feel the spell beneath your feet? I did. I'm surprised you didn't. Perhaps you're losing your touch," said Frin-Ghirzan pointedly.

"When you question my general you question me," Crilodach growled.

"Never," Frin-Ghirzan assured him, "but I'm not the one responsible for the success or failure of your assault. The general is, and he allowed this cheap Sangyma army to take the tunnels. I've lost my Brujan sappers."

"Have they all fallen?" asked Crilodach, Its eyes burning.

"I believe there are six in which the Brujans are still forcing their way forward. The others have all fallen and any men sent in will meet the enemy's final, fierce resistance," revealed Frin-Ghirzan. "We will beat them but we have lost any advantage the Brujans gave the assault."

Rataplan spat on the ground. He was certain Frin-Ghirzan knew more than he was saying. They had always been comrades but he sensed his old friend was trying to oust him as general. He had bided his time to the end and now vied for a supreme position to assure his own immortality. When this battle was over Rataplan would have to deal with Frin-Ghirzan. Right now he had a fortress to storm.

"I've dispatched support brigades into every tunnel," Rataplan told them, "if we can secure any of them we will." Crilodach looked at Trecrogo and roared. The general had said 'if.' A word unknown to It. A thought It had never touched nor sought to touch.

"What tricks, Lilah. You think tricks will stop me taking your head to posses the Sagitæ?"

Its voice carried over the noise of the battle. Lilah looked directly at It. She was mourning for Gertis even as she brought down Bofindle and snapped a siege engine in half. A rage of endless arrows and spears and men poured upon her and she whirled Bofindle above her head beating them back by making their own weapons boomerang upon them, savaging their comrades. Bofindle cleared a passage through their ranks which was quickly filled by the endless reserves at Crilodach's disposal.

"Why don't we fight hand–to–hand," It called out above the tide of battle.

A challenge. Did It want to end this quickly or did It see there was no end? All around Trecrogo now battalions were harrying the defenders. Still they danced the dance of death with them. Feet are very nimble when their heads are in danger of being cut off. Demeter could not protect all the Arvernat all the time and some were falling. Mojolo was standing her ground single handed against Ferveiss' manoeuvres, her hair, able to cover every inch of her side of the parapet, became an impenetrable fence. Even the Stagetes and others who, dodging Arvernat, charged her from behind were lifted by single strands and hurled against siege engines in front of her as if her hair had been a flail. She did not need to turn her head. Her hair saw everything. As if Sanjava stood by the side, stretched out his hands, and conducted every strand of hair like a vast, unyielding, ever-changing orchestra of defence. And then strands flew out across the armada, single thin threads of hair, gripped one of the engines and hauled the heavy engine off the rails and the entire apparatus crashed into the men below. The engines stopped trying to penetrate Mojolo's position. The Sangyma had planned well but unlike Crilodach, the defenders had no reserves and their numbers were dwindling, though their nerve did not break.

Lilah did not answer Crilodach's challenge. Let It rage and curse. Let Its anger boil away some more. Let It lose Itself to Its violent temper. Let It be gripped with doubt. Inside her a spell was forming. Its rage would fuel the power she would put into her magic, for as the fourteenth law states,

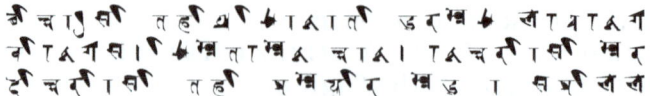

*'Because They Emanate From Living Beings, Emotions
Can Increase Or Decrease The Power Of A Spell'*

Her muscles tingled and she was almost thrilled at what
her spell might do. Before her a world of beings ranged
against her, beside her were tired yet steadfast allies. But
she knew Crilodach's armada would wear them down. One
by one. She knew they had to break off at some stage. But
not now. Not now she had heard It call out a challenge. It
was getting anxious. It loathed being frustrated when time
was pressing like a vice upon Its heart. It could not
countenance missing the opportunity of possessing the
Sagitæ. It did not want to think about fighting when the
prize was this close. The battle of minds was reaching a
crescendo. She took away the covers hiding the window.

"Very well then coward," It roared, "I'll give you a gift.
I'll allow you to watch each and every one of your friends
die before I kill you."

She smashed another siege engine with Bofindle in reply
and opening her fingers on her left hand like an enchantress,
she drew out the bodies of the dead men inside and flung
them at Its feet. They sank into the mud. Crilodach looked
at her and lifted Its foot and pushed the bodies deeper into
the mud.

"This I'll do to you," It cried out to her.

"And I shall avenge each and every one of my friends, and
each and every one of all those you have killed, and all those
who have cried in the night and in the day for the pain you
have inflicted. For all those who have cursed you and all
those who have feared you. This is your hour to feel their
sorrow."

Lilah lifted Bofindle after she spoke. She thrust the
weapon deep into the ground around the fortress like a spear
thrusting through a chest, and the weapon extended to the
bottom where the roots of Trecrogo winding their way
through the ground gave way to allow each huge hole to
form. As she drew Bofindle out again hundreds of men were
sucked into the holes and down into the emptiness of space
beneath. Some tried to crawl out but the roots of Trecrogo
plucked them up as if they were plucking hairs off a face and

dropped them down to follow their comrades. Her eyes, dark as night, looked at Crilodach and still she said nothing but lifting Bofindle she made another hole, and another hole. And siege drills were crushed as she ploughed through some of the tunnels. Though magically all Gertis' army caught in the attack were held by the roots and brought upwards to land on the parapet. Where the defenders had thought they had no reserves they were joined by hundreds of willing, weary yet ready, races. Fully armed. Glad to be out of the flooded sapper tunnels. Taking new strength from the stones of the fortress they ran or leapt into the rest of the fight.

Below them the armada began to lay iron bridges over the huge holes Lilah had made, and some pulled the sieges engines sideways so they fell making a walkway over, and along these they scrambled to the parapet able to stand face to face with the defenders. The armada were like ants traversing any–and–all obstacles to get to their food.

For the first time in Its long, long life. For the first time in all the days It had planned and plotted. In all the times It had won victories and created armies. For the first time, Crilodach felt a small amount of uncertainty. Her eyes were so steady. Resolved. Her silence gave quiet assurance. It knew Its whole armada could not defeat her. If she was to die and release the Sagitæ in her possession, It would have to kill her Itself. And at that moment Crilodach's armada finally became as nothing to It. At that moment of awareness, It changed Its strategy.

It swept all the battalions around It from Its mind.

Let them fight. Let the defenders of Trecrogo fight. There was another battle here. A battle beyond the mud. A battle with her. Not about Zaqui or the Sagitæ, but about power, the desire for which spawned all Crilodach's efforts. It had to fight Lilah one–on–one. For the first time in all the millenniums Crilodach wanted more than just to live forever. It wanted Lilah dead. Wanted her dead with a passion that filled Its entire body. Wanted her dead this second. It roared a roar of absolute rage.

Across the left flank of the fortress, Ferveiss, who had taken up Rataplan's position when he went to Crilodach's side, sent men in heavy armour to catapult over the walls. They landed on their feet, touching the stone with their protected, gloved hands and silver shoed feet, and then charging forward at whoever was nearest. Demeter created a corps of Arvernat that did not exist and for brief seconds these assailants hacked at images of their enemies and nothing more, wondering what their comrades had found so difficult to overcome in these weak, green men.

From the flank, Copret ran down the first of those catapulting onto the fortress with long, swift swings of his arms his claws ripped through them, many fell back into the struggling armada below, others landed near cockroach-army survivors from the tunnels, who fell on the struggling corps from Rataplan with the renewed energy of those who had won a victory and craved for more. The fighting was fierce and relentless. Copret's claws found their meaning and gave vent to his anger as he threw the new attackers back in twos and threes, disappearing beneath a mass of fifteen of them jumping onto him like a plague, only to come growling back and fling them dead from his fur, their lifeless bodies falling around him even as he strode forward and found more bones to break. His eyes blazed. His blood pumped. No one but Lilah had ever seen Copret like this. He was ready for anything. Ready for more. He stood astride the stones surrounded by those from Gertis' army and they all roared at the enemy. Showing how equal was their hatred for the other.

"Too many of them are able to stand on the fortress," he cried out to Lilah.

"Of course, Crilodach is protecting more and more of them," shouted Demeter.

"Can we do something about that?" Copret shouted, wading through more who flew at him from every side.

More Arvernat arrived and stood in the direct line of the catapults. The fourth wave of fighters did not get so far as the first. Lilah watched as men no longer fell down the large holes Bofindle had made, and yet more were bringing up iron pylons to help run over the muddy wasteland Mojolo had created, and without looking back at him she shouted back,

"You already are."

She looked at Mojolo standing her ground all by herself impervious to every assault, grabbing each and every weapon sent against her and throwing them back. Her thick hair as good as ten battalions, her lariat cutting through anything sent against her. This was the Mojolo of legend. The first companion to a Sangyma not trained in the academies. Filled with a love of the sea. Filled with a sweet song that made water into life. That made life into strength. That made strength into a bulwark against the armada. Lilah thanked Sanjava quietly under her breath.

Copret dropped dead men from his grasp. Somehow this was not enough. He wondered if there were something he could use to sweep more of them off at one time. Even as he thought this, a yellow light formed in his hand. Warm, filling his paw; he curled his claw into the warmth. The light widened and hardened, circled around his arm across his back and down his other arm. He felt the warmth in his fur. He looked at the men piling over the walls and he lifted his hands and clapped them together. The shock wave thrust forward and outwards sending out thousands of small, yellow daggers that sliced through the soldiers. Some disappeared completely cut to thousands of pieces. Others fell badly wounded, as their arms, heads and bodies were torn so deeply they could not stand, or see or hold their weapons any longer. Copret looked at Lilah who saw what had happened. She shrugged. She was not behind the magic. He looked over at Demeter but he was so busy he had not even seen what Copret was doing. Lilah stamped her foot on the stone and Copret looked down. She was right. The gift given to him by the power of Trecrogo. The roots were taking hold of the battleground and the defenders were finding Trecrogo was not only a fortress but also an ally. For the stones moved.

Should a sword get too close, a spear too near, an arrow be too fast to avoid, the stones on which the defenders stood shifted a little. Should the engines gain advantage the stones drew back and instead of landing on the parapet the enemy fell onto their comrades below. Crilodach's army could no longer trust their eyes to tell them where their targets were. Tegriel had left his gift in the fortress. The spell that made Trecrogo a bejal. Though how he had managed to make a bejal out of the creation of the bears they would never know.

Demeter was flying round the parapet helping the Arvernat with an energy and determination Copret had rarely seen in grown men, and never seen in a young child. As if he, too, felt the anger of the bears which had been driven into the stones of the fortress. An anger every bit as vivid as Lilah's and also directed at Crilodach. An anger that matched Its bitterest thoughts with ones full of sweet hope for a more temperate time. The noise of the armada was strong, raucous and persistent but there was another sound. The sound of those on the fortress. Drowned by the shouts of Its own armada but there nonetheless and, because they were there, their shouts drowned out all other sounds for Crilodach. The tired, strong, defiant shouts of the free.

Ferveiss waved a hand from the far side of the armada, and from the depths of the dark the defenders heard and felt a gale. A gale picking up, blowing down upon them, pressing against them, forcing them to stand forward, leaning like clowns pretending to fall over, just to maintain their balance. Then they saw red and white wings in their thousands mixed in with the gale, and the winged assailants circled them looking for advantage and a clear target.

"The Radizlain come," called out Copret.

Armed with sharp spears they threw them down in phalanxes and as they threw them new ones appeared in their hands like a torrential rain. The spears flew out of the gale straight to their targets. They aimed at one defender at a time and if they moved out of the way, they would find another phalanx of spears even closer coming at them. Six Arvernat fell pinned to the stones. But their dead bodies did not burn to ash. Even as they fell more Radizlain fell on them to cut them to pieces but something stopped them. Their weapons were blunted. They struck at the dead bodes but everything they used passed through the dead without touching them. In death Trecrogo had taken them to another place. Out of the reach of the weapons of Crilodach's armada. Slowly, the dead vanished all together. The spears evaporated. More fell. More men died. Copret raised his hands and clapped and once more streams of daggers flew from him and Radizlain had their wings ripped from their bodies plummeting to their deaths in numbers unseen since the dragon wars which decimated their numbers for generations.

Chloe aimed an arrow and sliced through a dozen that she could see as Mojolo, her eyes blazing with the inner magic Sanjava had instilled in her, moved her ground to the centre of the parapet and her hair began to grow, at home in the gale, circling their mistress. Twined into plaits, spitting out like a whip they lashed into the Radizlain slicing through wings as if they had been butter, cutting through the flying army unscathed by their spears. Screams rose from the Radizlain as her hair flew through them and the plaits loosened and entwined amongst them like ivy pulling them out of the sky as thousands of strands of hair, stronger than graphene, gripped them in unbreakable bonds. They cut at the hair with their teeth to no effect. Like a wild spirit unleashed in the gale created by their enemies, Mojolo let Sanjava's hair decimate another section of Crilodach's army while her lariat flew out wrapping round one siege engine after another. Arvernat grabbed the handle of the lariat with her and pulled the engines over. Everywhere the winged army tried to make a stand her hair ripped into them, and behind her hair, Chloe's magic arrows drove through their bodies. More blood was flowing from the Radizlain than spears. Crilodach did not roar. Crilodach was not interested.

With Mojolo away from her post Ferveiss urged his troops on, hoping to take advantage. Lilah was there now and he did not know which of the two, Mojolo with her Sangyma hair or Lilah with Bofindle, was the worst enemy to face.

Chloe was soon loosing her arrows freely, and her eyes were saturated with the sight of thousands of foes. Copret sent his yellow daggers into the storm cutting down some of the remaining phalanx of Radizlain. As he did so an iron arrow shot from a siege engine hidden behind the earthwork at the entrance to a tunnel, about the size of a stout tree, sliced through the air straight towards Chloe. She bent backwards to get out of the way and from that position, the iron passing over her small, thin body she saw creatures' hands on the battlement stones clawing their way over behind her, through a gap in the defences created by the defenders concentrating on the Radizlain. Even as the iron arrow passed over her, missing her by inches, she loosed an arrow as she fell backwards. The arrow flew at the invaders, cutting them down just as they attained their objective. Their weight as they clung to the stone mortally wounded, loosened the top stones and the group fell back onto their comrades below, sending them all falling into the mud. The stone dissolved, crashing onto the ground. Everything particles of stone dust touched burnt to ash in a twinkling. As Chloe lifted herself up to her knees and then stood up, the gap in the battlements re-grew. Soon she could never have believed any stone had ever been dislodged. She did not even have time to think about Trecrogo as a living, fighting ally but had she, she would have been more than grateful. She went to find an arrow but her quiver was now empty and she had given those arrows so much to do they were still flying through the enemy. She saw Crilodach catch one and break the shaft with his claw, snarling at her as It did so. She slipped her hand down to her belt to take her last arrow.

❖

Trecrogo's ability to regrow was becoming obvious to the surviving Brujans who had managed to dig into the walls. In the last tunnel, as yet, untouched by the cockroach army, Kilvan, who had been taken by Rataplan as a baby and brought up by two Elstin Witches who whipped him daily, spat and cursed as the drills wore out in seconds and, even as they were replacing them, seeing the stone whole again as soon as they were ready to restart the drilling. He struck at the wall in anger, burning his hand, and swiped at the cockroaches which fell around his feet from the roof. The hot tunnel smelled of burning stone and overheated bodies. His clothes stuck to him. Sweat poured into his eyes from his matted hair. Men rolled new drill bits down the tunnel. And as is the way with huge armies rumours were spreading that the other tunnels were under attack.

"Attack from wot?" he grunted.

"They don't say," whined the man who had spoken of running. "They say we're the last."

"Were yu born a coward Linlack? Is you too good for this work?" He lifted him by his neck and held him in the air.

"I isn't petrified," whined Linlack.

"Wot? Not even of me?"

"You's in charge. I knows me orders."

"More scared of me than an army wots attacking Brujans?"

"Yes, yes, more."

He dropped the man who scuttled back to helping put in the drill bit.

"We're the garbage under Crilodach's feet, we is," Kilvan shouted, "We're here to die if needs be. D'yu hear? Yu and yur stories and yur gossip. Gossip don't win wars but if yu goes on lis'ning to rubbish yu'll lose this 'un." He spat again. He felt a dryness in his mouth. "Water," he cried out. He snatched at the water bottle that was handed to him.

He did not look at the person who had handed him the water but something in his brain told him there was something unusual about him. The lack of smell? The soft touch of the skin on his hand next to the rough, worn, scaled skin of the Brujans. Kilvan, holding the water bottle in his hand turned to look as he swallowed down a large gulp. The coolness wizened up in his throat. He felt as if his teeth were all loose and his eyes were unable to focus on anything but the face he saw. He no longer heard the drill. Suddenly he was not in a tunnel but centuries and millions of miles away in another battle, at another place.

"Well, well Kilvan," said a voice next to him. "Yours is the tunnel I find myself in. Gertis has smiled upon me this hour."

Kilvan's grey eyes almost swivelled in their sockets. His scarred face looked into the steady eyes of a light brown animal whose human–like hands clasped a dagger in one hand and a long, curved blade etched in writing which both of them could read, in the other. The Brujans on the drill froze. They saw the metamorphosis of the cockroaches happen before their eyes. The throng of strong warriors, many of whom were from races they had never seen before, materialized among them as ghosts come back to haunt those they hate. A few wore insignias. The lions of Zandin, the women of the lost cities of the Dorwenda; these were places the Brujans had fought in and helped destroy. They did not exist anymore. The terror of seeing the dead rise, holding weapons, talking with real, bright eyes filled with fury, stifled every cry of fright.

"How?" gasped Kilvan, dropping the water bottle and gripping his armour. He was unable to step back because the drill was too close.

"Not as dead as you'd wish, am I?" he said.

"Not yet," snapped Kilvan, regaining his composure and with his huge hands lunging at his old enemy.

The others from the cockroach army ran forward without great shouts. They ran past Kilvan to get to the other Brujans. They tore into them in the darkness of the tunnel as the new drill bore into the stone trying yet again to gain entry into the fortress. Grinding smooth. Only this time Brujans did not stop and replace the cutting edge. This time the Brujans were dying and bleeding in the mud whilst the drill bit flared with red and then white heat turning the tunnel into a furnace. Still sword met neck and tooth met spear and the Brujans fell as if they were being reaped. Above them Rataplan's troops were still running to reinforce all the tunnels and 41st battalion were even then at the entrance to this tunnel. They heard the clash of arms as they raced towards the fighters.

Some of Gertis' last fighters still grappling with the Brujans, heard the reinforcements coming and turned. Six abreast. They knew the men coming would hit them at full tilt and they had to stop the rush, they had to break the charge or they would be pushed back against their own comrades and the throng would be so tight no one would be able to swing a blade. Crammed in the tunnel with the drill about to explode they would all die. Gertis' army did not fear death. They feared not living long enough to kill as many of the enemy as they could.

Crilodach was walking closer to Trecrogo all the time when from nowhere a tremendous quake rippled through the Rounds as the drill in Kilvan's tunnel exploded. Crilodach had to steady Itself from the tremors as mud and pieces of Brujans flew onto the army. The eyes of Tethval's men around Lilah picked out thousands of Gertis' army scrambling out of the cracks caused by the quake racing across the ground as fast as they could towards Crilodach. The men and women, the animals and magicians, the children, wise and powerful people, small and innocent people. Crilodach saw more of them as they ran at It. Its memory was long and It knew them all. Rataplan saw them and ran towards his master but Crilodach held up a claw in command. It said nothing, but Rataplan knew he was to press hard against the fortress and take Copret, leaving this rabble to It.

Some from Gertis' army ran in formation towards Crilodach. Did they think they could kill It? Did they think they could stop It? Did they think they could make any difference? In the heat of battle, with the sudden feel of weapons they had not been able to hold in generations, perhaps they did not think at all. Perhaps they just ran because they wanted to run. Perhaps they needed to have their lungs filled with air, to feel their nostrils flare, to know their hearts were pounding. From the armoury Demeter had sent a steady stream of weapons and the army within the armada formed and manoeuvred and burned a huge hole in the enemy numbers even as their own numbers thinned.

130

They got within a hundred yards of Crilodach. Close enough to smell Its detestation of them. Close enough for It to feel theirs.

Crilodach roared and Its roar hit the side of Trecrogo, but instead of cracking the stone open, the shock-wave bounced back knocking It backwards. It was learning how powerful Trecrogo was. Where had the bears gathered such unnatural power? As It pulled Itself up Its surprise turned to the inevitable conclusion. For only something unknown to It could have given the fortress such power. Only something unknown to It could have thrown It off Its feet, only something unknown could have given Bofindle such power and helped a few defend against the armada with such vigour and ability. In all the universe only the Sagitæ were unknown to It. A power unlike any other. After all they had survived other Zaqui. It roared loudly. Had the bears imbibed the secrets of the Sagitæ and planted them in Trecrogo? Was this fortress capable of surviving the end of this Universe? At that moment Crilodach for the first time wondered if It should be on the inside and not trying to destroy the fortress from the outside. It saw the defenders as doing what It wanted to do, living into the new universe with a ready-made home. They had the secret. They knew. They were trying to keep It away from Its rightful ownership of the future. And as It thought these things Lilah felt the change in Its focus. Attuned to Its every mood she was sensitive to Its mind. Soon, she thought, soon she could lure It into Trecrogo. It wanted her. It wanted the Sagitæ. The time was almost perfect. Its armada just had to see the window.

Rataplan, spattered in mud looking for a surprise attack to his left and right all the time, appeared in front of Copret who was spattered with blood, hot with anger and breathing hard. Beside the general were six men in black. They were thick-set and claw-handed. Copret had not seen them before in the armada. The bear swung round rising off the ground as his whole body twisted in a circle, his claw slicing through the air taking the head off an assailant who was coming up behind him, and then he deftly landed on his feet facing Rataplan and the six men again. The intensity of their gaze gave him no alarm. He knew what they intended.

"You're still fast," Rataplan spat at him.

"You're still alive," he growled back.

"Let's finish our war," suggested Rataplan.

"Who are your friends?" asked the bear.

"They've been bred for one purpose," Rataplan told him.

"What do you call them?" asked Copret.

Copret sensed the struggle ahead was going to be his last. He faced his enemy without fear but he knew with a sense he was born with. A sense that had helped him in many battles and in many places. He had given himself up for dead those long ages past when he had lost his daughter and his wife to Rataplan. They had been caught helping those who had fled from the destruction of the island of Poliman, a once beautiful place ravaged by Rataplan so that It could mine the ores that lay beneath the surface. Seventeen refugees had been found by his wife and she was tending their wounds when Rataplan found them. Leave none alive was the standing order. Three days later, alone and hiding from the thousands of Rataplan's soldiers who patrolled everywhere, he had found her body. He would never know the men who had killed her. He could never find them. So the entire armada was his enemy and his target for revenge. A revenge he had pursued in hundreds of battles since.

"Bear killers," Rataplan told him.

They were close now. Their outstretched arms could reach each other. The cries of the other fighters became distant. The whole battle crammed into the space the eight of them occupied. The battle between Copret and the men was fast and furious. They leapt upon him and he took to the air upon the Onäis as they circled him with great chains meant to immobilize him. Their armour was thick. Their heads small. They cut at him and he moved around them trying to keep them at bay as he picked them off one by one, sometimes at such a steep angle only magic could pull him up in time to avoid crashing into the parapet. They jumped at him and one of them coming in beneath the others, cut his leg. He growled but he held fast. Chloe from her perch worried for her friend, disregarded his warning, and sent her last arrow at them, slicing through their heads. But Rataplan, whose eyes never left the others on the parapet, was waiting for her this time. He had noticed she always kept an eye on Copret, as she had shown in their first battle. When Rataplan saw anyone show a habit he used that against them. In this case against both of them. As she looked up and aimed, her torso was the perfect target and he threw a spear into Chloe ripping into her heart and sending her flying onto her back, dead. Thrown so far she almost landed at Lilah's feet. The bow still in her hand vibrating from her last shot as the arrow flew to her targets. Her other arrows fell to the ground before they finished they work. As Chloe died they vanished. Their use over. Their time fled. Created specially for her, there was no one else amongst the defenders who would use them.

Copret saw from the corner of his eye the spear fly and Chloe fall and for a precious second he was distracted and the last of the men still alive dug a dagger deep into the bear even as Chloe's arrow sliced through his neck before disappearing. Life falling away, Copret snapped off his arm and sent him plunging to his death but the dagger had been well crafted for a single task. Mortally wounded he landed the Onäis once more on Trecrogo, panting out his last breaths. Rataplan from his distant aerie racing from the scene looked back at him.

"At last you die," he spat gleefully.

"I'd look to your master," coughed Copret, as he raised his hand from his death agony.

"You can do nothing to him," spat Rataplan. He was surrounded by a phalanx of his own men who bore the brunt of Lilah's fiery response to the sudden death of Chloe.

"Are you so sure?" asked Copret.

The bear grimaced and with his tired eyes he looked at Rataplan who swore at the dying bear and sped to his master's side. He would have preferred to see his ancient enemy die, just to be absolutely sure.

"Now might be a good time," suggested Copret, softly.

Lilah heard him. As she fought off the armada with Bofindle, shaking with tears she could not shed. As Mojolo's hair settled down having helped to clear the skies of the Radizlain. As Demeter looked for ways to rescue more of Gertis' army from the ravenous armada overwhelming them. As the surviving Arvernat began to falter and tire. He coughed. The noise and whirlwind of the battle was receding from him. Then he intoned an old saying,

"To lift an autumn leaf is no sign of great strength; to see your suns and moons is no sign of sharp sight; to hear the noise of thunder is no sign of a quick ear."

"Sleep well my friend," replied Lilah.

Copret could have sworn at that moment he felt her hand in his fur and her kiss on his cheek as he had often done after their fight practice. But she was standing far away. You would have been forgiven for thinking she was alone. Her face turned to stone, Bofindle balanced in her left hand. The whole armada could see her. And in her right hand to entice their enemy and draw It into the trap, she took out and held the Sagitæ they had found after the Earth was destroyed.

The cosmic jewel shone in her open hand as if she were offering a gift. As if It could just reach out and take this, Its greatest desire. Crilodach, beset by fighters on all fronts and an entrenched enemy, unable to make a breach, felt the aura of the Sagitæ and stared at her. It had been right. It was utterly deaf to Rataplan's commands. It was deaf to the noise It had created with Its armada. It was deaf to Its own heart beat as Copret had been in his last moments. It waded past the remnant of Gertis' army struggling in the mud to hold their position and being driven back towards Trecrogo. They tried to stop It but they were incapable. It moved as if mesmerized. It even stamped on Its own men who did not make way fast enough. It touched the walls of Trecrogo and burned Its skin. As It took Its claws away they left their imprint upon the fortress. At that moment messengers from Ferveiss came to It and reported there was an opening on the other side of the fortress. Mojolo was contained holding back the rest of the armada. A force could get through. Lilah had planned the timing perfectly. Even as she saw the plan working, even as she felt the small delight in Its doing as they predicted, she was shaking with sorrow. Copret lay dead, and at her feet a young child made into a warrior before her time would never move again. And this was not even the beginning of loss. To lose a single life is to lose everything and she had to be there to see every life lost. She barely knew how to stand anymore. If not for her magic at that moment, she would have given herself to deep and bitter sobbing.

"Together," cried Tethval, as with the last of his men he swept past her and cleared the battlements of the enemy around them. A remnant of Gertis' army found themselves penned in below. Tethval and his men let down ropes which would achieve very little but Demeter, seeing the hopelessness of their plight sent a siege engine crashing, allowing the machine to crumple up against the walls and instead of burning to cinders, the broken siege engine made a rough ladder. The beset fighters took their chance as Crilodach turned at right angles and ran to the rear of the fortress. Huge numbers of Its armada, who instinctively followed It, detached from the assault. The fighters started to scramble up the wreckage as many of their comrades gave their lives in a rear–guard action around the base of the siege engine to help their comrades escape. Arvernat helped them up the last few feet. No sooner were they on Trecrogo then they turned to face the enemy who were following them. Like the first survivors of the battle with the Brujans they could not stop to catch their breath.

Lilah watched Crilodach. With desire ripping through Its whole body It ran to the window, calming the wild sea as It did so, and, ignoring the pain of the burning because the window was too small, It smashed a way through and roared as It found Itself inside the fortress. The roar echoed below them and all the defenders knew It was inside Trecrogo. If Hagouti had gotten free and told It there was an entrance before the fortress was ready all could have been lost. A single entrance to a fortress like Trecrogo is obviously a trap, but to an angry and single–minded Crilodach, the window was only an opportunity.

"Be calm," Lilah cried out, "this was expected."

It was inside the final place left It knew definitely held a Sagitæ. It was meant to be here. The victory of victories was here. It sped through the room, followed by eager cohorts. It entered the complex fortress rushing down corridors and up or down staircases. So brazen was Its arrogance It thought this was the beginning of the end of Trecrogo. It thought this was the end for the insects that plagued Its right to rule all life. It had victory in Its grasp and immortality so close It could taste the satisfaction of a lifetime of waiting.

Rataplan looked for It and could not see It on the battlefield. His men looked for It and they could not see It. As is the way of armies some whispered It was gone. Some whispered It was lost. Some whispered It was dead. Some of them looked at their comrades as if asking for orders. Men landed on the parapet and, unsure of where It was, jumped back into the armada to escape the defenders. Without Its presence they became less enthusiastic and Rataplan had to shout more to keep them fighting.

Once inside Trecrogo, Its men swept out of the room Chloe

and Demeter had cleared of maps, and turned right running down a long corridor and then left down a small flight of stairs. Behind them other men piled into Trecrogo and turned to follow them and also turned right. Like a torrent they poured in. Then suddenly the men far back, running after those in front of them, came to a stone wall instead of a flight of steps. They stopped, confused. They could not see or hear their comrades who had gone before them. They hurried down open corridors to their left and right trying to find the others. Afraid that if Crilodach missed them they would die as a consequence. They ran down more corridors, and always those behind came up against a wall and turned another way and so the invading force was split into groups.

As they hurried down corridors that they could have sworn their comrades had taken, down or up, they met with walls. They could not go forwards. They could only turn. There was no other way for them to go. Then they began to notice they were smaller in number so then they turned after a while to go back and regroup but their way back had changed. The corridors changed even as they ran down them. They split up again and went down both ways and split again and again and slowly the thousands of men became hundreds of men looking less for the defenders and more for each other, and they became tens lost in an endless series of stairs and corridors so intricate they would never meet again in years and they had but hours before Zaqui. They began to shout for each other but heard no replies.

Their prison was sealed with frightening efficiency. As if the fortress was swallowing them up whole and no matter how many more poured in through the gaping hole Crilodach had made, the same fate awaited them. Slowly in their minds came the thought that the opening was not an accident and that the stone did not yield to the great might of their master, but was put there to entice them and capture them. And worse. Something was stirring in the fortress. Something left there by the Sangyma. Made by a disenchanted witch of Elstin who had worked in hiding with Filvani with exotic compounds, whose chemistry was unique, building something alive one atom at a time with atoms that had never been magical. Atoms collected carefully, slowly, by a dedicated group of thirty-six magicians. A perfect machine which had only one purpose, like the bear killers, to stop a strong enemy.

Crilodach was hurtling down one sharp turning after another following Its nose until It realized, with that same sixth sense that had forewarned It about many things in the past, that something was wrong. It stopped and looked back. About a thousand men were strung out behind It. No more. It ran back through them throwing them into the walls which burned them as It went, and looked down the corridors behind them. They changed even as It looked. It could have sworn in the depths of the stone It heard Its men running in other directions. It roared in frustration. Lilah, throwing Bofindle into the armada with renewed energy, heard It and smiled.

It ran down another way and stopped to look back. The corridors were meshing and changing as It passed them. It ran down stairs and up stairs and every time Trecrogo became different. It smashed Its claws into the walls but they did not yield. It marked them but could not break them.

"Find me a way out," It roared at Its men.

They hurried off in all directions. But the labyrinth was every bit as complex and intricate as Its own Hâgon had been and even here Its cohorts were finding that not only did Trecrogo change every second, imprisoning them in these corridors, but that the fortress contained a million traps set for them. The most frightening of which was the way the walls turned them to ash, even through Crilodach's protective gloves. All the time they ran trying to find a way to escape, more cohorts raced into the fortress through the broken window. Trecrogo was now a labyrinthine prison and every turn Crilodach took, the stones moved to make sure It could not escape. It knew It was trapped. It realized this had all been a trap. They had sacrificed themselves to imprison It. It stamped the floor, It cursed, in Its eyes It saw the Sagitæ burning like a false promise. There was more magic here than Sangyma. And in Its mind came the thought, the terrifying thought, that explained so much. It had never known what power held It at bay when It was ready to plunder the universe. Held It locked up as rock as other life evolved and civilizations rose and fell. But whatever that power was, the Sangyma used the same spells to imprison It here just as resolutely. It had been duped. From the first, drawing It into leaving Damkina, bringing Its armada, the sham ambush meant to prod It on Its way, and Lilah holding the Sagitæ for It to see just as It was getting more and more frustrated at how the defenders held Its armada at bay. Just as It delighted at the death of Copret and the girl who had taught the clone human child who handled the fortress with such brilliance. It roared. It held Its claws in front of Its face and It spoke a few words.

It stopped running. It closed Its huge eyes. It still maintained Its grotesque shape but now It was going to show how It too could plan ahead. Crilodach had an uncanny ability to get into people's heads, to know what gave them their greatest fears and why. Because Crilodach understood how beings think and how differently they think, It was able to play complex mind games. The more powerful you are the less you fear because there are fewer things in the universe that can actually hurt you. But the more powerful you are the more your brain has to work, and the greater your knowledge becomes the more you know that ideas can be just as frightening as real events. If not more so. A quake might fill Tethval with fear underground knowing he could be killed and those he loved could be killed or they could be trapped and die before being rescued or hurt and in need of medical help that could not get through. Lilah would never fear such a quake because no quake could harm her and she was powerful enough to make sure those near to her would be safe. But the idea that for all the years of her training she had been trained incorrectly, or that her training had missed an essential truth in the final battle, would fill her with doubts. The idea that they had misjudged Crilodach, missed a vital part of Its character, missed a piece of their planning, would blot out all other considerations. Crush her spirit.

Crilodach always knew that taking on the shape of a huge beast frightened people. It always knew that misshapen, ugly creatures instilled fear. Creatures everywhere were used to seeing the animals of their own worlds and anything that looked out of place, anything unknown, as scary. That was part of the reason It looked the way It did. The other part had nothing to do with choice and everything to do with Tegriel and the foul Bofindle. Nothing in the universe was quite like Crilodach but in hiding the fact that It could leave this body, Crilodach would now create a huge doubt in Lilah's mind. It too had been hiding. Using the beast as a protection against being touched. When Its spell ended and It lowered Its claws It gave Lilah doubt. She would know this was not over. The prison had only half–worked

Crilodach moved off down the corridors more slowly. Listening. It knew the place must be saturated with traps. Like a caged animal It trod Its prison. Every turn made Trecrogo move and slide silently into new places, stairs came and went, right turns became left turns or vanished, floors moved even as Its feet passed over them. At every change those with It became fewer. They did not know the fate of those they could not see. Trecrogo was like a huge, convoluted, endless puzzle with no code to break. Then It heard the screams. Its men were being picked off by ... what? It knew the defenders above had their hands full with Its armada so whatever was hunting the corridors was new. From the screams It heard the traps must be fierce but It could not get an image in Its mind of what was killing them.

Its eyes glowered. Behind It, Its remaining men huddled close, scared to touch anything. Their weapons held in almost listless hands. It could feel them shivering. If this place could hold Crilodach they knew they had no chance. They moved on after It to places that looked and felt the same but were not. For they passed by the hidden door that Mojolo had walked from and inside, as Crilodach passed, there was movement from the huge second container. The spells of the Elstin witch twitched into action at the scent of the enemy.

Eight of Jurveiss' men jumped down from a falling siege engine slaying two of Gertis' army before Lilah struck them down in their turn.

Demeter was noticeably weaker as his power was now going to contain and confuse Crilodach. She knew they had to disengage to stop more from the armada entering the fortress and give him time to concentrate his powers on Crilodach alone. Now they were reinforced by the final remnants of Gertis' army the parapet was fully defended. She called out,

"Now Demeter."

Demeter, who had dropped down to where Chloe lay, held her head in his hands, disbelieving what he felt and saw, crushed within himself as if all his life had been a stupid, not a glorious, adventure. For the briefest moments he had thought war was power and friendship, comrades fighting, hope against Crilodach's malicious intent. For the briefest of moments he had revelled in the resources Trecrogo gave him. He had marvelled at Copret's strength and Lilah's magic. For someone who had never known war or been in battle, he and his friends appeared invincible. When he had seen Crilodach's armada he had not balked at their numbers or their ferocity. He had been filled with confidence. In an instant his confidence bled to death with Chloe in his arms, Copret lying motionless not far away. The bear who wanted to see everything clearly. The girl who wanted him to pass his test. Dead. This pain was too much for him.

He seemed to hear Lilah call from a great distance. He looked up and, through his sadness, saw everywhere Crilodach's armada surging forward uncaring as they died in their hunger to win. Did they not have time to weep for their friends? Were they an armada that had no friendship? How could you defeat an armada that did not know the meaning of a friend being one's right arm. They had never walked through a valley with a friend, lit a camp fire and climbed endless steps relying upon someone else to be there if they needed them.

Lilah had grown up being watched over by Copret. The Arvernat were as close as brothers and sisters could be. Gertis' army had hungered and struggled as only families know how. But this armada, shouted, bellowed, cursed and threw themselves at the fortress in relentless frenzy. They had seen Copret fall and Chloe die. They did not count the cost to them in their own dead, they saw the deaths of their enemy as the victory they hungered for. They saw Arvernat fall. They knew the Brujans had failed but the cockroach army sent against them was vanquished. A Sangyma was dead. No matter how many of them died, if one enemy died the battle had been a good one. For though they had no experience of friendship themselves, they did know the meaning of friendship to their enemy. They knew the meaning of loyalty to their enemy. They knew the meaning of loss to their enemy. They had been trained by Frin-Ghirzan and he knew every life was precious to Its enemies. One life taken was worth worlds. So Rataplan ordered the armada forward, eager to kill Demeter, Tethval and Lilah and the last remaining fighters standing. Believing they could. Crilodach was no longer amongst them but inside Trecrogo. Soon the fortress would fall. They did not know yet Trecrogo had It imprisoned. They thought at any moment they would see Crilodach standing upon the parapet. They wanted to be the first to stand there beside It.

In anger Crilodach bellowed and the sound echoed throughout the fortress. Demeter heard It, also seemingly from a distance. He suddenly came to himself. Dazed. Something inside himself was no longer functioning. No longer there. He swept his hands out as he walked forward cleaning the parapet of the enemy and giving the defenders near to him, a few seconds respite. And in those seconds the remnants of Gertis' army clambered over the wall and the siege engine they had used as a makeshift ladder broke into dust along with the hundreds of the enemy crawling up behind them.

Midrak had crept along with twenty others. The walls did not burn them knowing the were allies. They climbed up between the soil and the fortress until they began to struggle not with soil but with bodies. The dead from Crilodach's armada who had been thrown off the parapet. They pulled and clambered through the mounds of dead struggling to get to the open, passed blood and stone–cold eyes, torn limbs and strange grimaces, until they managed to get to the top layers of bodies. The armada above them took the movement of their fallen comrades as the twitches of the wounded. They stepped on them anyway. The twenty survivors waited with Midrak.

"If we show ourselves we will be ripped to shreds," observed Midrak.

"Wait for a chance," replied Fulminar.

"I'm not sure we will have a chance. That crippled siege engine they were using for a ladder is gone," said Midrak.

"We could be seen at any moment if we stay here," warned Fulminar.

"They have more to think about than what may be under their feet. Tell the others to be ready to go. We'll have to be fast."

"But our comrades on Trecrogo may think we're dead. They may not help us and we will be in the open," warned Fulminar.

"Then this is where the universe ends for us."

"What about the bottle," nudged Fulminar.

"You will become known to all, not just those on Trecrogo."

"What do you have to lose?"

Midrak poured the liquid out, which, never reaching the ground, floated through the bodies above them. They were all tense. They waited for what seemed hours until Demeter swept the enemy clear from the walls in one violent effort. In that second the liquid threw up the remnants of the dead. And the Sangyma aura around Midrak became visible to everyone on the battlefield. Their way suddenly clear, Midrak and twenty others ran for the wall hoping Lilah or Demeter would help them up. But Rataplan looked across the sea of men and machines and saw the group dressed differently and running away. The aura of the Sangyma was clearly visible.

The general ran at the small group like an eager child anxious to join in a game but this child was armed. A Sangyma was a head worthy of his every effort to take. Two in one battle had only been achieved once before and never by the same man. He craved such a success. How could Crilodach leave him behind if he had done so much to give It victory?

Even as they made their way forward again all remaining siege engines rolled threateningly to the walls, the men upon them roaring out their threats. Seeing Midrak's group running to get to the fortress a few badly aimed spears were thrown at them.

From far away a second bellow answering Crilodach's was heard. But Crilodach was in the fortress. This second one came from outside. Not an echo but a response. Lilah looked towards the sound. Who? What? The bellow was definitely from Crilodach, though not as deep. How was that possible? Unless Tegriel had been right. The ancient fight he had described to her when she was a child, the way in which Crilodach became the beast, and why It feared to be touched. Had It reverted to Its original form? Crilodach's magic was working on her. She shivered slightly and raised herself with Bofindle to steady her bleeding arm. She looked at her defences. The remnants of her forces, Tethval and fourteen Arvernat, Mojolo, Demeter, and now some three hundred men and women Gertis had brought to them, heroes of the battle against the Brujans. Then, as she looked out to see where the roar had come from, she saw her own brother about to be submerged in the flood of the enemy with no less than Rataplan at their head.

"I am always saving you," she whispered to herself.

But her hand was stopped even as she raised Bofindle, by another bellow. She looked to see something she had hoped was not possible. There running up in the midst of the huge armada was a strange creature. It wore no armour. Its skin was grey. Its hair was white and long. It roared as It ran with determined strides. Crilodach was a man again.

She watched as It made Its way towards the fortress. Making an entrance any actor would have been proud to make. All eyes from the fortress were riveted on It. All except Demeter's who's eyes were on Rataplan, the general responsible for murdering Chloe.

The man was heading for the fortress. The man hidden within the beast. If It attacked from the outside and the beast attacked from the inside at the same time the fortress would fall.

Even as Lilah spoke to Tethval the door to the room Mojolo had awoken in was slowly moved out of the way by strong, alloyed hands. The heavy head turned on well-crafted motors, his matrix for a brain fully booted up, his green eyes focussed slowly to the room and the feeling of immense pain he felt bled power into his whole body. His eyes focussed. He saw perfectly in the dark. His hearing turned on. He heard Crilodach and his men pass by. So acute was his hearing he heard thousands of individual voices at once. In his head he could see the layout of Trecrogo, changing every second, and he could follow each and every person trapped as well as those fighting above. All this information he could process with ease.

Nu-An had risen quickly and jumped to the floor from his container. He had seen Mojolo's empty container and was glad she was awake. He looked down the corridor and smelled the armed men ahead of him. Then he walked in the opposite direction. In direct contact with Trecrogo he was being guided to confront Crilodach face-to-face. The Elstin witch had assured Filvani, Nu-An could withstand the power of Crilodach for one and a half days. Filvani believed her, but to be sure he gave the robot his own gift. Part of Filvani moved along the corridors. Hidden in the brain were all the laws and the history of the Sangyma. Filvani, of all the Sangyma, had been the one who used his magic the least. He had taught Tegriel that knowledge was a kind of magic, and he preferred to teach people that from knowledge could come wisdom, which was an inner magic. Nu-An was using that knowledge now as he hurried along the corridors. Once he engaged with Crilodach, Demeter would be free to carry out the final, irrevocable action of Trecrogo.

❖

"We can't even bury our dead," Mojolo complained, bitterness in her voice.

"There is no time for burials," Lilah told her. Her arm hurt. The wound bled slowly and she whispered a spell to stem the pain. "But they are not forgotten. Trecrogo is carrying them into Zaqui."

"What happens if Trecrogo falls?" asked Mojolo.

"We move to fight elsewhere," said Lilah.

"But we put so much into Trecrogo," said Mojolo.

"Our objective is to keep Crilodach fighting, not necessarily to keep alive," explained Tethval. "Isn't that right?"

"I never told you that," Lilah told him, watching Rataplan's battalions as they tried to become accustomed to the new man in the midst.

"I'm a leader of Arvernat, I can work these things out for myself. This is the only strategy that makes any sense of all this," Tethval told her.

"Demeter ..." Lilah called, wondering why he did not disengage the fortress.

Demeter was standing on top of the wall. His lips parted slightly as he looked at the torrent of savages that faced the fortress and the mud that was mingled in their blood and had turned a russet colour. Midrak and his comrades were back to back in a huddle totally surrounded, but as Demeter jumped down from the fortress he was not thinking so much of saving them. His thought was revenge. Lilah, who had been ready to fly to her brother's aid, watched, astonished to see him leap into the enemy.

❖

To instil terror you need to know something first. You need to know what keeps a person awake at night, unable to turn off their lights, or waking find themselves in a sweat filled panic. You need to know what their nightmares are, and to know that, you need to know the person well. For we all know fear but we do not all fear the same things equally or for the same reasons. There are those who believe in a higher power and if their fate is to die they will, and if their fate is to survive, they will. They can be visited with any calamity and they will meet the challenge calmly. This gives them an ability to explain and accept how great events have a very personal outcome for all of us. There are those who just run as fast as they can. There are those who stay put to give others time to run, willing to save the others at the risk of their own lives.

To know someone else well you have to be able to not only see the universe through their eyes, but be able to see into their hearts. To understand what they understand and why they understand what they do, the way that they do. To follow their reasoning. To know their childhoods. The Sangyma minds and hearts were all about life. Trying to understand those whose minds are all about hurt and pain, like Rataplan's, is not easy. The Sangyma know that when we die, everything ends for us. For Crilodach's general that knowledge was his only fear. He did not want things to end for him now he understood the immensity of everything.

The bears had always known the prison they had built might not be enough. As the fortress was there to play for time they kept an open mind about what additional strategy to follow. Far away they found the plans for an ancient mechanical weapon that had been lost and hidden by an ancient civilization. The disenchanted Elstin witch followed the plans and built one and placed him in the room next to Mojolo. She had called him Nu–An, part man part machine for he looked like a giant and was made to accomplish a great task.

You can never understand the fears of a machine.

Now, as Crilodach's presence rent the air and Its roars reverberated around the fortress, Nu–An waited. In the dark. In a long corridor by a long series of steps that led nowhere. He waited. The roars got closer as the beast was talking to the man outside the fortress. They were organizing themselves to attack the same spot in Trecrogo from inside and outside at the same time. The thump of feet got closer. Nu–An waited. He had waited a long time. He had known he was to be created when they drew up the blueprints. He had been in those plans. Felt them. He had ached to be built but they had never built him; they had feared what they had thought they could create. The Elstin witch built him for she feared nothing she made with her own hands. The bears had sensed the power he could bring to the battle. A robot of alloys, determined to be built. Nu–An made his hands into fists as he prepared to meet Crilodach. Deep inside his head he heard a voice. Filvani's voice.

"You're here then old man," he said.

"I told you I would be."

"I'm pleased to hear your voice again," said Nu–An.

"The beast is with us?" asked Filvani.

"Closing in now."

"Remember what I taught you."

"I will leave the magic to you old man," Nu–An said. "I'm metal and gears."

"You were always more than that to me."

"I judge myself by what I know myself to be."

"Then be as a son of the Sangyma."

Nu–An had felt every bolt and joint being made. He had felt them sliding into place. He had felt the strength building in him. He had seen for the first time. Touched at long last. Sensed the world that had been calling to him from the idea of himself. And then they had put him in Trecrogo to wait. Deprived him of the years of life he could have had because he had to be a secret weapon. He was not allowed to experience anything. So Filvani, connected to him and understanding him, had shared experiences with him in the vault, in the long-dark. Nu–An had lived a thousand lives while waiting. Seen planets, made friends, fallen in love with sunsets and skied past black holes. No one can be alive without memories. He had been built as a weapon but Filvani had given him a magical heart. And when Filvani was killed on that fateful Saturday when the Sangyma met to talk about Zaqui, Nu–An had felt the loss though not yet in the fortress. In the depths of his silence he had mourned and kept as precious that part of his magic which Filvani had left with him. A universe of experiences.

Nu–An was also filled with pain. For things he had lost. Lost because Crilodach was a beast. A power that had to be stopped. If Crilodach had never lived, Nu–An may have known what life was like.

Nu–An met Crilodach's forces who were eager to kill anything. They swarmed over him their metal weapons cracking upon his impenetrable alloy skin. As he ripped the men off his body with his strong fingers and smashed them into the walls where they burned to ash, murmurs ran up and down their lines that he was not real. These soldiers, who had fought all kinds of races, had heard of the robots that could not be killed. They had been told they were myths but here in this fortress, myths were becoming realities.

Nu-An walked forward without hesitation. His footfall light for one so heavy. Some thought he would walk past them and allowed him near them. They were wrong. He killed them without so much as a glance. Nu-An crushed them with huge arms and moved on looking for Crilodach. Always Crilodach. His arms spanning wall to wall so nothing would escape him.

They met on the stairs. Two Titans crushing everyone around them as they fought head to head, blow for blow. Neither would yield. Neither felt any pain from the blows of the other. Neither gave ground. The spot at which they met was the place on which they fought to the inch. Face-to-face without a shout or a yell. An astonishing sight to see. Arms and claws, straining muscles and alloy metal, struggling like sumo wrestlers without so much as a second's pause. And the small device Lilah had placed upon Crilodach's back burst into life at Nu-An's touch, threading through the beast's back and lacing into Nu-An's fingers. Crilodach felt the new spell. Knew what was happening. Nu-An's grip would not be broken for hours. Crilodach did not have hours.

Every ounce of strength each had was going into the fight. They performed a strange kind of dance for they could not move quickly, so strong was the power of the other. Crilodach whispered spells. But Nu-An was protected by the arts of Filvani and Zananto as well as the atoms of the alloys which were inert and did not respond to magic. For spells can only affect things with atoms of magic in them. The spells bounced off his alloy skin and his steady eyes met Crilodach's and they both realized they may as well have been in chains for neither of them could get an advantage over the other for long minutes of struggle, which became a half an hour contest, which became an hour. Nu-An sensed the slight lessening in Crilodach's power. He did not know the man had separated from the beast It had clothed Itself in since Its first battle with the Sangyma. But Nu-An knew It was not as powerful anymore. It could be controlled, even pushed back. Behind them Crilodach's remaining two men heard yells. Something was coming for them. Someone. Unable to get past Nu-An and Crilodach they turned, trapped, to face their fate.

Given to their own deaths the few remaining Arvernat would fight on. Engineered for and synchronized with Trecrogo, Demeter would fight on. Mojolo empowered by Sanjava, would fight on against all odds. But Lilah now had to activate the rest of their plans. With part of Crilodach secured inside the prison but his real self turning up out of the blue, they had to move away from this battlefield. To stay and fight the armada would be a waste of effort as Nu-An took over the fight against Crilodach below them.

But how much of Crilodach had they really captured? Could It be as strong an enemy without Its animal skin? Would they find Crilodach Itself was still active outside Trecrogo even though the beast was quelled by Nu-An inside. If It retained all Its power, Trecrogo would not stand. As if Copret and Chloe had died for nothing. As if Tegriel and Tobia had gone back in time to achieve nothing. The doubts It had created plagued her mind. This was Crilodach's ace card, and It was played at exactly the right time, which was, as It thought, the worst possible time for Lilah. She needed time to think. She needed time to plan. She called Tethval, summoning Copret's Onäis to her side.

"Come, we have to go now," she told him.

He jumped on the Onäis as she wrapped them in invisibility. The armada saw the defenders slowly vanishing and thought they were running because they were losing. They crowded closer screaming their victory songs.

Even as the others escaped on the Onäis that lifted them above the parapet, Demeter landed on the ground. In his mind he still saw Chloe. On his hand he still felt the touch of her as he had bent to touch her dead forehead. His body was small but strong. His heart was big, yet broken. He was so powerful now, his finger had burned a small mark on her skin and he shrank away not wanting to hurt her even in death.

With Its armada thrusting forward the white-haired man was screaming fit to burst wanting to free his beast-self. Demeter, the boy who had moaned about climbing up all the steps and fallen in love with Chloe raised his arms. He had leapt into the air still something of a boy, but landing on the stony ground around the fortress was an angry, vengeful man.

The armada raced to kill him but where he landed amongst them the force within him swept their lives away from himself for a mile around. Rataplan and his immediate followers faltered in their charge against Midrak, some even turned to charge at Demeter and were taken aback to see the boy charging not so much at them as through them. They did not even exist as he ran past them towards their general. Crilodach the man, saw the charge and shouted out orders to stop him but any who tried were thrown helplessly to one side. The force and skill of his run breaking their bones and avoiding their weapons in the same manœuvre.

Rataplan struck out at him trying to sidestep the lunge Demeter made at him. Demeter with his fist clench ducked Rataplan's first strike and punch his arm through the general's armour ripping out his backbone and dropping the bones from his fingers as they emerged from Rataplan's back, he sent out a shock wave that killed twenty of those who stood with the general.

Dying, Rataplan looked into Demeter's eyes and Demeter saw the general's coldness drain from his face, his demeanour changed and the man he had once been for the last time looked clearly at another living being. A child. Whole armies had fallen on him and he had survived, yet a child had beaten him. A child capable of focussing the immense power of Trecrogo through his body. He slid off Demeter's bloody arm and fell dead at the boy's feet. Without hesitating Demeter jumped back up to the fortress, taking Midrak and the twenty survivors with him in his wake.

"To the last Onäis," he commanded, "Go! Lilah will take care of you."

"What about you?" asked Midrak, still shaking a little from the hard fight.

"I'll be fine," said Demeter.

"But ..."

"Go. Now," he ordered, as hands from the hidden Onäis above them reached down and grabbed at the fighters.

Crilodach bellowed from within the fortress frustrated by the tactics of Nu-An. The white-haired Crilodach bellowed back like a brother answering Its brother's calls, and charged towards the remnants of the defenders of Trecrogo. The Onäis had all gone. Trecrogo stood defended by Demeter alone. He watched Crilodach leaping past the fallen general trying to get to the fortress but before he did anything Demeter called out,

"Your time will come."

Then the roots of the fortress broke through the ground and all the siege engines remaining were thrown into the air. The armada was lost in a muddy quagmire, blinded by soil and stone. Their cries of victory stifled in their throats. When the ground settled, the Rounds surrounded nothing. A vast hole where the fortress had been. A ready grave for all the soldiers piled up around the circumference who rolled into the emptiness and vanished towards Zaqui.

Crilodach screamed out from within the fortress but no answering call came to him. Utter silence surrounded them all. Tiredness suddenly consumed the armada. Another battle was over. The next battle was just beginning. Rataplan was dead. But before the white-haired man could appoint a new general they faced a new enemy.

The hole left by Trecrogo began to suck in the Rounds soon becoming a whirling wall of soil and stone swirling faster and faster, turning into a wall of matter streaming into the hole where the fortress had been. Like a whirlpool of atoms. Lilah leaned on Bofindle and whispered into her hands. Faster the bejal swirled. Invisible to the enemy the Onäis travelled away. The white-haired man leapt into the whirlpool and Bofindle struck him a blow to the head sending him flying back out, to land on his feet a little dazed, enraged and embittered. Lilah was pleased at the sight. Outside of Its beast's clothes he was not quite so powerful. The beast inside the fortress was not quite so powerful. They had achieved the near impossible. They had weakened Crilodach.

Yet even as she looked and Demeter took Trecrogo away with his prisoner, Lilah reached out with her mind and Hagouti, cramped and in pain in his cell felt her pull. His wispish self was sucked out of Trecrogo. He felt the presence of his master and he tried to fight being taken away but he didn't have the power to win against her. His tactics might get the better of a spellmaker but only ever once. Miss that opportunity and he would never have another one even if he had had all of time to plot and plan. Her mind flooded over him and he heard her orders. Understood her command to him. She wanted information from him. She wanted him to betray Crilodach. She wanted him to become her spy.

"Why should I spy for you?" he asked her.

"Because Crilodach lied to you. It would never keep you alive. It would never take you with It," she said.

"I know," he agreed.

"Yet you still served It?"

"Crilodach created me," he said.

"You are not Its servant now, look It is nothing but a man."

"They're one–and–the–same."

"But the Crilodach you know is in prison. It cannot escape Trecrogo."

"Why should I believe that?" he asked her.

"You doubt me?"

"You're running aren't you?" said Hagouti.

"I have what I wanted. Your creator in prison never to get out again, without any of the Sagitæ in Its possession and but two hours left to Zaqui. I want you to watch the man with Its armada. To tell me what It is going to do in those coming hours."

"If It finds out ..." he started.

"It will never find out," she assured him.

"What do I get in return?"

"The truth. That you cannot survive."

"You offer me nothing? Why should I do anything for you?"

"Because you would want to do something to get back at Crilodach. Look at It. It has no claws now. Is It so different from you? It has skin the same colour and narrow eyes. Do you not want some revenge upon this miserable looking, white–haired man who spent your lifetime lying to you?"

"What makes you think I should?" asked Hagouti.

"It created you to have pain. It did not need to. It could have made you better. It could have made you stronger but Crilodach would never make anything that was a threat to Itself."

"It told me I was incomplete."

"It lied about that just like everything else," she said.

"And you don't lie."

"I am telling you Crilodach will die in this universe. Nothing will save It. I have a Sagitæ, look. Your master is not all powerful."

Hagouti saw the Sagitæ in his head and the glitter from the jewel mellowed him.

"How do I contact you?"

"I will contact you," she told him.

"And I'm just to tell you Its plans?"

"Just stay close to It. I will know everything I need to know if you do," she said.

"I don't have to send you any messages?"

"You would be caught if you tried."

"Then I'll help you."

And with that Hagouti found himself on his hands and knees in the muddy remains of the Rounds beside the dead Rataplan. He looked at the face of the dead general and even Hagouti knew an era had ended. Something had changed. Crilodach divided, Rataplan dead. He a spy for Lilah.

"Life takes the strangest turns," he whispered to himself.

"What are you doing here?" snarled a voice.

He looked up and stared at the white-haired Crilodach, whose eyes burned with that same hatred Hagouti knew so well. How strange to see his creator so much the same yet so different.

"I was in a cell in the fortress. Now I'm here. I don't know what happened." Crilodach spat on the ground,

"Make yourself useful. Get up! Tell Ferveiss everything you learned of Trecrogo."

"Are you really Crilodach?" Crilodach bridled at his question.

"Never ask that again," It suddenly turned on him, Its nose up against Hagouti's, "or I'll show you just how much I'm still Crilodach."

Demeter, ripping Trecrogo from the battle, propelled the fortress through the blackness. The whole building trembled as the Ossendark opened. The vast fortress passed along and, as Trecrogo slowed, the Ossendark exploded sending flares into space like fireworks that were all light and no sound. Streaming tails of light that vanished in a second. The most ancient form of travel between worlds was no more. He talked to Lilah in his head, worried about her new plan.

"Will you be alright without me?" he asked her.

"We will be as we will be. You know your path," she replied.

"I do."

"Do not be afraid," she soothed.

"I'm not afraid." She could hear the depths, even in his thoughts, of his sadness.

"Keep alert. We shall see each other before the end."

"I'll wait for you."

And with that Demeter lost Lilah for a while, and he stood alone on the parapet. He washed away the blood of the fallen. He looked at the meagre shadows over the fortress cast by the only light left, that which came from him. He thought of fields and seas and summer days, but most of all he thought of one face. A smiling face. Sometimes stern. Teaching him. Talking to him. Her eyes bright. For all his powers, the child in Demeter wanted to cry. He could not. He had taken the same journey Lilah had taken. To be one of those who cannot mourn.

Mojolo peered at Lilah as they sat on the Onäis. She had fought the armada as It roared and cursed at them almost without a thought. Keeping her post as she had done on many occasions fighting beside Sanjava. She now calmly waited for what she knew would come. Lilah did not look back at her. She was listening to Hagouti. He got up and followed after Crilodach as It cursed and screamed. He scratched his left ear.

"I'd have threatened him," suggested Mojolo, knowing what she was doing.

"The way to control someone who is not by your side is to win their heart," Lilah pointed out, "no matter how twisted that heart may be." Mojolo could not argue with her logic but asked,

"What now?"

"Now," said Lilah slowly, "now we spring a trap we have not yet created. Now we hope Rimfelder has been successful."

"Another trap? Out of what, there's nothing left."

"Crilodach will go wherever Demeter takes Trecrogo."

"Where's that?" Mojolo asked.

Lilah pointed and far in the distance. The brief exploding lights flared and died. Everything else was darkness.

"It needs to reunite with Its beast if It is to defeat us."

"I should go to meet It there."

"It has not moved yet. I must shadow Its armada and watch

and wait."

"Why don't we take them on before they regroup?" said Mojolo.

"You're eager for another bout."

"I don't think we did too badly considering the odds," said Mojolo.

"Without Trecrogo we run too great a risk. We must be more subtle. As things stand Crilodach does not know I am not in Trecrogo with the Sagitæ."

"You planned for this?" asked Mojolo.

"Not exactly. Crilodach would have been scanning for our thoughts but Demeter and I were able to decide upon a course of action before It arrived. I first told him there may be two Crilodachs before the battle started."

"You knew," said Midrak, who was still recovering from their rescue.

"We had to consider the possibility. When we were building Trecrogo we had long hours to talk about everything. We all knew the beast was made in the first battle with Tegriel. What can be made into one can be pulled apart again."

"If Crilodach could not go back in time because It would meet Itself, how can It now live with two of Itself," asked Midrak

"This is something It only recreated when It realized Trecrogo was a prison. I felt something had happened I did not know exactly what for a few moments. Though both alive, both are the same being, and in that lies our hope because I do not believe either is as strong separately as they were combined. Keeping both alive has cost It some power."

"Do we know that for sure?" sighed Mojolo.

"I assume Hagouti may provide us answers?" said Tethval.

"More than likely Crilodach will give us the answers if we can get close enough," said Lilah.

Tethval, tensing his wounded hand despite the pain, said, "I don't like waiting."

"None of us do," said Midrak.

"Tethval, I think we should go and watch Crilodach. All our remaining forces can stay with Trecrogo. Rimfelder will appear there if anywhere and he may need to be protected when he arrives."

"Why him more than anyone else?" asked Midrak.

"Because he may be our key to victory."

"I thought we were fighting for time, not victory," said Midrak.

"That's about the sum of our efforts," winced Tethval.

"We survived this far," Lilah told them all, "we can survive the last two hours."

"Do you think Demeter can stand alone that long?" asked Tethval.

"The white-haired Crilodach will pursue Demeter. Demeter knows he will be coming for the Sagitæ Rimfelder brings. Our objective is to keep Crilodach imprisoned and Its white-haired self fighting. We know It will go wherever the Sagitæ are so I only have to appear for It to attack me. Like a moth to a light It will fly at me."

"Well," said Tethval sadly, "Copret and Chloe are dead, you and I are wounded, most of my Arvernat are gone. How much more do we have to give?"

"Everything," she replied.

The others moved around as directed to wait for Rimfelder. Lilah sat quietly on Copret's Onäis looking at the Rounds. Fulminar was here now. They spoke quietly to each other. They left more unspoken. Out of her pocket crawled a cockroach and she smiled.

"So, she said, "some of you were just insects after all."

Mojolo looked at Lilah and for the first time noticed the blood dripping from her hands as she held Bofindle. The acid of the weapons used against Lilah evaporated from her skin in a shimmering vapour. On the cockroach were a few hairs and Lilah picked at them. They were Copret's. She smiled a weary smile. She rubbed them into her wounded hand and murmured to herself and slowly her hand changed. Fur grew upon her skin and claws, followed by Copret's heavy pads. Part of Copret would live to fight again. Her hand became Copret's paw. In her imagination she heard his voice. That strong, fatherly voice with the hint of a growl saying,

"What now Lilah?"

"Now," she whispered as she stared at Crilodach and Its armada, "Now we fight."

How Dragons Die

Opiar's sudden death hanged like a hungry vulture gripping Rimfelder's head, demanding to be kept fed by the raw, constant surprise of the loss reverberating through him every few seconds with harsh, repeated blows to his forehead. As if his terrible death were a pebble thrown into a pond and the poet was being hit by every eddy, rippling through his being again and again, each eddy as painful as the first. Opiar dying over–and–over again. All around him shadows seemed to silhouette some part of Opiar: a wing, a neck, the face, a profile. Noises which echoed as the caverns deepened, seemed to whisper Opiar's name in his throbbing ears. The rock face wanted to bow inwards and crush him. The äis wanted to stop and drop him back into Phigata. His whole body ached with pain.

Rimfelder looked at the two remaining brothers like a man who endlessly looks for more than he can see. He felt that simply to live was to bleed, simply to breathe was to suffer and to go on thinking was to betray his comrades. Everything, everything, everything was wrong. He had had this same feeling just before meeting Lilah for the first time. A feeling that the juice from Vingura had deadened but now resurfaced with the insistent, shocking scream, *'all is death'*.

After all the fighting, Rimfelder was still unable to get used to either the smell or the sight of murder. He had forgotten during the rush with Lilah in the Ossendark (and the surprise of meeting Vingura), to be scared of having friends. So many had died he had tried to cut himself off from others to save himself more heartache. He could not count the familiar faces lost in the battle with the tyrant. The planet devoured. Tethval and the others sacrificed in the remains of the city, vanishing as quickly as you turn out a light. Tobia blinded. Midrak and Tobia plucked from their side. If he had known what was happening to his closest friends upon Trecrogo his pain could not have been any deeper. He felt as if he would never touch anything of happiness again. Unless he was with her.

Nor could he evade the brutality and often the need to kill as he had seen with Tethval in their struggle for freedom against the tyrant. The need existed even here in these caverns that curled and twisted as if Xibalba writhed in pain. There was no escaping the harmonics of pain as time and Zaqui held them in their vice-like, agonizing grasp.

Tethval had once told him that everything was gained in their life through blood, and though he did not want to believe him, he was slowly becoming convinced his friend had been right. This was true of the whole universe. If not true, then his fate was uniquely filled with bitterness. The hard, remorseless onslaught on their world by Crilodach's creatures. The awesome power of Lilah who killed because others came to kill her but who found no longing for blood in herself, even as death followed her everywhere. Vingura's garden healing so many who had all been wounded by so many others. The Gaddia telling him of battles he could not even see, wrapped in strange names that called to him, like the untranslatable calls of colourful birds, unbearably beautiful only because he did not understand them. Behind them all the whispered stories of the Sangyma and the war with Crilodach that began and ended with Zaqui. How, how, how could this be and he be alive when so many strong warriors were not?

He shivered once more seeing Opiar devoured by the lesser–toothed rock Irghwols. All wars, like all roads, are one. One leads into another, crossing worlds, solar systems and galaxies. As if one sword strike rattled enough atoms to send ripples through the universe urging others to kill with such authority they could not resist.

The smallest particles of magic in the universe, quantum magic, are all connected no matter the distance of their separation and likewise, blood and wars are linked across voids because armies are made of atoms sifted into bodies. Beings far distant, fighting wars unknown to others, none the less effect those others with a blood–letting beyond their understanding. War cries of one language give names to the heroes in another. Hammer blows in one world call those in another to fight. The passion of one animal can move another galaxy to rebellion.

What part could he have in such momentous events? Was he just there to feel the suffering and endure the pain? Was Opiar's death his failure? He wanted to cry out Opiar's name, to take back the last hour, to defy all the suffering in all wars by bringing Opiar back to life, but he could do nothing but feel the loss weighing him down so completely he simply did not have the strength to stand up. This is the seed of sorrow Crilodach had brought to life. The tears of others inevitably hidden behind every choice we ever make.

Opiar, who had waited longer than the mind can count to be rescued, forfeited his life so soon after being freed but by doing so proved he knew of a wider purpose. But then dragons have always been connected to quantum magic. There are no bejals they do not know. A knowledge Zananto gifted to them when they saved her life in the great war with Frin-Ghirzan when she was a young girl. A battle that showed she was a Sangyma, and how mighty the dragons proved themselves to be as friends. The battle which showed Frin-Ghirzan he needed more troops to deal with all Its differing enemies if they were going to survive Zaqui.

Such an incalculable loss thought Rimfelder. A double reason to mourn. His eyes should have been swollen with tears. The brothers should have been ripping into Opiar's murderers until none were left. But they had to concentrate on what lay ahead of them. This infernal place, plagued with traps and snares, wanted to devour them, to stop them from escaping, to keep Rimfelder from Lilah's side where he belonged. Phigata boiled with rage behind them. Only one had ever escaped from Xibalba before and she had been a Sangyma. Xibalba was so huge he wondered if dragons and a poet had any chance of escaping.

The silence, broken only by their beating hearts, said everything the brothers needed to say. Heartbeats endlessly thumping about injustice, heartache and pain. Like the silence of ink in a pen writing words against tyranny that would be spoken by millions. The beat that accompanies every sword thrust, every spell, every thought of every one. The beating hearts of the universe pumping blood through endless veins as everyone made their choice, as quantum magic bound them all together, as the war proceeded to the bitter end of all beating hearts. The pain of silence after the beating hearts of living things stop. The simple beating song of living carved by everyone out of hatred for Crilodach; battered by Its armadas, misshapen by Its purpose. The simple harmonies of hearts mercilessly beaten into battle cries. Opiar's heart was gone and there were those who knew and felt the loss. But none more so than those on this floating äis.

These were three comrades in mourning; three brought closer together by a terrible death; sharing a silence dressed in plain clothes ribbed with fresh wounds that were embroidered with glistening eyes. Just as Tethval and Rimfelder had fought harder because they had lost friends, so every death now made them more resolute. Even the äis was more determined. Something in the lines of the design appeared harder, less in shadow, almost weapon–like. Sharp. Fit for purpose.

Finally, as if he had just discovered he had a voice, he let out a groan that made no sense but was layered with meaning. The brothers turned to look at him in his misery. He looked into their sad eyes. Their proud yellow and black necks slightly arching forward. At times like this, strength of mind was all they could summon to their aid. Thankfully with dragons this was enough.

For the sake of all, they could not fail. For the sake of Opiar they could not fail. For the sake of Lilah he could not fail. He had to get back to her. To see her again. Even if only briefly. If everything was ending he wanted to be by her side in that last second. Not to make sure she was alright, that was absurd she had more powers in her little finger than he had in his whole body, but because that was his place. More, he hoped she wanted the same thing, if she wanted anything for herself at all. He wanted to look into her eyes before oblivion came to him in an even greater act of violence than had killed Opiar. For he knew neither his mind nor chance had chosen her side, but his heart. Just as Vingura had known. From the first time he had seen her and she had fought to save her brother and protect the city. She was the one who made sense of every battle and all his heartache.

Despite so many early deaths, far, far too many, he thought, he still had someone he loved. The darkness of the unseen was descending. He was voyaging far from her, with new–found friends in a distant sphere sucking them along burning, vile pathways as if slowly digesting them in ravenous, bubbling, hot juices. The very bowels of everything that was their natural enemy was disgorging upon them and even now, feasting on their dead friend. Working up the appetite to feast upon them in their turn. The sour air carried the sound of chewing to their tired ears.

The three of them knew eyes were watching them from behind every hiding place along the walls of Xibalba. The brothers, with their deep knowledge, knew the names of many of the creatures that had once lived here, feeding off each other. The vicious Irghwols who had eaten all the other species, now littered the caverns. The last creatures to torture the last travellers in Xibalba. Even as they floated above the barren, stony ground, Rimfelder felt as if the enemy brushed against his skin as they passed close to the cavern walls. He began to feel that Xibalba was scarring his skin. Cracking him open like an egg being broken, to get to the soft yolk inside. He felt very much in need of some natural sunlight, fresh water, the invigorating smell of fresh air and the smiles from friendly faces. The dragons were his friends but he had to admit they looked formidable. He did not think they would ever smile. But then what use were smiles in this vile place?

The closeness of the surroundings and the passing of precious time were eating into his mind, leaving room for nothing else but fear; held close like a corpse tied to his back pulling against his own movements with the stilted, freakish tightness of locked bones. Even the Gaddia did not comfort him for the minds that had created the book controlled him more than he controlled them. That they were moving forward was little comfort because he dreaded what lay ahead.

Opiar's brothers did not talk to each other that he could hear. They just sat on the äis, their eyes looking around, down and above. All that showed they were living to him was the occasional shake of their heavy, huge heads, or the almost casual flapping of a wing in irritation or flick of an ear against some distant sound to try to work out what they were hearing. Like two immense shadows so much a part of the äis they could have been made of the same stuff, on the same day, and probably were. Everyone else seemed to have been waiting for these days and these tasks. Not him. He was the outsider. The chance throw of the magical dice, the unexpected, who was as much surprised by everything and everyone, as Crilodach had been of him.

Their breathing was hoarse which Rimfelder assumed was because of their exertions after millenniums sitting doing nothing. Sudden exercise can bring on rasping breath but then he had never heard dragons stifling their sobs before.

160

He did not know that despite the passing of centuries, their muscles as dragons had lost none of their strength nor their claws any of their skills.

The brothers were not fools, they had known what was ahead of them from the moment the Gaddia had awoken them from their deep enchantment. If truth be told they had known this day would arrive from the moment Crilodach had imprisoned them. They knew the spells meant they would not die. They would be cut off from the world and be forgotten by all save a precious few.

They also knew that in choosing to lose their sanity when they did, their fate would be terrible if they awoke. Terrible because their sons had been kidnapped and turned to soldiers in Crilodach's army. The few who knew of them, and knew how dragons are connected to their children, might have wanted to spare them this dreaded fate. Rimfelder must be very important to have put the three of them through the misery of the past hours. They were able to survive what they were going through, after all they were dragons and very strong, but no one who loved them would have wished them to feel what they had felt since waking up.

Few people know a strange fact about dragons, that the fathers and sons, mothers and daughters, are telepathically connected. In the past of their great families when they were laying down the worlds upon which dragons would live, and laying down the laws they would live by, being able to see through the eyes of their children was always useful for fathers and mothers. In this way they could train them when they went on their long solitary flights, warn them of dangers in the places in which they arrived, advise them when they got lost and more importantly still, be there as a constant presence. Young dragons could range far and wide and still be within the family circle talking and listening in their minds to their parents. Hearing their parents talk to them when they needed to know something, feeling their guiding claw. In this way no dragons can be said to be truly alone. In the past, when some deserted their families for treasure and adventure, living isolated lives on barren islands and stricken castles, their greatest sadness was that their families knew what they had done, felt what they felt and were full of criticism for their wayward behaviour. When dragons talk to each other their songs are very long, longer than whale songs, can go on for months and span a galaxy.

Once Filvani was able in the Ossendark to listen to one of these songs. He said he had never heard anything so beautiful.

In older times when some ignorant men hunted dragons they commented how sometimes a young dragon would just stand there and not put up a fight. They never knew these dragons were suffering the sudden loss of a parent. An emptiness inside them which could never be filled again. With the loss they found themselves suddenly abandoned and easy prey to anyone nearby. Nor did men know when they killed their dragon quarry how living dragons far away, on worlds they could not even see, cried at the agony of the death of their child or parent. But then there are those who have ever been ignorant of how all life is connected. Worse there are those who knew and did not care, for the suffering of another meant nothing to them.

Fortunately, the worlds were few where dragons were not respected for their intelligence, devotion to friends and love of family. Anyone who saw the great battle when the dragons and Zananto fought Frin-Ghirzan to a standstill, would never forget the brilliance, strength and majesty of the dragon battalions, nor how heavy a price they paid for victory. For after that war the dragons were dispersed amongst the stars, always ready to help, always there in a crisis but never again to have their own world.

Because of this innate ability, all through their first ride on the ship, the brothers had been catching up on the lives their sons had led. A story kept hidden from them by their enchantment now flowed into them like a vast number of unwanted e-mails piling into their brains one after the other. One horrific action after another, far worse than anything they could have imagined, as the events and deeds of their sons overflowed their senses. They felt the hatred welling up in their sons' heads. The love of valour and killing becoming their only thoughts. Each and every act the sons had carried out, each and every thought, each and every second of each and every day they had fought and killed for Crilodach, obeyed the orders of Frin-Ghirzan or solicited honours from Rataplan, poured over their fathers and ate into their hearts like a virulent disease ripping them into pieces. The distorted lessons Frin-Ghirzan instilled in their heads. The wonderful strength of their arms brought down upon the weak and upon the free. The betrayal of everything dragons stood for since they first gathered, speaking to Tegriel and Filvani. Showing Filvani the first laws of magic he ever learned.

To ease their pain they sang softly to themselves as the foul deeds of their sons entered their knowledge, in the ancient singing tongue of their people, and one phrase they repeated over and over,

'Totanim Tu, Deik Oshanim Su'

Which translated means 'My son of sons, show them mercy'. But their sons never did. They had lost their fathers' guidance. The most important part of their education had been silenced. And they were so useful to Crilodach because It could replace that part of their brains which should be connected to their fathers, with Its own presence. Wherever they were It guided them, spoke to them and perverted the very essence of being a dragon. Nobility. Until they took on the appearance of others in the army for they had become one with them, delighting in their command of them and no longer wanting to remember their own people. In many ways that decision wounded their fathers more than any other.

Opiar felt far more than simple pain as he protected his friends from the Irghwols. He was flooded with the immense vacuum of death surrounding his son, that swamped his mind whilst still alive, the worst fate that can befall anyone with a little magic in their veins. To lose without a fight. To be corrupted without questioning. To kill without ever missing a victim. These were the thoughts that tumbled into the minds of the fathers from their sons. A dam of indifference. An unstoppable tide of darkness. They all felt the terrible pain because this was not how dragons should be. This was not their training, these were not their lullabies, nor the knowledge of the seasons and weather conditions on a thousand planets they would have been taught. Crilodach's stories were not the great noble stories of the dragon myths. Their sons had a warped knowledge of worlds and peoples. Their own history was a lie. Nothing they sought to believe was real. Feeling all this so vividly in their minds, so rapidly, was almost enough to drive the brothers truly insane. They were strong. They held themselves together. Almost.

They had given life to these sons but they were not dragons any longer. They had taken on a new form, fought with Crilodach's armies, rising to be lieutenants under Rataplan and striking terror into Its enemies. And how many dragons had been slaughtered by those seeking revenge for what these three had done? For no matter what form they took, a dragon always knows a dragon. A dragon dressed as a man still roars like a dragon and fire still comes from his mouth. For fire is just part of the many elemental forces a dragon can call forth. *'Totanim Tu, Deik Oshanim Su'*, was meaningless for their sons.

Opiar's death had been closer to suicide than Rimfelder would ever know. For there are few who could take this much pain and remain alive. Opiar was as filled with remorse as his brothers but more, he blamed himself for the fact they were ever caught. He felt he had let his brothers down, and by so doing lost them their sons. He felt that all the suffering their sons had caused was on his conscience. His brothers would have told him he was wrong but he did not share these thoughts with them. Whilst fathers and sons, mothers and daughters were connected, brothers and sisters could choose to share their minds or not. At the moment he died Opiar felt his death to be preferable to living a moment longer. His last thoughts were to Eldet and Clevian who were mortified he wanted to die, but they were too late to save him, they had to keep Rimfelder safe and so their lament was filled with the grief that maybe, they could have saved their brother if they had been faster.

The äis floated onwards, towards their uncertain future. The caverns burned different colours as they passed. Rimfelder's eyes caught every movement, every play of shadow that might be made by Irghwols trying not to be seen. He gripped the Gaddia so hard his fingers were becoming numb. The Gaddia gave off a comforting warmth. He could almost believe the book was breathing.

Rimfelder's skin felt the change in temperature. The walls were cold. Cold water lapped beneath them. Where had this dark and sinister change sprung from? He was scared to lose his new friends and be alone. Scared to fail. He laid the Gaddia on his lap. The pages turned softly. The äis skimmed the water and for the first time he felt they were bobbing slightly up and down. The brothers came out of their reverie with deep sighs. They blew icy breaths upon their claws and scratched their backs. Their tails rattled. Dipping their heads into the water they drank and washed their faces.

Then they hugged each other and took up stations watching fore and aft. So they travelled on for another hour, without a break in the silence between them.

Every few minutes Eldet gripped his claws against the äis, bent down dipping his head underwater scanning below them for signs of pursuit.

"They're not swimming after us," he told his brother, "yet."

"There," said Clevian, suddenly pointing with his head, as he saw what he had been looking for. Rimfelder looked up, rubbing his eyes.

"They muster quickly," commented Eldet. "How did they get ahead of us?"

"This place must be crawling with side passages," said Clevian.

"Or they're just another group of Irghwols guarding their territory and waiting for us to arrive," said Eldet.

The cavern ceiling was lower now. Drops of water mixed with saliva dripped onto them. Ahead of them, coming out of the water were large, faceless Irghwols with bulbous bodies, and long tails that split into three. These they used like arms and hands to climb the walls. They looked as if they had traded faces in preference for teeth. Golden teeth that stretched down half their height. Razor sharp. They made them look as if they had been cross–stitched into the walls. Their bodies swelled with each breath they took, making the shadows falling over them bubble like foam across waves. The smell from them was saturated with eye-watering venom. Slowly Rimfelder noted they were making a hissing noise, filling up the whole area with their sullen song that began to sound like a wail as their tails lashed like cats, in anticipation of their onrush. Above him he saw some doing acrobatics, swinging from one side of the cavern to the other using their tails like ropes latching onto each other and swinging from one to another. A ballet more than an attack strategy. He stepped closer to the brothers.

"What are they?" he asked, horrified by what he saw.

"Blood sucking animals that leech out your life–blood," said Clevian.

"Ours?

"Especially ours. These gold–toothed Irghwols were bred to kill dragons. A line of defence left here to make sure we never escaped should anyone be mad enough to attempt our rescue. They won't stop at tasting a poet if one's served to them," Clevian told him.

"They make me feel nauseous."

"I won't lie to you to make you feel better poet, they make us nauseous too," said Clevian.

"They were once great nomads of the seas. They knew how to swim to the deepest parts of the oceans and retrieve the precious rocks that fuelled their civilization. But they were never friendly. Cut themselves off from other people. Here they have become sallow. Probably even trained by Frin-Ghirzan. Wrapped up in what they have become, blind to the fact that their evolution has been perverted by It," said Eldet.

"What happened to bring them here?" asked Rimfelder, his eyes following the horde as they prepared their positions across the cavern.

"What happens to everything that It seduces? They took some prisoner and bred them on Ghirzanben, that putrid hole of a planet where It trains Its troops. They changed from curious fish to foul creatures doing another's bidding. Dragon killers," spat Clevian.

"Can you reason with them?" asked Rimfelder.

"No. See how they gather. The tails are deadly. Stay clear of their tails, especially the poisonous, central one. I've seen people boil to death after one touch," warned Eldet.

"They move so quickly how can I avoid them I'm slow enough but with this book I'm like a tortoise."

"I was forgetting you only have two feet," said Eldet.

"I'm scared Eldet."

"That's why we're here," the dragon told him.

"Are you ready?" asked Clevian.

"Always," replied his brother, stepping up and rearing his head.

He reached up as the äis suddenly rose like an elevator, and with a sudden sweep of his wings scraped six Irghwols off the walls. But he didn't kill them. They dived into the water and vanished.

"They feel bloated Clevian."

"On what?" asked his brother.

"Who cares. If they've fed well they may be slower off the mark and that's to our advantage. They weren't expecting us to get this far."

"Six of them to one dragon and they flee," Clevian said.

166

"We're in for a fight with the hundreds ahead of us. That lot won't run," pointed out Eldet.

They laid their necks on the floor and folded a wing each over Rimfelder who lay down between them clutching the book with all his strength. Their lives depended upon the Gaddia and he was not going to drop the book in a fight. Irghwols leapt out of the water, their slimy bodies glinting in the darkness their sharp tails looking for flesh to latch on to, but the dragons were too fast for them. Fire first seared, then shrivelled their skins whilst they were still in the air, they howled diving back into the water but along the surface, the especially hot fire burned the water into steam. Steam they could not pass without being scalded. Rimfelder started coughing but none of the hundreds of Irghwols who tried laid a finger on him. The Irghwols circled the äis and crawled underneath trying to tip them over by bumping against the sides but two pages of the Gaddia separated from the book, speedily passing in front of Rimfelder's eyes to right and left, growing and shaping themselves into floats like those on a trimaran they stabilized the port and starboard of the äis. The Irghwols were strong despite being surrounded with fat. As they battered the äis, the dragons created more steam, the Gaddia opened in Rimfelder's hands and he turned a page. He started to read some words.

One Irghwol managed to latch onto Clevian's wing. The creature's teeth broke through his scales. He flapped his wing wildly, smashing the beast against the roof of the cavern.

"Are you alright?" Rimfelder asked him.

"They sting but one hasn't enough poison to hurt me," he said.

Flames spewed from between his tongue until his teeth started to glow and his tongue turned redder and redder as with every second he directed the fire first left, then down, then right in concert with Eldet. The underside of the äis was red hot. The yellow and black of their skin glittered in the light, but the upper deck of the äis was cool. Still the Irghwols came. Until Rimfelder's voice echoed from under the protective wings of his friends,

> If I could be born renewed in loving
> You, and know as I once knew sunlit days
> And controlled the chances that lead the living

Out of Xibalba's caverns' deadly maze.
If I could walk or swim undrenched by hate
In palaces the sun built for my ease;
Would I have not inherited a State
And found the cure to Ghirzanben's disease?
Drink up the hope of epochs to be free
From all the chains that marry minds to death;
Then love as if love were your destiny
And live, for love has need of living breath!

Living this sunless life beneath the ground
Irghwols you have forgotten love's pure sounds!

The lashing tails vanished from the walls. Hundreds of Irghwols dived into the water not even trying to bite the dragons as they passed. Like flying fish jumping over the surface of the water they plunged through the steam and swam away. The water gurgled with their retreat and then slowly settled, the wavelets lapping the walls. Rimfelder looked out and up from beneath the dragons' wings.

"The Gaddia didn't kill them," he said.

"You sound disappointed," said Eldet.

"They wanted to kill us."

"That wasn't the book's teaching," replied Clevian, "They've been tortured to become the killers they are, we will always have the choice not to kill such as they. That is why the Gaddia chose to remind them of feelings. When you intend to kill you must first block all your feelings."

"I doubt the Gaddia would do more than needed, magic is an exact art not prone to excess," pointed out Eldet, flicking a golden tooth from beneath his claw into the water after the Irghwol. "As the Book of Derivations states, 'everything is in proportion.'"

"Besides why show them all we can do before we know the full extent of their power?" asked Clevian.

"So the Gaddia has a strategy?" asked Rimfelder.

"Definitely," nodded Eldet, "and who knows about strategy more than Vingura."

"No one?" Rimfelder guessed.

"Ah, you don't know," replied Clevian, "that when he was a young man before he learned the laws of magic, Vingura was a soldier."

"And a very fine one," Eldet added.

"He went up against Rataplan, and Rataplan thought he had all the aces. The high ground, greater troop numbers, better armaments. They had spied out the land the month before. Rataplan thought he knew everything. Vingura just stood his ground and Rataplan was unaware for two hours that the ground he was standing upon had been mined the week before. Because of that Rataplan had Frin-Ghirzan evolve the Brujans, battalions of Its own sappers. One of Vingura's finest victories. Reports from the battle say at the moment when Rataplan fell Vingura could have struck off his head."

"Why didn't he?"

"He said Rataplan had to die at Zaqui, because if he died before then, the poison in him would cover the universe and bring great harm and loss to us all."

"He always thought ahead," Clevian winced as his poisoned wing itched him more than he had anticipated.

"Deep bite?" asked his brother.

"You saw the tooth?"

"A good half," said Eldet.

"Any left in the wound?" asked Clevian.

"No," said his brother.

The äis floated out of the low caverns that had been perfect for the Irghwol attack. Behind them the surviving Irghwols looked menacingly from the water's side. As Rimfelder's words echoed in their heads they sank slowly back into the depths. The words had brought back memories they did not know they had. Memories that hurt and made them hunger for things they had long forgotten. They swam aimlessly no longer interested in the äis. They would leave them to the Irghwols further ahead. They did not manage to swim very far. As the äis vanished from their sight the water began to heat up and become unbearable as the laval ocean encroached with extreme speed. Phigata was on the move as never before and following the äis. Not one escaped.

Along the äis the steam had evaporated in the air and warm droplets formed in Rimfelder's hair. He saw huge droplets run off the dragon's bodies forming puddles around their feet which ran like small streams off the deck and back into the water. Irghwol skin was stuck along places on the äis, burnt off where they had come into contact with the surface. The skin gave off a musty, seaweed smell that made him feel a little hungry. He felt guilty for being hungry.

"I think you stopped them though, poet," congratulated Eldet, "Dead or not."

"Not me, the Gaddia," said Rimfelder.

"And what power would the book have without you?" asked Clevian, licking his wing.

"I'm sure others would have been as able as me, if not better. I wasn't even the first choice for this task," said the poet.

"Oh I doubt that. Vingura is not one to settle for second best," Eldet told him.

"I know I wasn't, there was another person who didn't turn up and ..."

"And you just happened to be in the right place at the right time," replied Eldet.

"Or the wrong place," suggested Clevian, "by the look on your face."

"I'm sorry if I look dejected," he told them, "I'm just not used to having so much resting on my shoulders. Every time I see an enemy I think I could die and not accomplish what Lilah needs of me."

"Death isn't a danger poet," Eldet told him, "Living without a greater purpose is far more dangerous."

"Well said," added Clevian.

"Do you think those Irghwols are finished with us now?" asked Rimfelder.

"No. There are more species of them that Frin-Ghirzan grew down here. I'm surprised we've not been fighting every inch of the way."

"I'm thinking as Zaqui draws close many will have left," said his brother.

"Leaving only enough Irghwols behind to stop us?" asked Clevian, wincing again as a pain shot across his forehead.

"That would be my guess."

"Do you need that seen too?" asked the poet.

"This is just a scratch," grimaced Clevian, showing off his teeth.

But he was beginning to realize the wound was far worse than he had thought. The Irghwols had been well prepared knowing that many of them would have to bite a dragon to bring one down they had bred a few Irghwols so full of poison only one was needed. Clevian's mischance was to have been bitten by such an Irghwol.

"The saliva of a dragon heals," explained Eldet. "That's why some of us were hunted by the ignorant. They'd cut off our heads, drain out the blood and eat our tongues thinking our meat would heal their diseases."

"That's terrible," shivered Rimfelder.

"For all of those involved, not just us. We died but in death our saliva becomes a poison. So they'd die in agony but then, finding such a strong poison, they cut off our heads to put our blood on their arrows, and in food, to kill their enemies. A drop of dragon blood fetched a high price on many worlds."

"I'm not surprised there are so few of you left," said Rimfelder.

"There are three who must be brought to account," Clevian told him.

"Two, for one's life did not last as long as the other two."

"Your son?" asked his brother.

"Yes," replied Eldet.

"When?"

"I felt him leave whilst we were fighting off the Irghwols."

"Then one of us should kill Opiar's son for Opiar can no longer carry out the task."

"Agreed," nodded Eldet.

As the dragon's shook their claws together in agreement, rock eating Irghwols, a vestige of Frin-Ghirzan's wish to have the ability to build watching posts high up in mountains without anyone knowing, were busy setting a trap above their heads. Alerted to the journey of the äis by the drowning of the island, they had set to work hours before, eating deep into the ceiling of the cavern. As the äis passed beneath them they finished their work of eating away at two huge, long pillars of rock that cracked loudly as they broke away each the size of the tallest skyscraper. The noise boomed, alerting the dragons who looked up. As the rocks gave way they plummeted down in an arc, striking each other half way down. One broke into three pieces and the pieces threatened to come down upon their heads.

Clevian, with his weakened wing beat, launched himself into the air and with his huge claws grabbed one of them and swung round in a circle, using the pillar like a slingshot, hitting the second large piece out of the way. The spines of his back shot up at the ceiling and the rock eating Irghwols, dislodged from their perches, fell headlong against the stony walls and thumped with loud splats onto the ground exploding and exuding a foul smell from their broken bodies. Irghwols leapt out of the water and pulled their dead bodies under, glad of the bonus food. Around them the huge pillars broke and crashed sending waves across the boat, but the third piece hit Clevian's head and left wing, crushing the bones at the shoulder. His mighty wings still trying to work, his head looking upwards as he fell and landed with a groan onto the äis sending Rimfelder and the Gaddia flying across the deck. Eldet threw the last piece of the pillar to one side and leapt to his side but Clevian lay motionless.

Behind them the pillar crashed to the ground. The ornate shape of the pillar crumbled into pieces a few glancing off the äis as Rimfelder crawled for cover. The äis moved forward more quickly to get them out of the danger zone, twisting around to avoid further attacks from Irghwols, skimming dozens of them off the walls.

Clevian was still breathing as Eldet spoke softly to him but Eldet learned from his brother that he was dying from the poison. His strength was diminished. He would not be able to stay with them.

"That was close," said the poet.

"We're not safe yet," replied Eldet. "Look back."

Rimfelder looked back to where the last piece of the pillar had fallen. He could see smoke. Then as he looked the pillar quickly evaporated in a way he had never seen rock evaporate, to be replaced with a bright, reddish yellow burning.

"I don't understand," he murmured.

"Phigata," explained Eldet, "is following us. Burning up everything behind us. The Irghwols have far more to worry about than us."

Clevian was in great pain as he dragged himself slowly to prop himself up on his right side holding onto his brother with his broken claw. The wounds from the pillars were deep. He was bleeding inside so much there was blood on his teeth. He looked at Rimfelder with weary eyes. The dragon was in pain but Rimfelder hoped he would recover. He willed him to recover. He could not bear to lose yet another.

"Is the lava coming for us?" asked the poet.

"Yes. Phigata's been following us since we crossed onto the land and the ship changed into an äis," said Eldet, "tracking us. Let's hope our path brings us to the way out because if we get trapped with that behind us, we're dead."

"I think Phigata's following us like a dog follows a master," coughed Clevian.

"Hush brother you're not strong enough to talk."

"I need to talk whilst I can."

"We still need you," said Rimfelder.

"I'm dying my friend and poet. I'll say what I want while I'm able. Phigata needs to get somewhere, just as we do. We're all being called. Maybe by the same force that drives the äis onwards. I don't know. But we're all being called, that's for certain."

"I thought the äis just knew where we were going," replied Rimfelder softly, unable to bear the loss of yet another friend.

"Haven't you noticed that we're not steering? I've seen a few caverns branching off, but we passed by never taking them. We're not in charge of the äis. We've been kept on a specific path never for a moment slowing up. So far this craft knows what to do and, like Phigata following us, I'm sure the äis is homing in on some beacon. How long that beacon will be there I can't tell you."

"Called by whom?" asked the poet.

"Someone strong. Maybe Lilah or some other."

"What would Lilah want with Phigata?" asked the poet.

"Her mind isn't open to us for me to be able to tell you," said Clevian.

"But if not her then ... who?" asked Rimfelder.

"Someone else, maybe even Crilodach if you're very unlucky," said Clevian.

"Then we're travelling into a trap," growled Eldet.

"There's nothing you can do about that yet," ended Clevian.

"Isn't Crilodach where Lilah is?" asked Rimfelder.

"If It were, and this is Its work, then we're being strangely used by our enemy," said Eldet.

"Then we must stop the äis," cried Rimfelder.

"But what if someone on our side is calling us to bring a powerful weapon to them?" asked Eldet.

"How can we be sure which is right?" asked Rimfelder.

"By going on and finding out," whispered Clevian. "Don't argue we've no choice. If events show you're being used against our allies, maybe the Gaddia will have something to say that helps us."

He coughed and slid slowly down again. His wing draped over the side of the äis, his head stretched out on the deck. His eyes were so bleary he could no longer see anything clearly. Blood oozed slowly from the pits in his back where his spines had been and his skin turned darker and darker yellow.

"But instinct tells me It is not the one calling us."

"Can you help him?" pleaded Rimfelder, kneeling by the dragon's shoulder, dwarfed by his wing.

"If I had just a few broken bones," replied Clevian for his brother, "I'm sure I'd heal but that poison was stronger than I thought. I'm bleeding internally too fast to heal myself. They've evolved since we last met them. They've become far more deadly. Be wary brother."

"We plan for tomorrows beyond our knowing, knowing they will come as surely as the suns shine," whispered Eldet.

"We were dead. The past hours have been a reawakening for us, brief and painful." Clevian coughed again. He felt a rawness in his throat.

"We've no way back and the Irghwols are picking us off one-by-one. This is a nightmare," wept Rimfelder.

"That is what Xibalba's supposed to be Rimfelder. Don't be surprised," Clevian told him. "You must get him to Lilah alone, brother."

"I'll get him there," promised Eldet.

"Can't we ease your pain?" asked the poet.

"I'm used to pain Rimfelder. I'm sorry I shan't be with you to the end."

Clevian couldn't move and lost all feeling in his broken wing. Blood oozed from his head and he lost the sight in his right eye. Rimfelder went to his head cradling the huge, gasping mouth in his hands and wishing he could do something. The äis moved softly on and none of their enemies tried to attack them, as if in their victory they also, strangely, mourned. Clevian couldn't speak.

As he sat there feeling small and scared Rimfelder was gripped by the feeling of flying through voluminous clouds, on powerful beats of outstretched wings with razor-sharp edges. He saw the clouds spread out before him as far as his eyes could see, like soft mountains undulating beneath a sunny sky. They looked so beautiful from his viewpoint stretching away from him while the shadow of his huge body undulated across their surface beneath him. He could feel his two wings beating through his powerful shoulder bones. He knew his eyes were shining as he swooped through the clouds losing visibility for moments, feeling the cold and wet wash his face and body, and down below the land suddenly materialized, as if set out upon a table. He was so

174

high-up everything looked like a model. Snow capped mountains looked like frosted desserts, the seas, blotched with low clouds, looked like a still life painting, and then with the incredible accurate eyes he had, he saw animals moving below. Animals that had no inkling he was watching them. Animals he had never seen before yet whose names he knew. From the four footed, grass eating Jukata deer, to the greatest of all snakes, the wise Dœnsol whose skin was grass green with three pure white stripes down the flanks. He turned on his back flying upside down. Above him he knew the stars in their millions were shining, almost inviting him to fly to them. He sensed he could if he had wanted too. He felt so strong, alive and wise. He knew so much without thinking. He could almost touch infinity.

Then, with an awful suddenness that made his stomach jolt and his neck bones crack with discomfort, he was back on the äis, forced out of the visions to the almost blinding darkness. A fierce heat wave hitting them from the encroaching lava. Aware that his body had two legs and he could not fly. His arms had not the strength nor means to support him in the air, he would never feel the thrill of flight or see with such clarity again.

Clevian was not breathing on his hand anymore. Yet the dragon's head was not heavy as part was rested on the Gaddia which supported most of the weight. Had Clevian's head been wholly on Rimfelder the poet would have been crushed.

The euphoria drained from Rimfelder like hope from Damkina as he realized these thoughts had come from Clevian. The dragon's dying gift to him. He was at one and the same time distraught that another of the brothers was dead and bereft that never again would he be so close to a dragon's experience of living.

"He's gone," said Eldet in his ear.

"I think so," replied Rimfelder.

"I wasn't asking you, I was telling you," the dragon replied, gently taking his brother's head from Rimfelder's arms. He laid his brother's head upon the äis with a broken heart.

"I ... ," stuttered Rimfelder, "I was flying."

"His gift to you. He treated you like family to allow you to see how a dragon feels and what a dragon knows. He would have hoped that made his passing easier for you to bear. We both saw how badly you took Opiar's death."

"But you barely looked at me," said Rimfelder surprised.

"We don't only look with our eyes poet, even the Irghwols felt your sorrow, your emotions are very powerful. I've a feeling that's what makes you special."

"Everyone feels."

"But not everyone can make others feel what they feel. To express so exactly how one feels is a gift. Our shamans told us the fundamental challenge faced by all life was to evolve to be able to feel what others feel. Poets like you are vital to the evolution of species."

"Evolution is over." He turned his head so as not to be looking into Clevian's eyes. "Just now, for that second, I was above a world I've never seen before yet knew so well. I felt so powerful, so in control. I've never felt that in control in my whole life."

"Describe what you saw?"

Rimfelder did his best. Eldet nodded his head and rubbed his eye free of some rock dust.

"That was no ordinary world. That was where we all grew up. I know exactly where he was flying. Such a beautiful world, I wish you could have been there poet. You would have had much to write about."

"I suppose those sights don't exist any longer."

"Oh, in our mind's eye they're always there. Those places, those memories never fade. Strange to tell you, when we awoke from our enchantment we all felt as if our homes were not that far away but that was probably wishful thinking."

"I wouldn't be so certain."

"You think entire worlds could exist in these caverns?"

"I've absolutely no idea, I just wouldn't be certain they don't. Appearances deceive, that much I've learned in the past days. We're here in the dark with Phigata pursuing us and for all we know this is all that's left of the universe. On the other hand we may be trapped in a small part of a vast eternity. How'd we know, we're told but half of any story."

"You think knowing more would make our journey easier?"

"Don't you?"

"A long time ago I did, when I was young. Many things should be known but some things, like those spells known only to the spellmakers, maybe are best left to them. Some knowledge is hard to survive unless you're taught well."

"This journey's hard. I'm scared we'll never get out alive."

"My brothers haven't."

"Is there some song to sing or rite to go through for the dead, I can help you with? I'm a fast learner."

"There are the songs one makes up. Since the days when we fought in our thousands with Zananto and lost our home we've become more solitary creatures living in small family groups. Wanderers. I don't think you'd find three of us who sing exactly the same songs."

"Isn't that a difficult way to live?"

"When you have deep knowledge of Crilodach, all living becomes a challenge. Crilodach's nature burns away optimism. Its promises are transitory, but what is one left with when one knows the first life ever created is so vile and filled with hatred?"

"Sadness."

"And, maybe, hope that sadness ends."

"I'm destined to see everyone I love die."

"There are worse destinies."

"Name one."

"To kill those you've loved," replied Eldet.

Rimfelder sighed. He knew now what Eldet had to do. Somehow, although he had only been flying in the clouds a few moments, so much more about Clevian was in his head than the flight. He knew about their sons. Because Clevian had shared his thoughts and life with him for those precious last seconds, Rimfelder understood for a father to kill his son was such a great tragedy Eldet would not wish to survive afterwards. Dragons love life so much they see another's life as precious. They delight in sharing existence. They kill only in extreme need, when those they love are threatened. That's why Frin-Ghirzan found their sons such a prize for not only did he get fine fighters, he also perverted the children of a race that had never bowed a knee to Crilodach or given It one soldier. For there was not a dragon anywhere that forgot that Crilodach destroyed their home, and each and every one of them in their own way fought against It. That was the one event that bound them all together no matter where they lived.

After their sons betrayed their people, and everyone knew that three dragons fought for Rataplan, there was only one race, the bears, that did not offer up their own traitors, for all those who knew dragons felt they must have crumbled before Its might. If dragons fall there was no way others could stand tall. The bears held themselves aloof because of Hiesia. Because she carried a great power.

"I'm being selfish. We must go on," Rimfelder said softly.

"If you hadn't noticed the äis hasn't stopped moving. We're nearing an end to this part of the cavern."

"How can you tell?"

"I hear the voice that has been calling us getting louder. So hard to catch sometimes. Almost as if ..." he stopped and Rimfelder turned to him,

"Almost as if what?"

"As if they don't know they're calling us. But how can that be? Oh don't say anything, I know, you think anything is possible in this place."

"How could anyone have the power to call us out of Xibalba and not know?"

"That would depend upon who she is."

"She? Lilah?" asked Rimfelder, excited.

"No. This is not a magical voice like that. She's not calling to us but behind us. She's calling Phigata and we're caught in her spell, but sometimes her voice disappears altogether and then comes back, that's when we pick up speed. Have you noticed the unevenness of our speed?"

"Not really."

"You should pay more attention."

"I've been a little preoccupied."

"We'll know who she is soon enough. Since we don't want to, and now can't, go back, we'll see what this is all about when the äis arrives."

"But this mysterious voice isn't calling us but Phigata," said the poet.

"Strange, don't you think?"

"I wonder if we'll ever get wherever we're being called."

"You'll get there," replied Eldet softly.

"And not you?"

"We were meant to make sure you arrived. The Gaddia and my brothers. Our strength in numbers is lessened but our resolve is not."

"But I can't get out if you die."

"Don't be so down beat, poet, what would've been better, to die fighting with you or for us to have died still locked in our own madness on the island without knowing Zaqui had come?"

"I suppose to die fighting because then at least you know.

Though I'm not sure anything good would come of the fight."

"Though I feel the pain of the loss of those I've loved since I was born, I can see that loss would've come anyway one way or another. Better the pain comes when I'm doing something worthwhile. Better they died defending you, fighting Crilodach, being true to the Sangyma, being one with the traditions of the dragons."

"Does that take your mind off the pain?"

"That balances my pain," said Eldet.

"I never learned the art of balancing pain," replied Rimfelder. "Though somehow seeing Clevian's mind for that moment has made his death easier to bear. I hope Opiar's thoughts were as wonderful."

"I can't say for sure they were."

"He shared with you?"

"Not in the same way."

"I'm sorry if his thoughts were sad, Clevian made me feel uplifted for those precious seconds. I can't forget that feeling."

"Which is why he shared them with you."

"If we don't get out of here I want to tell you, I want you to know ... I've been honoured to meet you."

Eldet didn't appreciate sentimentality at the best of times.

"The lava is moving more swiftly than we are right now," Eldet noticed.

"Is the äis not sure of the way forward?"

"The äis has natural defences that might be making her more wary of going faster or possibly Vingura and the others didn't expect this voice to be calling us and the magic of the äis is being cautious."

"But if Phigata catches us ..."

"Courage poet, we've a long way to go yet and you shouldn't waste energy worrying about things you can't change. Clear head, simple thoughts. That's my only order to you."

The two of them looked ahead as the äis continued weaving with the twists and turns of the endless cavern that occasionally opened up to vaulted ceilings and chasms that turned even the hot air behind them chilly.

Then the cavern would be enclosed again and blasts of hot air billowed over their backs reminding them of what was following and how Phigata was able to fill up the vast abyss behind in minutes. By all accounts, thought Rimfelder, they should already be dead. He began to feel that he was only half living. He was numb from the deaths of the two brothers, numb from the sight of the Irghwols, numb from the burning heat of Phigata. He sneezed frequently with the silt and dust in his nose, his eyes smarted from all the stuff continuously falling onto their heads. His hair was matted with rock dust. When Eldet occasionally shook himself, tons of rock dust flew into the air as if he had taken a dirt bath.

Then the äis slowed and stopped before a large number of entrances. The halt was unwelcome. The äis seemed not to know which one to take and Rimfelder had to awaken from his dream of a half–life to talk again.

"What now?" he asked, breathless.

"A choice. If I'm not mistaken about this place, there is only one right path for us. The äis has made all the choices up to now but now we have to decide."

"Why did the äis stop making the decisions?" asked Rimfelder.

"The äis is following a call. Maybe she who calls doesn't know there are many passages here. Maybe her magic is just to pull us forward which up to now has been along a simple, fairly direct route."

"How do we choose?"

"This is what we call a Gwedling problem," smiled Eldet.

"Gwedling," repeated Rimfelder in surprise.

"You know the name?"

"Vingura said that to me several times when we met. Before and after he gave me the Gaddia. He said Gwedling was the one who should have been there but he didn't turn up. A warrior trained to do what I've been doing. He tried to make light saying I'd arrived instead and that made me the man for the job."

"And you believed him?" asked Eldet.

"I'd no reason not to."

"You were chosen for this task, that's why Lilah sent you to him, even if you were chosen only at the last moment."

"Last minute choices are dangerous," warned Rimfelder, "I told everyone I wasn't able to do much."

"From the moment of Lilah's birth Crilodach would have been hunting for her, and who knows how many were slain in his efforts to discover where she was. We'd never have been able to train more people for all the tasks ahead and kept them all alive, but when the choice had to be made the right people appeared. It isn't the time of the choosing but the character of the person chosen that matters."

"Lilah appeared in my life out of nowhere. Right before her came her brother whom we didn't know was her brother. I know that couldn't have been coincidence but our fight with the tyrant happened just the day before. Are you telling me the whole thing was planned?" the poet asked.

"She knew you were there is all I'm saying," replied Eldet.

"Why would Vingura lie to me?"

"He didn't lie, he left you clues to what may lie ahead. Clues that we would need."

"Clues to what?"

"How many times did he mention Gwedling?"

"I don't know."

"Remember," ordered Eldet.

"About seven."

"Are you sure?"

"No."

"Our lives depend upon on your remembering accurately everything, every little thing, he said to you."

Rimfelder closed his eyes, he could see the table and the garden again. He could even smell the fragrances. He felt he could reach out and touch everything. He heard Vingura's voice clearly. He counted on his fingers as Eldet watched him quickly going over the conversation, and finally he said,

"Nine."

"Certain this time?"

"Definitely. Amazing I didn't think my memory was that good."

"He gave you something to drink whilst you were there didn't he?"

"Yes a cordial of the berries from a bush in his garden."

"That's why you can remember so clearly," said Eldet.

"You mean he enabled me to memorize our conversation with a drink?"

"Word for word. He may have ensured our success. When I ask, I hope you can recall everything accurately."

Eldet steered the äis towards the ninth entrance and they went into the maze. It was still dark. Here the fragrances were different. No Irghwols had been down this way. The rock changed and the waves of heat billowing from behind them heated up the air. Steam rose all around them. It was soon like being in a sauna. The water condensed making the äis slippery. Water dripped off Rimfelder's face, dampening down the dust until his skin was streaked as if he had been badly tattooed.

"How did you know which was the ninth?" asked the poet, seeing there had been about thirty entrances in all.

"I counted from the end of course."

"Then we might be in the wrong one because there are two ends."

"Certainly if you counted left to right I would've chosen the wrong one. Dragons count and read right to left."

"You're sure that's the right way to count down here?"

"Vingura gave you the clues. He knew you'd be coming for us. If everything went well he knew we'd be here together. I'm absolutely certain we're to count like dragons and that this is the right way."

"What's in those other caverns?" asked Rimfelder.

"We'll never find out," he replied. "But probably nothing worse than we're going to face in this one."

The äis took them carefully along the high sided, enclosed maze. Soon the ceiling was dancing with lights, like lightning above their heads streaking in zig–zags without making a sound. Flashes of colour momentarily caught their eyes as the light glanced off mineral flecks embedded in the rocks. For a few seconds the light display was dazzling.

"Now if we take a wrong turn at any time there's no going back. Phigata is on our tail and won't retreat. You must be accurate and swift in your responses."

"I understand," said Rimfelder, whose eyes were wide with amazement. He took a deep breath.

"Don't worry poet, you've been given all the weapons you need to help you."

"A drink and a book?"

"Wars have been started and ended with less. Open the book, think clearly and leave the rest to the äis and me."

"Where's Clevian?" Rimfelder said suddenly, looking for the dragon's body.

"A mist in the air, a memory, a wish, a thought. He's where all dragons go when we die."

"The body ..."

"Evaporated. He didn't want the Irghwols to eat him. He denied them their ounce of flesh each. Not that they'd have had much chance to eat, poor creatures."

"Poor creatures! How can you feel sorry for them?"

"Tell me you didn't?" Eldet challenged him.

"For a second but not now. They murdered your brothers."

"That's what makes them poor creatures. What would be better poet, learning from a living dragon or standing over a dead one?"

"Learning from a live one of course."

"All that companionship, all that friendship, all that learning, the Irghwols will never know," said Eldet.

"That's not our victory."

"Poet, the loss of our friendship is a great loss. Our enemies lose us as friends, and that's a great defeat for them not lessened by the fact they don't understand what they have lost. Now pay attention, remember well, which way left or right."

"What am I trying to remember?"

"Clues Vingura left you in your conversation."

"He may well have but we had a perfectly ordinary conversation in the circumstances, which were anything but ordinary."

"In our written language the number nine is a right angled line."

"That doesn't ring any bells," said Rimfelder.

"Quiet." Eldet bent his straining ears to the divided pathway.

"Is there nothing here to resonate with your memory?"

"I don't know what I'm looking for."

"I hear the song but, as I suspected, no more strongly in either cavern. We must go right. Continuing the Gwedling problem. Do you agree?"

"I would rather go wherever you're going and nothing, but nothing, is going to make me get off this äis."

Eldet gave a smile. Rimfelder saw that one of his right side teeth was missing. He wanted to ask him about the loss but somehow, he thought, this was not the place to remind Eldet any more of the past. They moved forward until they came to a blank wall. There were no turnings right or left, up or down. Rimfelder's heart thumped at the thought of being burned alive as Phigata engulfed him.

"Was that the wrong entrance after all," he said.

"Not so hasty poet, look here there are etchings on the wall."

With a soft breath Eldet blew flame onto the wall and the dust burnt away and there burning brightly were eight different designs carved into the stone.

"What's that?" asked Rimfelder.

"Clues, clues, clues. Did Vingura give you any lists?"

"Why would he ..."

"Just tell me if he gave you any lists," insisted Eldet.

"Not really. I mean only in passing."

"Such as?"

"He said 'a gardener is as much a soldier as a pilot or sailor once the decision to join up has been made.'"

"Did he now. Clever fellow."

"I don't understand."

"We have a series of images, look at them. They're etched into the stone, emblems of various things. All in a line like a list, yes?"

"Yes."

"Now let's see in the most ancient language of dragons, which Vingura would know well, A gardener is 'Aridot', and a soldier is 'Periadot', a pilot is a 'Sophridot' and a sailor is 'Acridot'. They are all related words because we view armies like gardeners, only they do more pruning than normal. Now then the first letters of those words taken in order spell 'Apsa', which is a very rare berry. Vingura being a great gardener would have known that well and here," his claw almost touched one of the flaming emblems, "is the emblem of that berry. It grows only on one tree in forests that were much loved by my people."

He took his heavy claw and pressed the emblem which sank slowly into the wall and the wall divided showing them a deeper cavern, out of which blew a cooling breeze. Rimfelder was not only overcome with relief, he realized that with the answers to the riddles being in his head, he was now Eldet's only hope of escape just as Eldet was his. The äis proceeded through the opening as Rimfelder looked back for the tell-tale sign of Phigata.

"I'm very confused," he said.

"About what?"

"About how emblems that mark the way forward only make sense in ancient dragon when we're escaping from Xibalba. What have your people to do with this place? Are they the builders?"

"Not at all but whoever did build Xibalba, and I don't know who they were, probably wanted to leave alive. That's the way of all builders and architects who lay the traps behind them as they make their way out."

"Then why did they leave ..." began Rimfelder again.

"They didn't leave the signs," interrupted Eldet. "I'd suggest the signs were put there just for us. Placed in the right place so as not to be suspicious to any other eyes and yet, with the right clues, our salvation."

"Placed when?" asked Rimfelder.

"Who knows? In the distant past, when Xibalba was built or a few seconds ago."

"All this was planned for so long."

"Magic has no time poet, but communes across the ages. Spells ripple through time like ideas from one person and one place to another. Things are not so much planned and expected, they're the everyday. Spells happen when they happen. There may be clues here for other races and other travellers we know nothing about. There may be clues we'll not recognize that have never and will never be used. Who's to know?"

"More magic than can be used," said Rimfelder.

"More magic than can ever be understood except by one person, the last spellmaker."

"What would've happened if I'd arrived here alone? If the Irghwols and those other things had killed all three of you?"

"You think you'd have died at the entrance to this tunnel"

"Exactly."

"Maybe you wouldn't have. Maybe Vingura's voice would have guided you, but that bit of magic hasn't been used because I'm here. Maybe the äis has some other uses not needed right now. Who's to know? Magic is a challenge, poet. You don't take up with magical folk unless you're prepared to suffer and take all the chances and hazards, all the threats that will fall upon you like a torrent. Think on your feet, or in my case your claws."

"That doesn't make for much happiness."

"Nor does writing poetry."

"No," he shrugged, "I don't suppose so."

"Happiness isn't what makes us strong," said Eldet.

"I guess if you're looking for things to make you happy then you aren't happy, and if you aren't looking then you're a dragon," said Rimfelder.

"Dragons have long been self-sufficient, poet. We live for a long time, we're virtually impregnable to non-magical folk, we can fly anywhere and our best friends are magical.

Not much to be down about in all that."

"My best friends are dead. Men and woman I fought alongside, sacrificed for this." He patted the Gaddia.

"That," said Eldet who caught the gesture out of the corner of his eye, "is worth dying to preserve."

Eldet's eyes never strayed from looking ahead. Time was not on their side. They were losing the race to keep ahead of Phigata. He heard many Irghwols behind them screaming as they were eaten up by the laval ocean's rapid advance, desperately scrambling to follow them, for even if they could not hear the voice, they could sniff out the äis which they sensed the dragon and the poet were using to escape from Xibalba. At anytime, Eldet thought, they may lose their fear of the spells of the Gaddia and his claws and swarm all over the äis just to get away from the lava. He looked ahead for any ambushes prepared in front of them. He clenched his claws.

They came upon sets of grey stones inset as barriers into the walls all around them, blocking the äis which could not pass through without scraping the edges of the stone. Needing them to be moved out of the way or broken to allow them to pass, the äis kept trying to edge forward but every time the stones touched them they were forced back. Eldet looked as Rimfelder reached out to touch one. The shock that passed through him shot him backwards into his back. Such a powerful shock would have killed an unprotected man but a spiral of smoke from the Gaddia that vanished even as he was sitting up blinking with astonishment and feeling he had been kicked in the stomach, showed Eldet the book had saved him.

"Touch nothing," said the dragon.

"I thought if the äis can't get through maybe we'd climb out."

"And what would you do the other side if there's hundreds of miles of more caverns?"

"Come back I guess."

"Let's not take that risk. If the äis can't pass through these stones because they're too narrow, somehow we must move them back or maybe chart a pathway as yet unseen through them."

"You know they remind me of something," thought Rimfelder. Eldet raised an eyebrow and lowered his long head to Rimfelder inquiringly.

"I am probably saying nothing but they look like the ferns back in Vingura's garden. I noticed as I walked there they were strangely patterned like these stones and they've the same kind of shape. If they actually met in the middle they would all mesh."

"Pattern. What were the features of the pattern?"

"I'm not sure."

"Think."

"They were surrounded by bushes, red, yellow, black and blue flowering bushes. Made them stand out in my mind."

"Colours, how do you find colours in the darkness?" asked Eldet.

"Can't you light the stones up with your fire."

"We need a flare," replied Eldet, taking out a thin spine from his tail he struck one end against a tooth and, alight, he threw the living flare high into the air. Slowly floating down burning like phosphorus, hurting Rimfelder's eyes with the brightness. Eldet's thinner inner eyelids came down and protected him against the sudden light. He saw clearly that on the edge of each stone were colours. He would never have seen them without the light. Nor would he ever have looked for them if he had not been alerted by Vingura that they were there.

"The äis must follow the colours in order red, yellow, black and blue. Down, lie flat poet, the clearance is very tight. Do not touch the stones with so much as a hair."

"Don't worry."

The äis moved forward almost scraping the stones as they slowly weaved up and down and round the stones as Eldet pointed out the colours one after another, the äis moved to his voice commands. It was almost as if the äis had ears. The coloured stones moved slightly into the walls as they neared to let them pass and then moved back. Rimfelder felt exposed and wondered what would happen if the Irghwols or some other creatures suddenly leapt out of the dark. They would be overrun in seconds. He did not see Eldet slowly dripping poison from Opiar's tail spines onto the stones. Only when they had passed the stones and moved on, as the Irghwols tried to climb through them, did he hear the screaming from behind them.

"Did you hear that?" asked the poet.

"Yes."

"What are they?"

"The greater-toothed Irghwols following us have found a present I left them on the stones."

"Greater-toothed?"

"These have teeth like tusks, and six hands. They dance so quickly when you've one by the throat they grab for your eyes and elongate their necks so their heads seem to float. Their bodies can break up into four pieces and each piece is lethal."

"They sound horrific."

"They've always been formidable enemies. Six against one dragon can't be beaten. Less than six, a dragon skilled in fighting has a chance. But right now they fear that book more than they fear me."

"How many are there behind us?" he asked.

"I sensed about eighty-three."

"Eighty-three. When did you first know they were there?"

"They watched as Opiar and Clevian died. Now they're probably thirsting to kill before they themselves are killed."

"You said nothing."

"Dragons avoid them like the plague and since you could do nothing against them we didn't think you needed to know about them. When they catch up with us I don't know if I can defend you. Perhaps though the Gaddia will have something to say before they do their work."

"Maybe the Gaddia can defend us both. After all we've thirty six magicians in here," said Rimfelder.

"Indeed we do and they've been working for us all this while. What do you think saved you just now from being electrocuted? What helped steer the äis across level ground? Or any of the dozen things that have made our journey less hazardous. Hold those magicians close poet. Hold them close."

The äis continued on for hours of wandering. The heat intensifying. The sound of the bubbling lava growing. Eldet's trap had hurt the Irghwols behind them. They did not attack but kept a wary distance. Sweat poured off Rimfelder. Eldet gave him water from the store. The water evaporated as soon as he splashed his face. Eldet did not take so much as a drop.

"Don't you need any water?"

"I drank when we were above the fresh water. I won't need to drink again for the rest of the day."

"My thirst is terrible."

"There are spells that can make you more dragonish if

you want, though I wouldn't recommend them."

"Why not?"

"It doesn't change the power of your mind. I don't think many people have the strength of purpose to be effective dragons."

"Has anyone ever become a dragon?" the poet asked.

"Some of the bears did."

"Bears?"

"Ancient and proud people, they say Crilodach fears the Sangyma first, then the bears and then the dragons. If It fears anyone."

"Will we meet any bears?"

"Who knows poet, who knows."

The poison had slowed the Irghwols but they now wanted Eldet's blood. They eyed the äis with envy thinking if they could float like that they could save themselves from the laval ocean. Tusks dripped with saliva as they burned with hunger.

The äis came to a full stop in front of a large, wooden door that looked ridiculously out of place surrounded by stone,

"That's unexpected," said a surprised Rimfelder.

"As you were to Vingura, supposedly. What did he say, seven times out of ten he got the unexpected."

"Yes."

"Why only seven out of ten, why not always?"

"Well you don't always do the same thing, just most of the time."

"And what if this isn't the time to go through the door. What if this is the three out of ten? Look at the designs; dragons and cups of wine. They don't go together."

"Do you think Vingura left us more clues about what to do next?" Rimfelder asked.

"Vingura gave you little more than clues, poet."

"Why didn't he just come straight out and tell me all this stuff."

"He spun you a yarn which is easier to remember. From what you told me you weren't very responsive to begin with and he had little time, so he gave you a drink to help your memory ... drink! Of course cups. Look the dragons are drawn but the cups are outlines with little points of gold. He said 'to the last point'. Now which is the last."

"Bottom left if you read from right to left."

"True but this is unexpected."

"I wish he'd given me better directions."

"Poet, he gave you the best direction of all. The book. Look in the book."

Rimfelder opened the Gaddia and the pages flipped past. A perfume filled the narrow place in which they were floating. He felt heat on his fingers and realized the laval ocean had not stopped flowing just because they had halted. His throat was dry and his cough hurt him as he saw the pages appear and the doorway they were in front of glisten in the dull light that emanated from the page. Painted in such perfect colours you could have taken the page out of the book and, replacing the door in front of them with the paper, seen no difference. Eldet looked and growled. Next to the door on the page, like a shadow, was a door made of darker wood, hidden from sight.

"The makers of this place knew people would come who used eyes to see. They prepared their traps for such, see a door that is not a door. Most unexpected."

Eldet breathed on the bottom of the doorway and pressed with his single left claw one of the points on the last cup in the design. The shadowed doorway opened wide and the äis floated through even though Rimfelder was sceptical they could get passed the opening was so narrow. Now at last they were out of the maze and floated above nothingness.

"Will the Irghwols follow us?"

"They were close enough to see where we went. They'll certainly try."

"Why didn't they make these doors so only the äis could get through?"

"Perhaps because other things have had to pass through as well in their time, for their reasons," said Eldet.

"Like Irghwols?"

"Like other thing."

"What is this place?" Rimfelder's voice echoed slightly. He longed to see Lilah's warm smile once more and be rid of these caverns.

"This is a void. We can't proceed easily from here there's no pathway nor any clues that could ever be given to us. The only thing that can lead us through this is the voice that calls to us."

"I can't hear anything."

"But I can poet. A woman's voice still strongest in that direction," he nodded.

"What about the Irghwols?"

"This place will unnerve them. They're creatures that need good footings and high walls, to feel earth and rock and water around them. They don't do well in nothingness. They can't float. With a bit of luck not all of them will survive."

"I don't think I do much better in this nothingness than an Irghwol."

"Quiet now poet, let's be silent. I need to listen to the voice. If we lose her we'll be lost."

Rimfelder stood on the prow with Eldet, in the shade of his wing. Like a friendly arm too big to be wrapped about his shoulders. He could not even hear the dragon breathing but he listened very hard in case the sound of tusks scrapping the sides of the äis came to his ears. He had never felt so scared and tired at the same time. Even so he decided his hands and body were trembling from the effects of the electric shock and not from terror.

Hiesia

Hiesia looked from the top of the southern-ash tree she had climbed, across the dense, multi-coloured forest into which she had fallen without warning. Her fractured existence in and across time had led her to develop a routine when she first appeared anywhere. Firstly, she checked to make sure she was alright with no broken bones. Thankfully the magic of time-travel had always been safety-conscious on her behalf. She was always alright, though often in terrible danger. Secondly, she gauged if there were any immediate threats from armed inhabitants or wild animals. Finally, she looked for a high spot to see what she could see of her new world.

She had been lucky in choosing this large-canopied, ancient, southern-ash, for its thick, round branches held her weight well. Though she had never believed in luck. The magic that had brought her here chose this spot for a reason. Her large paws had gripped its rough bark with ease as she had hauled herself upwards, quickly, to satisfy her need to see the lay of the land and get her bearings.

Though she could never fully get used to popping up in places across time, she usually had time to prepare for the journey, or even, on rare occasions, a choice of destinations. This time she had been brought here without any warning so she was being especially careful. Never before had she been unable to determine where she was within half an hour, but most of the plants on the forest floor were new to her. A world beyond her previous experience was unique.

She had felt pulled as if a mystic hand had reached out, curled her in a soft, huge palm and, like a Buddha, ferried her across space and time. Bears are rarely frightened by magic as there are only a certain number of spells that work on them and only the greatest names amongst magicians even know those spells. For the most part Hiesia's magic always kept her safe. Especially since her miraculous escape from Damkina where she had stolen the captive Sagitæ back from Crilodach by concealing the jewel under her skin. this

Sagitæ propelled her through time and had protected her cub from becoming one of Crilodach's soldiers, blocking Its spells with those older than this universe.

From her new vantage point she was able to see across the crowns of the forest trees for several miles to the thin, tall hills in the north, and to the sea in the west which she could not glimpse but the scent of the salt on the warm breeze was unmistakable. The ribbon of clouds in the clear sky barely cast shadows across the rich land. Yet something was wrong. No birds flew to their nests or across the sky searching for food. The sight was at once beautiful, refreshing and somehow intimidating. She had never known a forest not to have birds flying through the canopy before, nor be so filled with strange perfumes and so bare of animals. She felt as if the forest were waiting for creation. But that was impossible. Animals naturally developed alongside vegetation. At the same time. Not in sequence. Something had scared all the animals away.

She had landed on the forest floor amongst the fresh ferns and damp leaves without so much as a bump. As if she had merely jumped off a small rock. Her large paws barely made the leaves flutter; far less like falling and more like materializing. She had once complained to Sanjava that a bejal might take her places but Sagitæ magic never left her a note to tell her where she was. He had laughed at the thought. After he had stopped laughing he had said very seriously,

"Hiesia, we are not permitted notes. That is why we train so hard, so we can be of use to the bejal or magician that has called us as quickly as possible."

He had been right of course. Though she felt sometimes she was little more than a puppet, she knew the minute magical strings of her existence made her strong. Like parents you always argue with, they nonetheless gave her life, character and direction.

She felt she was getting somewhere. She was orienting herself. She could gauge direction accurately. She could also tell when a magician was within a day's march of her and right now she knew one of the Sangyma was on this planet with her.

But though she knew something was going on she still had not found out where she had landed after over an hour. This forest, filled with smells she did not recognize, was in a place she knew was alien to her, on a world she had never visited before, fattened with vegetation but not animals. She had never heard of such a place. She looked up. With her penetrating eyes she was able to look past the blue sky into the open space and view the stars. So many. And yet not one constellation she recognized. No smell, sound or sight came to her that made her fur hackle or her heart palpitate. Even so she was not at ease. Then the first breath of trouble came to her, vibrating on the air and making her ears twitch. Something else had materialized from nowhere. The Sangyma who was on this planet was being chased.

The branch she stood on now creaked as she walked along, her heavy, sharp claws helping her balance by holding the merest twig, so well was her body's balance centred. They said the bears could walk across the water without getting their paws wet and watching her you would have believed them, for she seemed to grow out of the tree and her head stretched forward so her nose could catch the tiniest fragrances on the breeze. Precarious though her position, you would have thought a tempest could not have moved her at that moment. Even her fur was still. She opened her mouth and tasted the air on her tongue.

As she turned away from looking at the mountains, far distant she could see the trees broke up, thinned and the land stretched out, flatter and more open, much like a savannah. That was the place from where she would be able to get a better idea of where she was and what, if anything, was going on with this Sangyma. She wondered if the Sangyma who shared this planet with her, had called her here but he was so far away she could not communicate with him yet. Why was he so far way, usually they managed to bring her to their front doors. The distance was worrying. Unless the danger was greater than usual. Unless he was deliberately blocking any communication. Only Crilodach's presence could have divided her from a Sangyma's mind yet she could not sense It at all. There was something like It here though. Maybe she was wrong and the Sangyma had not called her. Her fur hackled along her back and arms. Her teeth ached. Sure signs a fight was coming.

She decided to get down and to aim for the savannah. She let herself down with leaps and swings until she was near the lowest branch and then she leapt down, her knees bending to take the force of the landing and she rolled playfully, head–over–heels, in the fallen leaves enjoying her mastery of the surroundings. She sprang up. She ran forward scratching the bark of trees as she ran past, weaving here and there as the thick forest, lacking all paths, tried to catch her. She was too used to speed to be tripped and she ran over the strewn stones and leapt without stopping, old trees rotting slowly away to feed the new growth poking out from their decaying timber. Small forest flowers were crushed by her passing feet only to slowly spring back on their spongy, moss filled beds. Her feet beat out a tump, tump, tump as she ran and her controlled breathing carried the beat of her heart pumping fresh blood to her muscles. She was acutely aware of the fact that no creatures ran out of her way; no deer were surprised or startled by her; no squirrels bolted up trees, nothing living greeted her. Did they know who she was? Were they scared? For her to meet animals who feared her would be a new experience for most instinctively knew she did not eat them, and part of her essence, which was married to her time–travelling, made strange animals immediately relaxed in her presence.

There was something fresh about this place that made Hiesia feel young again. After an hour of running she did not feel at all tired and after three hours she reached the break in the trees. This was a young world. And because the stars were unknown to her she thought she must have come back far into the past. She had not come back this far before. She wanted to find out how close to the beginning she had materialized. She was excited.

The trees grew more sparse, the land opened out into flowered grassland, spattered with the odd rock and boulder, erratically placed. She was thinking deeply about what kind of world this was when she saw something that amazed, delighted and worried her at the same time.

Tegriel, whom she had met several times, two of which he had engineered and in one of which she had saved his life, was running like the wind. Next to him was a Ruzniel she did not know but she was impressed at how she kept pace with relative ease. She could not recall Tegriel having a Ruzniel companion in the long time she had known him. Close behind them reeking of the fireballs Tegriel had made to try to blind them to his destination, came two creatures that finally explained why her fur hackled, her claws and teeth ached for a fight and how Crilodach was involved. They did not belong to the smells of this planet. They looked demented, fitted out for war in their armour. They were not running with such ease. Their pursuit was heavy, determined but sluggish. She saw that they were not gaining on Tegriel and his Ruzniel so the danger was great but manageable. She sniffed the air. Her heart leapt. Kalevala was here. Her oldest friend. She had not seen him since the days of her imprisonment on Damkina.

The moment she saw the metal–clad sisters with their spines rattling, their teeth glittering and their swords flashing, she knew both the reason for her journey and what she had to do. She did not know she was on Samphin yet. There was no real reason that she should as this world fell to Crilodach long before the bears became allies. Why Tegriel should run from them she did not know for she was sure he could stand and fight if he had wanted to, but he must have good reason. She ducked back into the sparse tree line and outpaced them on their flank without them seeing her and came to a bend in the landscape just as Tegriel and Tobia ran past. She took up her place chanting quietly to herself and flexing her claws. She stood square in the path of the sisters, then vanished from sight.

The sisters could see their quarry ahead and even fooled themselves into believing they were catching them up, but as they rounded a hillock and went to leap over a small outcrop, they literally bounced off empty space, their armour clanking and their bodies reverberating with the unwelcome jolt. Freyom got the distinct feeling of fur on her face. Yaltha felt the toughness. Both were thrown onto their backs.

Their armour yelled as much as they did as they fell against each other and then onto the ground in an undignified heap. Both of them looked bemused at the empty space in front of them slipping in their hurry to get up, they used each other to stand up straight. Tegriel was getting further away from them and they immediately thought he must have laid another trap behind him to buy himself some time.

"That won't help you," screamed Yaltha at the distant runners, looking for her sword.

"The artifice of a desperate man," screamed Freyom, shoulder to shoulder with her sister.

So certain were they that Tegriel was running scared, and so complete was Hiesia's disguise that they did not sense her. They leapt after him with the energy of the huntresses they had been trained to be, only to hit the object again and be thrown down once more onto the mud.

"Now what?" snapped Freyom, as she started to pull herself out of the mud and shook herself like a dog. Frustration sped through their bodies as they looked around for the answer to the spell that stalled their hunt.

Freyom's lip was bleeding and her spine vibrated like a rattle-snake's across the back of her armour in intense anger. She caught her breath and her narrow eyes looked hard at the spot where they had been hit. She could neither see nor sense anything. She lashed out blindly with her sword.

Both of them were now certain something else was here and they crouched on the ground each balancing on their legs and one arm, Freyom holding her sword low against the ground thrusting her sword forward every few seconds trying to provoke an attack whilst her sister held her dagger having dropped her sword when she was thrown back against her sister. She looked for their enemy out of the corner of her eye but could not see anyone. She quietly cursed all the time, peering around them in case what they could not see decided to launch an attack. Nothing happened for the long seconds that passed with their quarry getting further and further away. Yaltha wiped her nose with her hand still clutching the dagger. Looking into the reflection on the blade as she did so, to see if anyone was behind her.

"This is all because you lost us the element of surprise," Yaltha snapped, thinking Tegriel had created a force field against their advance. "He's trying to imprison us here."

"Surprise is highly overrated," Freyom snapped back. "Nothing can imprison us. I felt something hit us that was very much alive. There's someone invisible out there."

"I can't hear a heart beat," argued Yaltha.

"You doubt they're there, sister-mine?"

"No, but what can hide from us; what has no smell; what has the strength to throw us both onto the ground at the same time?"

"Who knows what's in this foul place. We can take on anything that lives and a few things that are dead. We'll flush this thing out."

"Show yourself!" screamed Yaltha.

"I think our enemy wants to play games with us, back-to-back sister-mine."

They faced away from each other, each of them covering the other's back. Circling with careful steps a bit like a crab snapping its pincers together with loud clacks as their armour scraped against each other's back.

"Where's your sword?" asked Freyom.

"Something snatched the blade right out of my hand," replied Yaltha.

"Very strong to take away your sword."

"I said I wanted something better than a sword but you said they were unbreakable. As good as any weapon known you said," complained Yaltha.

"You lost your weapon to our invisible enemy, don't blame the sword."

"I didn't lose anything. Aren't you listening? I said my sword was snatched away!"

"If they can get your sword they could get anything," warned Freyom.

"The hammers can be welded to my claws. They would've been better for me. You know I prefer them," said her sister.

"I still have my sword why did they just take yours?"

"Maybe I was closer to the thing. I was slightly ahead of you anyway," Yaltha said.

"Are you suggesting I don't fight from the front?"

"I'm telling you I can't judge what an invisible enemy is going to do neither could you. They could just as easily have taken your sword."

"Never," hissed Freyom, gripping her sword more tightly all the same.

"Even now you have to try to pretend to be a better warrior than me," Yaltha cursed her.

"I still have my sword, you don't. The fact speaks."

Yaltha wanted to say something but she could not. She just locked away Freyom's insult for a later time when she could get her own back. The sisters had gone round in circles several times whilst talking but nothing moved. The ground had become even more muddy and they had sunk almost to their ankles.

"I've had enough," growled Freyom, "Come. Whatever was here is probably gone."

They both marched forward and hurried to follow Tegriel and once again a heavy presence sent them both sailing through the air though Freyom managed to take a side swipe this time but did not connect with anything, instead the sword swung in an arc and narrowly missed Yaltha's helmet.

"Watch out!" screamed her sister.

"Its a slippery beast," cried Freyom.

"Only cowards fight like this," screamed Yaltha, covered with mud and smarting from being hurled like so much dross across the ground. "You wouldn't have been able to throw me like that if I still had my sword." She waved her fist in the air at nothing she could see.

"If only you hadn't been disarmed so easily we'd have more of a fighting chance."

"You've lost more than a sword," intoned Hiesia.

Hiesia did not know who they were. Not that that mattered. They were Tegriel's enemies. That was enough for her to fight them, but her sixth sense did give her an indication of the kind of fighting techniques they would use. The smell of Crilodach was powerful now they were face to face.

In her experience Crilodach liked to use the crafty and cunning, sometimes the brutish and powerful, but most of all It enjoyed training individual fighters for specific tasks. In the case of enemies as strong as the Sangyma It had been known to train whole armies to take on just a single Sangyma. She could see these two were here to fight Tegriel. Alone. Which meant they were extremely dangerous, smart and had a good deal of magic in them. She also now guessed they were Its daughters but not because of what she saw and smelled, more because of what she knew. She had been a prisoner in Damkina and she knew. She too had been used for Its experiments and only the Sagitæ had saved her son.

The sisters scrambled to their feet, Freyom looking in the direction of the voice and propelling her body forwards at the same time. Just one voice. Was there only one opponent or were there more? If one they must be very strong, very daring and wholly unafraid of them. Maybe they did not know enough about the sisters to be afraid, or maybe they did. With Yaltha by her side they attacked the voice hauling themselves out of the muddy hollow they were in, across the ground and into mid air in one swift, continuous movement. They hit nothing.

"Thing's fast," hissed Yaltha.

Hiesia of course, was not even close to where the sisters had attacked. She had thrown her voice because she wanted to study the sisters from the flank and get a better

Yaltha and Freyom

understanding of their fighting prowess.

Freyom licked her wet lips and grit her teeth. Her sword hand tight to the hilt of her weapon, her other hand was in a fist, ready to parry any blows even though she had no way of knowing when they would fall. The blood drummed in her head as her muscles tightened with her anxiety. Her sister had a dagger in each hand now, balanced so she could strike in either direction or bring both weapons down on her assailant. They stared at the ground around them, to see if the owner of the voice moved so much as a blade of grass. Even though they were out of the hollow they knew the enemy was close. Almost imperceptibly they were walking in slow circles in a steady straight line away from the hollow. Any moment now they would make a break and continue running preferring to get Tegriel if they could, and learn how to fight their invisible enemy another day.

The sisters had eyes made to see the invisible but they were useless against the spells Hiesia was using. Although they were at the dawn of the time of magic, they were fighting a bear who had seen Sangyma die, Damkina from the inside and fought in so many battles they said she was second only to Tegriel in the harm she had done to Crilodach. She could feel them trying to find her but not so much as a hair would reveal her whereabouts.

"Close but not close enough," she told them.

The sisters stopped. Both of them stared in the direction of the voice for long minutes but did not attack. They were aware that whatever they were up against was watching them, gauging their strength, making them tire (though, as many had found out to their cost, making Crilodach's daughters tired was near impossible). Mud was dripping from their shining metal armour as if the soil were bleeding from them. They turned, keeping their backs to each other. They came to face the way they had been running and none of their senses picked up the slightest clue as to what they were dealing with. Freyom spoke softly but her spells did not reveal anything. Yaltha spat. In the first attack she had been so anxious to get Tegriel she had lost some of her craftiness, but now she had been forced to stay in one place for long minutes she began to think. There had never been much book learning in their training but some creatures they had been taught about because they were the creatures most likely to fight for the Sangyma. Amongst them were the bears, and amongst the bears were the five named elders they were told to be especially careful when fighting.

"Only one creature has no smell when invisible," said Yaltha.

"The bears can't be here," replied her sister.

"Why not?" asked Yaltha.

"We're long before their time."

"We're before our time, yet we're here," Yaltha pointed out.

"Why didn't our father tell us they'd be here," argued Freyom.

"Maybe It didn't know."

"Do you know what you're saying sister-mine?"

"The exact same thing I've always said, our father may not be the greatest or strongest creature in the universe," said Yaltha.

"If It heard you say that It would pull out your tongue," Freyom told her.

"Oh, shut up. Why'd It need us if It was so all-powerful?" asked Yaltha.

"Because It can't be everywhere at once."

"Yeah, right. So It 'births' us because It needs help," sneered Yaltha.

"You think you're so smart," said Freyom.

"I think Its not as smart as some of Its enemies, that's what I think."

"You better hope It doesn't hear you."

"I don't work on hope," shouted Yaltha.

"You should be quiet anyway because our enemy can hear us."

Hiesia stepped forward from her spell, her brown eyes large and angry, her clawed, broad feet immovably planted on the soil. In her left paw she held Yaltha's sword, twirling the blade between her claws as she would have a child's toy. She bared her teeth as the sisters snarled at her. Their suspicions were correct.

"I thought you were too engrossed in arguing to ever figure out who I was," she told them. "You two are a joke. I can't see Crilodach birthing two such idiots."

The sisters knew about the bears. The greatest magical enemy of their father after the Sangyma. They knew many of them by sight. They had been instructed to kill bears at every opportunity. Almost as if Frin-Ghirzan had a special vendetta against them. Hiesia had a unique life, popping into different times and places with lightning speed which often made accurately describing her impossible for her enemies. Her disguises had been excellent. The only bear whose fur was the colour of bright clouds, with a streak of silver around her neck. Now she was black as night with a white line going from between her eyes to the end of her nose.

"Do you have a name?" spat Freyom, twirling her sword in her hand with far more intent than before, sniffing at the blood that pumped beneath Hiesia's skin now she could smell her as she was visible. Hiesia let the blade of Yaltha's sword touch the ground, almost casually,

"Come closer. I'll whisper my name to you," she enticed them.

She did not intend to hold a long conversation with them. Nor did she know if she would have to kill them. She had not decided. They seemed a dangerous, odd pair. There was more going on here than she could guess. On the wildest nights and in the deepest fears of her friends, she had first brought them news that Crilodach was dabbling in hybrid creatures. Everyone was on their guard from that moment because no one knew why It would want children. It went against everything they knew of It. And though Hiesia had her suspicions she was still surprised to see the results of Its experiments. She almost felt sorry for them. Surely It could have sired greater fighters than these two, squabbling sisters?

Freyom levelled her sword and leapt at Hiesia with a sudden spring–like release of the pent up energy in her legs. The bear stepped sideways parried the thrust with Yaltha's sword, grabbing Freyom's shoulder as she missed her step and throwing her back the way she had come as if she were no heavier than a leaf. Then Hiesia moved back a pace to make sure she always kept both sisters in sight and stopped Yaltha's attempt to carry out her joint attack from the flank. Only having a couple of daggers Yaltha did not feel like taking on her own sword. Bears, she remembered, do not have a blind side. Freyom fell but knowing where Hiesia was she rolled and in one move sprang to her feet and again thrust at her. Yet her sword was turned with such power she could not follow through with her thrust, and she was again flung back this time rolling on the ground before finding herself on her knees, her sword on the ground by her side. Her clawed hands shook. She could not remember the last opponent she had had who had bested her twice in a row. Nor the uncomfortable feeling of her metal armour rubbing against her leathery skin as her body was jarred about underneath. She was not in control. This was not the palace. Hiesia was not an ordinary warrior. She snarled and thumped her fist into the ground so hard she buried herself up to her elbow, pulling her arm out again instantly, wishing with all her might she had thrust her fist into the bear's chest to pull out her heart.

"You're light and strong," she spat, grabbing at her sword and scrambling upright.

"Or you're slow and overweight," goaded Hiesia.

"How are you here?" questioned Yaltha, unsettled and not at all anxious to attack this beast. "The bears are not a nation yet."

"We're obviously a nation of one," Hiesia replied, twirling Yaltha's sword.

Hiesia took in everything the sisters had said. They were all far in the past. No, much more, they were in the universe's early life. That explained the unusual smells and her increased energy. That explained why the constellations were unrecognizable, there were simply a lot more stars at this time. That would explain why Tegriel was running because in one immense second Hiesia saw what was happening, understood what was at risk and what she was actually fighting for. Not the freedom of Tegriel nor the life of a single Ruzniel, but everything. She knew enough of the legends to know how important some things were, and the finding of Bofindle was second to none. Being the only being in the universe up to now that had dotted around the time-lines she recognized the Upala's magic. She instantly saw what Tegriel had done and what Crilodach had plotted. Knowing that the Upala was taken by Crilodach ages past in her memory she could but guess at how Tegriel and the Ruzniel had found the bejal. She did not yet know of her own part in creating the Upala because she was only now, about to do that. With her intuitive brilliance she suspected Zaqui and the beginning on Samphin were intimately connected through Tegriel's life and now she was part of that connection. The immensity of her deductions did not phase her. She was Hiesia, after all. She was constantly involved in accomplishing the vital.

She had never heard tell of these two but that hardly mattered to her. They were Crilodach's successful hatchlings. Because It could not use the Upala Itself, these were Its chosen emissaries of hate. It was trying to change the course of known history. She squared up to them.

"Maybe if we kill you the bears will never be a nation," hissed Yaltha.

"This world is too pleasant to be filled with the stench of Crilodach," she replied firmly.

Freyom screamed and swung at the bear who ducked and stopping Freyom's return blow with her elbow, dug deep into Freyom's armour with claws that matched the sisters' own, bringing them shoulder to shoulder. Freyom could feel the muscles under Hiesia's fur and she realized why the bears had always been such powerful enemies.

"I'll take your head bear," she spat into her face.

"And if I killed you here would your sister avenge you?" asked Hiesia, "What do you say?" she asked, looking at Yaltha. "Do you want her dead?"

Freyom wriggled but she was held fast by a strength she had never encountered before. As if she had been bonded to Hiesia with the strongest magnets. So strong was the bear's grip she could only just breathe and when she finally managed to feel for her dagger she found the weapon was gone. The bear had thrown her dagger onto the ground even as she held Freyom prisoner. Hiesia's mastery of tactics was formidable.

"Let me go before I rip you to pieces," hissed Freyom.

Hiesia kept moving round keeping Freyom's body between her and Yaltha making sure if Yaltha tried anything, Freyom would receive the blow.

"Hiesia is my name Freyom," she snarled back. As she spoke the black fur became white and the silver streak around her neck blazed out. The sisters both knew Hiesia. They had been warned about her by Frin-Ghirzan who carried the scars of his fight against her when she had escaped from Damkina.

Raising her shoulders and bending her knee she sent Freyom flying back into her sister who was trying to creep around Hiesia to grab at her from the behind. Yaltha grabbed her sister and dug her left leg behind them both to brace for the impact, stopping them from tumbling backwards and over each other. They were getting used to Hiesia's fighting style.

"The white bear," cried Yaltha. "The mystic. I was a child when you were already a myth."

"I don't believe you were ever a child," responded Hiesia. "I didn't think Crilodach's hatchlings needed to be children. You just need to squirm into life and fizzle out into the nothing of your vile existence."

"I'm his daughter," snarled Yaltha, "and I'll teach you respect."

"Nor do I think Its offspring fit teachers," replied Hiesia. "I doubt this is even your plan. Doing what Crilodach told you to do like servants. Running after Tegriel obedient to Its orders. What were you promised, a hot meal of his flesh? Power? Worlds?"

"How did you find a way to come back in time with us?" Freyom asked, moving slightly to Hiesia's flank.

"How do you know this isn't my home. From here I could have gone forward in time to be with my people and led them many times against your armies. I could be anywhere in the future and then vanish like a deleted icon to make sure you're stopped from pursuing Tegriel. Or didn't that occur to you two geniuses?"

Hiesia had one eye on Freyom and one on Yaltha. Tegriel was far away now. Soon, Hiesia knew, Kalevala would lead him to Bofindle. Kalevala had told her the story many times and she had smiled each time because Kalevala, bright and wonderful as he was, never lost the dog–like delight at how he found Bofindle by doing what dogs love to do. Not an ounce of magic involved. What changes had Crilodach managed to craft? What dangers faced her? She knew she could upset the balance of events just as clearly as Tegriel feared the sisters were doing.

"How could you do such a thing?" questioned Yaltha. "No bears ever travelled in time but you."

"Maybe I have a Sagitæ," she replied. The sisters visibly started. "That surprised you. I've travelled endlessly to different times and places, to worlds you've never heard of. Waiting. With Crilodach birthing Its plots in your miserable, foul lives. Where did It hide you? In what black, foul, stench of a hole did It put you and who did you feed upon there?"

"Our father's beyond you," screamed Yaltha.

"Being sisters and Its offspring explains the sameness of

the stench that rises from your presence. You're no more than creatures of Its future, fighting is your skill for murder is always your intent. Maybe I should introduce you to It now, and see how your father welcomes Its children with open claws."

"Do you think we're not prepared to meet our father in this time?" Freyom argued.

"Careful sister," warned Yaltha, "Say nothing more to her."

"Listen to your sister she knows me better than you do. Obviously Crilodach only gave one of you a brain."

"Give me back my sword and I'll show what fighters we are," threatened Yaltha.

There are times when dealing with creatures like Yaltha and Freyom that you must show yourself to be someone above and beyond what they are expecting and trained to fight. No matter where she was all times were Hiesia's future, as she was always living her life forwards (a confusion that Tobia was still dealing with). She had learned much in her long life, although officially, at this moment, she was yet to be born. She now did something the sisters were not expecting. She threw Yaltha her sword without a word and stood tall and straight with no weapon the sisters could see. Yaltha caught the hilt of her sword in mid air and thrust left and right for a moment, thinking the bear must have broken the hilt or booby-trapped the blade. She had not. She glanced at her sister.

The sisters were dumb struck. Of course they would both leap at the bear now, but they were confused. They had taken stock of their adversary. She was strong and quick and knew how to use the sword as well as they did. She might have held them off for hours. She might have even sent them off in defeat. The tactic of disarming herself and rearming Yaltha made absolutely no sense to the sisters on any level. They could not understand why she would deliberately leave herself open to their assault unless there was some tactic they were missing. Doubt stopped them attacking her at once. A little of their self-assurance drained away.

"Will you stay visible?" asked Freyom, missing how absurd her questions was. Her question was more like a child making sure of the rules before trying to get her toy back.

Throwing back the sword was a perfectly timed strategy by Hiesia, for the sisters were now slightly apprehensive.

When they made their attack they would be half expecting
something and that would blunt the ferocity of their lunge.

"Do you want to die?" Freyom added, slightly confused.

"No more than you," Hiesia replied. "Though I'd suggest
you think carefully before you give me up for dead. So far
you've been singularly lacking in the skills needed to so
much as graze me."

Hiesia did not speak idly. This planet had given her
renewed vigour. The magic in her cells felt the power around
her and increased with each passing moment. Particles of
magic were flowing through her cells at faster and faster
rates. She could feel how fleet and impervious she was.
When they had swiped at her she had seen the thrusts almost
in slow motion and was able to avoid them with acrobatics
she had not been able to do since she had been a cub. But
the youthful energy was also having the same effect on the
sisters.

Yaltha ran at Hiesia with her sword in the air above her
head, bringing the blade down on the bear's head. Except
when she struck, the bear's head was not there, nor was the
bear. Thinking she had turned invisible she screamed and
turned in time to see Hiesia was behind Freyom. Before she
could shout a warning the bear kicked the sister in her
backside sending her sprawling into the mud at Yaltha's feet.

"Why didn't you attack with me," cried Yaltha.

"Would I have made a bit of difference?" Freyom wondered.

"She can't escape a two pronged attacked. Get up."

Freyom dropped her sword, she cursed, turned and ran at
the bear her hands outstretched trying to strangle her as
she leapt and sailed through the air to where Hiesia's neck
had been, landing with a thud on her face on the ground as
the bear vanished. Yaltha twisted round quickly but Hiesia
was not behind her. Then she too felt a kick from behind and
though she slashed behind with her sword in a reflex action,
she went sprawling just like her sister without touching the
bear.

"Stay still you witch!" cried Freyom, who had never seen
any animal move so fast.

"Frustrated sister?" goaded Hiesia. "More used to victims
than equals in your fights? Perhaps you should've trained
with those well able to kill you. You can't learn to hunt
wolves by killing rabbits."

Their claws were dripping with mud. Yaltha handed her

sister her sword. Their claws gripped their hilts with fierce tenacity. Yaltha had one of her daggers as well, as the sisters started to circle Hiesia looking for a weakness. Hoping for a weakness. Their eyes blazed.

"We don't have to fight like this," Yaltha told her.

"No you'd prefer I just roll–over and die," growled Hiesia.

"Not at all. We could join forces."

"I doubt we've the same aims," said Hiesia.

"I'm sure you'd want to hold our father on a tight leash," said Yaltha.

"Stop with your plots," snapped Freyom.

"Oh, you are playing a dangerous game," warned Hiesia.

"Together we may all have a chance against him," said Yaltha.

"And who'd make that chance?" asked Hiesia.

Yaltha lowered her sword for a moment thinking she had Hiesia's attention,

"I'd fight with all my heart."

"Sister!" screamed Freyom.

"Silence Freyom. Better we fight for ourselves than for our father. Are we to be servants, we who've had a million servants and seen them die without shedding a tear?"

"Its our father," argued Freyom.

"And what does that mean to you?" asked Yaltha.

"I obey orders," she replied.

"See," grimaced Yaltha, "See what I've to deal with. She's no imagination. She can't see the bigger picture."

"Which would be what?" asked Hiesia, "Some more servants for you to toy with?"

"You have power bear. More than we knew. The bears obviously possess more magic than even we were told. You can teach us what you know and we can teach you about our father. Knowledge is power. We can share."

"Creatures like you never share. You see in me someone you can't bypass so you're trying to lure me into your deceitful schemes. You don't even know what you're plotting. Crilodach can't be defeated even by you."

"Then why do you fight against It?" asked Yaltha.

"Neither for power nor a tiny share in the magic of the Sangyma," said Hiesia.

"Bears! Always so noble," snapped Yaltha.

"Creatures like you know nothing about nobility. You want to kill me, now or later makes no difference to you. Lie your way to my throat or fight your way, your aim is the same. You've one purpose. You're as see–through as glass."

"I give you my word we'll not kill you," promised Yaltha.

"I give you mine you will. And my word to myself is more accurate. You'd betray your father and not me? Please!" scoffed Hiesia.

"Finish her off!" screamed Freyom.

Hiesia had watched them carefully. How their muscles were placed into position to take the strain of moving their weight in balance with every step. Sliding their feet more than lifting them, feeling for ground that would support their leaps. The metal shoes sliding sideways until they came to stony ground which they tested by pressing down hard, slightly bending their knees. She could see them thinking. All their training showed clearly in their stance. From where they were standing they could launch a strong attack. Was the bear close enough for them to get in a successful strike? If they missed was their lunge going to be strong enough for them to change direction and strike in two more directions within the second? Between them they thought they could cover almost a whole circle around Hiesia. All that remained was whether or not the sisters thought that was enough.

"Make your choice, join us or die," warned Yaltha.

"On the contrary the choice is wholly yours. Go now, and never return," Hiesia told them.

They did not retreat. They never learned how. From their first days of fighting with wooden sticks. Building up their muscle tone to take the weight of heavy metal swords. The expansion of their shoulder muscles and thickening of the neck muscles as they practiced every hour with hammers and heavy stones. The spines thickening early so they could withstand direct hits. Lithe and springy to add power to their moves. Being thrown onto hard rock until their skeletons shuddered. Endlessly learning what to expect from each of their many enemies. How to face magic with a sword, turn a hair with a dagger, stop a spell with their claws, match blow for blow. For all that training to have an effect now, they needed a foe they could lock swords with, parry dagger thrusts with, even wrestle. A foe they could actually grapple with in some way.

You could not train to fight Hiesia. She was beyond her age and charged in this newer, fresher universe with powers and knowledge the sisters had never been given. For with Its usual foresight Crilodach had given them one chance to surprise Tegriel and take him down. If they did that well they did not need to know that magic in this time was different. This world, where the gravity was changeable, where the bears had not yet reached their place amongst worlds, where Losek soil that was stuffed full of magic, where Bofindle had just been found and the first of the spellmakers was not yet fighting in the open, everything was different. Closer. Hotter. Faster.

They did not need to know half the things that were going on in the universe around them. They just needed to do one thing and if they failed, It would have put Its trust in the wrong daughters. Though maybe their determination and half formed plans of treachery in their minds, would yet take them forward. If Crilodach hated others to have life because they were unpredictable and would not bow down to It, It was even more suspicious of the children It created from obscure spells.

Hiesia sensed their hatreds and knew how to handle them. Using the same determination that had kept Crilodach penned-up, allowing races and species to evolve on thousands of planets before It had the chance to break out from the forces that held It in a magical vice. A determination that defied Its power to know, stemming Its yearning to experience total control. Though they had lost the first, long contest with Crilodach and It was free of them, the three Sagitæ were still strong.

The sisters did not know any of this. Nor did Hiesia know that Crilodach was at this moment on Its way. Neither did Tegriel. Such was the craft of Crilodach. It was coming to this planet having received secret communications on what was happening. Plots within Its plots.

The sisters leapt at her from two sides at once because that was how they had been trained. To take on an enemy from two sides so that one of them could get the deadly trust in and kill. She vanished. They bounced off each other just having the time to turn their swords away to stop striking each other, swinging round to see where she was, thrashing with their swords at empty space. They were bewildered. Their hunting instincts numbed. Their assuredness blunted. They stood back to back again, as if they were surrounded by many and not just one. Circling the emptiness around them looking for her, sensing she could attack them at will and they were open to being hurt. Fearing she could tear into them before they even knew she was there.

For the first time in their lives the sisters were afraid.

A killer can go on for hours. They can fight all day if they have to, taking on one foe after another. Their muscles are tired but their bodies keep on pumping out adrenalin and feeding blood to the muscles in an endless effort to stay alive. But even they are only able to go on because they see they are having some effect. Because, as their enemies fall they go onto the next one, instinctively counting not the numbers of dead but the successful seconds of fighting.

But Hiesia did not fall. They could not hit her even when she reappeared. In the half hour that followed, Freyom threw her dagger at her but she caught the small blade in her teeth and bit down, splitting the dagger in two pieces. When Yaltha dropped her sword and dagger and leapt onto Hiesia's back and they thought at last they had her. She found herself thrown over the bear's head, sailing through the air to land once again in the same mud she had been floundering in since the fight started. Deliberately thrown there by Hiesia to make her more mad. The sisters were sweaty, dirty, hot and frustrated. They were being made fools of and now they began to wonder if the ringing in their ears was from the many falls or some stifled laughter.

They had to put down their swords. Yaltha grabbed one of the spines from Freyom's back. Her sister screamed with pain. Then Freyom did the same to Yaltha. Blood speckled the ends of the two spines as they held them in their claws. Then they threw them at Hiesia's feet. In the soil the acid bones burned and grew all around the broad circle they had been fighting in. Great arches of bone stronger than stone. The stars were beginning to show above their heads so long had they been battling each other. More stars than the sisters had ever seen, but soon they were blotted out by the bones. The sisters yelled with delight for now they could run with swords held out and flail at Hiesia within the prison of bone. If the bear could not escape they were bound to cut into something. They charged at her and Hiesia stepped back against the bone wall, feeling the acid bite into her skin, and using her claws she bent down and pulled one of them out of the ground.

The sisters stopped stupefied at the strength. Hiesia

slammed bone against bone and the edifice crumbled as quickly as their bones had grown. If pulling the spines out had hurt the sisters the pain now in their back as the bones crumbled to shards was indescribable. They bent double and found they could hardly stand for precious moments. Tears welled in their eyes. With open mouths they swallowed some of the mud they were floundering through. Yaltha vomited. Her whole body revolted by the sting of defeat.

Such fighting can only continue if the sisters had the absolute determination to go on, but after all these hours, and the failure of their final attack, they did not. The one thing that sapped their energy was frustration at not getting their own way. Which, of course, was the marked difference between them and Hiesia, whose strength came from the conviction that she was on the right side not what happened during the fight. They wanted to see blood. They wanted to have an effect but they saw nothing and had nothing to show for all their effort. In training they had hurt people, killed huge giants, wounded a dozen strong men in one go, even sparring with each other they had taken pride in how many bruises they could give each other.

This bear jogged around them, vanished in an instant, knew what they were going to try before they even tried, and let them try, then showed them the fastest way to the mud. Worse for the sisters, if they had been Hiesia by now they would have been laughing, mocking the plight of their enemy and making their defeat worse by rubbing their supremacy in, taking out a nick here and there to let out some blood without killing them, to increase their sense of play and prolong their victim's death. But Hiesia said nothing. She did not call them names unless they called her names. She volunteered no curses. She did not jibe at them because she found them amusing. They knew after the first hours of this that Tegriel was far away doing the things he had to do. Starting the process by which their father was to be limited in Its successes. Their mission had failed. Yaltha had not even been given a chance to suggest her plots and plans to the Sangyma. All the times she had gone over that conversation in her head. All the variations she had used and always, Tegriel had seen her way, succumbed to her brilliant use of words and vivid reasoning. She had not been able to say one word to him. That rankled her too and made her want to give up.

Hiesia was their only consolation prize but they could not defeat her. She never let them get the upper hand. She never flagged or tired. She opposed them more implacably than a thick stone wall, or even, as they began to think, as if she had been their father, so futile seemed their best efforts. Their lungs hurt, their bodies hurt, their sword arms were aching.

"Why don't you use a sword?" Freyom said with disdain.

"You have them both," replied Hiesia.

"You don't want to fight do you?" spat Yaltha, "That's the truth. Sister she isn't here to kill us, she's here to stop us. She probably hates the sight of blood."

"Is that so?" asked Freyom, "You one of those mystics who believes in showing love to all?"

"You'd have no understanding of what I believe or what I am."

"I'll bet our father put you up to this," grumbled Yaltha. "Changed his mind and told you to keep us here until It arrived."

"What would make you think I'm in your fathers mind?" asked Hiesia.

"You're too wise to our fighting style. We trained in secret all our lives, there's no way you could have defeated us," said Yaltha.

"Frin-Ghirzan's training hasn't changed in all the years I've known him. You're simply poor soldiers."

"I'd throw those words down your throat if I could," snapped Yaltha.

"Our father will teach you a lesson," spat Freyom.

Hiesia knew the reason Freyom mentioned Crilodach. She had also just felt the foreboding. An incoming depression set against the sky turning the clouds into unkempt billows of untidy fog almost bursting with the throbbing blood vessels of a violent storm, sucking at them, trying to make them all lean forward in supplication. A weight so heavy was on their shoulders their heads ached. Hiesia knew this feeling. The last time she had felt like this devastation and slavery fell upon her head. Then she had been alone with work to do. Now she was never alone and had much more work to do.

"Father'll get Tegriel whatever you try to do," Freyom told her, in a futile attempt to sound as if she were in charge of the situation.

"Try?" Hiesia raised an eyebrow and, with the merest twinkle in her large eyes, said, "So far the only ones trying anything are you two. Neither of you are very good."

"You're not trying?" questioned Yaltha.

"Not to kill you no ... not yet. After all wouldn't that be what you expected me to do? Why should I do what you expect?"

Yaltha took one last leap and swung at Hiesia. The bear did not vanish but caught the sword in her claws. Yaltha tried to pull away but the bear held hard and Freyom, sensing she was occupied, thrust her sword at the bear's side. But Hiesia and Yaltha's sword were gone. The sisters turned round in circles again.

"Where are you?" Freyom screamed out. "How could you let her disarm you like that again?"

"I didn't let her. She's as slippery as an oil–beetle wrapped in snake blood."

"She won't give your sword back a second time."

Suddenly Yaltha's sword flew through the air and glanced off Freyom's helmet, digging into the ground at Yaltha's feet. Yaltha seized the hilt. She did not even ask if Freyom was injured. She held the sword between her palms and let the blade float in front of her, then divide in two and two again until hundreds of swords floated around her. Freyom knelt down to avoid the attack and Yaltha sent the swords in every direction at once. Her spell was a desperate measure and meant the end of her sword. If their spines could not imprison Hiesia she was doubtful striking every inch of ground at once would phase her.

"Not bad," smiled Hiesia, standing up with Yaltha's original sword in her grasp. "Had I given you back your real sword that might have worked."

"Where did you learn your cunning, witch," shouted Yaltha, shaking her claws at Hiesia.

"From your father. Many years from now. In Ghirzanben, in the mines, where It will burn prisoners for added fuel to stoke the fires that will forge swords like this one. In Damkina where It will conjure Its creatures from the arcane magic of Its own brain. Do you know your father has a hundred and eight uses for bear fat?"

"Good," cursed Freyom. "I'd give him one more."

"Really? I didn't think you had that much imagination. What would you add?" asked Hiesia.

"A celebration feast cooked over your death," Freyom said.

"It tried that," revealed Hiesia.

"Not over your death," Freyom said.

"Freyom, are you so blind? Do you think I'd travel in time and vanish in an instant if I were still only a bear?" Hiesia bared her teeth.

"What are you suggesting?" questioned Yaltha, peering at Hiesia less with cruelty and more with astonishment.

"Do you think I'm wholly alive?" asked Hiesia.

"She's playing with our heads again," warmed Freyom.

"Anything done to a bear dead or alive, is good," goaded Yaltha.

"The pity is you escaped our father," snapped Freyom.

"I was not a prisoner," growled Hiesia. "I was a prospective mother to one of Its children."

Freyom gripped her sword more tightly. Yaltha rasped as she sucked in air. They had suspected their father would have used more females than the Ruzniel who bore them but they had never had proof.

"We have other sisters?" asked Yaltha.

"I was not going to be the mother of such as you. After I left, Crilodach never had any more fat from my people."

"You seem to think a lot of yourself," Yaltha told her.

"No more than you think of yourself, who has never thought of her mother in her long life," Hiesia said.

"What are mothers to such as us?" demanded Freyom.

"Did you ever wonder why Crilodach, who can create beings like Hagouti, needed mothers for Its children?"

The sisters were tired, intrigued and confused in equal measure. Freyom rubbed the watery mud from her eyes. They had never given their mothers any thought at all. They hated hearing Hiesia's voice. They wanted to get away but nothing they did freed them. To make matters worse their father was coming and they still did not know if Hiesia was doing Its bidding or not. Freyom began to look at Yaltha and her plots as the reason their father could have betrayed them. Yaltha trying to convince her to follow her and not Crilodach. All the traitorous ideas whispered into her ears, started to bubble up inside her. She was getting angry with her sister.

"You see," intoned Hiesia, "It needed to know you would be weak enough for It to destroy when It had used you. Its own creations, It can never destroy. Though they wish It would. I've seen Hagouti's endless pain. Surely you must have realized you were born to be weak."

"Liar," said the sisters together.

"Why should I, who was there, lie to you who were not? What would I gain by lying to you?"

"We don't trust bears," growled Freyom.

The sisters stopped for a moment. They had heard a rumour. So long ago they had forgotten. So rare they did not need to remember. Of a time when Ghirzanben was in uproar. That prisoners had escaped and no one knew how. Crilodach had taken the heads of a thousand guards that day. Frin-Ghirzan had been locked up for his laxity for three months, and every man who walked over his head was ordered to spit through the grates onto their commander. So began Frin-Ghirzan's particular hatred for bears. They never knew how the escape had been organized.

"You brought them here," Yaltha realized. "That's why our father never found them, you brought them back to this time."

"Not quite this time. I did bring them through to a time before It could know they were here. I brought them back with knowledge of It. They prepared for It to come before we were a nation. This is why the fight will never end. This is why the fight is so hard for your father. Your finding your way here changes nothing. Not for me, nor Tegriel nor your father. All your training, all your lives in whatever place you spent them, count for nothing. You're nothing."

"No!" screamed Freyom, leaping at Hiesia as Yaltha dived at the bear's feet.

Hiesia was not there but this time she appeared between them and lifting them both up by their necks she flung them against the trees, casting a spell as they sailed in the air. The branches wrapped themselves around the sisters in a split second, holding them fast.

Then the grasses grew up and wrapped them tighter. The sisters' hackles rose and they wriggled to get free but the tree branches held them even as they gripped and tore at them with their teeth.

"Not so loud-mouthed now?" Hiesia observed.

"This is all your fault," snapped Freyom.

"Mine? How d'you work that out?" asked her sister.

"You and your plotting against our father has made us weak."

"Don't be ridiculous," argued Yaltha.

"When I see It I'll tell It. I want no more of your prattling about power. Father's not to be crossed," Freyom said, struggling.

"If you say a word It'll kill us both," said Yaltha.

"As long as It kills you first, I don't care."

Hiesia moved to a rock and sat down. She was tired of the sound of their voices. She reached into her fur and with her claws drew out the Sagitæ that had sustained her for all her years. She smiled. The sisters looked at her, their eyes widening with surprise. They did not know what the jewel was they saw but they knew this was the source of her power.

You see what you want to see when you look upon the Sagitæ. As with all the bejals. Hiesia saw much the same as Lilah saw, the whiteness and the beauty of a single jewel. The sisters saw something utterly different. They saw power, raw and untempered, that made them salivate and wriggle harder. A power that called them by name, so much did they agonize to discover the promise of eternal existence. The Sagitæ did not look like a jewel to them, but a metal claw that would replace one of their own. But only one. And for only one sister. The first to touch, to hold, to possess this power.

Hiesia knew, despite her saying the opposite, the trouble brought by the sisters could have terrible consequences. First she had to find Tegriel. He had told her all those years in the future she would hold this Sagitæ in trust, that this one cosmic jewel had been chased by Crilodach becoming many things throughout a long history. Now the jewel inhabited her. Now they crossed time together. She eased back her shoulders and looked at the sisters.

"Eventually I'm sure the trees will free you, or you'll die of old age, one of the two. I never heard tell of trees being found with skeletons buried in their trunks so I assume you get free somehow. More's the pity."

"You aren't going to kill us?" questioned Yaltha.

"Do you think I should?" the bear asked her.

"No," said Freyom. "Go and leave us alive but don't expect us to change."

"I'm counting on you not changing," said Hiesia.

"We'll fight again," growled Yaltha.

"I'm sure we will."

"Unless ... we were to fight for the same thing," tried the sister again.

"Sister be quiet!" stormed Freyom. "You've done enough damage."

"How would you betray Crilodach?" asked Hiesia.

"For a price we would do anything that needed to be done," replied Yaltha.

"And that price would be?" asked the bear.

"Power of our own, in a part of the universe far from you and yours."

"Yaltha, I'd never trust you to stay there," Hiesia answered her, "Nor do I think either of you have power enough to defeat your father. Nor would I allow you to subjugate others for my benefit."

"We could win with you, Tegriel and that claw you hold."

"Yaltha no," cried Freyom.

"See sense sister, we'd have everything." She turned to Hiesia, "Defeat our father and you save millions of lives bear. What d'you say?" Hiesia stopped for a moment, as if thinking. She replaced the Sagitæ and vanished.

"Exactly how many angles do you intend to play?" warned Freyom.

"All of them," replied Yaltha.

"Not if I'm first out of this knotted tree," struggled Freyom.

"Why? Are you going to run to father like a snitch?" writhed Yaltha.

"No I'm going to whip you until you bleed," promised Freyom.

And so they argued, and struggled to get free, with all their venom directed at each other. If Dalved had seen them, he would have rolled onto his back holding his legs with his thin arms, so deep would have been his laughter. And that was when Yaltha noticed for the first time that he was not there. In the battle she had forgotten all about him. She cursed him for not cutting her loose.

Tegriel stopped to catch his breath. He realized, from the lack of screeching from behind, that the sisters were no longer in hot pursuit. He turned round. Breathing softly he calmed himself down, he wondered if the sisters had gone another way to ambush them further ahead. Tobia, with no desire to be caught asked,

"Why have we stopped?"

"Because they have."

"Where are they?"

Tegriel opened his hand and from his finger a small, clear puff of air shot upwards. He could see through this spell as if his eyes were a mile or so above them. He surveyed the entire area. He saw the sisters being thrown into the mud by Hiesia. He allowed himself a small smile for he knew that this was not what had happened last time. He was very glad she was here. That he could have beaten the sisters was not in question but he simply did not have the time to have his progress checked. He did wonder if the Sagitæ had brought Hiesia here in time to help him, just as much as Hiesia did. He had always thought the Sagitæ were working away in the background helping the Sangyma but until now he had never had any proof.

"Hiesia is here fighting our enemies," Tegriel told her.

He did not tell Tobia about the Sagitæ so Tobia never knew that Hiesia carried a Sagitæ with her. In this way he tried to keep as much as possible the same as before because he still did not know that everything had, indeed, changed.

"She's here? How did she know, if this hasn't happened before?" asked Tobia.

"We are creatures of magic, Tobia, when we cross from one place to another, when we take one step, there is an equal and opposite step taken to keep the balance. For every magical action there is an equal and opposite reaction. Filvani called this the Theory of Moments. A self-sustaining balance built into the fabric of the cosmos."

"The same cosmos that allowed Crilodach to live in the first place?"

"None of us has ever discovered what makes the Sagitæ or Crilodach live," said Tegriel. "Nor could we change anything if we knew. We will never go back far enough to witness the mysteries that control all our lives."

"The cosmos that created Crilodach might not be on our side," she pointed out.

"Possibly. What we do know is that those sisters have changed history. So to balance the sisters changing events, the magic which exists in the cosmos had to bring someone else to this place."

"And that someone is Hiesia?"

"Yes," replied Tegriel.

"Is that how the Sangyma have always managed to be

wherever Crilodach is, brought there by the cosmos?"

He stopped to take his bearings before answering her,

"Actually usually a lot more planning goes into what we do. Things do happen by chance. We call such events 'ivatim', strange occurrences almost with the character of chance about them though we have never believed in chance. Crilodach has always kept Itself to Itself to prevent us from ever knowing exactly when It will strike. Coming out as It has, Lilah now knows everything It will try to do for the wake of magic around It will wash across her being like water over a beach. Magicians can only hide by not using their magic." They headed off again.

"I don't believe Crilodach could ever hide Its magic," she said.

"It never has but It has taught others to. Though they cannot hide from the Sagitæ. Perhaps, in truth, nothing is ever hidden from the cosmos herself, we are just able to hide things from each other. Events like today's are part planned and part the unforeseen consequences of those plans but being a consequence of magic means some spells, deeper than understanding, see them."

"Makes me feel as if I were being controlled."

"You should talk to Hiesia about that when you meet her. She says that is the most common feeling amongst all beings."

"Does she know we're here?"

"I could not hide us from her. She has dotted around time. Her travels would make even a Ruzniel head spin. She has an instinct for knowing who is around. A special bear sense only she developed. Come along we still must hurry," he said, rushing down a hill and across the small stream.

Tobia and Tegriel marched forward but her mind was still on the bear whose life was now intertwined with hers. She had seen her father's painting of Hiesia in the front hallway to the academy in her city. A dramatic piece depicting her escape from Ghirzanben on an äis with Mojolo and other bears by her side.

"Is she a Sangyma?"

"No. In many ways she is more like a bejal than a bear, more like a spell than a being. She never wanted to be one of us. She has always gone her own way, done her own thing. That is her strength."

"Doesn't she ever need any help?"

"Not in all the time I have known her. She is a creature of time and no place, quite wonderful actually. Endlessly interesting. She always has something to say for herself. I think she understands more about the cosmos than even Filvani. She may even have a part to play at Zaqui, she could get there. But many magicians have put time and effort into this war. Spells you have never heard of, places you have never been, all working away in a hundred different ways. All our allies. Layer upon layer of history like steps leading to the summit of achievement, the pinnacle of magic, becoming a part of each of us."

"Hiesia's magic is part of me?"

"The day is not just a day, Bofindle is not just Bofindle, Lilah is not just a spellmaker and Hiesia is not just a bear and you, Tobia, you are not just Tobia." They leapt another stream as they hurried on. "Now is a time when a lot of adventurers travelling to far reaches of space try to uncover some new gem, some new spell, some old magician. To tell you the truth, some of those legends were my own invention and they kept Crilodach's lieutenants very busy looking for people who did not exist. Just in case the prophecy was true and there was a mirror in which Crilodach could see Its own death, or a sea you can walk upon that gave the traveller healing powers. I might even add a couple more this time to keep It extra busy. I should certainly say something about the daughters It has. 'They will seek only to betray It.' That should make It stop and think awhile."

"Seems to me you enjoy making stuff up," said Tobia.

"All to a purpose Tobia, all to a purpose. Anyway Hiesia is one of the most brilliant minds of her people. Every bit Copret's equal. She has been able to appear at different times to guide her people, ever since Crilodach took them and imprisoned them in Ghirzanben."

"Who's Copret?"

"Forgive me, I forget what you do not know."

"I can see him. He's a bear too. But I don't know him."

"He helped build a great fortress, Trecrogo. The power that will break Crilodach at Zaqui. You will become close friends with his family in your later years."

"Later years."

"You say that with surprise," smiled Tegriel, "you will still age."

"Alive before I was born. When is my time? I span ages.

I'm now in the days before there were any legends before the birth of my entire people. Yet even here Crilodach's claws seek us out."

Tegriel suddenly said, interrupting her thoughts,

"Here is the spot. I hope I am not too late. There are magical moments in my lifeline that must never be altered by even so much as a second. Magic Tobia is fluid, if I cannot find Bofindle at exactly the same moment as before, the magic in the bejal might not be the same. Who knows what that could do? She may be weaker, or worse she may lack vital knowledge that helps us in a million ways down the ages."

He began an incantation. She could see subtle shifts in the soil and the rocks trembled slightly as if Tegriel's quiet spell was a mellow symphony making things resonate with sound. Even the sky above them began to move. Hiesia felt his magic as she fought the sisters.

Around Tegriel the elements opened up the ground and minerals began to combine atom by atom, the sunshine heated up the hollow in the ground. Tegriel had to protect Tobia from the heat. The ground rumbled. Tegriel began to sing. The stars appeared and disappeared in the sunlight, and the mountains seemed to vibrate until out of the ground ... came nothing. He had expected a small staff to form that glowed with the colours of the rainbow but there was nothing. The bejal should be cooling at his feet but there was nothing. His face lost all colour. He looked ashen. Tobia felt the Sangyma was weaker, shrunken, and changed as if the very life had gone out of him. Like a winded fighter he stood unable to move though he wanted to fall on his knees. He was stunned. Bofindle was gone.

Hiesia sniffed the air. She smelled a dog moving fast to her left and something else. The unmistakable something else she had never forgotten since her time in Its dungeons. It was here. It could free the sisters if It wanted. The trees could not stand against Its power. Kalevala had also smelled It, and he was running fast now with Dalved on his back riding as if he had been born to ride, which was strange to Dalved who had never ridden any animals in his life. Had he known he was only staying on because Kalevala wished him to, he would have been happy and scared at the same time. Magic does that to people.

"Who's that?" Tobia asked, seeing a slim, lean—muscled

man standing on the other side of a wide stream.

Tegriel looked up from his attempt to find Bofindle and stood stock still. In one horrendous moment all became clear to him. Bofindle was not with him, the sisters had been a diversion, everything had gone in Crilodach's favour. Did Crilodach possess Bofindle? He slowly touched her shoulder, his voice carrying an unusual air of foreboding.

"Tobia, whatever happens stay out of the way."

He handed her some pieces of grass and a few seeds.

"What do I do with these?" she asked.

"If I fall I have already made arrangements that the Ossendark will take you to another place. When you get there look for a place that is filled with blue grass and throw the seeds and the grass onto the ground. Sprinkle them around a bit. The spells will take care of the rest and you will be safe."

"What can happen to you? Who's that man?"

"No more questions now."

Tobia looked at the man who was motionless on the opposite bank and then at Tegriel who was not moving nor even blinking and hardly breathing. They were like two statues waiting for an horrific battle to bring them to life. She had heard of this before, the swift spells of the fiercest of battles amongst magicians. Lightning reflexes and split-second decisions. Only the finest magicians can fight this fast. Whoever the man was, he was a deadly enemy.

"What about all the other stuff, the prophecy and hundreds of years of work."

"You'll have to fulfill my work if I die here."

"No!"

"Do not be afraid. Stay hidden. Hiesia is coming. She will guide you."

Tegriel walked forward and the man glared at the Sangyma, without surprise or fear.

"Tegriel," It snarled. "Still trying to save meaningless creatures with your futile gestures."

"I did not expect you so soon," Tegriel told Crilodach.

"If at all."

Its lips were slightly parted in a sneer, Its long fingers flexing as It spoke, Its clothes untouched by any movement from Its limbs. Its heart beat was the essence of silence.

"What has worried you so much to have brought you here?"

"My worries are never your concern Sangyma. Now I've trapped you in your little plot, Tegriel the magnificent utterly defeated before he's had time to carry out one act of defiance against me."

"I was sure when you worked out the nature of the Upala you would come up with some notion you could change history," Tegriel said.

"As you always intended to do with your pathetic prophecies. I wonder you can sleep at night you plot so much for so many who will never give you any thanks. Your brain can have no grasp of reality you're so filled with connivance."

"I know you see me in your dreams. You hate me for stopping your scheming, but stop you I do," replied Tegriel.

"I never dream," said Crilodach, "I've seen your plots taking shape, they're vicious in their intent. You use people more than I and you call me the cruel one. Now every prophecy is utterly useless. I've bested you Tegriel before you can even make a start."

"And these daughters sent to kill me, what are they but a failed plan to prevent Bofindle being found?"

"Pawns."

"In a game you play with all life."

"Life is a game Tegriel, you never understand that. You play because I exist. Without me you have nothing. Without me you've no cause to champion. Without me your existence is pointless. You and all your Sangyma crowd. You're all slaves to my being."

"Your defeat is as assured as the stars coming out at night," Tegriel told It.

"We all know the stars will die first and I'll be there, master of the Sagitæ, lord of all and you'll never have even left Samphin. I'll blot your name out from all memory, I'll eradicate you from history."

"Who knows more about lying than you?" goaded Tegriel, circling closer to Crilodach.

"I always wondered what's in them, the ones who fight me. Why some cave in so fast and others fight me with their last breath. That's all you, filling them with fancies and giving them false courage. I always give exactly what I promise and I promise nothing."

"There is nothing false in their courage," replied Tegriel, "that is the very cosmos standing against you. As all things of noble power stand against you. You make us sick to the heart. You make us vomit from the stench of your words. You are as cruel now as you will ever be but in your twisted machinations is your downfall."

"The weird and wonderful fantasies of a defeated Sangyma," Crilodach laughed. "You know what I found out about my enemies? I found they believed in your words Tegriel, and so many times they were half true. I knew there was something at work, some force behind the scenes. I know you. Playing with time is a weak throw of the dice. Using, what do you call them, your bejals, as your weapons? Relying upon laws of magic to fight for you. I shall assign you all to nothingness and be done with you."

Tegriel did not yet know how Crilodach could see and understand so much. If they had been arguing at Zaqui he would have understood very well but this man was Crilodach as he had first met with It, before It became the beast. It had not travelled back in time with a store of knowledge. How could Crilodach know what was going to happen? Crilodach continued,

"You of all the Sangyma were the oldest, the adversary with all the answers. I knew you were a time traveller even before I knew the Upala existed. What a gift Hiesia gave to the universe. Why she gave such a bejal to you I'll never know. What a useful bejal to so adequately change everything in my favour."

"I have seen the poor creatures you used for your tests."

"I never believed only one Ruzniel could pass through the Upala. Besides you're so full of lies at my expense I only half believed the Upala could do what they said. I had to test the rumours out. Such a perfect beauty of a spell in a bejal. Ah, the mighty Tegriel is confounded. You haven't a clue how I know so much? Do you think you're the only one to hide spells?"

"Your daughters," realized Tegriel.

"Fighters that they are they had no objection to wearing the armour I designed for them. What better way to send a spell back to bring myself vital information, oh such a well of information. I've all the answers this time Tegriel, not you. Things will not go the same way. You can't fool me, you can't stop me, you can't hide from me, you can't defeat my armies."

"I never had all the answers Crilodach. None of us do."

"You don't know how this day ends."

"Neither do you," said Tegriel.

"The end will be absolute. The death of my enemies. The one thing I lacked, I have. I've seen the future more clearly than you. I have you Sangyma, I have you from where you'll never escape."

"You have been blind since the first day of your violent life," argued Tegriel.

"Your little speech about goodness already. You should save that for when I hold you by the throat and you need to plead for your life."

"I have no speeches for you, they would be as useless now as they have always been."

"You and your Sangyma have tried so many times to convince my soldiers of their better side," Crilodach laughed, "which is why I spend so much time eradicating their judgment before I send them on their errands. I have the dates and times of your fellow Sangyma's births. I can blot them out before they even begin to understand who they are. This knowledge makes me supreme."

"But that is the point, Crilodach, you send people, you have always been so scared to go yourself. That will never change."

"I fear nothing!" shouted Crilodach.

"No? Did you forget to send back your fear?"

Crilodach cast a net of burning fire into the air with flames of blue and green stretching out across the sky like a vast, intricate, hooked web, coming down around Tegriel threatening to cut through him as the silk fell all about him. He quickly knelt down on his knee and raised his hands to his ears. From his fingers shards as sharp as knives flew into the air cutting the net around him so the pieces fell onto the ground without touching his body, broken up into wisps with no more weight or power than flower petals. Where they touched, the ground bubbled and burned. Wisps of smoke filled the area with the stinging scent of acid that made Tobia crouch behind her rock with her eyes stinging.

As Tegriel stood up Crilodach attacked again from a different position, closer than It had been before, then with a swift leap It was standing in front of Tegriel and they locked hands. Writhing against each other's power, seemingly no more than two men trying to wrestle each other to the ground. Trying to trip or throw the other whilst from their eyes bolts shot like bullets flashing between them in myriad colours as they ignited on contact, any one of which getting through would have killed Tegriel. They came more rapidly than machine–gun fire and each bolt intercepted those from the other and exploded until neither Crilodach nor Tegriel could see each other.

And all the time their minds locked as fiercely. Crilodach taking to arguing and screaming, insulting the Sangyma. Castigating his weakness and pointing out his impending defeat. Tegriel laughed at him and told him nothing would change, that everything It knew would be next–to–nothing when they finished here. Both of them would know what was to come, so at every juncture their battle would rage even more strongly than before.

Mind and body locked in combat. Now their clothes, wrapped in spells Filvani had yet to categorize, tore into ribbons and became yet more hands wrapping around each other to stop them attacking the other. Tearing at each other like serpents bent on murder. From nowhere the drumming rose. From the clash of bright bolts and spells ripping into each other, the rocks about them started to smash together on the ground and in the air. Sounding like a deadly symphony berating anything for living. A little way away even Bofindle hummed.

The ground reverberated beneath Tobia's legs and she actually felt herself being thumped by the pressure in the air. Frozen behind a boulder, watching in her mind. This was not the Crilodach of her nightmares. This was not the sinister creature with strong teeth and claws. This was a person as tall as Tegriel, grey skinned with bones that jutted out. More than that It did not look so evil nor was Its voice the rasping growl that had been described to her so many times before by those who had heard the beast. How could this ordinary man be the first creature to have been born? How could magic have touched someone so ordinary, so normal? It even had hair that shone white with cleanliness and wore clothes that could have been made on any loom.

Yet here It was fighting the greatest Sangyma, the strongest and kindest man, this fight alone told her this man was Crilodach, and was her enemy. At that moment anyone seeing them without knowing them would not have been able to discern much of a difference. Definitely not the life changing difference that would have told an onlooker which of the combatants would destroy, and which one would save, worlds. Which one only had hands and which one concealed claws.

Kalevala came up, running hard to the knoll on her left, with Dalved now running by his side as he too had been imbued with strength from his new found freedom and his body exalted in the freshness of the air and the coolness of the breeze. Kalevala had told him to jump off and stay concealed as they came to last mile before catching up with the fight but Dalved had refused. He was delighting in every new sense and with every passing second the palace and all the drudgery fell from him as if he were shedding a skin.

The dog took in the scene in one moment and growled to himself. Dalved, who had expected to see the sisters in all the noise and lightning, was at a loss and scratched his head. Then he saw Tobia crouching behind a rock and pointed. Kalevala ran down to her with Dalved in tow. The man fell behind the rock as stray bolts bounced around him, almost laughing with the sheer thrill of the fight. Dalved had lost all fear.

Kalevala sniffed her hand. The wetness of his nose and the smoothness of his voice came to her like a song across a great distance, with catches of a melody she knew well. Waves of heat flowed over them as Kalevala said,

"Hunu seeds and Abin Grass. Tegriel has been busy despite this attack. I doubt they would be useful without Bofindle."

"We came to find the bejal but Crilodach was here." Looking over the rock at the two fighters he said,

"Looks like Tegriel can hold his own against Crilodach."

"But we have a problem," she said, "Tegriel had time to call forth Bofindle but nothing happened."

"He did, did he," said Kalevala, cocking his head and straining his ears in the direction of the fight.

"That Crilodach walks a twisted path, Its trying to talk to me even as It fights Tegriel."

"What's It saying?"

"It wants to know what I've done with Bofindle," Kalevala said.

"You?" said an astonished Tobia.

"Me."

"You have Bofindle?"

"Dug up and hidden two days ago. Got this sudden urge to dig just where Tegriel has been working. Took me two days to dig down and then I found this tiny, little stick.

Don't know why I wanted to keep the thing but I grabbed the staff in my teeth and filled up the hole. Ever since Tegriel got here Bofindle's been humming and snapping, and moving around in my fur. If the staff was a flea I'd scratch."

"Do you know how powerful Bofindle is?"

"The thing's been talking in my ear all the time. Things about being a bejal, the Sangyma and spell–making. Quite a tale."

Dalved's heart sank within him at the mention of Crilodach. Was he in truth not free at all? Would his new friends crumble before the father of his mistresses? He looked from his position low to the ground and watched. He had expected to see a monster. Then he said softly,

"How could that give birth to Freyom and Yaltha who are part beast?" asked Dalved.

"Why shouldn't It?" asked Kalevala, "the magic in It is as twisted as ivy climbing a tree. It has appeared to others as a beast because that instills more fear. Bofindle tells me It cannot hide what It is before Tegriel. It will never give life to anything normal. It created Its daughters when It was a beast. The children of magical people take on the essence of their parents." He growled, "Tegriel doesn't seem to be getting anywhere. I need to help him."

"This is Crilodach not one of Its lackeys," said Tobia, "Tegriel is about the only person here who'd have half a chance against It."

"Its daughters are half women, half beasts, filled with strength beyond even the strongest men, with back bones that bristle with poisonous spines. I've hated the sound of Its name all my life," said Dalved, almost to himself.

"Watch and wait Dalved, you'll learn. For now, stay down with Tobia. I'm going to help Tegriel," said Kalevala.

"You don't trust me to help?"

Kalevala looked at the thin, pale man who had never been free of servitude, licked his teeth, and replied

"I expect you to do what I tell you to do. That's all."

"I won't retreat," argued Tobia.

"What can you do from here?"

"I don't know, but I must stay to be of use," she said.

"You'll only be in the way."

"Since when is a Ruzniel in the way of her master?"

"The wrong move could hurt Tegriel," warned Kalevala.

The two men continued fighting hard as Kalevala tried to

dissuade the others from helping, sweat pouring off them both until finally Crilodach spoke,

"With all that power you can't escape my grasp ..."

Before It could go on It was suddenly taken by surprise from the flank with a mighty leap from Kalevala who threw It across the ground. Its hands reached out but Kalevala had timed his leap to perfection and twisted his body out of the way. Crilodach went one way and he another. By the time Crilodach had regained his footing Tegriel had blown sheets of fire around It like the bars in a prison. A fire that could burn It as easily as burning a person but a person would shrink from the pain, Crilodach walked into the flames and, though they were thick and It had to spend several moments burning up amongst them, It kept walking, coming out scarred and on fire. Its skin blackened, Its eyebrows and eyelashes burned off. Even Its lips were smouldering.

"Again Sangyma. Again. Bring your bears and your dogs, you've nothing, nothing that can defeat me!"

"You will be defeated at every turn," cried Tegriel, "in a thousand worlds and in a million battles your armies will retreat from the might of those born to be your enemies."

"Not this time. You don't have Bofindle. You can't surprise me. This time I'll kill you where you stand."

"Even here I am many and you are but one," shouted back Tegriel.

"I smell my daughters coming. They've escaped Hiesia. Oh, don't look so surprised I sensed her here. How could I not, the magic in her is strong. Her offspring will not fail me and she will not escape me this time. This time the bears will be in my army. With them I shall win every battle."

"Let us finish with this one now," called back Tegriel.

Tegriel ran at Crilodach but Kalevala who had heard Crilodach mention Bofindle knew two things immediately. Firstly that he had been drawn to dig out Bofindle because somehow the bejal knew Tegriel might not have the time, and secondly that Tegriel needed Bofindle because with the weapon, he would defeat Crilodach. Even as he pulled the tiny stick from his shoulder fur he did not know what 'this time' meant exactly but he understood enough about their time travelling to just accepted everything any of them said.

When you know two things like that, and you do not know a third, you had best let others do some of the work so as Tegriel leapt Bofindle twirled through the air towards him, finding his willing hand and stopping his leap.

The mighty staff rose from Tegriel's hand, grew like a tree, and threw Crilodach upwards and backwards, and as It scrambled to Its feet like a wild animal baying at Its enemies, Bofindle broke upon It with repeated strikes in Tegriel's hands. Tegriel did not question where Bofindle had sprung from or what had happened. He had been very fearful of the outcome to this fight when they started, but now he was just eager to finish. Matters had not gone as they had the first time but still Bofindle was found and Hiesia was nearby so the Upala had a chance of being finished. The spellmaker Kalevala was by his side and Tobia was still alive.

"Feel the power that will defeat you Crilodach. Feel the magic that you cannot break. Feel the soul of the Sangyma."

But before he could land more blows Crilodach vanished and appeared again flaying at Kalevala's skin causing the blood to flow on the dog's back legs.

"No," cried Dalved, seeing Kalevala wince and fall, "No!"

Dalved could not stand to see the dog who had shown him the first trust and kindness he had ever received in his life, hurt by the monster he hated through knowing Its daughters.

Tegriel turned in time to see Dalved creep out from behind the rock, crouch and leap onto Crilodach's back. Tegriel reached out a hand but he stopped. With Bofindle in his hand ready to strike again, he stopped. With Tobia running to Kalevala to see to his wound, he stopped. He stopped because Crilodach stopped.

Tegriel had always known of the man who was inside the beast they had described and painted for many to recognize and fear down the ages. He knew Crilodach became that beast soon after their first battle. This was now their first battle. Though not in the same place or same time. But, as if some things had to be the same no matter how clever magical people became at changing the past; as if some events still flowed into the matrix of experience; as if to balance the hidden spell that told It all that was to come, the cosmos had brought Dalved to be a hidden weapon secreted in the heart of Its empire for Its whole life. As if a living being could be a bejal only if that being were Dalved. One change changes everything and one can know what all the changes will mean for them.

Crilodach was never meant to live as a man nor live without fearing the touch of others. Already in the heat of the battle, as Dalved scrambled on Its back to pull It backwards with both hands tight around Crilodach's neck, even as the old servant failed to make any impression with his poor strength, he had already effected Its change by his very touch.

Crilodach could not be touched. By warning Itself of what was to come It had changed how things would be, but Crilodach had not given Dalved any thought. It did not know the sun had changed him. It did not even recall his face or name. Its only consideration about Its daughters was their mission, what they did in their palace was of no interest to It at all. It did not see the magic in Dalved as Its mind filled up with the facts of Its history. It did not recognize that Dalved had come back in time with them when that was not Its plan. By missing him It missed the possibility that Dalved was a secret weapon.

Touching It made It change. Weakened It for a moment. Stopped It fighting. Until It arched Its head back and screamed. Dalved held It as tight as he could closing his eyes as he expected claws to instantly rip him apart. His heart pounded. He wanted to shout to give himself more courage but his throat was blocked by his pulsating heart. His lungs wanted to burst. His skin was on fire. He held on as someone on a mountain side holds onto a frayed rope knowing the long fall is coming at any moment. What Dalved didn't know was just how long his fall was going to be.

No one until Zaqui would ever know what Dalved felt, or how he felt, nor what he cried out in his head but the three of them saw what happened. Saw the skin wrap Dalved and Crilodach into one. Saw the claws and the eyes and size of the beast Crilodach emerge from Its contortions and screams. The servant vanished. A few seconds later Kalevala, balancing on Bofindle drove the staff from above It into the ground deeper and deeper until even in Its pain Crilodach's strength managed to stop the thrust downwards but by then It was deep below the surface. Bofindle rose up out of the ground and the hole closed over. And below them fighting Its transformation Crilodach wailed and writhed. Creating a labyrinth of tunnels as it tried to fight the pain. Samphin was becoming Damkina.

The last thing Crilodach did was to roar in pain. Then the noise stopped. They were left with the beating of their hearts, the sweat of their bodies, their fear, the sounds of the battle in their ears and the pungent odour of the spells on the breeze.

"The fool," moaned Kalevala, limping from his wound, "I told the man to stay out of the fight."

"Don't judge him hastily," said Tegriel, "The Crilodach I have fought is that beast. Events may have changed but we still fight It. It knows so much that events will not follow the same pattern but matters will not go Its way either."

"I wonder if Dalved lives on or even knows what he has done," said Kalevala.

"Better by far for him that he be dead," replied Tobia.

"For him yes, but this is new to me. This is not how this happened before. This is not how the beast we know was created," said Tegriel.

"The beast we know?" asked Kalevala.

"Will come to know," corrected Tegriel.

"How can things work out the same if they've not happened this way before?" Tobia asked, almost scared to speak.

"I am not sure yet. Inside It is a man trapped where he should not be. There is a great deal we do not know about Dalved."

"He came here with the sisters, what's to know?" Kalevala licked his wounds and stopped the blood flowing as he spoke, "Though Dalved seemed pretty normal for someone who's lived all his life in their company."

"There must be something in his life that made him deadly to Crilodach. We must find out what," said Tegriel.

"And how do you intend to do that if we can't ask him?" asked Kalevala.

"I do not yet know. Unless there comes a time when he is again separated from Crilodach, we can't ask him directly but I sense we have to find out because the future hangs in the balance," said Tegriel.

"Surely he's dead?" asked Kalevala.

"Crilodach is fighting the transformation, Its not in control and since we may assume Dalved would not want to be in Crilodach's skin we may assume he is not in control either. Whatever magic drives this metamorphosis between them may not kill Dalved," explained Tegriel.

"Poor man to be trapped with It?" said Tobia.

"Your wounds heal fast," observed Tegriel.

"Not that I get many you understand but in general I heal very well," replied Kalevala.

"And Bofindle," twirled Tegriel, "How did you get this?"

"Out of the ground two days ago."

"Two days. We were in the Upala two days?"

"What?" Tobia asked.

"The sisters using the Upala changed everything. And the balance I told you about, must have kept us all travelling two days, allowing time for Kalevala to become a spellmaker without me by using other spells."

"A what?" asked Kalevala.

"The first of the spellmakers," repeated Tegriel giving Bofindle back to the dog. "I need to think about this for a while. Come, Hiesia is close. We must get into the Ossendark and away from here."

"What about the sisters following us?" asked Tobia.

"Let them meet their father in their own time, I am sure they will find the reunion to their mutual distaste," said Tegriel.

The Ossendark opened up before them as Hiesia appeared across the river and, leaping over vanished for a second in mid leap to reappear again beside them all. She hugged Tegriel.

"What's happened to It?" she asked, "There are signs all over the three of you that It was here."

"A man touched It," said Kalevala.

"What does that mean?" she asked.

"We don't know, Dalved has the secret" Tobia told her. "He's the man who touched It."

"Fascinating," she grinned, her large teeth shining in the sunshine.

"But we don't know why," suggested Kalevala.

"And we must know," replied Tegriel. "We have a powerful weapon against the beast if we can find out what that touch meant."

"Here come the sisters," warned Hiesia. "Want me to kill them this time?"

"Bofindle is found. Hiesia, you must go back to complete the magic in the Upala. The time has come for us to leave," pointed out Tegriel. "Crilodach now has the form in which the universe shall know and fear It."

"This is the time for me to use those spells you taught me?"

"Yes," Tegriel told her.

"I can see why you never elaborated on the circumstances,"

she grinned.

"If you're going back I will come with you," insisted Tobia.

"If we three use the Ossendark now the sisters will assume we have all gone. That will give Hiesia time to evade them and finish her work here before following us."

"I wouldn't argue with him," said Hiesia, "there isn't any time."

She clapped her paws together to usher Tobia in, turned to see the sisters, waved at them, stepped back, and vanished with Tegriel and Kalevala, so easily she looked as if she had walked into the Ossendark whereas she had stepped aside and started to run towards the mountains. Before leaving she would use the Sagitæ to complete the magic of the Upala and send the bejal to safety even as Samphin began to turn grey under Crilodach's influence. She would also gain the vital knowledge that would save her and her family when they were imprisoned on Ghirzanben.

Running up to the spot Freyom cried in anger after the dagger she had thrown at the vanishing Tegriel missed.

"There's been a fight here," sniffed Freyom.

"The one we felt before. Look at the scorched soil." Yaltha sniffed the burnt soil and looked at her sister,

"This is father's spell. I recognize the scent."

"Where is It?" asked Freyom.

"Do you think they took It prisoner?" asked Yaltha.

"It was not with them when they entered the Ossendark."

"But Its been here sister. Why'd It be here if we were the ones who were sent to kill Tegriel, if not to kill us?" asked Yaltha.

"Maybe It ..." she stopped. Freyom could not answer her sister. The idea that they had been used as decoys foremost in her mind.

"I don't know about you but I'm tired of being used. I say we follow Tegriel and finish the job we started," snarled Yaltha. Freyom hit her fist into her sister's palm in agreement.

"At last you've got things straight," she said. "And if father used us we can deal with It later."

"Agreed," snarled Freyom.

Rebellion

Frin-Ghirzan was more than unhappy. He was hot with rage, like so many in the armada, still suffering from the shock of another defeat; going over their failed tactics in his head until his brain hurt. He had spent his whole existence training soldiers only to see them do what their training made them do and still fail. His heart sank like a piece of stone inside him. His hatred for the enemy was greater than ever. First, he cursed his bad luck, then he cursed a certain manœuvre he knew had not gone well, then he thought of his general, wondering if Rataplan had been up to the job because Frin-Ghirzan was not honest enough to find fault with himself.

He had to admit that Rataplan had always been adequate, even though they argued, and seeing him killed by a child made Frin-Ghirzan's head reel. How could Rataplan be dead? Demeter's crime seemed unbelievable to him. Now he looked at their commander–in–chief whom he had always feared and always obeyed, appearing somehow weaker Suddenly changed. Changed at exactly the worst of all times. Changed when they were at their lowest ebb. Changed when change meant defeat. Changed when he was not expected to ever change. When Its changing was not even the spark of a possibility in their minds. But then, Crilodach being trapped inside Trecrogo was not something they expected either. Along with seeing that Lilah possessed one of the Sagitæ and Sangyma magic thrived everywhere they looked despite the Sangyma having been thought dead.

Twice now the stunning fortress Trecrogo had defied their attacks; he had lost more soldiers than he had ever lost before in any single campaign; his ears rang from the endless noise and relentless efforts of the past days. He wanted to get rid of the armour that chaffed his neck and knocked against his knees and elbows as he walked. He had lost weight during these hours. The armour did not fit him snugly. The clothes he wore against his skin were dripping with his own sweat but he had no time to rest. He knew the fight was far from over. Yet he was also starting another fight. One within himself. One of doubt mixed with horror. One of disbelief mixed with anger. One of shock mixed with betrayal. A sour taste on his thick tongue seemed to drip bile into his skin and through his veins until he wanted to vomit. Repeating the same question over and over. Is Crilodach strong enough to win?

He scratched his unshaven face which was another annoyance. Rataplan had never grown any beard so the men were accustomed to shaven faces. Frin-Ghirzan hated shaving. He was walking briskly to see his fallen general's body. Like every good leader, he felt the feelings emanating from his troops as clearly as if he had asked them their opinions as he briskly marched passed them. He read everything there was to know about their thoughts by the way they held their bodies, by how they were cleaning or not cleaning their weapons, by the look of their eyes and the sunken disbelief at what they saw and did not see. He felt the livid doubts in his troops chiming with his own. Like a swift moorland mist wrapping around their legs and filling their nostrils until nothing could be seen except the mist that curled around them from nowhere, refusing to go. Clammy, formless yet blinding, doubt was sweeping through the ranks like the rank smell of rotted food or the foul stench rising from week old dead bodies as the men stepped on them and broke their weak bellies open. The putrid, rotted core of the army was billowing outwards until all of them were covered by the stench and growled in revulsion. A rotten fog of doubt dripping with one question. Is Crilodach strong enough to win?

At first he thought the cause was because they had been defeated twice by the same enemy, but then he saw what they had seen. He hurried even faster wanting answers for his armada. For he thought of the soldiers as his armada. He trained them, shared billets with them, saw them die, he even brought many of them up when they were brought to him as children. To refer to them as his armada was his secret pride. How much more were they his armada now, after what he had seen. After Rataplan's death. After Crilodach had changed, split in two, becoming something so much less than the mighty beast. Casting doubt over them all like a fisherman casting a net over a shoal of fish.

To make matters worse when he reached Rataplan, Ferveiss

and Jurveiss were standing almost as still as statues watching Crilodach's every move. They too could not believe what they saw. What they all saw. Like schools of fish pointing in one direction, the armada stared, the lieutenants looked and from a little distance, cloaked on an Onäis, other eyes looked. Crilodach did not care for a second what they were thinking or what they thought they saw. It never cared what others thought because It never feared what they could do. It was always indifferent. Tegriel had always said of Crilodach that Its greatest weakness was that It never changed. Fulminar added if that was so, then that was Its only weakness.

Thousands had seen with their own eyes. One moment Crilodach and thousands of Its armada were cramming into Trecrogo and victory was assured. Then the battle seemed to reach a stalemate. Everything teetered on a moment of apparent stillness in the blood–drenched fight. Suddenly everything went wrong. Rataplan dead. From nowhere the armada were left hanging on the Rounds, a gaping chasm appeared where the siege engines had been positioned, and a strange man was ranting in their midst. Unafraid. Unarmed. Unrecognized though those close to It felt there was something about It that reminded them strongly of Crilodach. The eyes. The eyes had not changed. The way It had run like a maniac towards Trecrogo spitting bitter insults as the fortress pulled away and vanished, the roots of the fortress like a living being, tearing themselves free. Those nearest had seen some of their comrades entwined in those roots being squeezed to death. Crilodach's beast–self inside the fortress and the man–self outside, did nothing. Nothing. How is that strength?

Perhaps they were suffering from a trick cast by the spellmaker. The sudden disappearance of the creature they had followed all their lives to be replaced by a lone man not quite like them, not quite unlike them. Naked and glistening without so much as a single line or wrinkle on skin almost painted onto the bone. Skin that seemed to have never needed to move an arm or bend a leg. Crease–less. This Crilodach had no hair, no claws, no huge teeth and was hardly taller than any of the men in the armada. This Crilodach did not look so impressive as their armour clad general Rataplan, or even Frin-Ghirzan despite his tiredness. This Crilodach looked vulnerable. Weak. Killable.

Instinctively, they disliked what they saw. No, much more than that, they hated It. Upon It they heaped their reasons for their defeat, their tiredness and their pain. Surely this being, this lesser-Crilodach, was not strong enough to win.

Though those cold eyes were the eyes of a being you could not defy. Those startling, yellow eyes. The frenzy It displayed as It marched up and down, demented, dictatorial, shouting, cursing and plotting, told them this was indeed Crilodach. Their leader. The beast for whom they had sacrificed everything. The beast who had promised them immortality and their choice of dominions in the future. Had It lied to them? Had It hidden away Its true nature all this time? Was It, in fact, possible for Crilodach to be beaten? They were not strong enough on their own to win but did following It make any difference to the outcome?

One soldier thought for a moment It was not Crilodach. If he had had a thought. He deliberately barred Its way, questioned and was throttled with one hand even as his feet shook in mid air as he was held above the ground. Then his body burned to ash whilst Crilodach still held him allowing the flames to curl around Its wrist and arm. Its skin untouched as the flames melted the very armour the man was wearing. A perfect display of power and anger. Not a word was said. Not another man moved.

All questions vanished from the armada about who It was, but the uncertainty was replaced by a certain resentment. At first, nothing more than shock, then the idea took hold that any of the men in the armada, their general or any one of Its lieutenants, would be a stronger leader if they had had Crilodach's magic. Frin-Ghirzan never hid who he was. Never lied to his men. Led from the front. He had been wounded many times. Crilodach, who had promised them all so much, had been defeated by their enemy on Its first campaign from Damkina. With fewer soldiers the enemy had thrown back the glory of Rataplan's army from the fortress. The fault had to lie with Crilodach. This Crilodach had enough power to kill them but no longer enough to capture their loyalty.

Frin-Ghirzan felt this resentment. So did Ferveiss and Jurveiss, who had never faltered for a second in their allegiance to Crilodach, but found themselves unable to fully comprehend the enormity of what had happened; wondering for the first time in their long lives, if they looked foolish for following a mere, naked man. If Lilah's objective had been to show Crilodach for what It really was and sow seeds of dissent in the armada, she had succeeded.

Though It hated and feared being touched by anyone in case a new change should take place, Crilodach was glad to have burned the soldier to death. It knew It was being seen by Its troops for what It was and not as they had been used to seeing It, indeed what It had become used to being since that fateful day when Dalved had attacked It. It did not like looking like the men in Its armada any more than they appreciated looking like It. The fact that Lilah was still alive and Its beast-self was caught by Nu-An was revolting to them all. How could It have allowed the enemy to set a trap like that? But just as Frin-Ghirzan felt a change in the air, so did Crilodach, but Its was a change of plan.

Allowing this armada to fight for It, using Its precious energy to drive these men into battle and keep them fighting, was not worthwhile. They had not brought It the Sagitæ. Nothing else mattered. The plans of the bears, which had been centred upon depriving Crilodach of time, had driven a wedge between Crilodach and Its armada more swiftly than anything else they had ever done.

Crilodach knew the beast-like appearance was part of Its power. It revelled in the fear the mere sight of the beast had instilled. A fear that had vanished in the seconds in which It had been split from Its beast-self. It thumped Its fists together and let out frustrated grunts that made no attempt to be words. The split had been Its only option. It did not want to become a man again. It still did not know what Dalved had done to It or how. Its anger could have flooded worlds, the heat of Its nature was as hot as ever and those standing near It had to stand back, avert their eyes and bring their shields up to protect themselves.

The armada did not know yet that much of Its power was locked in Trecrogo, held by Nu-An, a machine which would never move. Or that Trecrogo was hurtling to one place and one place only, Zaqui. The final battle ground where all magic and all matter would meet. Where all the laws would twist and change in death and birth. Crilodach knew Its enemies would sacrifice themselves there rather than let It join once again with Its beast-self. So It now had a choice to fight for Its other body or let go and concentrate on just getting the Sagitæ. Without Its full power that would be even more difficult yet at Zaqui the need for speed and cunning was more useful than raw power. The more It thought the less It wanted Its armada around.

The mood in the armada moved through shock, to resentment, to fear, to slow rebellion. Some muttered softly that if this was truly Crilodach then maybe It was not as powerful as they had been led to believe. Others pointed to the dead man saying that he had been burned up in seconds. They were answered by those who said that was only one man. Others whispered under their breaths one man was enough for them, they did not believe Crilodach the man was weak. Unspoken and unformed ideas were taking shape in their minds. No one with ordinary hands could win the Sagitæ from the spellmaker. If they were to live on, they needed a champion who did not get beaten. Someone who kept Its claws intact. Who was this brittle looking, smooth skinned Crilodach to order them or take the prize from them. More and more said that their defeat was to be expected when this was their leader. They should not follow such a brazen liar. Had It flown after Trecrogo? Had It been able to drag the enemy down? Had It saved Rataplan's life? All It did was curse, rant and kill one of Its own soldiers. Any one of them could do the same. They concluded, more loudly, this man–like Crilodach was not strong enough to win.

The armada began to look to Frin-Ghirzan. What would he do? What would he say as Crilodach strutted around the abyss hurling threats at the vanished fortress and cursing Lilah and a host of other named enemies some of whom the armada knew but many they had never heard of before. This shouting was accomplishing nothing. Crilodach was a man defeated, with no new ideas or places to go. The resentment in the army grew quickly, rippling out into Frin-Ghirzan and the lieutenants, Ferveiss and Jurveiss.

Then some men close to him nudged each other and pointed quietly at Frin-Ghirzan, who looked shocked. He never looked shocked. This man they knew well. There was no soldier in the armada who had not seen him train, had not seem him work until he almost dropped with tiredness. This was a real soldier, strong, born to fight, born to rule. He led from the front. He never gave up. His cursing meant something. They were his troops. This was his armada.

Though these thoughts permeated the whole armada no one dared make a move. They all knew Crilodach could hear their merest whisper but equally they did not stand in complete silence anymore. More and more of them clustered together ready to face Its ire rather than be led into another defeat. Crilodach knew what was happening. Their resentment clothed It like a suffocating straight jacket. It did not care. It no longer believed that the armada had the prowess to bring victory. They, It knew, would never win. And though It was no longer a beast It was also no longer plagued by Dalved's presence. It clenched Its fists.

A light had penetrated their darkness. Everything was changed now their leader was a thin, bony man with grey skin. No claws to tear into flesh. No teeth dripping menace. The only thing that kept anyone from fighting It, was Its apparent indifference to what they thought and Its complete lack of fear of them even though they were in their hundreds of thousands and heavily armed. Even as a man, Crilodach was able to imbue a measure of apprehension if not outright fear.

Crilodach knew the loyalty of Its armada was dead. It had been hoodwinked by Lilah and Trecrogo. It saw that with a few strong allies Lilah had turned the tide in the battle, outwitting It by playing to Its desires and not by breaking Its unmatched military strength. A stone fortress had shown more resilience than Its entire armada. The men lumbered, were weighed down with too much equipment and were not able to improvise. It needed to be lighter. Lightness was speed. Speed was strength. Strength was victory.

Its chest heaved with the huge breaths It was taking as It ranted on. Slowly Its anger subsided as It realized It could do nothing in an instant and slowly Its eyes focussed upon their armour. Its nose once again smelled them. It saw men standing aside to let It pass. A sea of men. It had never really seen them before. Every one of them had a different face. It was surprised to find them so diverse. In the past It had merely told Frin-Ghirzan how many men It wanted and then dispatched them. Rataplan dealt in numbers. It had only met with the brothers because they were the sons of dragons and It hated dragons with every fibre in Its body. Crilodach saw weakness in this difference. If Its men had been stronger Its beast-self would not have been caught in Trecrogo. The success of the trap was their fault.

Crilodach had not foreseen that the fortress was no more than a prison for Its beast-self. A brilliant deception had been played but It also knew that alone of all the Sangyma,

Tegriel knew Its true identity and It must assume that Tegriel's plan did not end here. Tegriel had been there when It became the beast, and now Crilodach was sure his magic had been responsible for the change. It wondered how Freyom and Yaltha were doing. Was anything changing or were these setbacks the result of sending them back in time? It cursed Its luck for not dealing more harshly with the bears when It had had the chance, for not getting to Earth earlier, for not being aware that whilst a living being could not match It muscle to muscle a manufactured one could if they could build such a robot, and they had, with the full knowledge of Its powers. Its anger and hate could not have been greater than at this moment when Its armada seemed a poor substitute for time. Time, the invisible product of energy. It needed time to win. It did not have much left. The universe was dark. It let out a huge yell in a language none knew but the power, passion and frustration in the sound hurt them all to the core. Far away Demeter heard It, and the boy wondered if Chloe's life were worth such a scream from their deadliest enemy.

Finally, It remembered Its general and lieutenants. It needed to plan. But quickly. Quickly. For the last hours mattered and the enemy were prepared. That creature that had touched It in the battle with Tegriel upon Samphin. Had they sent him to that time? Had they planned for It to be a beast all these aeons? It needed to find where the body of the accursed man had gone. It needed to know how his touch had changed It long ago. In that It was sure to find what Tegriel knew and had taught Lilah. They knew everything about that man. That made It bitter, and for once, a little fearful. It had hurt every day of Its existence unable to rid Itself of his closeness. Dead, that man had been Its curse.

It had to be careful. It could not tell Frin-Ghirzan or Hagouti or anyone why It wanted one particular body. Crilodach was sure Its enemies would also be looking for him because whatever power the man possessed might be employed to work against It again. It remembered how that felt. The utter powerlessness It had felt at the touch, the pain of the man against Its skin and how It had fought against him to stop him dissolving into Its skin. The shock of failing. The vile blow from Bofindle. It had taken days before It could stand. Crilodach had had Tegriel on the ropes, It had worked everything out, and then that man had appeared and worse, It had no idea how he had appeared on Samphin. How had he been waiting to pounce? How had Tegriel known? What power did that man possess to have changed Crilodach so completely? Tegriel had kept so quiet none of those Crilodach had tortured knew anything. There were no pictures of him and Crilodach did not know what he looked like. All this time It had feared any man in case he was like Dalved or worse. Nothing Its daughters had done ever revealed the secret.

Finally, Crilodach came upon Rataplan's body. The soldiers around him had lain his broken corpse out and covered him. They stood around him looking at the dead, stern face. Crilodach looked down at the general. It spat on him and ensured the poison gases in him did not seep out too soon.

It saw the men clearing the battlefield. Picking up the dead, awaiting orders to throw them into the depths of space where they would crumble to dust and vanish. Everything that was not fixed to the Rounds was being ripped apart by a terrific force of gravity. It did not want to draw attention to why It was now a man, for none in the armada knew the story. It wanted to keep things that way. It would merely command that any fallen soldier that was not in armour be brought to It. If that man was here It would see him for the first time. Would that make a difference? Was It clutching at straws? Was It tasting uncertainty?

Frin-Ghirzan bent his head and looked at the ground, as he finally joined Ferveiss and Jurveiss, as if he were ashamed. They looked up at him as he approached, for he was now their general. The general whose eyes read Crilodach's thoughts, because they were close to his own. The great general who planned well and expected the best from his men. The general they had always relied upon. They had never been friends. In Crilodach's armada friendship was not something you looked for. Here everyone was out for their own ends, to get on and kill for their master. But at this moment Frin-Ghirzan and his lieutenants were closer in their feelings than they had ever been. All were playing the 'if–only' game in their heads:

If only they had had more men.

If only Hagouti had been successful.

If only they had prepared better.

If only they had realized Gertis had a secret army.

If only they had known earlier that a human had been

cloned.

The death of Copret gave them no satisfaction at all. All the victories they had ever won, suddenly felt bitter in their mouths. As if the bear were laughing at them from the graveless death they had given him. Worst of all, through all those years of assault and pain and effort, had Copret and his friends known the truth about Crilodach? Was this their plan all along? Not only to show Crilodach as It really was but also to show Frin-Ghirzan and Its lieutenants how they had wasted their allegiance? Did Copret know that they had followed a mere man all their lives, whilst the bears had had Bofindle, Sangyma and the spellmakers? Had the Sangyma known? Had the whole universe which Frin-Ghirzan had fought to bring into obedience before Crilodach, really been sniggering behind his back?

As Frin-Ghirzan approached them, they took off their heavy gloves and exercised their clawed hands opening and closing them as if crushing an imaginary throat. They growled unusually low. The Sangyma had one thing in common, he thought, they were steadfast. They were a constant in the sea of change around him. Clever, adept and rigid in their ethics codifying the laws of magic. Sharing their knowledge, not using magic to create their own empires. He had always thought them dreamers. Despite their power he had never taken them seriously. No longer. They had shown themselves to be adaptable, imaginative, intelligent and strong.

The laws of magic effected Crilodach as much as everyone else. Effected this man who was still their leader. All these years the Sangyma had known what Frin-Ghirzan and the others had never known. Even in his victories he had worried some of his enemies had been quietly laughing at him. Now he was certain. They had been planning the greatest change-around in history, knowing that Crilodach was not above the laws. That, for all Its immense power, It too could be brought down. That It was a mirage, a make-believe, a self-creation dominating those around It by the power of their own imaginations. What they thought they saw, they feared. What they saw now was a man. Such a man could be defeated. Such a man was not worthy of leading Frin-Ghirzan's troops. Frin-Ghirzan's growl was unusually low too.

For the first time in his long life he questioned his loyalty. How could he possibly have spent his military career following this unimpressive creature. This man with his grey skin and thin-lidded eyes, frothing at the mouth in an impotent display of anger. This man whose bones looked as if they could be broken by his own clawed grasp; whose head could be split in two by a blow from the most unskilled swordsman. This man who spat upon Its own general. But looks can deceive. Even now, Crilodach was still a force to be reckoned with. Frin-Ghirzan might have felt his stomach wrench at the thought, but right now It was still his commander-in-chief because one thing had not changed. This man was as brutal as Its beast-self had ever been.

"Did you ever know?" he asked Ferveiss.

Frin-Ghirzan was amazed at the audacity he had in asking. As if he could not believe that though he was whispering, he asked such a question out loud. Ferveiss looked at him quickly, and then darted a glance at Crilodach. He knew what Frin-Ghirzan meant. He wanted to reply immediately but you do not get to be a lieutenant in Crilodach's army by speaking too quickly. Lieutenants know without having to say, believe without looking for proofs, and he knew both that Frin-Ghirzan was shocked to speak to him about what he saw at the same time as knowing they could both be killed by Crilodach, where they stood, if It once suspected what was on their minds.

If Crilodach looked at them, their heads close, looking at It with narrowed eyes and furrowed foreheads, speaking in whispers, Its suspicions would be instantly aroused. Man though Crilodach was, Frin-Ghirzan was doubly careful, smelling the smoke from the roasted soldier. So Ferveiss shifted on his feet and walked away saying hurriedly as he went, in a whispered reply,

"No."

"Neither did I," said Jurveiss, who had been scratching his ear as Frin-Ghirzan approached, self conscious about the depths of his own suspicions about Crilodach.

Not seeing exactly what had happened he had caught snippets of words and mutterings from the men as he came towards his cousin and then he had seen Crilodach the man. He had felt sick. All the envy he had ever felt for Crilodach's power, all the fear he had felt, all the sacrifices he had been prepared to make in Its name, vapourized on the over-heated air. What was this? What had happened? Was this a spell cast by Lilah and her cohorts? Had his cousins sacrificed so much for this? Had Arnveiss died for this? He had run to Ferveiss to find the answer and then he heard Frin-Ghirzan. His universe of illusions evaporated like the stars.

Just as suddenly, without a division between his reaching his cousin and the realization that Crilodach was a man, he was stunned to see himself on a boat surrounded by darkness and Irghwols. Aching in pain from his shoulder, with a Tsarbo he had never seen before standing nearby holding a book in his arms that was almost too big for him to carry. Only the book was not a book but vapours and mists that swirled around the äis they floated upon. The smell was of berries and trees he had forgotten he had ever known, from when he was a baby and could not even speak. Deep memories that layers of training had overpowered but never extinguished. Then just as suddenly the vision vanished and he was himself again still marching beside his cousin but as in a dream because he had no recollection of his legs moving or of how far they had walked together. He looked at Ferveiss. He could see he had also seen something. Been part of something. They shivered.

"Are you with us," asked Frin-Ghirzan, as if he had been asking him several times.

"Sorry?" queried Jurveiss.

"How many times do you need to be asked?" said an exasperated Frin-Ghirzan.

"You suddenly looked as if you'd seen a ghost," Ferveiss replied.

"I'm ... alright."

And then Crilodach called for his new general Frin-Ghirzan to come to It. Even the voice was different. Rough, loud but reedy. Powerful but no longer backed by huge lungs that could roar across planets. This was too much for them to take in all at once, as if Crilodach's change to a man had changed something inside all of them. Frin-Ghirzan's question to Jurveiss, about why his men were not helping clear the Rounds, went unanswered.

Frin-Ghirzan turned his steps towards Crilodach, giving them all time to talk for a few seconds for nothing was untoward in Its general and lieutenants coming to talk to It as a group after the battle. Such a walk was not even unusual. What else should they be doing but making their way towards their Commander-in-Chief.

"Crilodach's change has affected you too," Frin-Ghirzan

asked Jurveiss.

"I don't know, I think probably no more than anyone else, but I suddenly thought I was somewhere else. Or a part of me was."

"Somewhere else?" asked Frin-Ghirzan.

"Yes, almost as if I wasn't here."

"I know exactly what you mean," replied his cousin.

Frin-Ghirzan looked at him and stopped marching. He knew of the connection between dragons but he also knew Ferveiss' and Jurveiss' fathers were in a place that could not be reached. But these were strange times and if beasts could be men, then prisons were no longer the prisons they once were even if they were Xibalba. His suspicions were raised. Three dragons were a formidable enemy at the best of times, but those three were special. If they took over their son's minds they would lessen his chances of success.

"If you have any more such visions I want to know," he demanded.

"I'm sorry general, the visions lasted but a moment," said Jurveiss.

"I want to know. You will tell me immediately. That's an order."

"Yes sir."

"Why are illusions so important?" Ferveiss asked.

"I'll decide what is and what isn't important."

Ferveiss made no answer but the sudden stiffening of his back was answer enough. He might be angry but he was a soldier who obeyed orders.

"And stop your men muttering. I don't like the feel of the armada right now," he added.

"An armada needs a leader," said Jurveiss.

"We have one," replied Frin-Ghirzan.

"A leader they can trust to deliver," added Ferveiss.

Ferveiss made no bones about what he meant for he was looking directly at Crilodach as he spoke. The words hanged between them until coming out of the air around them Hagouti materialized. Jurveiss and Ferveiss grabbed at the swords but they stopped before they drew but they did not let go of the hilts. Frin-Ghirzan just looked at them with such anger that they took their hands fully away. His eyes said everything. What were they thinking? To fight here in front of Crilodach. What better way to inform It of their thoughts. The glare also threatened that Frin-Ghirzan would fell them where they stood if they dared to strike at Hagouti. They stood back and waited to find out if Hagouti had heard their seditious talk.

Hagouti smiled at the new general's glare which he, too, understood. He was not to be killed by the likes of Ferveiss and Jurveiss. Half formed, the vapours floated around his legs and Jurveiss seemed to think the vapour looked like the mist around the book he had seen in that strange Tsarbo's hands in his vision. The half–smile, looking awkward on his sallow face, reminded Frin-Ghirzan of an old adage he had heard on a planet run by humans long ago, 'like death warmed up.'

"You still have your wits Frin," Hagouti congratulated him, using his nickname for the general that the general hated, "Makes up for what you lack in military skills."

"We're tired, the battle has been long, I've no time for your butter–cunning," said Frin-Ghirzan.

"What's tiredness to Crilodach or Crilodach's armada? You've never complained of tiredness before. Perhaps you should be replaced," argued Hagouti.

"You don't get to choose who commands here," snapped Ferveiss.

"Others have been replaced," Hagouti said.

"I don't need lessons from you. Nor your ice–jibes at Crilodach," snapped Frin-Ghirzan.

"Did I jibe at Crilodach, my maker and master?" asked Hagouti.

"Don't test my patience," argued Frin-Ghirzan, "I've never heard a word from you that didn't have two meanings."

"I'm as my master made me. Though my master seems unmade," Hagouti said.

"When will you turn into someone else, grave–eater?" asked Jurveiss.

"Is that your problem?" asked Hagouti, sweeping round to glare at him. "You don't like how our master has changed?"

"What we like or don't is no concern of yours," snapped Ferveiss.

"Perhaps the changes you see around you have unsettled your fighting spirit," said Hagouti, adding, "Even made you think the unthinkable."

"What would death know about our thoughts?" asked Frin-Ghirzan.

"There are ways to regain what you think you've lost, Frin,

many ways," offered Hagouti.

"What have I lost?" Frin-Ghirzan demanded.

"Your sense of power. Your need for might. Certainty. Even Rataplan is a loss right now you could do without."

"You seem to be doing a lot of thinking for me mist-walker," replied Frin-Ghirzan.

"I can help you," offered Hagouti.

"What can you do to help us?" growled Frin-Ghirzan.

"You admit you need help," said Hagouti.

"We admit nothing," snapped Ferveiss.

"Your betters are talking Ferveiss be quiet." snapped back Hagouti.

"Enough! Speak or go Hagouti. I've no time for your oily tongue," said Frin-Ghirzan.

"I've been closer to Crilodach than any of you. I know his mind in a way you couldn't even guess. I might even explain what's happened in terms even you could grasp," revealed Hagouti.

"So we come to the truth," said Jurveiss, "death wants to be our comrade."

"I'm merely voicing what's in your minds, after all this wouldn't be the first time you've replaced a leader."

"You'd seek to replace Crilodach with yourself, grave-eater," sneered Jurveiss.

"I'm not leader enough," said Hagouti, "I don't even look like as a leader does, do I?" he sneered. His head and shoulders vanished and swirled around them coming to form again by Frin-Ghirzan's side.

"What do you mean by that?" demanded the new general.

"Don't try to play the fool with me," Hagouti replied.

His legs took shape enabling him to walk around the three of them as he spoke whilst still remaining mostly a putrid, smelling wisp of mist. His face appearing and disappearing, coming close up to each of them as he spoke. He was dancing around them. He knew Crilodach was watching but the mist he created kept Crilodach from seeing exactly how their lips moved or what they said. Not that It was thinking of needing to know. Rebellion was far from Its thoughts at this moment. So far that It did not pay particular attention to Its new general. After all It had now decided what to do with the armada and since It had no more use for them they were all as good as dead.

"Do you think I can't hear you when you can't see me?"

251

goaded Hagouti, "Do you think Crilodach can't read your thoughts when Its minded to? Even now as you go to It, It knows what you've half–planned. Half–wished. It knows the questions you're asking yourselves as you look on It. Is It as powerful as It was? Is It as strong? Can you challenge It? Will you try to betray It and take the Sagitæ for yourselves?" Hagouti spoke with conviction. Knowing, even fearing, that Lilah heard him too. But somehow he liked what he was doing. He wanted Crilodach to fall. For the first time in his long life he knew he could choose a side. Though neither side wanted him.

"You've become a gossip grave–eater," snapped Ferveiss.

"He's right," nodded Frin-Ghirzan. "Crilodach knows us better than we know ourselves. We either stick with It or fight It now."

"Fight It," Jurveiss looked at his general. "Do you have any idea what you're suggesting?"

"Of course he does," replied Hagouti. "He makes perfect sense. Crilodach has betrayed us all."

"I despise you Hagouti," answered Frin-Ghirzan.

"Nonetheless, Frin, the thoughts come don't they?" smiled Hagouti.

"Just look at him, a man, no more than one of us," responded Jurveiss, "bested by Lilah and her fortress. When It left Damkina I thought we'd be supreme. I didn't think anything would be able to stand against us. They ripped away Its beast. Its not even worthy of armour."

"Despite the dangers, Frin," smirked Hagouti, "they're almost decided."

"If we take Crilodach on now we could all die," warned Frin-Ghirzan.

"The whole armada looks to you now," said Hagouti, "They all share the surprise to find Crilodach was a man all this time pretending to be some beast. Not even a man as tall as you Jurveiss with your dragon father, nor with an arm as strong as yours Frin with your endless military training. A man you've followed believing It to be so much more than a man."

"What do you know of my father?" asked Jurveiss.

"More than you, of that you may be sure. I may even know where he is," Hagouti suggested.

"Silence Jurveiss, you've one father and that's Crilodach don't forget that," ordered Frin-Ghirzan.

"Fathers can change," replied Jurveiss, who had never answered Frin-Ghirzan back before. The new general turned on Hagouti suddenly aware of the depth of danger his talk was taking them all towards.

"Why are you here Hagouti?" he demanded, "To spy on us? To betray us to Crilodach? To taunt us?"

"Come Frin, surely we need to take stock of your position. The enemy is strong but their strength isn't what we should think about but their mission. They've beaten us back twice. Time runs thin and with time Crilodach's promises vanish."

"Their mission is to take control of the Sagitæ before we do. To stop Crilodach from living for eternity, to break our backs and strip us of our power. If we can't defeat them with Crilodach as our commander, we'd never have success without It," argued Frin-Ghirzan.

"Their mission, Frin, is to remain free and nothing less. Its mission is to get life for Itself. You think any of them care about you? Do you think our enemies even care about themselves? We're fighting the enemy of enemies. These people have been trained to be selfless just as you trained your troops to be utterly selfish, thinking that was the way to make them strong. These people are free to go, but they didn't go; instead they stood upon Trecrogo and defied us. They bubbled up from the ground. They stand in their own right against everything you've worked to create and so far they're winning. They don't quake before you, they don't tremble at your words or hide from your weapons. They're children, animals, magicians ... they're at your feet and throat and stand before you defiant to the end. Did you see Copret die? Did you see how he accepted his death wishing only to protect Chloe? Did you see how she, a child, a female child, fought? Even Crilodach's own daughters could not have fought so well at her age. These people are made strong by their absolute commitment to what they believe, not by the orders they've been given. That's the real strength we lack."

"You've become quite a little speech maker since we last met Hagouti," growled Ferveiss, "What's changed you?"

"Maybe your time in the spellmaker's clutches has changed more than your words grave–eater. Maybe you seek new allegiances," said Jurveiss.

"My time there was torture Jurveiss, as I'm sure you're pleased to know. I wasn't allowed to become a mist and I was stuck in a prison cell made by the bears. Anything that's changed in me changed a few minutes ago when I saw ... that."

He pointed in front of them towards Crilodach. They all focussed ahead of them. For truth–to–tell they had not stopped walking towards Crilodach the whole time they talked though they were not actually looking where they were going. They were vaguely aware of their men making a hole for them to walk through but they were not hurrying. Not that they did not want to reach Crilodach quickly, but they instinctively knew that by the time they reached It they had to have come to a decision. To die fighting Lilah or to die fighting Crilodach. Even with the pain of defeat and the shock of Crilodach's change the decision did not come easily to them.

"Crilodach's never given in, I always admired that about It," commented Jurveiss, "It'll not share the prize you're right there. We'll be left to die. Crilodach is as much our enemy as Lilah and her cohorts."

"I don't follow It for the prize but for the power I have," snarled Frin-Ghirzan. "And I won't see that power threatened whilst I've breath."

Frin-Ghirzan already wanted to rebel but he did not want to be the one who suggested the action. Had Rataplan been alive this conversation would have ended here. He would never have rebelled openly or sacrificed everything without any gain. But the armada was being led by others who were already forgetting about Rataplan.

"Power It gives you," pointed out Hagouti, "without It you're nothing. Spite It and very soon you'll have nothing. Don't spite It and Zaqui will take your lives as easily as you squash an ant."

"I can still break your neck claw-stealer," threatened Frin-Ghirzan.

"Think of having that power in another universe with no Crilodach. Wouldn't that be more power than you've ever dreamt of?" Hagouti asked him.

"More power than you can give," observed Jurveiss.

"True, but gifts sometimes depend only upon which side you choose. Why not use your natural talents for your own ends for a change?"asked Hagouti.

"Are you suggesting ..." began Frin-Ghirzan.

"Nothing more than what you're thinking," smiled

Hagouti, "nothing more."

"Grave-eater, I should rip you into shreds where you stand," said Ferveiss.

"You should, but you won't." He vanished into his gaseous form and his voice added, "I wonder why?"

He wafted across the army thinking to himself how best to play the situation in his favour. Lilah was a strange one. He could not fathom her at all. Had she let him go, thinking he would do her work? He had to be careful. He might find in playing Frin-Ghirzan and the others against Crilodach he was not serving his own ends but hers. But how do you out-think a spellmaker? He had to be very devious. He knew the times were rushing together, Zaqui was upon them and old alliances meant little in the chaos around them. For all his bluster and plotting he knew he could be blown apart as fast as anyone else unless he had help. But who would help death to live? Hagouti, knowing no one wanted him, had chosen his own side. Himself.

"Frin-Ghirzan," said Crilodach, as they finally arrived at Its side.

The new general stood before a man he could look in the eye. For the first time he thought that if Crilodach went to strike him he would fight back. He wondered if he could draw blood from this grey, sweaty skin beneath which the veins branched out across the body. He had never thought like this before. He had oozed fear before the beast. Made that extra effort when he had felt all his muscles would give way if he swung another blow. If the only way to the enemy was over a mountain he had climbed that mountain, fearing Crilodach's anger if he didn't. Now he was thinking Crilodach could lose this war and if It did, how the armada could still win something despite Its failure. The scars with which Crilodach had lacerated his body felt sharper than usual. In a strange way he envied Rataplan's death. He was free. Jurveiss and Ferveiss who had stood in front of It but a few hours before trembling at their defeat, lacerated by Its tongue, now stood in front of It with an armada at their backs that It did not control. Still, something more was needed to start the rebellion properly. The visions of Jurveiss, the disbelief of Frin-Ghirzan, the goading of Hagouti, the shock of Ferveiss, and the revulsion of the armada, would not be enough. But Crilodach Itself would light the final spark. For in common with all those who cease to feel for those around them, they act without regard for the suffering of those closest to them. Soldiers don't need magic to rebel but only an unheeded wish, an indigestible command or a thoughtless action. Given one of those they will hazard any odds and face certain annihilation just to be heard and treated as equals.

"What do I do with the armada?" asked Frin-Ghirzan. He expected orders. Details of the next push against the enemy. He expected deployment and action.

"Do what you wish," replied Crilodach, annoyed that Frin-Ghirzan had even mentioned the soldiers, "They're of no use to me."

"We can't go against Trecrogo without the armada," complained Jurveiss.

"I don't need any advice on tactics," replied Crilodach.

"I ... I'm sorry," said the lieutenant.

"I didn't ask for an apology either. No wonder your cousin is dead you were always a mealy mouthed trio. I knew nothing would come of Frin-Ghirzan wasting good time with you. Dragons have always been a foul species."

Jurveiss controlled his anger as he always had around Crilodach but his blood pumped strongly, and his head felt explosive. Ferveiss was also angry at the jibe but he stood very still. Hagouti's words echoed in his brain. The visions of an äis in the darkness were with him all the time as he began to realize what they meant. And instead of being angry that his father was travelling towards him to kill him, he was glad.

"The fewer I take with me the better," growled Crilodach.

"Isn't going against Trecrogo with a few, where hundreds of thousands have failed, reckless?" questioned Frin-Ghirzan.

"Hundreds of thousands did this to me. Do you think this would have happened if I'd been less occupied with Grafiers, Brujans or hidden hordes of cockroaches?"

"What exactly has happened?" asked the general.

"Where do you get the gall to ask that of me?" It snapped.

"I ask because I don't understand."

"What have you ever understood?"

"Your orders," he answered It.

"Then my orders are to carry on without the armada."

"We leave the men here," asked Jurveiss, "to die?"

"You can stay with them if you want. I need killers with

me or no one."

"You'd go alone?" asked Frin-Ghirzan.

"Rataplan was weak but at least he acted on my decisions immediately," Crilodach hissed then he shouted out, "Hagouti! Hagouti!"

"Yes," said Hagouti, spiralling into form near his master's shoulder. Crilodach looked at Hagouti with fire in his eyes.

"What have they been whispering about?"

"What do you mean?" asked Hagouti.

"What is this, are you all sleep-walking?"

"Who do you want to take with you?" asked Frin-Ghirzan, trying to ease Its fury.

"I'll show you who I want. I want those who live after fighting me. Come on who's first, who's first to feel my might?" It challenged.

No one moved though many wanted to. Crilodach marched around them and they turned to face It as It circled them. Something they had never done before. Not a man had a hand near a weapon.

"You can talk revolt but you can't summon up the courage to do a thing against me. I should have trained you all myself. There might not be much left of you but what there was would fight me now."

"We don't want to revolt," interceded Frin-Ghirzan, "we only want to understand so we know how to make you better."

"You think I'm ill?" It asked.

"We don't know why you're a man," said Frin-Ghirzan.

"I was always a man but idiots like you follow beasts more readily than men."

"We'd always have followed you," Jurveiss told him.

"Only because behind me is the safest place for nobodies like you. Come on Jurveiss, let's see you strike first."

Crilodach turned Its back on Its commanders and stared ahead. It saw Frin-Ghirzan grab Jurveiss' arm to stop him from trying to do anything. It saw many of the armada lean forward and hold their position watching their general. It saw Hagouti look at Frin-Ghirzan and Frin-Ghirzan held his gaze. It saw Ferveiss with visions crossing his eyes. Without looking It saw all and It knew. It knew they hated It enough to try. It looked at the men in front of It and their weakness dripped out of them, distilled in their sweat. Yes they were fearsome, yes they could quell whole planets but against

Bofindle and Trecrogo they were next to useless. Lilah knew that. Capable generals could sacrifice one part of their territory to save the rest, and that was what Tegriel had done. The planets Crilodach had conquered were not gains, but gifts. The real places of power like Ruzniel and Earth were defended or hidden from It. It looked on the armada and saw what Its enemies saw. Nothing but numbers. It turned back after a long few minutes. It spoke to Jurveiss,

"Lack of courage, strong enough daggers or support?" It asked him.

"I only live to serve," the lieutenant replied, bowing his head and wanting to tear into Crilodach with his every sinew as he felt his father, Clevian, dying from the battle with the Irghwols.

"We'll not be left behind!" shouted a solitary voice from the ranks of the armada. Crilodach looked behind Its commanders at the army and told them,

"You'll do as you're ordered and when we've completed the task we'll return to get you."

Even as the words left his mouth everyone who heard them and everyone who was told them knew that Crilodach was lying. They did not believe in this man who ranted at Trecrogo but did not pursue their enemy. The armada had already invented ten different reasons why It was a man, why what had happened in the fortress had happened and why none of their comrades had escaped.

"I remember at Sindal Hills how we defeated an entire battalion with six men. If we could pull that off we can win today," said Frin-Ghirzan.

"I recall that too, but Trecrogo is hardly in the same category. They've designed this fortress to perfection. Look what they did to you," added Jurveiss.

"What did they do to me?" asked Crilodach, menacingly.

"You can't deny you're changed," replied Frin-Ghirzan.

"I've changed back to what I was."

"A big change," observed Jurveiss.

"Think that makes me weaker? I'd break any and all of you."

"We never ..." began Ferveiss.

"Spare me your excuses. I'm not interested. This armada is meaningless. Of the thousands inside the fortress I doubt one will manage to so much as graze the skin of a single foe. We must move and move quickly. Hagouti, Hagouti where are you?"

"Here."

"Stop disappearing when I'm talking."

Hagouti winced and his eyes watered. He knew Crilodach had already decided all their fates.

"I want to know more about Trecrogo. Everything you learned," It ordered Hagouti.

"I wasn't there long, I mayn't know enough."

"What's with you? I made you, I know what you're capable of knowing." It stopped and looked at them. It sneered. "You want me to prove I'm still the leader of leaders. Am I still as capable and mighty? Am I the demon you feared? I care nothing for what you want. Follow me or go."

"You can't leave the armada here," said Frin-Ghirzan

"Can't?" It hissed.

"I say can't. You must take them. At the very least they can form a diversion."

"You dare question me," raged Crilodach.

"I dare," said Frin-Ghirzan.

The men who moved closer to Crilodach may just have been going to move away from It and took a step to ease the crush from behind them. They may have been going to protect It from Frin-Ghirzan who squared up to Crilodach as if they were equals. They may have been going to attack It. They may have just wanted to move a bit as only one in the armada had been saying or doing anything since the general and Crilodach started talking, and more and more men from the outer rim of the army had pushed in bringing the closest soldiers even closer.

Whatever the reason It cut them down with one swing of Its hand. Cruel speed. Slicing through armour like cream, and as they fell the troops behind them feared they were next and instinctively defended themselves. Ranks closed, weapons were thrown, shields were up, then the whole armada moved forwards with those at the back pushing forward not seeing what was happening to those in the front.

Like ants swarming over their prey, as if a scent had been left on Crilodach's body they could not ignore and had to bite, the armada swarmed with crushing force against It. Where It stood became a mass of bodies and blood endlessly frothed upwards and outwards, like a bubbling vat of fat growing too hot. Frin-Ghirzan took out his sword and ordered them to stop but no one was listening. Jurveiss was pushed aside. Ferveiss joined in the fight. The army knew they were nothing but dross to be thrown to one side when It had finished with them, but they would finish with It.

The surge went on. Crilodach grew tired of the smell of Its own men and lifting Its uncut arms It swept with broad arm strokes as if reaping. Men fell for as far as the eye could see. Rising above the crowd of bodies, sweeping one way and another until only his commanders were standing. Within seconds all that Lilah and the others had stood against, every soldier, was dead. Ferveiss lay wounded with his men. Seeing him lying there, Jurveiss lunged at Crilodach.

Crilodach held the lieutenant with Its hand taking the full force of the blow of the sword which could not cut into the skin. Frin-Ghirzan swiped at Its side and It held him with Its other hand in a vice from which the general could not even squirm, and then Ferveiss with his last strength lunged, only to be held in mid air by the power of Crilodach's mind, unable to move or get any closer. It held the three of them, Its mightiest warriors, like puppets. Far away Eldet saw the whole thing and Ferveiss let out a roar as of a dragon. Crilodach knew the dragon brothers were free. Another twist in Its heart. Another plot of the Sangyma falling upon It like hail.

The armada was destroyed. The Rounds vapourized with the bodies, and the atoms in formation funnelled away into the distance, like water going down a storm drain, towards Zaqui.

"See that," snapped Crilodach, "that's where we're all going. But my commanders are weak, infantile men who saw the beast but don't see the beast in the man and so fall at the finish."

It dropped Its hands and the three of them fell back. Hagouti trembled at Crilodach's feet, not daring to move. Crilodach made them all look at It and Its eyes bore into their brains, burning away all sense of self, all sense of freedom, all thoughts and doubts. The eyes overwhelmed their minds until Crilodach was in their brains and there It put Its Lazab.

They didn't take long to overcome the minds of Its commanders, and soon virtually nothing of who they were remained. Crilodach released them from Its gaze and they got up, changed and enhanced. Frin-Ghirzan was given two more arms, detached from his body but able to fight just as well as his own two arms. Jurveiss was given back the fire of his dragon self which burned out his teeth immediately because the Lazab could not control the fire properly. Crilodach bent down and ripped out a tooth from Ferveiss and plunged his hand into the bodies of his army retrieving Rataplan. He replaced his spine with the tooth and the old general stood again. A copper-coloured ooze now issued from Rataplan which could dissolve anything with the merest touch. His eyes were two stones. His body as cold as marble. So would a dead general and his dead lieutenants fight again.

None of them felt any pain. Crilodach controlled them yet they moved independently of their commander-in-chief. Not a step slower or a whit weaker. It told Its mind-imps what It wanted them to do.

"Hagouti," he said slowly.

"Yes."

"Why didn't you warn me of their treachery?"

"I didn't know," he lied.

"You talked with them before coming over to me."

"They don't confide in me, they hate me. I told you, from always they hated me. If they planned anything I'd never know."

Crilodach looked at Its creation.

"Did Lilah promise you anything?" It asked.

"What could she offer that would interest me?" asked Hagouti. He was certain Crilodach knew but his real astonishment at the question saved his existence for Crilodach assumed this idea was new to him. It did not notice Hagouti quaked because he was always squirming when he was not a mist.

"I don't trust you," Crilodach told him.

"I don't trust you but I do fear you," Hagouti admitted.

"A pity the armada didn't share your feelings."

"You pity those you've killed? You never used to."

"Keep your tongue to yourself," said Crilodach, "I don't want to hear another word about how changed I am."

They stood upon the last of the Rounds. Crilodach turned towards the final showdown with Lilah. The place where the last of all life would be found. The three Sagitæ would have to be there.

Crilodach had his last army. As a man, in charge of these five fighters, with a close-quarters fight to the death, It was as devious as ever. But It knew It was not quite as powerful.

Hidden, watching everything, Lilah spoke softly, whilst far away Eldet wiped his eyes with the softest part of his huge, front feet and quietly promised his nephew and son an end to their suffering.

Pashtul's Secret

On the Onäis, lying flat on his stomach, his muscles tense and his nerves steady, Tethval looked at the sea of moving bodies that made up the remnant of Crilodach's armada. Though remnant was a ridiculous description for so many. They did not mill around as crowds that have no purpose move. There was still a good deal of discipline in their ranks. All the captains doing their work with the minimum of orders. Just like Frin-Ghirzan though not from as close, he, too, felt the mood of these troops. From his hiding place in the darkness of space watching them every second, breathing so softly in case he should give himself away, he thought he was watching an armada preparing for more fighting.

The wounded along with the dead, were being thrown into the darkness without a second glance. Like all the soldiers in Crilodach's armada the dying knew to shout out or ask for mercy was useless. They fell into space as they were tossed over the edge of the Rounds without a sound, carrying their deaths in much the same way as they had carried their weapons; with bitterness. The grimaces of pain from the wounded as they were thrown away were not lost on Tethval. If they had not been an implacable enemy who had wiped out thousands of his own people he would have whispered something to Lilah about the cruelty being shown to them; how shameful to treat anything living in such a way. He kept silent. He knew what they were like to face in battle. He quietly gave thanks for Trecrogo's weapons that had wounded them, and the fact that their numbers, though still immense, would be less in the next bout of fighting.

Lilah had told him to speak in his thoughts alone. He was not too sure why he was with her watching the armada. He noticed Demeter's face, when he had departed with the fortress, was like stone and Mojolo had looked as if she were in great pain. He could not help them. Each person had to deal with the losses and struggles of war in their own way.

He did not mind being chosen by Lilah for this task because he respected her. He even thought he understood what a spellmaker was but that might have been a residue of the magic scattered by Bofindle. There was only one man who truly understood Lilah and right now he was far, far away fighting for his life with Eldet. He was struggling with all his might to get to Lilah knowing all he would find was more fighting, more bloodshed. Not because his love made sense of everything, not because his love lessened his pain, but because his love had become his only focus. The only emotion he had left. The strongest thought in his reason.

The broken siege engines were also discarded in like fashion by the armada, misshapen pieces of metal and stone tumbling over and over with the soldiers like so much rubbish. The work that had gone into making them, the effort that had brought them into the battle, all vanishing swiftly to Zaqui. The men who carried out these tasks were automatons. Occasionally they would spit on the ground but none spoke. Something was happening to them even as he watched and he searched the scene like a good hunter, eagerly looking for the reason to explain the change.

He did not know why yet, but Tethval could tell that even as he looked the fight had begun to go out of them. The dream that had kept them focussed on their slaughter had shifted. They were not waiting for another battle but for answers. A sense of calm was everywhere, mixed in with the eddies of warm air on his forehead and across his eyes. On these waves of heat came a smell they had not had in the battle. Like rotten meat. Worse. He was fascinated by what he was sensing and exhilarated by being so close to the enemy without their knowledge. There was no ambush this time. He had time to watch. They were not looking in his direction. No look-outs were posted. The armada did not expect spies to be nearby. He would have posted look-outs. You always expect an attack when on a campaign. What could possibly have happened to Crilodach's commanders for them to forget such a basic principle of war?

"What's that smell?" he thought. Lilah, close by, answered without looking at him,

"Crilodach still scorched with the burning separation from Its beast-self."

"Why didn't we smell that before now?"

"The smell takes time to waft across the armada."

"Even Its smell is vile," thought Tethval.

"It did not choose to lose Its beast-self. That was Its

264

answer to our surprise imprisonment. I was hoping Trecrogo would be Its death–knell but the fight goes on."

"That can't be helped," he answered her.

"The weakness in all plans is that events are changeable."

"Its still in control of the armada."

"That is not particularly good for us. At the very least we have shaken a little of that self–confidence It always shows, but I doubt that is enough. I can hear It ranting."

"I can't see what they have done with Rataplan's body."

"I am more curious as to what It looks like now. I cannot see anything unusual, can you?"

"They're clearing the battleground, getting ready for the orders, I presume. Nothing more."

Lilah, who was kneeling low in the darkness, had one hand on the Onäis to keep her balance as they moved around in the dark, always shadowing the sea of men, always facing them. She shook her head slowly and pursed her lips.

"I am not sure," she answered him. "There seems to be a restlessness in them I do not yet understand."

"Like they've been deflated."

"Almost. Then again I sense an anger that could only come from Crilodach."

"One minute I thought they were getting ready to fight us and then, they changed. Now they don't feel ready to continue to fight us at all."

"Someone is getting ready for something otherwise why throw out the wounded and the dead?" she thought.

"Do you think they expect us to attack?"

"I have no idea, that is why I am also watching and looking for Frin-Ghirzan. If anything happens now the action will come from him."

"But you said Crilodach is still there, isn't It their leader?"

"Frin-Ghirzan is now their general, he is the one they see fighting day after day. He is the one who gets them food, walks their ranks. Crilodach just terrifies them."

"Wouldn't we do better back on Trecrogo?"

"No, my brother and Demeter can take care of things there and anything Rimfelder brings when he arrives. I want to keep a close eye on It for a while. I also need to keep tabs on Hagouti. I hear him moving about. Something has piqued his interest. Let's move over and upward we will get a better view from there."

"What are Crilodach's choices now anyway with Its beast–

self locked in the fortress?"

"It is weaker but still dangerous enough to get the better of us if we lower our guard. This setback won't change Its strategy."

She lay Bofindle on the Onäis and lay flat without taking her eyes off the armada,

"It will be angry but I have a feeling the first thing It has to do is make sure of the loyalty of Its troops," she thought. "Ah, there, see." He looked where she pointed. "I see some smoke. A man has been burned to ashes. And there, see, a space in the middle of the smoke where none of the armada are standing. I know Crilodach is in there. I wish I could see more clearly."

"Last time I saw Crilodach It stood high above Its armada like a mountain, now Its dwarfed by Its own men." Tethval's thought was muted, almost as if he were whispering.

"Things are not always as they seem. There. Look. The man Itself."

Tethval looked and they both saw the naked man ranting and shouting. Lilah, using her powers, made Its voice ring more clearly and Tethval, looking towards the middle of the armada saw Rataplan's dead body. He touched Lilah's arm and pointed. Frin-Ghirzan was marching through the ranks. She nodded. Now they had a clear view of the players.

"Crilodach was challenged by a single soldier," she explained, "There you are. That is what we have been feeling, their anger at finding Crilodach is just a man. Now then Frin-Ghirzan, let's see you do something."

"How can he do anything and not be killed?" thought Tethval.

"For certain that will be on his mind. There's Ferveiss and Jurveiss with him. What an interesting conversation they must be having. I can almost taste the words."

"And your spy?"

"You can always rely upon Hagouti to take advantage of any situation. He talks to them. Jurveiss is distracted. I know why. Rimfelder is doing his work."

"I am glad my friend is still alive."

"He thinks you dead. The lieutenants do not know why Crilodach is not marching off after the enemy, eager for blood as always, leaving them to follow as best they can. The battle has stalled. They have been hurt. They are stunned by Crilodach's appearance. Listen you can hear their questioning:

'Is this defeat or is this part of Its plan?'

'Is It weaker now?'

'How powerful is the spellmaker to change It?'

Crilodach had to kill one of Its own. They cannot believe what they see. Frin-Ghirzan now suspects we always knew It was a man. He thinks we have played him for a fool. His pride is hurt. Rebellion is in all their hearts."

"So quickly. After so many years of fighting when they followed Crilodach to the death?"

"It taught Its troops to hate without reason, such hate can turn in seconds. You see they look on It now as more of an equal than before. What is to stop one of them being the commander–in–chief if Crilodach is just like them?"

"They don't have the power," doubted Tethval.

"But the power exists. What if Frin-Ghirzan had a Sagitæ? Could Crilodach stand up to him then?" He looked at Lilah as she thought this and then back at the armada,

"Just because It appears to be a man they think they can successfully challenge It?" he asked.

"If we are lucky. Certainly they are unhappy right now, but they are also unsure. Remember they have only known the beast and they have spent lifetimes being scared of Its power. The armada will not move in open revolt unless they can see It is weaker or unless Frin-Ghirzan moves against It."

"What chance do you think there really is that they'll fight It for us?" he countered.

"Eventually, they all would betray It, if they thought they had a chance to live forever. Who is faster in betrayal, that is the only question, Crilodach or Its new general. I would not back the armada."

"Are you thinking what I'm thinking?"

"Knowing you Tethval you think we should plan an attack on Crilodach as soon as we can and show It to be weaker than It used to be. That way we might initiate the rebellion against It and we can leave them to kill each other."

"You sound sceptical."

"Surrounded by Its armada It will not be easy to get too and futile for us to call them to help us fight It. We are still the enemy. They would instinctively attack us. If they are

267

thinking about rebelling, It will know, and act. If they are going to fight each other I am not going to give them a reason not to by giving them us to fight."

"So we wait."

"For the moment."

"Stuck on an Onäis not daring to show ourselves isn't my kind of fighting," he thought.

"I will have need of your eyes before we leave."

"So, you do have a plan?"

"I would not be lying here without one," she told him.

Tethval looked at the thin, gaunt, naked man who marched amongst Its men sneering as It went. Even as a man Crilodach showed Itself to be filled with a natural disdain, which poured out of It for Its own men as much as for everyone else. Tethval could not understand why any one would follow a leader who treated them that way.

"That's the torment of the universe?" he thought to himself.

"Its original self," she replied.

"I'm not surprised It created a beast to hide inside."

"It did not choose to be a beast. The beast came to It because It had to fight to survive. Because of something that happened that even Tegriel, who was there, was at a loss to explain."

"Survive? I thought It was invincible."

"It can be hurt and It was. But Its fearsome reputation was enhanced by the fact It built Damkina and never appeared again. Making such a terrible name of the once beautiful Samphin. A place to fear, with a hidden labyrinth below from which none ever escaped. Kalevala, the first of the spellmakers was there that day. He limped all his life from the wounds he received. He said a man touched Crilodach. A man changed It."

"Another great magician?"

"No. No one really knew him. He seemed weak and powerless. In fact when Kalevala first met with him he thought he was working with Crilodach. Shows how wrong first impressions can be."

"Anyone who can make Crilodach afraid is worth knowing."

"There lies the problem we do not know him and we do not know what power he used. Kalevala knew his name but would never tell. Something about changing the future, he said. Tegriel also said something about keeping the name a secret from Crilodach. But I have always wanted to find out."

"Is that why we're here? Are we waiting for him?"

"I am working in the dark here. Tegriel said whatever the magic was the man fused with Crilodach. Possibly, now Crilodach has split in two, the man has also separated from It. We just have to wait to see if we get a chance to find out and finally solve a mystery as deep as the magic in the Sagitæ."

"You think he's down there?"

"Whatever was done to him we have undone. Crilodach is a man again. If that man exists who touched It, and I can find another weapon for our arsenal in him, I fully intend to."

"All these stories, all this power and all this fighting. Amazing to think I'd never heard of Crilodach before we met you."

"It was coming your way sooner or later, time merely caught up with us all. There were a few we managed to keep free of It."

"We were only spared because of the work of the Sangyma?" asked Tethval.

"You were not spared. The tyrant was Its machine. Ah! they go to It. Look how they are walking slowly like men suspicious, unsure of their place. Hagouti is a wisp of smoke. Their hearts rebellious. I wish I could get closer."

"It wounded you last time you got close. Are you sure we can take the risk."

"I am rarely sure of anything. They never held so much as a single class on certainty on Ruz."

"That I can't believe."

"When you came out of your mines to fight against the city did you know if you would win?"

"No. We just knew we had to fight."

"It does not know either. Certainty is a fiction the powerful instil in the powerless. And such certainty has begun to leave Its general and lieutenants. They were always so sure of themselves. How satisfied I feel to see them uncertain. How Copret would have enjoyed this sight." She clenched her hand, now Copret's claw, as if sharing the moment.

"Well I can see the reason, they're strong men. Crilodach as a man doesn't look like It could take much punishment."

"You are deceived by looks. I just told you a man who looked weak turned Crilodach into a beast."

269

"How do we recognize him?"

"All I have to go on are the snippets Tegriel told me."

"What are they?"

"There was a battle when Tegriel first met Crilodach. On the fields that were to become Damkina."

"That's the Rounds in front of us?"

"What's left. Crilodach plundered the planet for buildings and the labyrinth in which Kalevala buried It. It created the labyrinth as It ate Its way out of the depths of Samphin, until, darkening the very sky with Its presence, It escaped. Not a stone in the place did not feel Its teeth marks. But on those green fields and hills before becoming Its home, Tegriel fought Crilodach whilst Hiesia held Crilodach's daughters at bay."

"Daughters?"

"Fierce fighters, who almost caught up with Tegriel and stopped Bofindle from being found. The whole of history would have been different if they had succeeded but they did not. In their surprise attack there was a man. A strange man no one really knew well. Hiesia had never seen him before and Kalevala barely had time to speak with him. He was a servant who had been afraid of the sunshine. He did not appear to be on Samphin by his own free will. Kalevala said he was slight, not strong, but he had a way about him. As if he had been waiting a long, long time. Grey skin from being indoors too long. Medium height. Thin hair. None of them expected him to attack Crilodach. He had no weapons. He seemed to have no training. But when Kalevala was wounded, and Tegriel faced It alone, he attacked Crilodach by jumping on Its back. Now an unarmed man could do nothing to Crilodach and for a second Tegriel assumed the poor fellow would be gutted right there as he gripped tightly to Crilodach. Instead Crilodach reared up possessed, and as It did so It took on the form of the beast and the man sank into Its skin, trapped. Vanishing from all discourse with us. A prisoner of Its flesh. Caught in the magic which shielded Crilodach from the man's power, for all time."

"A horrible way for anyone to die," thought Tethval.

"He might not have been killed. Not immediately. He might not even have realized what happened. He might have lived through everything Crilodach has lived through just barely conscious. Or he might have vanished into the beast losing his personality entirely. He might have died in a few minutes or a few years. We do not know."

"He would have been driven mad if he lived."

"Maybe, but his life may also have made him the most knowledgeable person in the universe about Crilodach. When you live that close to someone you do not need special powers to read their minds."

"Well if he's still alive he wasn't just a man."

"Perhaps not. Perhaps he was another being hiding as a man. Perhaps he is somewhere over there. The soldiers would not know in the general debris of dead and machinery. They may be stepping on him without knowing. I think Crilodach would be interested in him. On the other hand he may still be trapped in Its beast-self, in Trecrogo, unable to move."

"I would want to know who the man was if I were Crilodach.

"Does It have the time to find out?" she wondered.

"When I touched It briefly, nothing happened to It."

"What makes you assume nothing happened?"

"Well I didn't stop It or send It into hiding or have It change Its form."

"You could not do what that man did because Its beast-self already existed, but you may well have started a chain reaction in Crilodach. It has always feared being touched. When Nu-An grasped the beast It could not escape. All It could do was recall Its old shape. It doesn't know if that is because of Trecrogo, your touch, or both"

"So something else might be happening to It?"

"I have no idea. Nor does It. It hated being touched enough to hide away in Damkina because It never wanted to be close to anything living It did not control. It may have been touched by others. How are we to know? The man who changed It might know. He may be down there somewhere, what's left of him, in amongst the armada's debris. Perhaps the greatest man who has ever lived."

"Crilodach will have him murdered if he's alive."

"I cannot say if he is alive or dead. Recognizable or just a lump of flesh. Like looking for a single beam of light in a bright sun."

"One dead body amongst many, or if not dead, wondering where he is. He may have lost his mind," said Tethval.

"He has not been thrown over the edge. I have been monitoring them and everyone so far has been a soldier," she told him.

"Look, I could catch one of those soldiers being thrown out and take his armour. Then I could ..."

"You would not fit any of their armour Tethval. Nor would their metal shoes cover your feet. Half of them have their helmets up and none of them have lights for eyes. If anyone does anything, I will."

"I should at least go with you."

"And give the game away?"

"You can't take on the entire armada alone," he argued.

"I very much hope I will not take on anything. I need to see where the man may be, search for clues, and then go quickly to retrieve whatever is left of him if he is there. Now, while the armada is concentrating on Crilodach. Meanwhile you need to keep looking and perhaps guide me to any one you see who looks different."

"Couldn't we go and sift through the dead as they drop them over the sides. They're throwing them out right now, we might catch him before he dissolves."

"What if he is alive and they find him?" she asked.

"They may take him as one of the wounded, he can hardly be in any fit state."

"And if they do not?" she asked.

"Well the soldiers being discarded are all wearing armour. Was this Dalved wearing armour when he attacked Crilodach?"

"None. If one naked man stirs up the entire army you would think another man without armour would have also peeked their interest, if they had seen him," she observed.

"So no one has noticed him," concluded Tethval, "or he's in armour, or not there."

The Onäis slid along the flank and under the army and Lilah reached out a hand and caught one of the dead men being thrown over the side of a Round. She took the armour off him as quickly as they could. It was a bad fit but good enough for the few moments she hoped to pass as a solider in the armada. She tested the helmet then moved the Onäis away as if pushing a boat from a mooring.

Tethval who had been watching the soldiers intently pointed to the last group of dead and wounded being made ready. What he saw was a naked, unclad foot on the bottom of the pile. Lilah's heart leapt.

The men who were moving the last of the dead hauled a group of bodies up and dumped them over the side pushing the pile with their big shoulders. One of them slipped, and looking at the ground sniffed.

"What's this?" He kicked the lump on the ground.

"Dead un," said his companion.

"Like a roach."

"One ov 'em?"

"Can't be. They's gone. I went to pick up one of their lot. Impossible. Melted away in me 'ands."

"Over the side then."

"He don't look like no fighter."

"Orders says injured and dead over the side."

"He ain't wearing no armour."

"Big deal. Over the side. Don't make me tells you agin."

"Who is he then? We don't know what rank or division he belongs to."

"You care?"

"Not so you'd notice. Odd though, mighty odd."

"That man over there talking to the general. That man being Crilodach that's odd. This is just a dead un and I don't find that a bit odd after a bloody fight, k?"

"I guess. Little one ain't he though?"

"Can't be an easier duty that clearing up the dead and you've got to go make a big deal outta arms and legs."

"I wasn't making no big deal."

"I says you is."

"I'll throw him over, k?"

"What you two jawing about?" barked a third voice.

Their commander looked at them from a few feet away his visor down, his gruff voice loud and angry.

"Nothing," they both said together, driving their heels into the man on the ground and kicking him backwards.

"Wait," their commander ordered, walking over with long strides, "let's be having a gander at that one."

The commander looked at the body of Dalved as the Onäis moved quietly below the Round out of sight. He picked up Dalved's bare arm which was lifeless. Sniffing and spitting on the ground the commander said,

"Lot of use that one was in battle," and rolled the body over the side.

The men shrugged and carried on their work. The commander walked away suddenly to be faced with Hagouti appearing in front of her.

"The clothes suit you Lilah," he told her.

Without a moment's hesitation she flicked Bofindle which became long and thin as a needle and sliced into Hagouti's half body, half mist form. He winced but found he could not talk, nor could he move, nor could he change. Ever since his attack on the parapet Lilah had never let down her guard expecting him back at any time and here in the enemy camp, though he was spying for her, she would not trust him for a second. Lilah's scalp given to Crilodach would crown his achievements. The only thing stopping him from betraying her before confronting her, would have been his uncertainty that Crilodach as a man had power to overcome the spellmaker.

"Don't even think of betraying me," she warned him.

He shook his head and winced pointing to his mouth. She pulled Bofindle out of his body,

"That hurt," he whimpered.

"I should hope so," she hissed.

"I don't intend to betray you."

"You know what will happen to you if you try."

"I bring you news," he said.

"And what is so important you needed to hunt me out?"

"I didn't hunt you out. You're the only commander here not looking directly at Crilodach."

"The sooner I leave the better."

"I know you have one. A Sagitæ. Jurveiss told me he thought he had seen one."

"Where?"

"In his visions. He said he had been having strange visions the past few hours. He says he sees places, faces, a book, and he's floating on one of those things you Sangyma use."

"How does he know what he is seeing is a Sagitæ?"

"Like me they're the only bejal we wouldn't immediately recognize."

She smiled. She had seen some of this in the cousins, but she put on a stern face and said,

"You better not be lying."

She let him go. Barely suppressing her thoughts. She knew Ferveiss and Jurveiss had seen Rimfelder and she was delighted by Hagouti's confirmation. She marched away.

Like all subordinates the men around her did not look up to listen to their 'commander's business' with Hagouti. Meanwhile their commander made her exit never to be seen again in their armour and even Crilodach was unaware that

274

she had stolen away with Dalved before It had the chance to issue any orders to reclaim his body.

The body fell into Tethval's hands and he laid the broken and dead Dalved on the Onäis. A few moments after her conversation with Hagouti, Lilah joined him and they both looked at the silent, brave servant.

"He's never going to talk again," thought Tethval.

Lilah agreed with him but she would not part with the body. At the very least such a man should go into Zaqui upon Trecrogo, next to his true allies. They sped away to join Demeter.

The deliciously warm, scented air vibrated with yet another huge quake that reverberated throughout the unwalled room, shaking the bejals and shifting them uneasily from their various places, rattling out sounds Pashtul could hear as if from a long way away. Her own body shivered uncontrollably because no matter how many of these quakes she experienced without injury, she still expected the worst.

Nothing broke. When the first quakes had hit them Pashtul had run to catch objects that appeared to be falling off shelves, but she soon learned that in this place nothing got broken. Disturbances were fleeting. They were more like leaves falling off a branch slowly wafting down to the grass where they gave an occasional tremor in a passing breeze but otherwise remained unhurt. Even though Matymus' hands, with their graceful, long fingers and long fingernails which he held above the table like a piano player about to strike the keys, shook, making the skin slightly shimmer. Like plasticine that was being pulled into shape by an unseen sculptor then eased back to being a perfect hand again within seconds. Everything in this place had a form that could not be altered. She had no idea what protected them. The quakes were fierce but no matter how much more frequent they were becoming nothing here was shattered in the violence.

Matymus' arms also felt the quake but only his silk clothes seemed to show unease as this quake continued for longer than the others. A few more objects left their appointed places and floated across the room but these were not leaves and there was no ground upon which to fall. So they floated until the quake passed, then they continued to float for a while before finally settling back into their accustomed places along with Pashtul who tended to close her eyes during the quakes because she did not know if she should be sitting, standing or running. Almost as if the quake shook up her thoughts. Thoughts that were already unsettled enough.

Matymus was a delicate, long faced man who appeared to do much thinking. He was quietness personified. His presence was very hard for her to define. He was like the darkness in a mine, the scent in a chase, the heat from a fire. That which dictates caution and direction without actually being independently alive. His eyes looked at her often but she never settled on their colour. She heard him speak yet never saw his lips move. His voice was mellow, almost like her father's. Sometimes she could swear he hummed but she was unable to pick up the tune. She was tall for an Arvernat and she thought he was as tall as she, but when she looked at him from a distance he looked small. Tiny. There was not one of her eight senses she could use that gave her an insight into the magic of this place. She was not trapped but she felt she was enclosed, swaddled like a baby all wrapped up and unable to move without help. The light from her eyes illuminated nothing and seemed to waver and flicker, along with everything else.

Of course this was not really like a room at all. From whatever direction she looked there were differences in colour, and when she looked again the open space changed, though she could never quite say how. The bejals seemed to have the appearance of jars, books, boxes, photographs even a kettle, but not one of them looked exactly right. When she tried to fix on any of them with her eyes, they would wobble out of focus as if the air were shivering. Nothing in this place could quite make up their mind to stay put and who could blame them when they were being hit by quakes from every direction every few minutes. Sometimes she felt the room went on for eternity. That was impossible but for those scary minutes she felt blinded. Her heart rate increased but like everything else here that, too, was protected and though she felt anxious, she calmed down, the quakes passed and the space became still.

You might assume the tremors that oscillated through Bofindle at irregular but frequent intervals made everything seem out of focus, but you would be wrong. Bofindle was doing two things at once, creating a semblance of normality around Pashtul to reassure her, whilst keeping her safe as the battles raged outside. Nothing was real inside, which was one of the most magical places in the universe. Apart from the Arvernat no living being had ever been taken inside Bofindle before. All Bofindle knew was that the Arvernat had been needed and Pashtul still had a vital task to perform. A task she was soon to fulfil. Matymus himself was only in this form to make Pashtul feel more secure. For in this space inhabited by the presence of Matymus, reality was all made by magic.

Filvani would have found so many answers to his perplexing puzzles if he had ever been able to visit this place. He would have realized just how much magic and reality were intertwined. In fact Bofindle was wise never to allow Filvani inside because, in all probability, he would have been so fascinated he would never have left. A primaeval netherworld not yet reality but far more than dream.

Not that this helped Pashtul get her bearings for she was an alien in this world. While the likes of Tegriel and Lilah could have stayed inside here without going mad and would have had no need for Matymus, Pashtul was doing brilliantly to have survived so long. That was down in part to her strength of character and in part due to the fact Bofindle had been able to send her fellow Arvernat away relatively quickly so giving the bejal a chance to concentrate on her needs. She missed the other Arvernat. She missed her father. She felt strongly she should be by their side facing the dangers they were facing.

This latest quake started without warning, like all the others, and ended as suddenly. Matymus placed his hands once again on the table that did not appear to have any legs, until the skin under his fingernails turned a deep pink. Pashtul would have been astonished if he had told her that the whole room had somersaulted, twisted right round, balanced on a corner that was not really there, gone up and down like a fair ride on rails, shrunk in size until smaller than Pashtul was tall, and struck whole planets with enough force to shatter them to bits, all during the quake. Upsetting though the tremors were they were nothing so extreme as to give her any idea of the fact that they were caused by Bofindle's battles. He did not explain. There was no need to. The most important part of bejals was that reality was different inside them and Pashtul needed protecting because in this place where nothing was fixed, the dead could live. This fact would make her the most precious messenger ever to have lived in the universe. Even if she felt disorientated and lonely.

His lips gently parted a little as he intoned a new tune. Matymus enjoyed making up music. Often the glasses around the room would ring with notes and he would make up a harmony to go with them. Soothing the tumult of the quakes. Sometimes he even had a few words to add to the music. Words that he knew had meaning somewhere, but they were just sounds in this place, as hard to define as everything else. Pashtul got the sense that nothing here wanted to be known. That somehow the very shadows of their existence gave them a strength she would never possess. Sometimes Pashtul thought she was more like a fish swimming through the dark trenches in the depths of the sea, than an Arvernat walking this way and that, waiting for her chance to leave and join Tethval. Of course, at this moment, she still did not know she was being held safe inside Bofindle, as Tethval now knew, just as Tethval did not know the battles and the mighty weapon Lilah wielded were causing so many quakes inside Bofindle. Pashtul, not knowing where her people were, clung to the hope of seeing them all again. That is often the way when we are alone. Hope is all we have.

The magic inside Bofindle was as old as Crilodach, still attached through magical energy, like an umbilical cord, to the primordial universe. Born in the midst of a fight, dug out of the ground by Kalevala, the first spellmaker. Spellmakers had many secrets they taught to each other about this bejal. How much stronger they felt just knowing Bofindle was there, how their spells came to them from nowhere so much more accurately when Bofindle became theirs. No one knew if Bofindle had thoughts. Some of them assumed Bofindle talked to them. But Zananto had warned Lilah to take care for if she believed Bofindle was talking to her she might go crazy. The bond between a spellmaker and Bofindle was intense. They relied upon each other. The death of a spellmaker, they say, badly affected Bofindle. The bejal did not weaken but some said they had seen Bofindle weep, though no one knew what they meant for how could a weapon weep? Unless in those rare moments of quietness, when a spellmaker holding the staff in their hand just looking, beneath the suns of Juloro, had an idea put in her head that when a spellmaker dies their essence sinks into Bofindle and she was holding the minds of every spellmaker who had ever lived. A thought so immense she cried. Then she knew how Bofindle wept, because Lilah felt the bejal using her tears as the weapon remembered passed friends from universes unknown.

Matymus hummed his music, until the sounds of the quakes were simply a different phrase of the tune, a contour in the rhythms that made up the main melody, and then a second melody seamlessly started. Cadenzas shifting back and forth just like the objects in the room. His music was a counter-point to the wild noises outside. Perhaps he was here to make her feel less angry at being left behind. Perhaps the idea that she was waiting for something was given her by Bofindle to get her ready for leaving. The Arvernat had spent their lives in mines, with no other friends but each other. Friendship until death. They were like a huge family and none of them were used to being this alone, even in the dark.

She listened to his music. She noted how the melodies sounded like Arvernat songs and she wondered how he knew their music. She sighed once or twice in the lulls between the quakes, curling up like a baby ready to go to sleep. Almost floating in this netherworld. A sleepy being of deep sense and deep strength in a strange reality created for her; because of her message.

This place was less a limbo and more a place of ideas, the certain ideas of all bejals emanated from this room to the outside universe, where the ideas of objects became solid, where real planets orbited and huge quakes tore worlds apart, upturned and broke everything. Here everything prepared to exist without actually existing yet. Nothing could be lost here as all was captured on the notes of gentle music hummed in the hurly-burly of tremendous quakes that struck and struck again. But once outside the objects were still linked to Bofindle becoming the bejals prized by magicians and non-magicians alike.

Matymus finally rose and with a small flick of his wrist all the remaining objects still floating in the air, went back to their places. Then, through an opening in the room no one would have noticed, he walked towards her. He looked at her. Here was another music. The fall of feet on the smooth surface of the perfectly flat floor that was there when she put her feet down, but did not seem to be anywhere else around her. Her heart pumping her blood to the easy rhythm of her breathing. She also had words. Some he understood. Some he guessed at but her feelings and thoughts were many and those he knew well. He had been impressed by the Arvernat, her father Tethval, and all he could hear and see of them.

Matymus was not the intelligence inside Bofindle, but part of the weapon's being. Found in the myths and legends that no one knew and had never been written down. Neither magician nor living animal, Bofindle created through Matymus an essence that could communicate with those who were not spellmakers. He changed as seasons change, always coming back to himself.

Kalevala, with the instincts of a dog, had said that Matymus had become such a part of Bofindle they could not be separated. He talked to Tegriel about the presence inside Bofindle. He remained a mystery to them. In fact Matymus' essence helped to make Bofindle indestructible for Matymus had been born in the first universe of all, and so not being truly alive or a part of the atoms of this one meant he could not die in this or any other universe. He experienced time after time the torrent of struggles against Crilodach. You might think that would make him somewhat one sided in his opinions but you would be wrong. He had never lost his belief that his struggle and that of all the spellmakers was to make things better. He alone of all those who fought Crilodach had some idea how well the fight was going. He alone knew the secret of the Sagitæ and the reason for the deaths and rebirths of the universe. He alone carried with him the names of all those who had fought against It. He could never go outside to tell anyone but because he remembered so much history he was, of course, so much greater than history for his wisdom was fathomless.

"Welcome Pashtul, welcome. What brings you to me?"

She had queried him before about why he said that when he walked towards her but she had never been given a straight answer. How could he give a straight answer when nothing was straight in this place.

"The quake?" she told him, brushing back her long, green hair with her hands, exasperated by the wait being forced upon her. Working long hours in the dark the Arvernat had become adept at knowing how long a time has passed without looking for a watch. She knew she had been here almost two of her days. She was getting very fed up.

"Surely you're used to them after so much time here," said Matymus.

"Too many," she complained.

"Quakes or days?"

"Both. I want to know what's going on with my father and the others. I want to know why I was kept here when they were released."

"This isn't a prison."

"I know but ..." she tried to be nice about her feelings, "I feel like I'm in one."

"I'm sorry for that. That isn't meant. I can tell you all about your friends," he suggested.

"Yes."

"There's no music around them, everything's hurtling to Zaqui."

"Are they alright?"

"Many have gone. I hear names and voices but they are less than when here. Many others have gone from other peoples. A few great friends have come back to us. I'm sure you want to go and see for yourself."

"You know I do. My place is with them."

"And will be," he assured her.

"Why not now?" she asked.

"We had to wait."

"You've been waiting too?"

"Of course. I've taken advantage of your stay to learn more about your music Pashtul. I've a need to hear your song for a little longer so I can understand you fully."

"But I've sung nothing."

"Not what you call song," smiled Matymus, "the deep song of your being. The songs that are in you from the chords of the cosmos. The songs that made you fight for your freedom, the song that makes you want to leave to be with your people though you know you'll find only death."

"My place is with my family," she said.

"The song of place! Perfect. I need to know where you fit into creation. I'd like to know what this idea of place means."

"Why?"

"So that I may make music," he said simply.

"Don't you know about place?"

"I only know about all places. I've been everywhere, I don't know how to be only in one place."

"My people are dying and you talk about things I don't understand."

"Everything dies Pashtul. You know that. Tethval knows that. Everyone knows that."

"Is my father ..."

"No, I still hear his music. They speak his name with love. Already he's done great things. His song is of hope. Hope is a great song Pashtul but not the greatest of songs. Crilodach's song has lessened. It has been hurt. So long I've heard Its song I can strum every chord."

"Surely I'd be better use out there ..." she pointed vaguely having no idea where 'out' actually was, "fighting with them?"

"You are fighting Pashtul. Fighting with all your might."

"You can't convince me I'm fighting when I'm barely moving."

"You're part of the struggle just by being here. Crilodach doesn't know you're here."

"I'm no great, big secret."

"The quakes have been violent haven't they?" said Matymus.

"Yes."

"But nothing has been hurt or broken in here."

"No."

"That's because of your desire to win."

"What? How?" she asked in disbelief.

"Feelings are mightier than actions. Feelings are the magic of living things. Your power to be with your people again, infuses us all."

"How can someone like me make this place any stronger?"

"Not physical strength Pashtul. Your determination, your focus upon one aim. Bofindle's joined with your mind because you have been here longer than anyone before you."

"I've felt helpless ever since arriving. I'm waiting for something momentous that never comes and now all of a sudden you're telling me I'm part of that ... thing ... Lilah brought to my city."

"You're not helpless Pashtul. You're strong. I knew that when I saved all your people. Few survive here. When they felt my song they added their own. So very strong. So many songs have been sung down the ages that I've heard only from the outside. I'm sure I've not collected them all and for so many I am too late."

"You could bring anyone here you wished," she pointed out.

"Not even the spellmakers come here. Nor the Sangyma. You need to have something very special. No one sings with me in here. My existence has always been set apart, an outsider who knows so much. Tegriel does not even know how I could exist. They have wondered what makes Bofindle so strong but none of them know. Not even Crilodach can crack the secret."

"Are you keeping me here because you're lonely?"

"Is that what you think?" he asked her.

"I don't know. You sent the others out and not me. You study me like some specimen and you talk in riddles. I've no idea what you're telling me half the time. I just assumed you needed to talk."

Matymus floated slowly over the floor. As he did so the place changed. Everything changed when he moved. Nothing here stayed the same even when there were no quakes. When they had first arrived, Tethval had called them all together fearing they were in the afterlife. How they had feared they were all dead, or worse in some trap Lilah had not seen, created by the enemy that had brought the rocks of their world to life. The enemy they could not defeat.

They had heard the stories they told in the cities. There were certain places of torture people went to as ghosts. They thought they were in such a place and for what seemed a long time they had waited, clustered together, wondering what new terrors were coming their way.

Yet no torture started. Then the quakes hit them and they braced themselves only to find out they were being protected. She had been the first to notice that none of the other Arvernat dead, ones she had seen fall, were with them. They had concluded they must be alive.

The quakes became relentless. There was no space for rest. They all stayed together, linking arms in case anyone got sucked away. Suddenly a great light hit them from somewhere and an Arvernat shouted out that she saw something. They started running forwards and each one let go the arm of the one next to them so they could run faster until there was a steady flow of Arvernat heading for what seemed to be an opening. As she ran to go with them, something held her back. She was running, she knew she was running yet they all outpaced her vanishing one after another and though she ran harder towards the vision of a stone parapet, lit up with the sights of a huge battle, the light vanished. She fell forward but did not fall. She floated alone. She had seen the parapet of Trecrogo, she had seen Arvernat feet land as the others leapt, she had heard the raging battle, but her own feet never touched the freedom her fellow Arvernat enjoyed. They had pulled away from her as birds blown by winds her wings could not catch.

Around her, as Matymus moved, as rooms vanished and new ones appeared, as things were made and unmade in seconds, she began to wonder if she really had died and if her people had ever been here. She was in a dream. When he was not near she could not bring Matymus' face to mind. All she could see were his hands. Those elegant, shimmering hands. She was not even sure she heard his voice except in her head. He existed like a ship far out at sea passing by so quietly that only those who were actually looking would ever see him. Matymus was as strange as this whole place and she gave up trying to focus on anything. She just wanted to join her people, to be out there, wherever 'there' happened to be. All their lives the Arvernat had fought to be free of cages and perhaps she was a little sensitive because being here was like being in a magical land, where she did not see the magic. She only saw her loneliness. She saw how alien the surroundings were to her.

Matymus had sent Tethval and the others out. At least that is what Pashtul thought had happened but now she tried to remember, things had happened too quickly to recall clearly, and Matymus had not been there so maybe he was not in charge at all. She was sure he had always been with her. Frightened, bemused, alone, unsure as she was, he had walked to her side. He was a comfort to her. He sounded so sure of everything. Imperturbable. As Tethval had sounded that day that seemed so long ago but could barely have been more that a week ago, when in the darkness of the mines he had spoken to them all of freedom, of how they had trained for the war and built up arsenals of weapons. They had walked out in legions towards the city to fight their enemy filled with his words.

Lilah had also seemed, when she walked into their lives,

284

one of those rare people who never panic. Someone you wanted to follow. Who held out no promises of riches or power but you knew promised something far better; the chance to be right. The possibility, for the first time in her life, simply to know.

"Hello, did you decide to stay?"

Matymus had asked without moving his lips or blinking his eyes. Those eyes that made her feel like a small animal seeking comfort. Such an ordinary question and without thinking, without understanding why, she had not shrunk from him, or asked who he was or where she was, she just answered his question as if she were living in an ordinary day,

"I wanted to follow the others but they were all too fast or I was too slow, I'm not sure which."

"You should stay, I think."

"Why?" she had asked.

She had no way of guessing what had happened. Seeing and knowing are two completely different things. In those last hours of pain when the whole world had been destroyed she had almost ceased to think. What was the point of trying to make sense of such madness.

"No one knows why Bofindle does anything but, Bofindle does, and that's all, and what the bejal does, well that's all, too. Still, I'm glad to enjoy your song. Your music is deep and lasting. Soothing. Wondrous. You have some dark motifs yet you carry such light in you. Like joyous cadences. Such a charming change. I've no shortage of harmony here but little change. The Arvernat are unique."

Matymus had not changed in the days she had been here. She could still smell the salty, rich odour of Crilodach's minions in her nostrils as they had fought them hand-to-hand. The dry dust from stone was still on her clothes. The feel of their unbreakable might still on her fingers.

She never asked where the quakes came from, so she was not aware that she was never that far away from Crilodach's armada or even that her father was always by her side. The odour wafted around this place with the crazy song of the enemy, songs that Matymus listened to once and then put away, devising harmonies for them in his head that did away with terror. She had felt the great surge of power around them when they were near Trecrogo. Like a roaring waterfall drenching them in a lust for being alive, a love of speed and freshness. Her skin had shone, her hair glittered as if braided with lights, her whole body felt as if she could run and never stop, lift whole mountains with a finger, defeat any enemy, stop any hazard and accomplish any task.

"I should go," she had said, "I don't belong here."

"If you should, you should. But for the present we're together and I welcome you." Always he would agree yet nothing was done and she stayed in this nether–world.

That had been the end of their first conversation. Always his voice was quiet, even when she was consciously waiting for the next quake, his voice was in her head. Calm. Composed. She still felt as if the quakes were trying to unsettle her very being, to stretch her as if on a rack and test her, but not as a quake should. She had felt those rumbling from deep below her feet, pulling down the rocks in the mines, opening up and ripping Arvernat from their families never to be seen again. They were to be feared for the Arvernat had nowhere to run. The quakes here did not make any noise but seemed to be fierce, frightening, threatening. Then Matymus would be standing nearby. Only his clothes moving. Slowly she had begun to see that this place was like no other. Elemental. Shaking not because of the quakes but in unison with them. Harmonizing with the magic in the cosmos.

"You will get used to that after a while," he had told her the first time.

Matymus brought her back to the present, and her reminiscence evaporated as quickly as silence at the end of a lesson.

"Bofindle fights you see," Matymus said softly, "Fights and struggles with the atoms in the universe It tries to use. They struggle with each other. Always fighting, exploding, merging, passing through each other, justifying their existence. The magic flows from one to another and back again, like endless fireworks going off mixing up all their fire and smoke until you cannot tell which is exploding or where, or what kind, or why. The atoms of magic are wayward and messy." He moved closer to her and went on, "The art of the spellmakers brings understanding to the chaos. Come see."

She saw darkness where she had been sure she had just seen a bookcase. Then she saw hands in thick gloves rummaging through garbage which she realized was not garbage but bodies. Gloved hands with heavily armoured arms, lifting piles of bodies. Dozens of hands. Hundreds of fallen soldiers. She moved closer to the images watching in horror as the bodies were pushed together, rolled over the edge to vanished into space. Heaps and heaps of bodies. She gasped in horror. Armour, weapons, metals and bone. And she watched horrified not knowing whose dead they were. Not hearing a sound. Perfect silence. The bodies fell and vanished. Lost in the darkness but she thought she could see a flow of something, like a river, snaking into the distance. She did not know what she was seeing. She would never have guessed they were the atoms of the dead flowing to Zaqui. Nor would she have taken in the streams of atoms from galaxies that existed no more, all flowing in huge transparent, elegant spirals.

The Arvernat had buried their dead, taken time to collect their comrades who had died in the rebellion, and buried each one with reverence, said their names, found their living brothers and sisters, wept over them. These gloved hands moved without resting as if they were clearing up no more than rubbish left behind after a storm. Then she saw him.

A body unclad in armour, crippled and thin, with wisps of grey hair on his head. He was being hauled onto an Onäis. This body was different, he did not seem to have any strength or power which was out of place in the armada and he was a good head shorter than any of the soldiers she could see.

"He's no song," said Matymus. "His suffering's been long indeed. He's old beyond the counting of all memories."

"I can see Arvernat hands," she cried out.

"They want to speak to him. They need to know something but he can't hear them. He stopped hearing long ago but what happened to him kept his body intact. His spirit you see, is locked away. Come Pashtul, hold my hand, let us see if we can make him speak to us and find out what they want to know."

"Why hold my hand?"

"He needs your song."

"Is he dead?"

"Very much so."

"Then I can't help him."

"By yourself maybe not, but with me you can and I can't without you, so ..."

For all her readiness to leave, Pashtul was not scared of

287

Matymus or of this place, so she took his hand. His fingers were strong. Warm. Real. She was surprised at how real. Her eyes looked at the äis and she saw the long, strong green arm of one of her own and she felt grateful to know that Arvernat were alive. She felt she was finally close to leaving. She watched with fascination as Tethval's profile came into view and with a sudden rush she knew she was close to him. All the songs she had heard since arriving came to her in one soft harmony and told her a great truth known to every soldier since the beginning of time; the mind is the greatest weapon. She felt Matymus reaching out with his mind. She looked at the dead man in Tethval's arms, and she called to Dalved, because she knew his name. But her call came out as a song.

All Tethval and Lilah saw was Dalved begin to shimmer. For a moment Tethval thought he was going to burn to ashes and he looked at Lilah to see if this was her magic. But she was surprised as well.

"What's that?" whispered Tethval.

"Nothing I am doing," she told him.

"Then ..."

"No, this is not Its spell."

"Could this be how he managed to change Crilodach?"

"Let's wait and see," she said.

"What if he blows up?"

"We blow up with him," she said.

"What if he can change you into something?"

"A risk I am willing to take," Lilah said.

Dalved's body shimmered just as Pashtul's had, as if he were caught in the quake with her and part of the image of Dalved turned, stood upright, opened his eyes and walked towards her though his shimmering body remained on the Onäis. Slowly, he found himself in the bejal with them as they held hands, standing upright though his legs and arms lacked all strength. He looked at the room, at Matymus and Pashtul, at their hands and faces, like a man who had forgotten there was a world. He sighed. In his head he remembered Kalevala, the pain of the touch and then he began to remember terrible things. Struggles. Agony. As if he were being dragged along rough stone pathways year after year. He felt his bones bleed. Voices. Many voices. Shouts and screams. But they were all his own, all inside his head. A universe of pain and sorrow, of loss and finally...

"Am I dead?" he asked, looking at them both intently.

He could focus his eyes easily. Though she tried, just as with Matymus, Pashtul could not see Dalved's lips move as he talked. He did not stare. Almost as if he was only half with them.

"No one dies here," replied Matymus.

"Where is here?" he asked them.

He turned and saw his body shimmering, prone and cold. He recognized himself. He took his hand from Matymus and reached out but he could not touch anything, as if he were a film of himself. He looked so thin. He recalled being a child, and some woman whipping him. Yaltha. He saw her face. He shivered. He heard her voice and saw her naked back rippling with spines. Then he saw the sunshine. The brilliant sunshine.

"I don't understand what happened," he moaned.

"Do you wish to?" asked Matymus.

"Very much. I feel so tired," he admitted.

"Hold my hand again, let my strength become yours. There. What is the last thing you remember?"

"There was a fight. A great fight. I'd been running with a dog. A brave dog. It was there, the father of my tormentors. The father of Yaltha and Freyom. I sneaked up behind It when It was all fire and rant. It had a man there It was going to kill. I didn't want It to kill him. I jumped. Then fire, great fire, and pain, such pain. I touched such utter darkness and coldness. I couldn't move. I couldn't breathe."

"And after that?" asked Matymus.

"I don't know. I longed for the sun. I thought I was back in the palace. I thought I was in a dungeon. I thought I was alone again and all my thoughts were overheard. I didn't know. I felt so lost."

"And then?"

"Long night. So long. No voices, no nothing, just cold. Bitter cold. I ... died, didn't I?" He turned his face upwards to look at Matymus.

"You've suffered long," Matymus told him.

"I'm not the only one," Dalved replied.

"You've a good heart Dalved."

"How do you know my name?"

"I saw your battle. I saw your leap though you didn't see me. I've known about your life and your trials. I've seen many things. Those who fought with you that day kept on fighting, but nothing ever matched your bravery."

"I'm not brave."

"Sometimes Dalved, to go on living is the bravest thing anyone can do. In the darkness and the long, long nights you didn't give up and there were those around you who took strength from your sacrifice. Who felt, without knowing, what you had done."

"But I died," said Dalved.

"Yes, you died but you did not give up," said Matymus.

"How am I here now?"

"Because the sunshine sustained this part of you," Matymus told him.

"So much darkness, so much coldness. I was never able to move but I could hear. I could hear growling and screaming. All the time. Sneering. I couldn't move. Why was that?"

"Do you want to know?"

"I need to know," he said softly.

"You became part of their father."

"Part?"

"Bound beneath Its skin."

"How is that possible?"

"It grew a skin to protect Itself from your sunshine. The atoms in you were filled with a magic from ancient times. You did not know when you saw the sunshine from the palace that the light sparked more than hope in your mind. You became someone else. The light was like a seed growing in you. That's why Yaltha never killed you. Her desires were blunted by the sunshine. You became someone they couldn't control yet believed they did. You became a living element, able to change events just by being there, driven to take your place amongst the legends of those who fought Crilodach."

"And the coldness?" asked Dalved.

"Your body was frozen in Its fight to protect Itself."

"And the fear?"

"Everyone feels fear in the presence of Crilodach."

"No, Its fear?"

"Its fear?" asked Matymus.

"It feared me. I'm not sure why. I touched It and, as I touched It, I felt Its fear. Substantial. Deep. It didn't know what I was. I did more than change It, there was more to the magic than that."

"It didn't know what you were?" repeated Matymus.

Matymus let go of Pashtul's hand and taking both Dalved's in his, he looked into his eyes for the longest time. There were no quakes now to disturb them and Pashtul was sure Matymus became slightly more real. She could see his face. A serene, bright face with unlined skin.

"Are you a man?" he asked Dalved.

"I think so."

"What was your mother called?" asked Matymus.

"I don't remember."

"Do you remember anything about your childhood?"

"I was born in a village. There was a huge lake nearby. We always had fresh fish. I remember a lot of rain. Almost daily. The houses smelled of cedar wood. There were animals everywhere. That's all I recall."

"How did you get to be a servant?" asked Matymus.

"I don't know."

"Dig deeper. Remember."

"I don't know."

"Remember Dalved. Remember." Dalved concentrated, closed his eyes and then said,

"I was sold."

"Are you certain?" asked Matymus.

"Yes, I was sold. By a woman. A gentle woman," cried Dalved.

"Your mother?"

"I don't think so. She was taller. She was different. She had a lovely smile. She told me I had to be a slave. I asked her why. She said because I would free everyone else."

Matymus nodded and showing Dalved the palm of his hand the face of a woman appeared.

"Is this she?"

"No." The face changed on his palm but that was not her either, but on the third try Dalved nodded,

"Yes, that's her. Just like that. With her hair done up behind her and that shining smile."

Matymus turned his palm towards him and looked at the image of Zananto. Of all the Sangyma she had always been reticent to talk about her travels. Gertis called her Aneginel, a woman of too many secrets. Matymus clapped his hands together and the image faded but now his eyes were wide open. They were black as black pearls as he turned to look at Pashtul.

"How well were the Sangyma chosen. How fine are our

champions. Pashtul your time here is over you must go now. You must go to Lilah. You must tell her we know why Crilodach fears being touched."

"Very well."

"Tell her Zananto touched Dalved. She sold him into the slavery, she always knew you see. Her champion in the heart of the Crilodach's plots was a slave. Dalved carries a spell inside his very being, he will become a great and powerful incantation against Crilodach. Every cell of his body is magic. That's why Crilodach felt such power when Dalved touched It. Zananto's magic changed Crilodach into a creature, drove It to hide Itself for fear of being touched again."

"I see everything. Wonderful, fabulous Zananto. She found in Dalved the exact number and matrix of cells she needed, to hide the spell in his body. Each and every cell broken up into millions of parts but taken together, with something to unify them like the moments in the sunshine, they became a weapon. Dalved is the only bejal that was a living being. Run Pashtul run and tell Lilah, Dalved does not have the secret, he is the secret. Run Pashtul and do not stop running until you have told her."

Pashtul turned from him and ran, without saying Goodbye. Without looking back. She ran into the light that did not recede from her this time but turned to darkness. A darkness she knew. Like that around the city at the end of the battle The darkness of space. And there was Tethval. Near by him she saw Lilah, the wonderful woman who had saved her brother and saved them from their greatest enemy. At last she would be with them. This time she would not leave. This time she had the message that would make all the difference because inside Bofindle a dead man could talk and an Arvernat could survive for two precious days to bring news of the bejal that would stop Crilodach.

"Meeting Hagouti was useful, if nothing else," said Lilah, kicking the helmet off the Onäis as they travelled a safe distance from the armada.

"You were pretty calm up there, what if their real commander had turned up?" Tethval asked her, able at last to talk softly.

"The commanders are itching to have a go at Crilodach

and not paying attention to anything else."

Dalved was dead. His weak, pale body did not seem to Tethval to be of consequence. His grey head and sunken eyes gave him a ghostlike appearance. Lilah was unsure her attempt to find him had been worthwhile. Then she noticed his skin glistened and Bofindle slid from her hair and floated above the body. Lilah knew this feeling now and she realized someone was coming out the bejal.

Pashtul was running hard as she left her friend Matymus in the space that vanished behind her. She ran so fast she bumped into her father who was stooped over Dalved's motionless body. Tethval grabbed at Pashtul's shoulders almost catapulting them both over the side but Lilah was standing there stopping them falling with her strong arms.

"His body," Pashtul said breathless into Tethval's ear, "his body is the secret, father."

"What?" said Tethval amazed. "Pashtul. I thought we'd lost you for good. Have you been inside Bofindle all this time?"

But even as he spoke Lilah had heard her and touched Dalved's head with Bofindle and his body changed. Where there had once been a dead man slowly the cells merged and moved, the hands slid into his sides, the legs became a single branch, the skin turned yellow, blue then gold, hair sprouted from his chin and wrapped round him like filigree work on a pillar. The body rose softly off the Onäis and turned with the winding hair until Dalved was like a cocoon. They could just make out he was still a man.

"What did you do?" asked Tethval, still holding onto his daughter's arm.

"Pashtul what else do you know?" asked Lilah.

"He was sold into slavery by Zananto. He's a bejal," said Pashtul.

Lilah's forehead furrowed. What a terrible fate for a man to suffer so long and not know why. To be so powerful but only for the benefit of others. To never use the magic in his being to free himself. To never know freedom or witness the magical things that would be done, could only be done, because he had lived. Always a slave, always giving to others their salvation. For the first time in her life she knew someone else had a similar experience of life as hers.

"Does this weapon have a name?" asked Lilah.

"Dalved," replied Pashtul.

At least, she thought, Dalved would be remembered after all this time by his real name. Of all the works of the Sangyma this was the most ingenious. The cells were too disparate for Yaltha or Freyom to ever understand. The cells could only show their magic because selflessness was part of his touch. Something the sisters never experienced. When Dalved jumped onto Crilodach he was acting in defence of his new friends and the spell within him activated, fusing onto Crilodach's skin, burning It with the misery of feelings. Feelings It had to protect against.

The beast, once born, carried the remains of Dalved with It until Nu–An trapped It. Crilodach carried throughout Its long life, inside Itself, the seeds of Its own defeat. Of all the Sangyma, Zananto had the greatest imagination to even think of such a plan. Cut off from It by Its own spells, the beast never found out what Dalved had done or where the man's power had originated.

Changes were Crilodach's enemy. Changes made It mad. Made It forget to be careful. Changes that throbbed in Its throat and made It yearn for vengeance. Changes that eventually meant that when Hu–An stopped It, It tore Itself asunder and Dalved's cells flew from the beast. Once again Crilodach the man was born, but It was not used to being a man anymore. It was not used to the feel of being a man. It preferred to be the beast. At Zaqui It did not want to be reminded of what It really was. As a man It feared being touched even more than as a beast. It ranted. It felt nothing but the power in Its arms and the hunger for revenge.

"What's happening to him?" asked Tethval, unable to look away from Dalved's metamorphosis.

"He is becoming a spell even I would never have thought of making," replied Lilah.

"How?" asked Tethval.

"Magical people resonate in their cells with the magic of the cosmos. The more cells that contain magic the more power their spells have, the Sangyma are powerful but even Tegriel only has about ten percent of magical cells. But Dalved had almost ninety percent. The energy of his spells would have a magic multiplied by the square of the number of magical cells in his body. Billions of cells. Power unknown."

"That's a lot of power to hide away."

"How well you were hidden," she said. "Even I did not

know. Zananto never said a word to anyone, yet from her hands flows our victory. This is why Crilodach changed when Dalved touched It. Crilodach was fighting Zananto's spell."

"If Bofindle had not rescued us, Pashtul would never have been alive to bring you this message," Tethval said.

"I know Tethval, but the magic runs deeper than even that. If you had not been enslaved It would have conquered your world and we would never have met."

"What do we do with Dalved?" asked Pashtul.

"We must get back to Trecrogo," said Lilah, "After all this, if Dalved's cells do not change fast enough into the bejal he is now becoming, fusing Zananto's spell with Crilodach's spells that surrounded him for aeons, we still could lose. We are dangerously balanced on the knife edge between victory and defeat."

"You mean after all we've been through, this weapon may not be ready?" asked Pashtul

"Time is never anyone's friend," replied Lilah.

The Ruzniel

Tegriel was thinking on the move. To have been surprised by the sisters followed by Crilodach, yet to have escaped, seemingly with minimal damage to the progress of events, was more than ordinarily magical. He was still worried about the unsettling eddies that would emanate from this fight across the future. He had not cast any spells apart from those to protect himself. That should reduce the adverse effects. Bofindle was found. Samphin was lost earlier than before but nonetheless lost to Crilodach. However, Crilodach's store of new knowledge of what was to come presented Tegriel with huge challenges. Not the least of which was to find out how much It knew. But how can a Sangyma pick Crilodach's mind?

He felt nothing unusual in the Ossendark believing he was on the way to Phindalt, a planet where he once foretold a man would come one day whose hair was alive, aided by a woman who commanded the sea and they would save the planet from a horde of slavers. How many of his prophecies would he have to change? He had to find out all that the sisters were doing, quickly, to make doubly sure he was safe to repeat his immediate prophecies. Their activity had certainly changed events. If he kept a close watch on them the fallout might be manageable. He was certain Crilodach would not have shared important foreknowledge of events with them because that would make them too powerful, but Tegriel knew he would have to kill or imprison them to break open the spell their father had hidden in their armour to find out all It now knew. At least he hoped that was all he would have to do. Much depended upon him finding out exactly what they knew before he made any decisions.

Feeling this uncertain about events felt very strange.

The journey did not take very long. He stepped out onto the grass with a dozen plans in his head to take every eventuality into account. He was so busy thinking he did not realize what had happened for several seconds. He might have even taken longer to realize if he had not seen the look of radiant delight and recognition on Tobia's face. Time was playing with them. They were on Ruz. He knew that was completely wrong for his timeline. He knew that Ruz was not even populated when he had originally found Bofindle and explained to Kalevala that he was a spellmaker. He knew this was not where he had appeared before in the scheme of things that made up his life. The shock flooded through his mind so completely he felt his legs buckle. Was this because of something he had done or some fresh trick Crilodach had hidden in the Ossendark?

Tobia recognized this part of Ruz the moment she arrived. She was unaware Tegriel was staring at the countryside around them with his mouth open. Even stranger was Hiesia arriving right behind them despite the fact she had been many hours working on the Upala while the sisters, who were hot on their heels, were nowhere to be seen. Hiesia waited for him to tell her what was happening because she did not know anything was wrong until she looked at his face. Even then she did not know they had advanced far into the future.

Tegriel remembered how he had helped Tobia with the plans for the first Ruzniel city, Auleed, in the west. They would not need help now. He had been unwise to think Crilodach's tampering with the Upala would be contained by Its new defeat upon Samphin. There was a huge shift in the magical currents in the cosmos. Perhaps too huge and too fast a change for him to manage. The sisters had only just fought with him, how could that have caused a whole planet to be created ages before time. What was going on? He drew his hands to his face and a skein like a spider web spread out before him. The same spell that Midrak would use in the last hours of Ruz. He looked. This was not a mirage. This really was Ruz. A huge chunk of his previous life gone by in the twinkling of an eye. Things had not been done that were vital to the struggle. Whatever else had happened he knew now he could not use his knowledge of events as a sure guide.

"I'm sure I know this place," said Hiesia softly, standing on her back legs, sniffing the air.

"We had a brief commemoration dinner here after Gertis became a Sangyma," replied Tegriel, lowering his hands, confused and perplexed.

"Of course," she smiled, "I only ever came to Ruz that

once. We were by the sea."

"I've heard of this place" sniffed Kalevala. "Bofindle told me I was to come here in a dream. I didn't think I'd live long enough to get here when Crilodach injured me."

"Is that leg hurting you?" asked Hiesia.

"I'll live," Kalevala told her.

"You've dreamed of this place?" Tobia asked him.

"Spellmakers have wonderful dreams," Tegriel told her, walking around, taking in the view from all sides, "Though they come from different people with different abilities the two things they have in common are their command of Bofindle and their dreams. Please do not wander off."

"I'm only going to look over there. I haven't been home in what seems like ages."

"There is no one you know here."

Tobia was already twenty paces off on this very young, vibrant Ruz. A fresh, lush, bush–filled Ruz that seemed to dance all around her.

"Let her be," suggested Hiesia, "this is her home. She'll be safe."

"Her safety is not what's worrying me," Tegriel replied.

"Then what is?" she asked him.

"I do not know why we are here. Things have changed too much, and if things have changed this much, my power to contain Crilodach will have been severely weakened, perhaps beyond my repairing."

"Why shouldn't we be here?" asked Kalevala, scratching his ear with his good back leg.

"I need to keep events on track. There are a million and one things I needed to do, people I needed to meet, spells I needed to cast, long before coming here for the first time. Tobia is supposed to be the first woman leader of her people, we worked together here, Fulminar came here and stayed to design their capital city. I have not even met him."

Somewhere Tobia heard water flowing. That beautiful, gushing of a waterfall over smoothed boulders. Tegriel heard the stream too but he was too busy talking to Hiesia and Kalevala to go sightseeing. Tobia drew further away until she lost sight of her companions. Through the sparse trees, round the base of the mountain and along a small gully filled with spring flowers she followed the sound. Her heart leapt at the sight of flowers she knew well. Smells she loved. If her parents had walked over the crest of the hill with a picnic basket or Yomiel had called out to her to attend classes she would have felt everything was perfect. But she knew that was impossible for this Ruz was filled with strangers, if there were any Ruzniel here at all.

She found herself striding over wet, white rocks, at the bottom of a pure white froth of water that drenched her five minutes before she arrived at the banks. She washed her face in a constant shower of warm water droplets that dripped onto her lips and tasted a little like lemon and honey. She let the water slide down her throat. Her whole body felt light. She closed out everything from her mind except the sound of the water and the taste in her mouth. She had never thought she would see Ruz again. She coughed as some water went down the wrong way.

The others were still talking. Hiesia was looking directly at Tegriel scratching her nose.

"Do you think Its daughters have forced these changes in our timeline?" asked Tegriel, who valued her opinion.

"The thinner one, Yaltha, she has big plans for herself. The other, Freyom seems wedded to her father but given the chance I think she'd go against It if, and this is a big if, she thought their plots would work in her favour."

"Did they spring some spell I missed? Have they been overrunning the universe for millenniums while we have been trapped in the Ossendark thinking only seconds had passed?"

"I felt nothing," replied Kalevala, "and Bofindle would have responded if anyone had cast a spell on us."

Tegriel was grasping at straws. They could tell he was deeply worried at the enormity of the dilemma. They shared those worries. A lot of time had passed since they fought on Samphin. Time in which the enemy could have grown unstoppable through Its knowledge of the future.

"It would certainly have started to gather armies the moment It got free" Hiesia said. "It obviously hasn't destroyed Ruz so that's a good sign."

How much might be changed?" said Tegriel, "We may already have lost the war! Crilodach laughed saying It knew everything, that It had sent back information on all our allies. All the Sangyma. We may be the only survivors of a war we never took part in. We need a miracle right now."

"I didn't think you believed in miracles?" Hiesia observed.

"That does not mean we do not need one," responded

Tegriel.

"There's another way to look at this," suggested Kalevala.

"Such as?"

"You're sure this isn't right. We shouldn't be on Ruz?"

"I don't forget things. Knowing is my chief weapon. I made a particular strength of my memory."

"How exactly did Crilodach change into the beast before?" asked Kalevala.

"In the dark days when Crilodach first appeared like a thunderbolt, people were falling to his promises. Whole solar systems collapsed and the Sangyma, trying to find out all we could about Its power, discovered patterns in Crilodach's behaviour. I did some experiments which I tested with the Sangyma Cawitle. He began to deduce the laws of magic. Kalevala, in those days, you created the magic of invisibility and saw Ghirzanben being built. Cawitle found a bejal hidden in the centre of a galaxy, a single planet over which It fought still as a man. The fight was long and the bejal was destroyed but Crilodach was changed forever."

"And while It was changing you went about your work?" asked Kalevala.

"I certainly did. I know too much about It to stay idle," said Tegriel. "I do not know where the magic came from this time or what powers Dalved possessed to force the change upon It."

"Maybe you don't but something that had to happen still did despite Its attempts to change history," said Kalevala. "There's a confluence of magic in the cosmos, a balance that can't be altered. Which means that being on Ruz at this time could be a part of that re–balancing process," he suggested.

"So quickly?" wondered Tegriel, "Crilodach was here and then the answer was here in the form of Dalved, though he travelled with Crilodach's own daughters, our sworn enemies. How did he fool them? And you Hiesia, you came along immediately to fight by our side but I never called to you. Sometimes the very magic I am part of astonishes me," said Tegriel. "But where, oh where, do we go from here?"

"We're all fighting in the dark," said Hiesia, "until we know where Crilodach is and where Its daughters have ended up."

"Where has our Tobia gone, I can't see her?" asked Tegriel.

"She's by a waterfall," Kalevala told them. "Washing her face, unaware that she's being watched."

"Watched?" asked Tegriel sharply.

"Ever since we got here in fact, we've all been watched. One saw us and immediately others appeared very quickly to track us."

"Are we in danger?" asked Hiesia.

"I don't know," sniffed up Kalevala, "my nose says only if we appear to be a danger to them. They show curiosity, especially in Tegriel. In shape and form they're the same as Tobia. I assume we are dealing with Ruzniel."

"Are they all Ruzniel?" asked Tegriel

"Certainly."

"They were never a shy people. What makes them shy?" he said.

"We won't get answers by standing around wondering," Hiesia suggested. "Come on lets go and join her, if we need answers like as not the Ruzniel will furnish us with them."

"Who could have all the answers to this," muttered Tegriel.

He could see that if Hiesia was correct, he no longer knew exactly what Crilodach would do. Fighting It would be oddly different. Many of the same people would be in his life but they may act differently. New people, whose actions he would have to assess as he went along, might become important to the war. Events had changed but the overall results had be the same. They would have to keep It guessing. If he saw a chance to prophecy he would and sometimes he might still be right. This was not the future he had anticipated. He was vastly less effective as a Sangyma.

While they were talking and walking to catch up with her, Tobia felt a slight movement behind her and turned as suddenly as a rabbit might, when her fur is caught by a shiver of a breeze across a woodland. Inside her head she saw images of a young boy who looked, well, exactly like a young Ruzniel with the chin hairs yet to fall out and the slightly puffy cheeks yet to grow thinner. He looked at her quizzically through his brown eyes. He obviously did not recognize her but thought he should. He eyed her clothes which were all Ruzniel in a strange way. So they should be, they had been made-to-measure for her on Ruzniel looms, but even she could tell his style was slightly different. No rounded hat on his head and his curly hair was unbrushed. He was not a student yet he was not carrying any materials of a trade. Ruzniel his age were always apprenticed to someone. The colours he wore were more vivid than hers, the buttons made of metal rather than wood. This surprised her as Ruzniel have used wooden button, out of respect for nut trees which gifted them to them, for generations. She herself had spent many happy hours choosing the right buttons for her clothes from fruit trees.

"You with them then?" he asked, jabbing his thumb back in the direction from which she had walked.

"Who wants to know?" she asked.

"That thing you came in, what was that?" he asked her, showing no interest in answering her question.

She did not like his rude way of answering her with another question. She decided to answer him in the hope he would do the same.

"The Ossendark."

"That's a name but what does the thing do?" he persisted.

"The 'thing' is the way Sangyma travel from world to world," she explained, "If you paid attention to what went on around you, you'd know that."

"World to world, now there's a thing. How comes you can see me 'cos I can see you're blind?"

"I see you in my head."

"That's a neat trick fer a Ruzniel," he said.

"You're very rude for a Ruzniel."

"You're dressed funny but I don't go 'bout saying as much."

"I don't think you're very well brought up."

"I don't think I'll apologize for that neither. You being the ones stopping by uninvited an' all," he argued.

"I don't need to be invited to my own world."

"So says you but you might be one of them hiding things."

"Exactly what are those?"

"Things that look Ruzniel but ain't."

"I didn't know such things existed," she said.

"Not such an idiot now is I?"

"I never said you were an idiot."

"And don't you neither."

"I'm sorry if I'm a little bit sharp. Last time I was on Ruz I was alone. I escaped with Midrak just as everything was destroyed."

"This is Ruz," he pointed out tutting and raising his eyes skyward, "still 'ere. That world to world stuff made you dizzy I shouldn't wonder? Escape from what may I ask? The grass growing?"

Tobia turned her face to the sky and there above where the two suns of Ruz. All very calm. But she had seen those suns destroyed. She had been thrown into the Ossendark to save her life. She sounded crazy to the boy because this was not her Ruz, but a younger planet. She took a deep breath.

"I'm sorry, of course none of that has happened yet."

"Well then, that explains that." He shook his head as if she were the saddest girl he had ever met and rubbed his cheek with his finger.

"No need to be so sarcastic. If you don't believe me, that might only be because you're ignorant," she told him.

"That's true that is," he agreed, "If you know about things to happen you might want to come back to town and chat to the elders. Escaping Ruz sounds pretty serious to me. 'sides which yer mates are on their way here so you should all check in. Just so we know you're not the ones we'll be escaping from. If you gets my drift."

"That's not going to happen in your lifetime," she explained.

"Ain't that a relief now."

Tobia and her new Ruzniel friend, who was called Chuff and had, she soon found out, a very big idea of himself, met up with the others. Kalevala had been tracking her to the waterfall with his sensitive nose. The dog was delighted to give them an accurate description of everything that was happening to her. When he was asked how he knew what was being said he told them he could hear them, not that he could smell words. That skill belonged to another spellmaker who would come after him.

Here they were, on Ruz with a thriving Ruzniel community all around them. Kalevala must be right thought Tegriel, unknown magic must be involved in helping them. Hiesia, who was so much more practiced at jumping through time, was less concerned. She believed things had a way of working themselves out if you tried hard enough to help them along. Although when you consider just what Hiesia was capable of doing, this was not like any ordinary person trying their best but more like an artist doing what they did well with the natural ease of inborn genius.

As they neared the town Tegriel and Tobia noticed more and more of the things that made this Ruz unlike the one they knew. The Sangyma had not only visited that planet in the heat of the moment anxious to find answers or in need of a companion, they had also spent many months in the quieter times talking tactics with the scholars, and travelling around the cities from Auleed to Motil in the south–west. There were strange differences in this town of Motil as they walked through the streets. For a start they had built on the east not the west of the range of mountains that bordered the ocean. Then there were the houses. So many were two storey as if Tobia's father's eccentric design had become the norm. The Ruzniel wore different clothes as well and if all that were not enough, as he told Hiesia as they walked,

"I understand that Crilodach's having detailed information of the future would enable It to change things, so why not stop Ruz being created? This place has been here generations. When I first came here bringing Tobia, Crilodach had been active for a long time and we were looking for a teaching centre. Thinking of all the planning that went on here and what this planet has enabled millions to do, this would be the prime target for It."

"You're worrying so much about not being able to do things in the right order, you're missing the opportunity to simply do the right things. You are, after all, alive and as informed of one future as It could possibly be," suggested Hiesia. "Whatever It changes you will know, It cannot hide any changes from you."

"As always," he responded smiling, "you are right. I need to calm down. If Its using new spells we need to know what they are. I need to find Its daughters and deal with them."

"Do either of you feel different?" asked Kalevala.

"No," they both told him.

"Well something weird happened to me, because I smell different," he said.

"You?" asked Tobia.

"Yes, me. I smell strange. Not at all new and Bofindle is hot. Feel."

Tegriel touched a finger to Bofindle behind Kalevala's ear. The bejal was very hot. Even Hiesia felt the heat through her claw.

"I think she's been busy," Kalevala told them.

"Why did I not feel this magic?" worried Tegriel to himself.

Confused as they were for the moment, what was not in doubt was the friendliness of the Ruzniel and their innate understanding of magical people. Once they had realized these travellers did not want to attack them, they were welcoming. The elders of the city sat with them, eating flowers heated with fresh water from yellow water springs that made fragrant soups. Hiesia could feel her muscles relaxing. Kalevala started to play with some of the children who had never seen a dog before, with Bofindle carefully hidden in his tail for safe keeping. Some Ruzniel brought herbs to plaster his wounded leg and so was born the story of how they saved a spellmaker's leg from being amputated and though Kalevala was more than able to heal without their help, he never contradicted them. Sometimes the stories we tell ourselves are more important than the ones we are told.

"And this Ossendark, explain that to us," said a portly, red faced elder called Fraylight, during their conversation in what would become the very Choosing Rooms where Tobia had first met Tegriel.

"We travel from planet to planet in the Ossendark," said Tegriel.

"Which just appears when you call?" asked Fraylight.

"We are linked to the web connecting galaxies together," said Tegriel.

"I am sure we are but what does that mean?" asked Kikkelrick, another elder with a delightful smile that lit up the entire room.

"In a manner of speaking, we were brought here," Tegriel replied.

"Must be a fascinating way to travel. Though if you end up in the wrong places not very practical, if you don't mind me saying," said Fraylight.

"When you know where you're going travelling's less fun," Hiesia told him.

"You don't seem very surprised by our appearing here," Kalevala observed, shaking his body and pulling at a ribbon one of the children had tied behind his right ear.

"We have had visitors before though never through this Ossendark," Fraylight told him.

"So we are the first magical people you have ever met," said Tegriel.

"I didn't say that," replied Fraylight.

"Well, are we or aren't we?" Tobia asked.

"You must know many places in this universe of ours," added Kikkelrick, quickly.

"To tell the truth we do not," replied Tegriel, seeing the elders wanted to learn more about them before revealing any secrets about other magical visitors, "I mean from what I know you should not exist yet," answered Tegriel. "Time is complicated," he added at their quizzical looks.

"And yet you say we're companions to magicians, with vast academies and a long history?" asked Fraylight, turning to Tobia.

"I was taught at them," she told him.

"This creature of whom you speak changed the past so we're not aware of our own academies?" asked Kikkelrick.

"We can only guess at what more has changed," said Tobia.

"Maybe we should show you what we know," suggested Kikkelrick, "That way at least you'll be able to get your bearings."

"Show us what you know?" asked Hiesia, intrigued.

"He means to take us to the large domed hall in the centre of the park on the south side of the town," Kalevala said.

"And how d'you know that?" asked Fraylight.

"Smells of more magic than I've ever smelled in one place, ever. Almost overpowering." Then he turned to Hiesia and whispered, "Bofindle has more power but doesn't have such a smell."

"I must travel with you more often," she replied, "I would never go wrong with someone who can smell everything so acutely."

"That much has not changed," smiled Tegriel, who heard everything despite the whispering.

"I've the best nose you can have for smelling out magic," said Kalevala.

"Sounds to us like you're still getting to know each other too," smiled Kikkelrick. Which of course is true because no matter how long a time you spend in the company of magical people, you are always learning new things about them.

From the future Choosing Rooms they took a curved, short pathway and walked through the front, iron doors of the dome. They walked into a round room which was circled by balconies, connected by steps, all overlooking the central open space. They went right to the top, looked down and there in front of them floating in the air in myriad colours, Ruz appeared orbiting other planets then receded and soon more planets and more appeared. By reaching out and touching them they could turn the view and travel around the universe, and so slowly Tegriel gained an understanding through this planetarium of what was in existence and what was not. Several important things had changed but more than that he noticed Damkina was not shown. Hiesia knew much of this map by heart and as far as she could see nothing much was different but she noticed Damkina was not there too. Crilodach's lair was the marker they always looked for first to remind themselves of the reason for their existence. The planet had a unique outline, because Damkina had no sun to orbit, but hanged in space with just Ghirzanben nearby. Turning slowly and maintaining orbit and gravity through Crilodach's will. It had used the energy from the destroyed sun to create Its first creatures.

"Where did this come from?" Tegriel asked the elders, as he looked at the huge map of the universe, "Have you travelled the universe to gather all this knowledge?"

"Not at all, we can't leave Ruz, we don't know how to though we know such a thing is possible. Now we've seen the Ossendark we know you've got the gift," said Fraylight.

"This map was given to us," explained Kikkelrick, "We were told by a traveller who first came to us, before I was born mind, to build the dome after which he placed these images here. We've been taught what the worlds all mean, their names in several languages, we know of the peoples on many of them, but we don't know why he gave us this knowledge."

"You know all this?" asked Hiesia astonished, "and you've never visited one other world?"

"And we teach what we know. Every Ruzniel knows every planet and world here, every sun and all the distances between them. In fact you might say this planetarium is as close to the academy you talk about as we've managed to build. Not bad though I say so myself," said Fraylight.

"Why do you learn so much that's of no use to you?" asked Kalevala.

"We were told one day, the 'why' would be obvious," answered Kikkelrick.

"By the traveller who brought this to you?" asked Tegriel.

"The same," said Fraylight.

"What was his name?" asked Hiesia.

"Fulminar," replied Fraylight.

"Fulminar!" Tegriel exclaimed, happily.

"You know him?" the elders asked him together.

"As well as I know Ruz but he will not know me, we have not yet met, though we should have long before Ruz was born."

"As I said, the balance has been kept, even without you being here," observed Kalevala.

"How could Fulminar have found Ruz without you?" Tobia asked.

"Whatever the sisters being here changed was more than just in the fight with us. Ruz must have been created earlier because the Ruzniel had to be made ready and we were kept out of the fight until some equilibrium had been reached. This is one of the things that cannot be changed because Tobia was at the fight against Crilodach and her past is fixed. So her father and mother must be born. We all live our lives forwards, so everything we have all been through to get here must either be fixed or changed so little as to make no difference."

"Including all the millions we have touched and known throughout all our lives," said Hiesia.

"So in trying to change the past to Its advantage the laws of magic have ensured It created destiny," said Tegriel.

"But not everyone's. Things are very dangerously changed," suggested Kaveleva, "As far as I can see no one here even knows who Crilodach is."

"That can only be because Its still trapped," said Tegriel, "still about to create Damkina. Maybe, even as we are speaking, It has broken free and created Hâgon."

"Unless this planetarium just doesn't show Damkina," suggested Fraylight.

"This isn't a model of the universe. Everything that is happening, happens as you watch in real time," said Kalevala, "If Damkina existed now we would know."

"Even those bright explosions?" asked Kikkelrick.

"Even those, they are exploding stars. And here look, look at this thread that appeared, can you see?"

"No," replied the elders."

"I can," smiled Tegriel, "The Ossendark. Someone is out there doing our work even as we are standing talking here."

"Does this explain why Fulminar came here without knowing you?" asked Fraylight.

"He is a Sangyma," replied Tegriel. "He would have had good reason."

Kalevala took Bofindle out of his tail and showed the

Ruzniel a small toothpick size bar and then, smiling, he threw Bofindle into the planetarium.

"Remember this is an image to the real universe," he said and then he snapped his teeth together. He sat on his haunches and watched.

The toothpick grew right along the planetarium until the bejal stretched from one end to the other. The two Ruzniel looked and suddenly realized,

"Your magic spans the whole universe," said Kikkelrick.

"This one bejal does," said Tegriel.

"You must be the ones," said Kikkelrick.

"Ones?" asked Tobia.

"Fulminar said a magician would arrived who knew of him. He said we could trust you as much as we trust him," said Kikkelrick.

"You assume he meant us?" asked Hiesia.

"He said this traveller would be accompanied by a Ruzniel like us," said Kikkelrick, "Now seeing as we can't leave our world and we know our own very well, and this little one is new to us yet one of us, I think we may safely assume he meant you."

Tegriel drew the map towards him and scanned the planets for a long time. Another world was showing that should not be created for many years yet. Then he said softly,

"The heat you felt from Bofindle, Kalevala. Could we have been in the Ossendark for millions of years?"

"Not impossible," said the dog."

"That would explain why, despite what It now knows, Fulminar was still born and he made his way here. That proves It must have been trapped during the time we were in the Ossendark," said Tegriel.

"Unless It tried to kill Fulminar and failed," said Tobia.

"Well Fulminar and Ruz at least met, which means others may be around whom we need but they will not have all the information they need. Troubles may already be starting even without Damkina being the centre of Its operations. For all we know Crilodach decided not to create Damkina this time."

"Where would It have found a planet to train Its soldiers if not Ghirzanben?" asked Hiesia.

"Why would It need them if we haven't been here?" Tobia asked.

"And even with It trapped, the sisters have been working

away. What have they managed to do?" said Tegriel anxiously.

"Maybe trying things slightly differently this time will benefit us all."

"You think I failed before?" he asked her.

"I think we've as much chance of success now as we ever did," Tobia replied, "because whatever Crilodach and Its daughters have done, if anything, we're still in the fight."

Tegriel paced up and down and then his eyes sparkled and he said,

"We can only be here now because the magic working for us knows Crilodach is coming. I know what to do next."

"What?" they all said together.

"I must go to Rûel."

"That's important?" asked Kalevala.

"Rûel, second only to Earth, hides a great treasure," said Tegriel, "I need to go to find out what is going on there."

"Are we safe to divide our forces," asked Kalevala.

"We have no choice but to split up and gather as much information as we can. Maybe meet back here at a later date," said Hiesia.

"We must find out how much information It sent back with Its two daughters," said Tegriel, "We must ask the elders to keep secret everything about this day and all they have been told. And, if we can, how Dalved caused Its unexpected change."

"My ramming It into the planet didn't help It much," observed Kalevala, with a doggy–like smirk of satisfaction.

"Let me understand you," said Fraylight, slowly who had been listening intently, "You're saying certain things haven't changed even though Crilodach sent Its daughters back in time and tried to change everything?"

"Yes we are," said Tegriel.

"Didn't Filvani say that what is done is done? I remember talking to him about the Upala," said Hiesia, "He said we only think we go back in time, but since we are always living our own lives in a forward direction, what we are doing is always in our own future. So, even if we are in the past of the universe actually where we are is always where we should be."

"Up to now Hiesia you were the only one who dotted around time and though you made a difference none of us felt the universe changing around you to balance out any changes you made. Now we will all feel those changes," said Tegriel.

"Crilodach tried to make Its future a past It had never had whilst It still existed in that past, and came unstuck," surmised Fraylight

"We have all become unstuck," replied Tegriel. "That leaves us vulnerable."

"But we must still keep everyone else's interest at heart," Tobia told him.

"She's right," agreed Hiesia, "the only thing you can do is be true at all times to your calling."

"But that's quite a thing," smiled Kalevala, "Crilodach thinking It was so clever and getting far more than It bargained for."

A Ruzniel joined them in the planetarium and almost ran up the stairs to them. She whispered to the elders and they nodded, patted her shoulder and turned to their visitors. Kalevala who had heard what she said gave a slight shake of his head and Bofindle flew out of the planetarium and back into his tail. His hackles rose.

"You could make a start by fighting with us," suggested Kikkelrick. Tegriel, Tobia and Hiesia all looked at the elder intently.

"Those sisters you've been talking about, Yaltha and Freyom, we think they're here," said Fraylight.

Hiesia interlocked her claws and clicked her knuckles. Fighting those two sisters was the one thing that would make her feel better after all Tegriel's talk of not being sure about this and that. She remembered all she was and all she had gone through on Ghirzanben. Every victory, every cut, every time she stopped Its plans, she gained a little revenge for those who had died saving her. For the cruel and unnecessary experiments she saw, for the nightmares she still traded for sleep.

"So much for them not knowing where we'd gone," said Tobia.

"There are things I have not yet understood about our situation Tobia, just give me time," Tegriel said.

"If they can track you through the Ossendark then Crilodach's given them more power than they showered on me," Hiesia told him.

"*If* they tracked us," said Tegriel.

"What else could they do?" asked the bear.

"Maybe they planned to destroy Ruz if they were unsuccessful in stopping me," Tegriel replied.

"And find us in the future, to the same day and within a few hours? That's no chance," she growled, "and as far as Crilodach would have known, Ruz was not to be created for aeons so It didn't send them. How did the sisters find us?"

"They are subject to the laws of magic just as we are, they may have wanted to go to Ruz at another time and been brought here to be stopped by us. The Ossendark is working to rules I have yet to gauge," said Tegriel.

"Or something else is using the Ossendark to help us," observed Kalevala. "Either way they're here and that means we fight. Bofindle gets to thrash the whole family, that's something you Ruzniel can tell your friends about."

"Do you think they've met their father?" said Tobia, as they walked out.

"Not if they left soon after us. Crilodach wasn't going to get out of that planet fast, not in the state It was in," said Tegriel.

"From Hiesia's description they wouldn't have wanted to meet It too soon anyway,"said Kalevala.

"This affords us a perfect chance to find out what's been going on," said Tegriel, "if I can access Freyom's or Yaltha's brain I can unpick some of their knowledge. Find out what they know, read the armour find out what information Crilodach sent back. If we know what It knows, we are back in the fight."

"That means killing them and getting to their brains fast," Hiesia pointed out.

"Can't you cast a spell and take them over?" Tobia asked.

"Do you think that would be any easier?" asked Kalevala.

"Might save a fight," Tobia said.

"The magic we could use to invade their brains would kill them instantly and remove any chance we have of questioning them," said Tegriel, "To use the spells I need to be within touching distance and then we could only get to one at a time, unless we were lucky. Once one of them was dead the other would fight with even more ferocity. If either senses what we were trying to do, they might kill the sister we trap, then run."

"Or they may be like the Waliro," said Hiesia. Then she added for those who did not know them, "They're a people conjoined psychically since birth. They never leave their dead on the battlefield. When one falls another recreates the body instantly with their thoughts. To kill one you have to kill them all. They cannot be beaten by conventional armies. If the sisters are able to do that they would continuously recreate themselves, making battles endless."

"The best way to take over their brains is to get to them in the last moments of life. We must capture them alive. Both of them. Even though that's the most difficult strategy," ended Tegriel.

"I didn't kill them before because I thought their power was still growing and I didn't know what I'd unleash. I remember the creatures of Crilodach that exuded deadly plagues when they died, or whose shed blood turned into yet more creatures," Hiesia added. "They'll never be taken alive. In that close a fight the difference between wounding and killing is not so much as a bear's hair's breadth."

"Talking won't get the job done," pointed out Kalevala growling, "How far away are they?"

"A few minutes. Our first soldiers are already outside waiting their arrival," said Kikkelrick.

"Keep your people back," ordered Tegriel, "they would not have a chance against the sisters."

Fraylight made no response to the Sangyma. The Ruzniel Tegriel knew fought bravely with magicians but on Ruz there had never been an army. This was not the Ruz Tegriel had helped to create. All over Motil, Ruzniel were taking up defensive positions. And a corps were assembled in the fields in front of the gates, armed and ready.

Tegriel walked briskly with Hiesia and the elders through the city streets where the militia were assembling to protect the houses. Living in the refined atmosphere of the Academies, Tobia had never seen her people going to a fight. The Sangyma had protected their planet for so long the Ruzniel used nothing more lethal than a hammer. Tobia looked at the young solders and observed,

"We have weapons."

"Of course," responded Hiesia, "there are no spells protecting Ruz yet. Fulminar has been wise enough to keep them on alert without interfering with Tegriel's work."

"How did he know to do any of this?" asked Tegriel.

"We'll ask him when we get to meet him," said Hiesia.

"Who are our enemies?" Tobia asked Chuff, who was geared out in protective steel with a tight fitting helmet

313

through which his ears stuck out.

"All we know is we 'ave to be ready like," he told her. "Fulminar said we'd have to fight for ourselves if help didn't arrive."

"That sounds like Fulminar," agreed Tegriel."

"Knowing him," responded Hiesia, "I'll give you evens he greets you by name before you say a word."

"If he does, matters will be in more assured hands than I think they are right now," answered Tegriel.

"If that happens I'm going to need a lot of explanations," Tobia told him.

Tegriel had to be so careful, so very careful, not to upset matters even more. Magic may be in balance but he felt totally out of sync with everything. For the first time in many ages Tegriel was not sure of his footing, not sure of his next spell, not sure of his next action. Yaltha and Freyom held all the answers he desperately needed. But then he also realized Crilodach's knowledge was only of use to It if everything stayed the same. If nothing were the same there was now a balance of ignorance between them.

The sisters arrived on the rise outside the city and saw lines of Ruzniel to their left and right. After their fight they had cursed Tegriel and Hiesia and wondered, briefly, about trying to free Crilodach, but Yaltha persuaded Freyom not to bother. Telling their father they had failed was not something either of them relished. For all her talk, when Yaltha had had a chance to confront her father she did not feel ready. The sisters still needed a lot more magic on their side before they could be certain of beating It in a fight.

They had a struggle with the spells and had to try four times before the Ossendark opened and allowed them to travel. That annoyed them. When they arrived they had no idea where they were, until they saw the Ruzniel lined up in ranks. Unlike Tegriel the sight did not make them apprehensive because they did not know the time–lines for the creation of Ruz and the founding of Damkina had changed. They recognized who the Ruzniel were and that was enough for them.

"We're in the heart of enemy territory," said Freyom.

"Scared sister–mine?" Yaltha asked her pointedly, still fuming at Freyom's words when they were bound to the tree.

"The day I fear our enemy is the day you can bury me as deep as our father," Freyom replied.

"They're waiting for us on the hill. This time I think they mean business," said Kalevala sniffing the air.

"And they didn't last time?" Tobia asked.

"They're ravenous," he added.

"Anything else you can tell from the smell?" asked Tegriel.

"They still smell of Samphin and the palace they lived in all their lives. They've not travelled anywhere before coming here. Like us, I think they've been brought here across time by the Ossendark's magic."

"Last time they were just as interested in working against their father as against us," warned Hiesia, "Now they know they can never do that, they'll come at us full force."

Yaltha was the first to strike. The moment she saw them she flung herself across the ground as if she had wings on her feet, revolving in mid-air, landing on Kalevala's back raising her sword to thrust into his heart before he had time to twist and bite her. Tobia leapt up at her and hit her in her face with both her hands feeling the stone–like hardness of her skin. In Tobia's mind Yaltha was not as tall as she really was, nor as powerfully built. Something in the armour was trying to block her senses. Tobia was taken by surprise as she bounced off Yaltha, but the attack made Yaltha close her eyes for a vital second giving Kalevala time to jump backwards and raise his back, forcing her momentarily blinded strike to miss his shoulder by a whisker. He threw Yaltha off with a roll. She sprang back up looking for Tobia but the Ruzniel troops had run up and covered Tobia with their shields. Fraylight had already told them not to fight the sisters directly, but to protect the flanks and backs of their allies. They ran about the battle ground in groups moving with incredible speed, far faster than the Ruzniel Tegriel remembered.

Even so the sisters fought with such blistering speed they found difficulty in keeping track of them. No longer wary the sisters threw themselves at their enemy with a potent blood lust. Whether they were thrown to the ground or pushed back they rolled and side–stepped with aplomb so that an attack from the right would soon become a secondary attack from the left, so that a miss would become another strike a few steps away in the same, smooth movement. Their eyes were swift and their arms swung like thunder bolts. But the sisters soon got fed up with their swords hitting shields instead of flesh and they started kicking out with their metal boots, sending one or two of the Ruzniel flying.

Hiesia becoming invisible, grabbed Freyom from the back but Freyom was waiting for such a ploy. She jumped up, somersaulted backwards and brought her sword down so fast Hiesia was almost cut on her arm. The sisters were not shouting or screaming, they were not calling out or cursing, they were just intent on fighting and fighting again, and cutting away at the energy and will of their enemy. They were ferocious and tireless. They had learned their lesson from their first fight with Hiesia. More than that they had seen their father struggling as It transformed and two things had struck them as they ran into the Ossendark to follow their enemies. Their father looked like the slaves they had been used to maltreating without a moment's hesitation. The beast was hiding a man. Something they never knew. They also heard It screaming in pain deep below the ground. They did not know how long It might be struck there but they had no wish to free It. Suddenly they were in command and they knew that if they could beat Tegriel and his few friends they would be able to rule over entire galaxies. Maybe they could find the Sagitæ.

Overcome with selfish desire they fought with terrifying determination.

Freyom lost her sword to a parry by Tegriel, who seemed to have unseen weapons that sparked and struck at her like knives. Every stroke gave off a sweet perfume because Tegriel's magic was mixed with honey and jasmine. The sisters had to struggle to stay focussed as they breathed in this sweet scent.

Freyom found herself with Kalevala's mouth round her arm but she was half Crilodach and her own teeth bit into Kalevala's side. Both drew blood trying to drag the other to the ground, before breaking off panting with fur and skin on their teeth. She took out her knives and leapt at Tegriel who lifted a hand and sent her flying to his left. She landed on her back, rolled, sprang up as if she had developed springs on her back and threw both knives one to his left and one to his right. They spun past his face as he turned sideways and he watched one fly across his line of sight so close he could feel the warmth of Freyom's skin still on the handle.

Hiesia caught one and Tobia caught the other. Tobia grimaced from the heat.

Tegriel realized these knives were forged by Frin-Ghirzan and since they survived the journey back he understood from the laws that that meant Frin-Ghirzan would still be born and work for Crilodach. He inwardly smiled. As Filvani had said to him once, 'time, like a river may alter course a hundred times, may even flow upwards, but the water can never stop flowing. Even if turned to ice, the glacier just flows more slowly'. Such is the nature of destiny.

Tobia felt the knife burning as the handle tried to twist her hand forcing her to cut her own throat. A claw took hold of the dagger. Her heart leapt in fright but Hiesia's voice came to her,

"These weapons will fight on by themselves. If you keep hold of one you'll die for sure. If you put one in your belt they would slide out and stab into you at the first opportunity. Only spells can hold these weapons back."

Tobia let go and Hiesia gripped the dagger with her greater strength. If only Tegriel had said they could kill the sisters. This would be so much easier. She just wanted to see the last of these two women. She had fought them to a standstill not a few hours before and now here they were, filled with renewed energy. The sisters joined closer together. Their spines rattled. Behind Tegriel a line of Ruzniel stood on one knee, shields up, looking at the sisters. Yaltha wanted some blood for all her efforts. She laughed as she attacked them. She knew about the Sangyma and their precious allies. She knew Sangyma took the death of others hard.

Tegriel looked back trying to save them but he need not have worried. The Ruzniel were well trained for soldiers who had never seen Crilodach or fought any of Its creatures before. Their weapons had the form of shields but the shields were magical, emitting powerful waves that pounded Yaltha with the force of her own attack, and made her bones shake even as she ran towards them. She was thrown off balance and rolling stood up and stepped back to take stock, then Bofindle thrown with perfect aim by Kalevala sent her flying. Hiesia took the chance to throw a net over her.

Hiesia was not only mistress of her own invisibility, she could make someone think everything else was invisible. Suddenly Yaltha, who could not see or feel the net, was alone. She was not only shielded from seeing the world around her clearly, she could not feel, smell, hear or sense anything in any way. She knew this was magic and she tried to find the spell that was attacking her, but the spell was not attacking her. The net was merely changing the atoms closest to her in the air and since she did not know that, she assumed something was touching her skin, some magic was attacking her sense. She twisted and turned this way and that but every one and everything had vanished. She could not feel the ground under her feet but did not fall over anything. She could not hear her sister and though she shouted out her name she was not heard by Freyom or anyone else. She ran, becoming disorientated. Breathing hard she swung wildly to no effect. Hiesia focussed all her attention on keeping Yaltha out of the fight. Cursing and shouting Yaltha ripped out spines and threw wildly but she could not see where the spines went or what they did.

They flew out of nowhere and almost hit Hiesia who for one heart–stopping second thought Yaltha could break her spell but soon realized as other spines flew out in other directions that the sister was throwing them blindly. Nonetheless the Ruzniel came in a broad circle around Hiesia and stopped a few of the spines which lodged into their shields and melted them utterly away. They dropped the vanishing shields and turned their heads away from the sickening smell. Not a few of the Ruzniel were grateful for others to be fighting these ferocious sisters.

But though Yaltha fought and cursed, Hiesia's magic saved her life for the moment Yaltha disappeared from her sight was the moment Freyom died. Freyom looked for her sister and thinking she was taken prisoner she flung herself at Tegriel who caught the full blow of her strike with his arms, protected by his spells. Her sword broke into three pieces, one part of which flew upwards and cut into Freyom's neck. She fell forward onto her stomach her head hitting the ground so hard she sank half way into the soil. Kalevala ran up striking her with Bofindle, Tobia bent by her side.

"Quickly Kalevala take her and Tobia back to the city, get her to the surgeons. We need her brain active, I must be able to talk to her. Then strip off the armour. Don't let her die yet."

Lifting the body of the dying Freyom onto his back Kalevala and Tobia ran back to the town in seconds. Tegriel then ordered the Ruzniel back behind the gates and when everyone had gone he and Hiesia looked at each other. This was going to be tough but now they did not need Yaltha they could fight her to the death.

"Now?" Hiesia asked.

"Now," agreed Tegriel, facing Yaltha whom he was well able to see thanks to Hiesia.

Yaltha suddenly saw everything clearly again and saw Hiesia and Tegriel standing in front and beside her. She looked around. The others had gone. Her sister was gone. She spat, gripped her sword, bowed her shoulders slightly, ready to take the repercussions of the heavy blows she was about to inflict.

"Before you attack you should know your sister is dead." Tegriel's words were not forced or breathless but strong and clear.

Many times over the years both sisters had wished the other dead. They shared little love for each other and wondered if being alone would be better than being together. Yaltha might have carried on fighting but, somehow, now she was actually alone she didn't like the odds of fighting these two by herself. Freyom might not be dead, the Sangyma could be lying, but then where was she? She could not sense, feel or talk to her in any way.

"Liar," she spat.

These were the first words she had uttered since they had started fighting. Tegriel picked up Freyom's broken sword and threw the pieces, one still blood–stained, at Yaltha's feet. She looked down. She bent down keeping them both in sight and touched the blood. Her sister's, and there was a lot. The liquid scalded her fingers. Spoke to her. She could feel the life force draining from Freyom.

"With her dead we might be able to work together against your father," suggested Hiesia.

Yaltha twisted her neck to get rid of the ache and stretched back her shoulders. She knew she could go on fighting and maybe land a lucky strike or two. She would have to be very lucky to wound either of them enough to claim any kind of victory. She wanted to maintain her anger but suddenly she could not, suddenly she felt as if there had come a time for a new way forward, a change in her actions. A plot to get what she wanted another way. Should Crilodach ever find out she could protest she was spying on them to find out how they killed her sister, or even better spying on them to bring her father news of Its enemies. In all events she was facing the two people who had killed her sister and she was no more powerful, faster or a better fighter than Freyom had been. Killing them would take planning, especially if she was going to live on afterwards. Neither of the sisters wanted to throw away their lives for each other or their father. Besides, with all the training Crilodach had given them they had failed. Her father was not as clever as It made out. Its plans! Its big ideas! She blamed It for everything that had gone wrong and in that way she could justify any of her own actions.

Tegriel and Hiesia did not hear any of her thoughts they just saw Yaltha sheath her sword and click each of her fists with either hand to release the tension in her claws. Her thick tongue licked around her teeth and lips.

"I told you we could work together," she reminded Hiesia, "Pity you had to kill my sister before you realized how good an idea that is."

"I doubt you have any pity for you sister," replied Tegriel.

"I've none, but two of us as allies are stronger than one," said Yaltha.

"One is all we need," pointed out Hiesia.

"And what happens when you don't need me?" she asked.

"This is more like a truce," Tegriel suggested, "which will help us both make sure we can control Crilodach."

"You can't control a beast that has reason. You found that out in your dealings with Earth," she argued.

"What do you know of Earth?" asked Tegriel.

"Our father taught us well, we had the time to learn much," she said.

She liked the way she could keep them interested in what she knew. They wanted information from her, not her fighting skills. Keeping them guessing about how much she knew would keep her alive long enough to engineer their deaths.

Tegriel was very aware that Crilodach might have been able to get a message back to the sisters that the Earth was in fact a Sagitæ hiding from them. Might have told them about the humans and the clone. He would have to be very careful how he handled her especially as he had decided to go to Rûel next to find out what was happening there. Not taking her with him was not an option. She was too dangerous to leave to her own devices on Ruz.

"I am going to see the Elders. They insist on burying your sister," Tegriel told her.

"How noble of them," sneered Yaltha.

❖

Everyone was under strict orders not to let Yaltha know what they were doing with Freyom. To aid the deception they buried her body with Yaltha present and even gave Yaltha permission to light the pyre. But they kept Freyom's brain in the surgery where Tegriel could analyze her thoughts. He took two days to interrogate Freyom.

Yaltha believed what she knew was her trump card. He had to allow her to think she knew more than he did. His first priority was to work out just how much to tell Yaltha and then to get her away from Ruz. To do this effectively he walked with Tobia one drizzly morning two days later having formed a plan of action.

Birds were flying everywhere. After the long struggles of the past days Tobia looked brighter now she was at home. He smiled when he greeted her. Tegriel had never had a home. He did not know the feeling. Homes were for others. Of all the Sangyma Tegriel was the one most alone, most of the time.

"How have you been these past two days?" he asked her.

"Busy," she told him. "And you've been hiding away since the funeral."

"Trying to find out how best to proceed with Yaltha," he told her.

"I thought you'd decided you were going to Rûel."

"That was an easy decision. There are many more to make. We have to try to ensure the Sangyma thrive and the Ruzniel strengthen their Academies."

"Oh, the mythical, blind Ruzniel who was me."

"Is you. You are here, the Ruzniel are thriving and the foundations of the Academies already exist. That said, what else has been done that once was, and what is left to do, are vital questions I have yet to answer. However, thanks to Freyom, I know much of what Crilodach knows."

"But not everything?"

"I cannot assume to know everything anymore. I have spoken with the elders here. Apparently two of them worked with Fulminar and know what kind of people the Sangyma are, but if this is to work I need you to stay here."

"To teach them all I know."

"You knew what I was going to say," he smiled.

"I came to the same conclusion. I've been talking to a few young people and they're very enthusiastic about being companions to magical people like you. I can teach them all I know, that way the Academies will be similar to what you expect them to be. You and I are the only ones who know and you have to go elsewhere, I understand that. I can also be here when Fulminar next arrives and if you haven't met with him by then, I can tell him about us."

"I will leave you with some suggested courses of action for him and a letter for his eyes only."

"I've never met the other Sangyma, except Gertis and he said he was the youngest so he isn't expected for a while yet. How will I recognize any of the others if they turn up?"

"Sangyma recognize each other, there are no signs or symbols Crilodach could fake. We are born, Tobia, not made. If Fulminar and I meet soon, together we can protect Ruz, then you won't have to worry about attacks. Until then all I ask of you is, be very careful."

"My middle name," she told him.

"Then that is settled. You will stay here. We will be apart for a while. I hope when I return I will have news of Crilodach's activities."

"What about Freyom's remains?"

"I am going to leave her brain here. We may need to search for more information yet."

"Leaving a part of Crilodach here's like lighting a beacon saying 'come on in.'"

"She cannot communicate with any one. Hiesia has hidden her in a net so the brain is unaware of everything going on outside."

"Does she know she's dead?" asked Tobia.

"She thinks she is enchanted in some way. I could not risk her anger at knowing we had defeated her. She thought I was just a voice in her head. We told her I was dead."

"She must've loved that news."

"She did until I told her Yaltha had killed me. I could feel her aggravation." He shook his head.

"So, I'm to leave her alone."

"Make sure she is secure, Hiesia will teach you to check the enchaining spell, but do not speak to her."

Hiesia was walking in the spring air. She did not enjoy seeing Freyom's brain captured, floating in the spells Tegriel had cast. Having been in prison she had an instinctive dislike of any spell that smelled of confinement. Freyom was never to be fully alive again and, since she had no way of realizing her complete defeat she would relentlessly struggle to break free. Hiesia felt the inescapable vice of her fate.

Seeing the two of them walking together, she wandered over and hugged Tobia.

"Have you found out everything?" she asked Tegriel.

"It sent back details of many battles, names of many magicians and leaders in her armour. It does not know all I know but so much of what I did must change now. It sent the sisters back with accurate accounts of almost all our lives. They were to scavenge for us like a pair of vultures. I know of the places in which It will be waiting for you."

"So It knows where and when every Sangyma was born just as It boasted?" asked Hiesia.

"Yes It does," he admitted.

"That's terrible," said Tobia.

"It worries me not as long as I possess the Sagitæ," said Hiesia.

"Crilodach must have been badly affected by Dalved because I still cannot trace any recent activity anywhere. It does not know the Earth will be a Sagitæ, It probably did not learn that, if at all, until the sisters had gone but It knows about the bears. It knows you escape from Damkina. As soon as Its free It will move against whatever and whoever It can," said Tegriel. "I just do not know how long we have to prepare our defences."

"We've got to warn the other Sangyma," said Hiesia.

"First to Rûel, then to find out where we are in time and who exists."

"I think you'd best leave today," said Tobia, "we can't risk It being free unchecked."

"I know," agreed Tegriel. "I am taking Yaltha with me."

"You must never trust her," warned Hiesia.

"That much I know without being told. I am leaving Tobia here. I think you should stay for however long you can and help them with the Academies. The bears were always friends of the Ruzniel. When you feel the need to go, or are drawn away, try to let me know."

"We're always bumping into each other," Hiesia joked.

"My biggest worry is using the Ossendark in case I jump far into the future again."

"You have no choice but to put your trust in the magic

working to keep the balance of our destinies," said Hiesia.

"No one here trusts Yaltha," said Tobia, "As the Academies are not even up and running she doesn't actually know any more than she knew from her father."

"Except the fact that the Academies are not here yet. That piece of information could be vital for Crilodach," said Tegriel.

"True," Tobia conceded.

"The sisters were under orders to destroy Ruz. With me dead Crilodach did not want any of the other Sangyma appearing and taking my place," Tegriel told them. "but that should have been two battles separated by a long, long time not taking place within moments of each other."

"Ruz is the heart of the Sangyma. Are the sisters aware of all the fighting the Ruzniel did and of the three lost Ruzniel," asked Hiesia,

"Yes. Its experiments will still take place to birth Its daughters so two of those Ruzniel I cannot help."

"The only ones ever tortured in Damkina to keep their secrets," observed Hiesia.

"You did," Tegriel said.

"I escaped before they killed me. To hold out after death, against those foulest of spells, that takes a very rare strength. Were the sisters on their way to the bears after Ruz?"

"Not to the bears, no. Crilodach did not make the sisters strong enough for that but after destroying Ruz they were supposed to create an army as quickly as they could. It had long term plans for Its daughters. It thought they would make better commanders than Zibanda, Rataplan and the dragon cousins."

"All of which was just to keep them from challenging It," said Hiesia.

"I have to go. Chuff wants to know all about you, and the elders want to discuss the foundation plans of the Academies," said Tobia, seeing the morning sun climbing towards lunch.

"Don't forget the gardens," said Hiesia, "whatever else changes don't leave them out."

"I won't," promised the Ruzniel.

"Stay well and be strong. I will see you as soon as I am able. Now where is that Yaltha?" said Tegriel.

"Over at the barracks asking lots of questions about

weapons," said Hiesia.

"The sooner I get her away from here the better," he muttered.

Tegriel and Hiesia walked on in quiet discussion for half an hour then hugged goodbye and Hiesia left him to deal with Yaltha alone. Hiesia too had places to go and later that year, after Fulminar had visited and explained many things to her that just raised even more questions, she disappeared for nearly ten years appearing unexpectedly again, as usual, just when needed

Yaltha was practicing jumping over spears which she had set in the ground, making the jumps as hard as possible by setting them in the soil uphill and jumping from the bottom. When he came towards her she walked over, her arms sweaty, her back almost healed from the battle wounds. Silently to herself she promised she would deal with Hiesia and get even. Not yet and not here. She needed their help just to get away as she could not create the Ossendark without Freyom. Another limitation for which she hated her father.

Her narrow eyes searched Tegriel's face. She was looking for signs of worry, smelling for recent spells he may have used. She knew she was being kept in the dark about many things. She had to put up with that for now. She was wondering, with some fear, if there were any signs of her father. No matter how glib her tongue, explaining why she was working with Tegriel would be a hard task with her sister's death unavenged.

As yet Yaltha did not know either that Freyom was still in part alive, or that they were far into the future from where she and her sister first met Hiesia. Keeping these facts from her when they left Ruz was going to be difficult, she was no fool, and she would soon begin to see what she had been taught and what she was experiencing, were out of sync. Once she knew that she would become unmanageable, thinking that she had much to benefit from the chaos.

"Her ashes were scattered?" she said.

"They do not like the way the ground has burned, killing all the flowers where the ashes fell, but they said all things must be remembered. I told them nothing would grow there again."

A patch of ground that would have great significance for all the graduates from this day on, because here they would see Its absolute destruction of life, which they defied.

"I bet that made them regret their kindness," she sneered.

"They are a people of great heart."

"Except the one you travel with."

"Tobia comes from another time, as have you. Everything has changed because you came back."

"That worries you?" she asked him.

"Your father will be more worried. I do not desire complete control. It does."

"I've a good side you know but with your attitude I keep myself guarded."

"Yaltha, you have no good side. You are here because working with me is worth your while. You are playing along. The moment you can, you will take advantage."

"That's what that bear tells you."

"She is never wrong." Yaltha shrugged and said, "Have you learned what my father's doing yet?"

"No. I have things to do and people to see."

"What happens to me?" she asked.

"I intend to take you with me."

"I thought I was a prisoner here," she said, surprised that he would take the risk and answer her honestly.

"You will be more use where I am going."

"You think I'm a threat to Ruz don't you?"

"Always."

"And keeping me by your side is a good way to keep an eye on me."

"If you say so."

"What if I want to stay here?"

"I am not giving you a choice," he told her. She slowly nodded and said,

"Am I to be armed?"

"Only if I think we are heading into danger, which we are not."

"I'm not used to being unarmed."

"To begin with Yaltha you will do as I say. I will leave you on any planet I choose the moment you try anything."

"I doubt you'll pass up my usefulness. Just as I doubt you'll ever share any of your plans with me."

"You will learn a lot on our travels," he told her, "what you do with that knowledge is up to you.

"Everything I learn I'll have to dig out for myself. You don't fool me Tegriel. You'd just as soon kill me as talk to me."

"If I had wanted you dead you would be."

"Readily spreading my ashes on Ruz like Freyom's, no doubt."

"You did not mourn your sister's death very long so why should I be sorry she is dead."

"She wouldn't have mourned mine. We're like that in my family, we tend to move on quickly."

"A touch of tenderness would make you understand how I work."

"I can understand everything by watching."

He caught the ice in her voice and silently cursed her father for changing events so much that he had to travel with this cunning creature.

"I am going in an hour, be ready," he said.

"Intriguing you want to get me away so fast, is anything happening here?"

"I told you I have things to do."

"I trust I'm still allowed my armour."

"That has been cleaned of all spells. Freyom's stays here, the Ruzniel want to understand Frin-Ghirzan's design techniques."

"The Ruzniel keep the possessions of the dead? How morbid. And you tried to tell me your people are different to mine."

"You do not have a people."

"One day I will Tegriel, and what then? D'you think you'll teach me to love you enough to fight alongside you?"

"You are indifferent to tenderness Yaltha, you will never love and you will fight on the side that offers you the most."

"You know what father wanted to know more than anything else?" she said.

"What?"

"How to find the spellmakers as children." Tegriel looked at Yaltha without answering and nodded.

"One hour," he reminded her and walked away.

He was slightly astonished she had admitted that to him. She was telling the truth. He had found the same orders in Freyom. At first he had been surprised thinking the Sagitæ should be Its primary target, but Hiesia has reasoned that It wanted to defeat the Sangyma and rule in this universe just as much as It wanted to rule in the next. The Sagitæ might not help It do either but defeating the spellmakers certainly would advance the former.

He began to worry that Yaltha suspected what he had done and was testing his reactions. This was going to be a very difficult journey. He found himself hoping she would try something quickly so he did not have to put up with her too long.

Tegriel's discussion with Kalevala was longer. He was still talking to him right up to going and had no time to say farewell to the elders. To which Kikkelrick observed that was just how Fulminar kept coming and going.

Yaltha stepped into the Ossendark with Kalevala and Tegriel and they all vanished with Hiesia waving a heavy paw as they went. She laid the paw on Tobia's head as the Ruzniel hugged her leg.

Tobia felt lonely for the first time in a long time and that feeling would stay with her for many years, until other Sangyma arrived to adopt companions from the first graduates of the Academies amongst whom was a certain Chuff. Then she met Sanjava's grandfather and he walked around the halls amazed at what the Ruzniel had achieved in so short a time.

By that time Crilodach would have been active in hundreds of planets, Damkina would be half built and Yaltha, well Yaltha would have found out her sister was still partially alive and be trying to save her.

Eldet's Thunder

Neither of them could decide which way of the two, to take. Eldet was using his claws like a toothpick in frustration, making scraping noises that echoed around Rimfelder. When he had first stepped onto the äis he had felt apprehensive, when he had found the brothers he had felt elated but now, after two deaths, with Phigata getting closer and Irghwols screaming in the darkness, all he felt was foreboding. Polluted water dripped rhythmically onto the deck. He hugged the Gaddia for comfort.

The widest route forward was to their left, through which you could have marched ten shire horses abreast but the tunnel sloped down into severe darkness looking more like a throat than a pathway. Branching off to their immediate left, was another way, small, flat, shallow, and perhaps a little cleaner; both were open, both were dark. Eldet sniffed them and shook his head indecisively.

"Again, they smell the same," he complained. "They might meet up again further down I suppose. I can't be sure though."

"So we can take either?" said the poet.

"There's no ambush waiting whichever one we choose, that's all I can tell you."

"Are you sure you can't make out any clues to tell us which might be the better choice?" asked Rimfelder.

"Can you think of anything Vingura said that we haven't already used because I can't."

"No, not a word," confessed Rimfelder, "I've repeated the whole conversation until I'm blue in the face. Unless looks mean anything?"

"Any looks in particular?"

"He seemed quite amused most of the time we talked. He smiled, waved an arm here and there to show me some special herbal bush or just to magic things away. Nothing else."

"There's nothing in that for us," said Eldet.

"Strange to bring us all this way, then not help us at a

fork in the road like this."

"That's what worries me," admitted Eldet.

"Maybe we could take either," suggested Rimfelder.

"Maybe. Maybe I'm missing something so obvious Vingura knew he didn't have to leave a clue to help me. Let's take this one and see what happens."

"Isn't that risky?"

"Do you want to take the other one?"

"I'm useless at choosing. Whenever I make choices I end up floating on an äis with a dragon being pursued by molten lava and Irghwols, using a book as a shield."

"The Gaddia hasn't failed us yet," Eldet reminded him.

"I just hope they never do."

Eldet clicked his claws for the last time and placed his feet on the deck, shook his head and replied,

"In either way could lie danger. There are no easy choices for us."

The äis finally moved down the wider of the two as Eldet quietly hoped to himself that he had chosen wisely. Since either route would seem to do, choosing the easiest appeared the best for two reasons. This way was wide so he could react to any attack with ease, and flatter so they could travel faster. The äis went downwards quickly, having time to make up because they had taken so long to decide. They were well above the ground floating along a dark but airy tunnel so steep the äis was almost at right angles to the ground as the bejal maintained a level pitch.

The going was easy. To begin with Rimfelder felt confident Eldet had chosen well. However Eldet paced the äis worried, flicking his head and sniffing the air every few seconds, grumbling under his breath. He walked in broad circles around the deck from prow to aft and back, stepping over Rimfelder when he came up to him. He was anxious for the moment but not about his decision. If he had chosen wrongly they would simply have to deal with whatever happened and since he had no idea what that might be he was on his guard. He was more troubled about what he knew he would have to face if they did get out.

The loss of his brothers was a great weight on his heart but more importantly to him the revenge he had to seek on their sons both pained and perplexed him. Would he be able to carry out his brothers' last wishes? What father can kill his child without thought? Without regret? Would those regrets make him hesitate as their sons, trained to be Frin-Ghirzan's killers, certainly would not? Being imprisoned in Xibalba, host to a spell that made him deranged, facing death helping the poet; was as nothing compared to this punishment. Would their remaining sons beat him now he was alone? Was there a way before Zaqui to bring the two living sons back from Crilodach's grip? At times like this he missed the counsel of the Sangyma. So he paced, unable to concentrate, filled with worries that buried themselves into his chest as if making an open wound. Worries that had made him make this terrible choice.

Perhaps there were small clues he missed. He would never know and Rimfelder would never remind him, not because he was forgiving but because there would not be the time to accuse Eldet of nearly getting them killed without the Irghwols lending a hand.

Filvani said that time has magic and being. Permeating the whole cosmos with a unique presence that rules both the Sangyma and Crilodach. They knew time could twist and turn and to a certain extent they could twist and turn alongside, but ultimately time was their master. Filvani first recognized that the laws of magic existed within time and that made time magical. Not in the sense the Sangyma understood magic. Zananto had asked once if they could harness time in their spells, and Sanjava in his younger days had spent many years experimenting to see if such a thing were possible, but his tests never got further than altering a second here or there. As Filvani told him, his experiments were like setting a small stone on the ground and then looking around for anyone small enough to think he had planted a mountain. You cannot fool time and if you get a second to repeat, though clever, that does not mean that every second all over the universe can or will repeat individually or together. Because to manipulate time, not the simple trick of travelling through time but changing how time works, you would have to be in control of the entire universe.

Time was running out more swiftly than Rimfelder knew. So swiftly that far away, though she now knew Rimfelder and Eldet were travelling towards them, Lilah was not counting on them getting through. Crilodach was closing fast, Trecrogo was in place for the final onslaught. Equally, though Rimfelder did not know, the magic in the Gaddia was also running low for each of the magicians could only help him with a single spell.

A little while after they passed down their chosen path, a remnant of the greater-toothed Irghwols slid down the walls, their skins drying out in the heat, cracking and bleeding, allowing their translucent, thick blood to drip from them onto the stone floor, as if they had been covered by boils that were bursting. They looked at both ways forward and sniffed the one Eldet had chosen. They knew he was down there. But they took the other route without looking back, almost sad for the fate that awaited the äis. As the last tail slid eagerly into the darkness, they were followed by the first searing waves of heat that touched the entrances momentarily, like a hot breeze on a dark night in high summer burning up the dust in the air making the sparks look like bright insects. These were followed by the first licks of Phigata that crept up the rock face burning into the walls, widening small crevices into caves and filling the whole area with the stench of a white heat, creating alloys out of the minerals that leeched out of the stone, and then carrying them along in the flow in such abundance that the surface of Phigata now had a skin of bubbling metals, making a grey-and-gold, superfluous, molten armour, blistering, cracking, and reforming with the relentless progress of unleashed magma.

Small pieces of rock on the wall crumbled away in the heat, revealing two signs Eldet and the poet would never see. One showing the right way to go and the other telling them not to take the way they had chosen. But these were not signs of a magician or of the Gaddia but of some long distant traveller, someone who knew that one pathway led to a dead-end and the other led onwards to freedom. That traveller had used signs that were used throughout the universe, a small tick etched into the stone the way the Irghwols were taking and a small cross on the wall of the way Eldet and the poet had taken. What the traveller had gone through to make those marks no one would ever know. Nor who they were or where they had come from. Their fate, like so many, was to be unknown and unmourned yet, quite possibly, what they achieved helped millions.

They floated on for a full hour until Rimfelder was unsettled to see the äis scraping the sides of the tunnel walls as they rapidly narrowed from both sides, at the same time the ceiling came sharply down and now the heat seemed to be coming from ahead of them as well. They did not know the Gaddia had sensed this pathway was wrong and was making plans.

"This is becoming too narrow," he said, "are you having difficulty breathing?"

"A bit. If this tunnel doesn't open out we'll get stuck here," warned Eldet, who stopped his pacing and lay on his stomach his head stretched out to avoid hitting the ceiling. "Maybe I should walk on ahead and see what's happening."

"Is that safe?"

"Safe from what, poet?"

"What if the Irghwols attack you?"

"Then I'll fight."

"What if the äis turns round and heads back?"

"I'll run after you, just give a shout."

"What if you're so far ahead you can't hear me?"

"If I can get that far away I don't think we've anything to worry about." Rimfelder shrugged. Eldet jumped down and said,

"Don't worry I've acute hearing."

He walked ahead as Rimfelder watched until he could no longer see his tail swishing from side to side. He had not liked to admit to Eldet that he was frightened of being alone. As the dark took hold without anyone to talk to, he gripped the Gaddia not daring to move or even to breath loudly. He felt intense fear. He started to count the seconds to take his mind off the creaks and moans that came to his ears from all around. If any sound of the dragon fighting had reached him at that moment, he might very well have had a heart-attack.

Eldet knew he was scared. He knew all the risks. His gamble to choose the wider route so they could see where they were heading had failed.

Rimfelder thought of Lilah. Her tall, strong figure so assured, so sensitive. Her voice calm and determined. Once again he calmed down as he remembered her. He concentrated on the task ahead. To get out. To see Lilah again. He began to feel less afraid but even so, his body stiffened at the sound of every rock falling. They were only tiny little pieces but as he looked up specks of dust caught in his eyes. He looked away and coughed slightly wondering why the dust was falling at all. He peered into the darkness and imagined he could see a shimmer behind them. Like a flickering swarm of insects. He shuddered. He was looking at Phigata. Sweat poured from his scalp and dripped into his eyes.

"Come on Eldet," he whispered.

He wondered if the äis would go ahead automatically and follow the dragon. His cough came out strained and rasping. He feared he had just given away his position. Trying to stop himself he succeeded in hurting his throat.

"Those creatures, he said to himself, "those creatures are creeping along the walls."

"I think not," said Eldet jumping back upon the äis.

"Well something is dislodging the rock above our heads," complained Rimfelder.

"They're not following us. Seeing that this path leads nowhere my guess would be they've gone the other way so are now probably in front of us. The heat is causing the rock dust to fall. No point in sugar coating a bad situation poet. I chose wrong, I'm sorry."

"You've no cause to apologize to me. I wouldn't have travelled this far without you and your brothers."

"I should've realized when the voice calling us got softer. I had a bad feeling about this even as I chose, I should've turned back sooner."

"I never heard the song in the first place. You made a simple mistake that has cost us nothing but a little time," said Rimfelder.

"Time we don't have," Eldet said.

"If we simply get out alive I don't think I'll complain about how long we took."

"Did you suspect we'd gone the wrong way?" asked Eldet.

"Me! What do I know? If you're not sure I'd never know. I couldn't see any difference between the two tunnels."

"Pity we couldn't have had the luck to choose right. If we continue we'll get wedged in and won't be able to move. We'll be burned to a crisp. We'll have to go back, if we can, and even then we may not get very far."

"After all our efforts, the loss of Clevian and Opiar, you think we'll fail?"

"We haven't failed." Eldet lowered his head, "But we might have to stop breathing for a while," he half-joked.

"Why?"

"Well, you know what's back there," Eldet reminded him.

"Phigata!" cried Rimfelder with horror. "But this tunnel's

too narrow, we can't bypass the lava."

"Less than minutes behind us I'd have thought, so when we turn round we're going to only have seconds. You up for that?"

"But we can't survive floating through lava," said Rimfelder gripped with terror. "I mean I can't. I suppose the äis and you will be alright"

"Phigata was created to be the enemy of everything. Nonetheless there's nothing here for us. We have to go back."

"Can't we blow our way through the end of this tunnel? Or dig our way upwards."

"How far? What with?

"Can't you use some magic?" tried the poet.

"For a while yes but when I get tired and we're still trapped what then? We have no choice but to go down the other tunnel."

"How can we?" asked Rimfelder.

"Come, come poet never say die. We have a chance because we know the odds."

"And what are the odds?"

"Near to nothing, I would say, against us," said Eldet.

"I guess I've faced worse."

"That's the spirit," Eldet said.

Rimfelder opened the Gaddia hoping to find something but nothing appeared to him. He looked at Eldet who was already facing back the way they had come. He felt as if someone had taken away his stomach. Was he to be burned to a crisp? He could feel the heat blistering his skin now. His feet felt uncomfortable as if his shoes were tightening and becoming firebrands. His throat was so dry he was unable to swallow. His hands were shaking. He had to close his eyes because they felt like hard marbles in his head. His eyelashes were literally singed off his eyelids.

The äis started to race back. Knowing their lives were now at risk, Rimfelder moved aft gaining a little comfort at being at the farthest point he could possibly be from the lava into which they were being propelled. His fingernails were heating up and burned his skin. In fact he felt very close to how someone would feel who was being tortured. Not a part of his body was untouched. Even his clothes steamed as the moisture they had absorbed over the journey, evaporated. When all that moisture was gone, the material cracked from the heat. Buttons split. His singed hair curled. He lost his eyebrows. He felt Phigata was cooking him.

Eldet chose to stand at the prow. Like all dragons he faced danger head–on. He wanted to show Rimfelder he was unafraid because he knew if they were going to get through this the poet had to help, and to help he had to concentrate and not be defeated by despair. The Gaddia and Rimfelder were linked and worked together. One without the other was next to useless.

Rimfelder, despite the pain, opened his eyes and noticed he could see more of his surroundings. A yellow and red glimmer decorated the uneven walls; light reached them as the lava appeared ahead welling up like milk boiling over in a saucepan, taking up all the available space. Hungry. Burning. Bulging with consuming fire. Rippled through with melting rock, curling like a distended stomach rolling over everything in a famished desire to gorge. Phigata was the perfect weapon for Crilodach, unthinking, unconquerable, turning everything into white–hot liquid. Moving very quickly. Rimfelder's eyes were drying out. He had to turn away.

"We're finished," he repeated, scared to hear how hoarse his voice had become.

"Look in the Gaddia again," ordered Eldet, "they may be our only chance I don't think the äis has any power to help us."

"I looked, there's nothing there," coughed Rimfelder.

"Look again as we get closer they may respond to the crisis. Look at the book not the deck. Now!" ordered Eldet.

Rimfelder opened the Gaddia with shaky fingers and this time the book skipped a page and slowly words came to him. Merging with the heat haze, forming across the ivory–coloured page. An emergency spell, a fail–safe Vingura had written into the paper. The additional page was purple and the words were almost floating off the paper in ivory white.

"Is anything happening?" asked Eldet.

"Yes something's forming."

"What do the words say," he asked.

"I can't see any words yet," said Rimfelder.

"Hurry up."

He willed the words to form. He pleaded with them to form. The lava was almost upon them. The äis was shaking trying to hold together in the face of the blistering heat.

Rimfelder tried to clear his dry throat. Eldet handed him some water which was almost too hot to drink. He swallowed. The cup was hot and hurt his fingers.

Rimfelder found his voice as Phigata's bubbling was all he could hear; as even Eldet had stepped back from the furnace, his wings close against his sides to give them some protection.

> Phigata burns all hate enclosed in time
> And captures like an insect all the food

He coughed, his eyes filling with sweat from his forehead. The words were moving as if they, too, were trying to keep away from the heat and still give him time to speak. Even as he said them they began to vanish, melt, replacing themselves with new ones struggling to survive. He was not going to have a second chance to speak them, he had to get this right first time. But his eyes burned and he felt his voice going. The book was heavy. The heat unbearable. His scalp seemed to be burning off his skull. He wanted to scratch his head but his fingernails were bent with pain.

"Don't dare stop!" cried Eldet, who shielded the poet with his body. The shadow of Eldet's body made him feel even hotter but also gave him confidence. He could feel the powerful dragon breathing.

> That feeds such hate and turns life into chyme,
> Despite how well the äis may be crewed.
> Before this flameless fire friends have to do

He drank some more water. He was using his voice muscles to almost shout as he looked into Phigata, but no matter how loud he still only sounded like he was barely whispering against the roar of the lava. The hot, aching gluttony of the approaching lava soaked up all other sounds. He did not dare to look up but hoped with all his might something was happening to save them.

> All chance, time, title magic and cool charms
> May give to them to do, even though few;
> Rimfelder is the shield against all harms.
> This enemy with violent flows burning
> Everything to death that tries to outpace

He coughed violently and felt a claw hold him steady. The words were still flowing but he could barely see them. His speaking had slowed down. He finished all the water and some drops dripped from his lips to his shoes where they turned to steam, hissing. He could no longer swallow. His hands shook as he held the Gaddia open. With painfully cracked lips he said,

> Phigata, the place of no returning
> The bitter foe that's never had a face.

"I can't see the last words! I can't see the last words!" he called out.

His eyelids were tight shut his eyes hurt so much, his lips were bleeding, he could hardly hold the book up. His hands were over his face. He dropped the book which stayed open on the page, the last two lines clearly visible. The äis shook more violently. Eldet leaned over his shoulder for being a dragon fire was his friend and his body much more able to cope with this intense heat. Hoping the Gaddia would understand he finished the poem, in an even, strong voice that had his characteristic touch of defiance,

> A bubble will protect you from this fire
> Bubbling all around with devouring ire.

As he finished he wrapped his wings around the poet hoping to spare his life for a few moments more. Phigata came upon them and rocked the äis from below, pressing upon them like a high, huge wave ready to crash down over them. But even as the lava touched them a shield grew, around which the advancing lava crept, under and over, until they were inside the flow, watching the lava pass them on all sides from within a translucent, spherical bubble.

Rimfelder, who had been counting in his head the seconds he thought he had left to live, neither felt nor heard anything. Gingerly he opened an eye and reached out to peer from the side of Eldet's huge wings. He saw Phigata pressing against the skin of the bubble, swirling and moving across their path, shining with hundreds of colours, unable to keep still, perfectly forming around the sphere and covering every direction in which he looked. He stepped out from under the wings. Still hot. The äis was moving through the lava, buffeted like an aeroplane passing through turbulence. He felt humming beneath his feet. He leaned out to touch the bubble but Eldet stopped him.

"Curiosity killed off many spells," he warned him.

"I only ..." began the poet hoarsely.

"I know, you only wanted to touch the bubble to see what magic feels like but what if the substance of the bubble is allergic to your skin?"

"Is that possible?"

"I've learned long ago to just go along with spells, don't ask too many questions and above all, never touch anything. The desire to touch has worked in Crilodach's favour in the past. Besides this is a spell I've never seen before and I don't know what we're dealing with. Before three seconds ago I wouldn't have even imagined this was possible."

"Vingura and his friends are amazing," said Rimfelder quietly.

"I for one never knew they had the power to create this. The bubble isn't even very thick, is as clear as glass, yet the pressure from the lava must be tremendous."

"The heat isn't as stifling in here either," said the poet.

The äis made slow progress against the flow of lava, bucking a little when half melted rocks hit the bubble but somehow the äis and the bubble worked together. When Phigata ran into the dead end of the tunnel the flow lost some strength and they gathered a little speed in the undertow. Eldet was sure the bubble was actually rolling through Phigata. He kept himself close to the deck, lowering his body and lying fully stretched out giving the spell less to surround and, he hoped, making the magic stronger as a result.

"I really couldn't see to read," he apologized.

"Stop worrying. I'm just glad my words were enough to finish the spell."

"My eyes were so painful."

"You said enough to make all the difference."

"But I failed at the last moment. I wasn't strong enough to complete the spell. If you hadn't we would ... well I'd be dead," whispered Rimfelder.

"I've ceased to count the number of times I've missed death by a whisker. Right now I have to say, I praise Vingura's name."

"The book knew our every step," said Rimfelder.

"Magic is dynamic poet. The Gaddia are with us through the book, they see, smell and understand all that's around us. That's what makes them powerful allies, along with whatever else they worked this magic with. Even luckier the spells suffer no time delay otherwise we would've been in trouble."

"Spells have time delays?"

"Of course, the further the distance they have to travel the longer taken for them to take effect. There are some spells that are even affected by the gravity of suns, they have to travel so far. That's why, sadly, sometimes spells don't work. They say that Tegriel cast a spell at the dawn of time that is still moving."

"So this bubble was created by the book which was only a few feet away from the lava and therefore only took a second to form."

"The book is the conduit through which the spells flow. The spells were created by the pages which are all linked to someone else, someplace else."

"The room where they're all sitting beside Vingura's garden?

"To begin with yes, the power came from there, but by now I suspect that room and everyone there has already gone."

"Then where did this magic come from?" asked the poet.

"All I can tell with any certainty is, not far away," said Eldet.

"Why not just have the magic in the book? That's the obvious place."

"And if the book falls into the wrong hands?"

"Ah, the magic doesn't."

"Exactly. Always plan for the worse when you are travelling through lands Crilodach has touched. Then, when the worst happens you don't entirely lose."

"Is your magic inside you?"

"Naturally, but living things are different from bejals. If I were caught, Crilodach could never use my magic without killing me first and once dead the magic in me would evaporate into nothingness like so many soap bubbles."

"The more I learn about the art of magic the more I'm in awe of you all."

"And yet poet, I think there are many of us in awe of you."

"That's absurd," Rimfelder said.

"Why? You have no magic yet you side with those who do because you were simply asked. You put your life in danger, you fight every inch of the way, just to get back to Lilah. No other reason. I can name only one other I've met in my long life whose wishes are as simple or as generous."

Irgwhol

"I don't deserve any praise, the Gaddia does everything."

"What use is a door without a key?"

"I'm a key?"

"I think so."

"A key to what?"

"That I can't tell you. I'm just sorry I almost got you killed just now because of my bad judgment."

"But we're getting out now."

"This won't last long." He gestured to the bubble with his claw and Rimfelder saw the inner surface rippling like water from the strain of holding Phigata back. "If you had finished the spell maybe the bubble would be stronger. We'll only get out of here, and on the right pathway before this bubble is destroyed by Phigata, if we can move faster. This lava has gone a long way down the other path and we are still going uphill, if we run out of time we may yet be consumed."

"I wish you hadn't told me that."

"I can't afford for you to become complacent," replied Eldet. Rimfelder clambered over the dragon's huge feet to get to a clear spot where he could sit down.

"I can't see anything but the lava. I'm hot enough to melt again. The bubble is weakening as we speak," worried Rimfelder.

"With every second," agreed Eldet. "We'll follow the flow of the lava down into the other tunnel, when we get there we'll start moving faster. Phigata, too, is being called along with us and senses freedom."

"Phigata has senses?"

"Rich with them. Sucked out of every victim, learned over millenniums of existence. All that activity and all those particles flowing through a lava that knows we're here. Phigata's exerting great pressure and all possible heat onto the bubble. No one has ever gotten away from Phigata before and she doesn't want us to be the first."

"Is she ... alive?"

"Not as you or I know life; Phigata has no thoughts. Crilodach doesn't make things that are good at living, but things that swallow up life and delight in death. In this burning heart Phigata shares her master's desires to eat away at everything until there's nothing left. She is also home to many dragon eating creatures. They would show themselves if we were not enclosed in this bubble."

"What about your planning for any eventuality?"

"All the planning in the worlds count for nothing if Crilodach has planned better."

"Ah," said Rimfelder, "well at least ill-luck seems to be a universal."

"Ill-luck is merely the absence of any luck," replied Eldet, "still," he went on, "look at what we have instead."

He looked at Rimfelder and the poet hugged the Gaddia closer. Although the book had saved them he still thought he only had a tenuous link to the magic. How could anyone think he was in charge of the Gaddia? If there was anyone left in the universe who did not have a clue how he was doing what he was actually doing, then that person was him.

"If that's true poet," said Eldet without looking at him, "then you must be very, very lucky."

Rimfelder sat bolt upright and stared at the dragon. Why had they not told they could read his mind. But he didn't have time to wonder at what Eldet must think of him for all his uncertainty over the past hours.

The äis turned suddenly as they shot out of the tunnel, swung left and went with the flow of the lava for the first time, racing down the throat of the other tunnel. Eldet even saw the remains of some fresh Irghwol dead who had not been fast enough to escape. Their twisting skeletons were vaporized in the blink of his eye.

The speed change was noticeable. The äis seemed to be moving more smoothly. The malleable contortions of the lava against the bubble changed. Everything was moving faster. Things began to get so fast small spaces appeared between the lava and the bubble as if the lava were having trouble sticking to the bubble, almost as if the äis were going faster than the lava. But how could that be? Eldet sniffed the air and got as close to the lava as he could. Raising his head, his nose twitching. The Gaddia were doing something. They were using the lava as a protective covering, taking advantage of the thickness and the heat. But why? He had no answer whilst trapped inside a bubble inside the lava.

They could still only see lava outside the bubble. They were rushing forward so fast Rimfelder could not keep his balance when standing and he had to hold onto Eldet's clawed foot. Buffeted by the speed of the flow just as Eldet had hoped they swung from side to side as if on a slalom threatening at times to loop-the-loop entirely. But the Gaddia managed to keep the äis merely rocking from side to side. They never somersaulted. Rimfelder held the Gaddia in one hand and Eldet in the other with such tenacity Eldet could feel his grip through his scales. Rimfelder was hanging on for grim death. Large boulders hit them and Rimfelder was mesmerized by the sight of the bubbling lava that surrounded them taking huge boulders and melting them into pebbles and finally into dust and nothingness in seconds. Parts of the bubble began to sag inwards but nothing ripped open. Eldet noticed these rocks were not those of the caverns. That had been black stone this way grey streaked with white.

Eldet knew this was going to be a close run thing. He kept his gaze to the front hoping they would overtake the laval flow and break free before the bubble burned away. Phigata was endlessly changing and turning, constantly licking at the bubble as if trying to find out why she couldn't burn through, seeming to be unconcerned that she could not get at the fleshy fruits within. As if Phigata knew all things burned and sooner or later the bubble would be breached. She was in no hurry. Phigata too was heading for Zaqui. Everything would be hers. He saw water vapour condensing on the inside of the bubble from his breath and Rimfelder's perspiration. He clicked his tongue. The speed with which the vapour turned to steam showed the bubble was about to break.

"Stay close," he warned Rimfelder.

"I can't exactly do anything else."

"Under my wing."

"I can't see under there," complained Rimfelder.

"If Phigata breaks in, that's the safest spot for you."

"What about you."

"Don't worry about me."

"Of course I worry about you, we're in this together."

"Just stay where you are. If the lava overruns us my body will keep you alive for a few more minutes."

"There are some things worse than death."

"And exactly how does that bit of wisdom effect sitting under my wing?" asked Eldet.

"If I live and you die I'll never get back to the others."

"You don't have much faith in yourself do you poet?"

Before they could continue arguing, as if a huge storm were blowing, the lava split in two and then just as quickly as Phigata had enveloped them she began to recede and the bubble flew out of her grasp like a tiger shark coming out of the sea in pursuit of a penguin and landing on the shore, bursting out at speed and sending refreshing, fresher air over their bodies. Surprising them with the freedom to move and feel the openness around them.

They sped forward leaving the lava behind them as the bubble finally broke, peeling away from above them, and the last drops of lava fell onto the deck of the äis, sizzling like cooking fat. A burning portion of lava fell onto Rimfelder's clothes burning a hole through the fabric but luckily dissipated before making any burns on his skin.

"If I'd known I could survive I'd have tried to swim," he said, surprised not to have been badly scalded.

"You couldn't survive. The äis can protect you from small amounts like that," Eldet explained.

Rimfelder's hands had burn marks he had not noticed before on the back and palms and even the Gaddia's pages had turned brown on the edges. Eldet had no marks or discomfort at all. They both looked at Phigata behind them, still following, still threatening, still powerful. Roaring as if hurling a curse at them for escaping. Eldet noticed how the walls had a burnish that gave off light rather that sucked the light away as in Xibalba.

"I never want to do anything like that again," said Rimfelder.

"What you want as a poet and what you'll get as Lilah's ally, are very different things," said Eldet.

The äis spun upwards. Remnants of lava on the äis evaporated as Eldet managed to look around beginning to wonder how exactly they would get out, when he noticed there were no Irghwols to be seen anywhere along the walls. Eager to make sure he opened his wings, flew upwards from the äis, and flew around. He found nothing.

Eldet came back and sat on the äis as they moved rapidly, crossing the uneven ground. Rimfelder looked ahead into the darkness wondering what more there was to go through before he got back to Lilah. He felt uncomfortable, like a man who did not think he had a right to still be alive. Clinging to a life raft in the midst of a huge storm, knowing all that kept him alive were the plans and efforts of others. Maybe that was the reason he wanted to see the others so much. To be with the people who made these kinds of things look easy.

These tunnels were broad. Phigata followed them swiftly but the äis was in clear air, well out of danger. Eldet heard the song quite clearly that was bringing them along, but he could not pinpoint the language. A bright song, melodious and sweet, that seemed familiar to him but from where or when he did not know. He scratched his cheek with his claw and shook himself until the spines along his tail rattled. He had to be wide awake, they could not afford another mistake. His eyes focussed in the dark. He saw shadows below them.

"Look below," he pointed.

Rimfelder peered down and thought he saw the tops of towers. Hundreds of them rising up a huge mountain side that reared ahead of them, growing out of the darkness like a legless giant sleeping in their path.

"Where are we?" asked Rimfelder, who had not expected to see any buildings in this place of all places.

"Some kind of ancient city. I didn't know there was anything like this in Xibalba or that any people ever lived here that could build. They are empty. No people live down there now," said Eldet.

"Whoever they were they only built towers," Rimfelder said.

"Is that significant?"

"Strikes me as strange."

"Unusual, not strange."

"What's the difference?"

"I've seen more strange things than you."

Eldet looked at the towers with great interest because he knew something out of the ordinary was going on. No Irghwols and now these towers. The äis flew towards the top of the mountain. The towers clustered below them with no particular overall design. Some so close Rimfelder could not have walked between them. Many overshadowed by those around them. Some even appeared to grow from the foundations of those closest to them like old trees growing out of stone walls.

"So many different styles," he observed, "no two are the same. Look ahead the towers rise up the mountain side, and see they're all different as well. Different stones, different designs. Some leaning over as if they will fall soon, others look well kept and new."

"Maybe the people lived from the bottom to the top of the mountain building new towers as they progressed upwards," suggested Rimfelder.

"Why the changes in design?"

"New building materials, different architects."

"Most of the stone didn't come from here, the rock is uniformly grey or dark silver all along the tunnels here," said Eldet, "There's no marble, but I see marble in many of those towers. There's a little agate, not enough ruby for a toothpick, and limestone would disappear here within a hundred years of forming. Slate roofs when there is no slate in Xibalba nor sandstone, yet all are in those towers down there."

The äis went through an archway built into one of the towers and above them they saw broken windows and stairwells, carvings in the stones of creatures so ancient neither of them recognized any of them. The courtyard was not overgrown because no flowers, lichens or mosses grew in this place. The lack of flowers gave Eldet the first inkling of what this place actually was. Tall or short, wide or slim, made of stone, grown from wood, or built of metals the towers flocked the mountainside as if collected. Each one had a set place. They were all near to each other, some almost touching, but none of them were connected by so much as a rope bridge. He knew no one would build like this.

Words, deprived of meaning they were so old, were carved into corner stones. Many different kinds of stone, worked in many different fashions, some Eldet knew but many he did not. The ancientness of the place belied the newer designs higher up the mountain. He had seen societies where they had rebuilt upon old foundations, he had seen changes in styles and building methods over generations, but he had never seen anywhere where the old survived so completely and the new used none of the designs at all from previous builders. No matter how good the architect, stone eventually will wear away and have to be replaced. But these towers showed no signs of such wear yet they spoke of age. Almost as if they were preserved. Not by the magic that moved the äis because the bejal was not strong enough nor by any magic in Xibalba which was too selfish.

"Look," he pointed, "I know that tower. I've seen a hundred in the towns near to where I spent a summer when I was a teenager. But this is impossible. Those people never lived here."

Behind them the lava slowed for a moment. The äis rose upwards. He saw more and more towers of places he had visited in his life and slowly the truth dawned upon him. The excess speed of the äis in the bubble was due to their escaping from Xibalba into some other realm. Some other place. He knew that the laval ocean had brought them to this strange place. That the remaining Irghwols, not protected by the bubble, had all burned to death. That going the wrong way was somehow planned because they were always meant to travel within Phigata. That was the only way to get to these towers. He could clearly see there was a time-line in the towers on this mountain. Not of one civilization or one people, but of all civilizations and all peoples. A history of life in this universe.

"These towers were not built here, they were brought here," Eldet told him.

"By whom?" asked Rimfelder.

"I've no idea. Look behind us, even the lava from Xibalba has stopped flowing. There's some power here holding Phigata back. Buying us time."

"For how long?"

"Who knows Poet, but some magic wants us to be here."

"So this place is our destination?"

"I don't doubt for a second there can be nothing comparable in the universe to this place."

Phigata had hit an invisible obstruction and was not even touching the first of the towers far below them but slowly rising vertically against the unseen wall that halted the lava's progress like a dam. Eldet wondered if the Gaddia had transferred their efforts to this invisible wall but somehow he thought the Gaddia must have had help from the magic hidden amidst these disorganized towers. Vingura could do many things but even he and his friends could not hold Phigata back.

Eldet wondered who would call to them across a magical landscape like this? Was he wrong, maybe the song was not for him at all? He shook his head irritably. Whilst the song continued Phigata would rise to the roof and then at some point the immense pressure would burst and would descend upon the towers like a burning tsunami. He had to make sure that did not happen before they had uncovered the truth.

"We daren't stay here," he said. "We must find a way out."

"Can you still hear her singing?" asked Rimfelder.

"Clear as a bellow from my father. Though his were louder, they were not more urgent. We're close to our journey's end."

"Is the song telling you that?"

"No, the Gaddia is glowing," said Eldet, nodding at the book.

"I hadn't noticed," said Rimfelder, who was enthralled by the towers and how beautiful they all looked saturating the mountain that climbed as high as he could see, "What's happening?"

"Something is going to happen, the whole book is suffused with an aura," said Eldet.

"There," pointed Rimfelder as they went between a granite archway and down over a bridge that linked two towers that were exactly the same. The äis turned as if new to the manœuvre. A slow, arcing turn, tilting them slightly as if looking, or waiting, for something. Then, levelling off, they shot forward like a speed boat as the Gaddia glowed gold and red.

They found themselves before a very different, perfect tower. The glass shone as if freshly washed and carefully dried leaving no spots or dust behind. Eldet stepped off the äis for a moment and dug at the stones at his feet lifting the huge flagstone as casually as you would pick up a sea shell on a beach. He grabbed at the rocks beneath with his claws and dug into them pulling out a handful, and lifted them up. The flagstone dropped back into place and Rimfelder could see Eldet's eyes shining even from where he was sitting far below him. The tall dragon bent down, opened his claws and showed Rimfelder the rocks and soil.

"Rubble," Rimfelder shrugged, "and loam."

"To go through a whole life without a dragon's sense of smell must be terrible," replied Eldet. "The 'loam' is Losek soil. This soil grows into the foundations of whatever you build. Forming a strong, magical, natural foundation, giving buildings roots. You haven't seen the fortress yet poet but if you ever see Trecrogo, that too was built upon Losek soil specially taken to Earth. This place poet, this place is ..." he stopped speaking as if overwhelmed for a moment and then went on, "Tegriel told me this place existed but I never knew if he were spinning one of his legends or telling me the truth. Here, on a mountain of Losek soil, the only such mountain in existence, one part of every world that has ever existed was brought as a record, as a memory of those who had lived and built in each world. Think of that, every world, ever! And this mountain," he gestured with his wings, "this mountain has grown upwards as the number of towers representing the people's of the universe has evolved. Think poet, everyone who ever lived is somewhere in these towers, the room and stairwells heave with knowledge. Think what must be here. This isn't just a library, their hands are here touching the stones, their thoughts are here, their very way of life emanates from these towers. This isn't just a place to learn about them, this is a place to be them. You could stay here ten lifetimes and never come to the end of the magnificence."

"But how do these towers help us to get home?"

Eldet stopped whirling around in his new found delight to look at Rimfelder eye to eye,

"I don't know whether that is the most ignorant thing I've ever heard anyone say, or a testament to your resolute determination to get back to Lilah."

"The latter," Rimfelder defended himself, "I understand what you're saying but this is just a sideshow right now."

"Did you ever stop to wonder why you were parted from Lilah? Don't you think your journey has a bit more meaning than the wayward chance that you happened to be available?"

"You seem to think I was meant to have the Gaddia. Lilah kept saying she had come for me and made my words powerful. Everyone tells me I have a job to do. To find a Sagitæ. I just want to get back to Lilah."

"Why did the Gaddia take you to Xibalba instead of straight back to Lilah?"

"I don't know."

"Why bring us here?" tried Eldet again.

"This was our way out."

"No, we left Xibalba's tunnels when we were in the lava. This is a different place, definitely set apart from Xibalba. A place so hidden only by swimming in Phigata could travellers ever gain entry here."

"No one would swim that lava."

"Exactly. We're where no one could ever be."

"With the best will in the world, I can't take an entire mountain with the knowledge of the universe to Lilah; if that's what I'm supposed to be doing."

"After all the wonders you've seen you still think in a narrow, practical way. You must stop believing in the strength of your two hands poet, your two hands can't lift so much as a flagstone here. But your mind, working with the magic of this place, what could that lift? In your mind you can lift the entire universe."

"Well if this place shrinks down to something I can put in my pocket I'll happily take everything," replied Rimfelder, "since you think I should."

"Poet you've no idea," smiled Eldet. "This mountain has grown, hidden from Crilodach. A brilliant and clever deception. It never looks here. It never visits here. The Irghwols could never come here. The way here was hidden within Xibalba only opened when Phigata followed us. We've travelled so far, so very, very far, through the imagination of great magicians.

"We still have a way to go," added Rimfelder.

"Maybe the death of my brothers blunted my instincts. We're dealing with forces whose power even I can only guess at. What place could be this vast."

"Or this secret," said Rimfelder.

"Indeed. Something very powerful is calling Phigata forth."

"Who, in their right mind, would call forth a laval ocean."

"I am sure we will find out. Here is the treasure Lilah wanted you to reach. Here is where we and the Gaddia were supposed to bring you. When I went wrong back there the tunnel squeezed us back because I was going away from this mountain."

"Tunnels can think?"

"Everything is responding to you Poet. Everything. We were dragged back in fear of our lives because we had to come here. You had to come here. That's why I was confused and didn't see what the towers were for a while, I thought we were still escaping Xibalba. Crilodach doesn't know of this place."

"So our next stop is Lilah?"

"I don't know for certain what our next stop may be."

"For one minute there I thought we'd see Lilah and the others come out of one of the towers to greet us," sighed Rimfelder.

"You never give in once you have an idea fixed in your head, do you poet? Maybe not getting carried away with things like this is a good thing, but this is a once in a lifetime experience. Besides us I doubt anyone but Tegriel, has even been here. Could you imagine what Crilodach would do in this place?"

"Destroy every stone?"

"It isn't that stupid. This would become Its trophy room. It would topple each and every tower as It conquered the worlds. These towers would provide It with knowledge about how life developed before It freed Itself from beneath Samphin."

He climbed back onto the äis which took them through

the archway and across a level courtyard. Rimfelder opened the book but no new pages opened. He looked at Eldet who lowered his head and said,

"We cannot expect everything to be in the Gaddia. I can feel the thoughts here of trillions of people. Think of the writings, the wisdom that exists here. Simply tremendous."

"And the wars."

"Not all people were moulded in wars, many of the peoples I met were peaceful people. Imagine whole worlds where no one ever made a weapon. How they managed, the secret of their laws will be here somewhere in one or more of these towers. So many secrets, so many lost names all saved here. The Sangyma, all of them will be here. Lilah's birth, even your own past."

"I can see a reason for them being here but what reason could there be in showing them to us when we have no time to search through them all?"

"Reason?" asked Eldet.

"Yes, why save everything just to sit here in the dark. Where are the scholars and students learning from all this knowledge? This entire place is empty of anything living but us. Why bring me here with you when we know there are only hours before Zaqui. Like holding candy out to a child – just out of reach."

"Something here must be crucial to our plans."

"At least the äis seems to be sure of where we're going," said Rimfelder, who had had enough of burning heat, their long escape, sacrifice, riddles and everything to do with Xibalba. He already felt he had stayed far too long amongst these towers.

"These towers aren't standing by accident. Anything that can ensure their survival here must have a reason for being hidden and have a reason for waiting for us," mused Eldet. His eyes looking all over the place for the slightest clue.

"If this place holds all this knowledge could there be dangers here for both Crilodach and Tegriel."

"Clues hidden here might lead to spells that could defeat them. Perhaps we're here to unlock their very meaning."

"How?" asked Rimfelder.

"I've no idea. Keep your eyes open you never know what will strike out at us."

"I thought the Irghwols were all dead."

"They are but that doesn't mean there isn't something

else guarding this place," said Eldet.

The äis had taken them right inside the unspoilt tower. Light from Phigata, which was growing ever upward against the invisible wall that was holding the lava at bay, blazed in through the stained glass windows, painting the walls red, yellow and blue. There was nothing about this place that reminded Eldet of their allies; no smell of bears, no sense of dragons, no memory of the Ruzniel. No Sangyma or dragon had ever walked here and left behind an essence of their presence. Although they were at the top of the mountain and by Eldet's judgment the most recent tower, the place did not look built at all. Almost as if this tower was only there to symbolize every tower. One stone from all the others was a part of this singular tower. Everything quivered in the intense waves of heat that washed over the towers from the laval ocean. Like a headache without any pain the pressure built up behind their eyes as if Phigata had a living will, bearing down upon all other living things, making him wonder if he were seeing things that were really not there.

The song calling them forward was unmistakable. Inescapable. Amplified by this tower, that, transcending the grandeur of crowns, swallowed the stature of the entire mountain.

Eldet wished his brothers could have seen this. The äis moved with perfect poise and brought them through the tower to the courtyard on the other side where an old fountain stood, silenced by the loss of water. No water had ever flowed here. Eldet muttered,

"See I was right, no one would build this here where there's no water. These towers have been built all over the universe and grown here maybe as peoples were dying, or maybe when they had their golden ages. Who knows?" He touched a stone as they passed, "Have you noticed this tower is different from the others?" Eldet said.

"We're at the top of the mountain and this is the last one."

"More than that. This is the key to the whole place."

"How do you know?" asked Rimfelder.

"Ordinary folk didn't build this for their habitation. Everything is unfinished and parts of all the other towers are contained in every wall."

Eldet stared hard at the place around him as his mind put all the facts together. He flapped his wings making a breeze that gently whistled through crevices.

"Why didn't anyone leave us a message here. They must have known we'd be strapped for time," Rimfelder said.

"Have you learned nothing poet, that you complain about your great success. Things that are hidden from the wise have been revealed to you. Dragons have given their very lives to protect you. Magicians have endowed you with gifts, yet you complain you can't make head nor tail of a mountain of towers."

"Phigata is going to break through and roll over this place at any second," said Rimfelder.

"You escaped Phigata once."

"Eldet we can't take this mountain with us however grand and exceptional Losek soil is. Everything is being destroyed this is just one more place that will be lost."

"You will get to Lilah faster without rushing."

"They're fighting for their lives right now ..."

"And we're not?" argued Eldet.

"Your mind seems taken up with wondering about these towers instead of concentrating on where the song wants us to go."

"The song brought us here. Phigata is being prevented from encroaching whilst we're here. Now think, poet, what force could do that?"

"I don't know. The book?"

"Nothing in the Gaddia has that power. They only just managed to protect us from Phigata. I know of only one power. One power that makes sense of everything. Of everything that has happened to you and why you had to free us."

"You think the Sagitæ is hidden around here somewhere?" asked Rimfelder, looking utterly lost at the thought of having to search millions of towers.

"I need to walk around," Eldet told him, jumping down and walking beside the äis. "I need this place to feel we're here."

"Feel?"

"Yes. Although hidden from Crilodach you could not let such a jewel lie unprotected. The towers, the mountain, might be discovered. So whatever is hidden here has to know only those who are chosen are here, before coming to them."

Eldet did have a point. As his back paws touched the stones, the whole place shuddered and shook. Loose stones fell from the other towers, smashing onto the ground and breaking into millions of pieces outside. The ceiling high above them creaked and the mountain side seemed to breathe every so slightly.

"What's happening?" cried out Rimfelder, looking up at Phigata and being swamped again by the terror of being burned alive.

"The mountain's responding to feeling my being walking upon the stone," replied Eldet, "I feel enlivened by the touch. The stones are cool. The tower knows who I am. But I am not enough. Jump poet, jump. Take off your shoes. Let your bare feet feel the Losek and the Losek feel you."

Rimfelder was too used to the strangeness of his life to complain or be surprised. He slipped off his dirty shoes which were still warm from the heat of the laval ocean, and jumped down. The flagstones were very cool on his blistered, bare feet. They trembled as he walked beside Eldet, refusing to let go of the äis in case he needed to jump back again in a hurry.

"I know this feeling," called out Eldet, as the stones tumbled down from hundreds of towers and the mountain seemed to heave up as if waking from sleep.

"You do?" Rimfelder's voice rose about the growing roar.

"Magic's in the air, poet, great things are happening, this place is about to change. You started this. I was right, these towers and this mountain has been waiting for you. This is the additional magic my brothers wondered about that protected the äis."

"Can I get back on now?"

"No, keep your feet on the flagstones. Let the magic that has waited so long engage with your being."

Rimfelder did not feel inspired by that idea though he could see Eldet was enjoying the show. To the dragon what was happening confirmed everything he suspected about this mountain. Everything around them was trembling and moving violently. He felt very unsafe and ill at ease even with the dragon's huge body next to his. Visions of Eldet being thrown and squashing him against the äis, or of the ground opening up and him plummeting into this living rock, filled his mind. All in all as the stones broke free and towers crumbled, with the laval ocean now as high as the mountain, he wished the entire place had been a myth. He wished his journey was over. He had thought the day and night of fighting the guards was the worst day and night of his life, then he had met Lilah and he had been shown how wrong he had been. Every step he took things just seemed to get worse. He was hungry, burned, hot and tired. His eyes ached. His bones no longer seemed to fit his body as they clicked so much with every step he took. He must have aged ten years in the last two days.

Eldet had been treading carefully on the stones but as he saw the dangers increase he judged whatever magic they had started was now in train and would complete without more help. He lifted Rimfelder without warning in his claw, and gently placed him back on the äis. The poet grabbed his shoes, but couldn't stuff his painful feet back into them. He picked up the Gaddia and huddled against the äis, barefoot, like a trapped animal hoping the hunters would just go away. Again the tower shook, this time back and forth like a dog shaking the water out of his fur. The shake was uncomfortable and made Rimfelder roll from side to side with the äis. Eldet had to flap his wings to maintain his balance. The Gaddia opened and a page began to shine. The light lit up the ceiling and bounced off the falling stones lighting up Eldet's scales and Rimfelder could see for the first time no two were the same colour. The light spread across the äis and touched the Losek soil that was exposed all over the ground where the flagstones had cracked and broken.

"Watch now poet, watch now and you will see how a mountain can fit into your pocket."

"You think that's what's happening?" called Rimfelder, at the top of his voice.

"I feel the answer coming to us. The mountain felt your call."

"And yours."

"I was merely a shudder or two because the magic knows who I am, you're the one who made this happen. The spell knows you're here and knows I'm your guardian. This magic knows the Gaddia are with us."

"All because I took my shoes off?"

"Losek soil was worked into the buildings," shouted Eldet over the cacophony of tumbling rocks, "Ancient stone-workers knew each stone's song, the inner beating at the heart of Losek's very atoms. The most precious soil in all the worlds. But here, there's not just a small amount broken off and crashing into a world as a meteor to be found by some fortunate mason. Here the whole immense mountain has a heart! I've never seen so much Losek."

"You want to know what knowledge does poet? You want to feel and see why knowledge is saved here? Why this was done for you to find? Some towers so old they are from the dawn of time, some so new they are barely a year old. These buildings are more than a record of everything. They are the universe of living things. Grown here as each civilization grew, mirroring their evolution."

He finished speaking. Everything began to collapse inwards faster. The äis took to the air to avoid the falling stones but did not move far away. Hovering safely out of danger. Eldet flapped up to join them and landed on the prow. Now everything happened below them in such a controlled way that not so much dust rose where they hovered.

Around the hull of the äis, the largest boulders caved into a huge hole that opened up across the ground splitting the mountain into five pieces. The flagstone floors gave way and all the arches and towers crumbled and the debris spun like a tornado. The äis would not move even as the debris rose around them and circled them making them the centre of a wild maelstrom that blotted out the laval ocean and everything else including the walls of the cavern. Ice cold air blew across his face as he watched.

"I don't have to shield my eyes to keep the dust out," Rimfelder said,

"That isn't dust poet."

Eldet folded his wings. He sat with back straight and roared loudly, enjoying the thrill of the noise. Enjoying the wonder of what he knew was happening. What was coming. He would see the jewel. He roared again like a wolf welcoming the pack home. He had been right. His people had been right. His brothers were not sacrificed for nothing. He bellowed again like a young dragon trying to get attention. He was joyous.

Rimfelder moved to the edge of the äis and reached out to the maelstrom around them. Unable to see anything he leaned out and touched something with his finger tip. Eldet remembered he had tried to touch the bubble and he knew that something in the poet was driving him to do some of the things he did. Perhaps he also heard a song but did not recognize the tune. Perhaps he needed to connect with the things around him to make sure this was all really happening. Perhaps the poet was just not well versed in magic and the dangers inherent in touching things he did not understand. Perhaps he understood everything on a different level of reality.

No sooner had Rimfelder touched the raging storm, than the maelstrom vanished. The sudden loss of pressure around him made Rimfelder totter over and for one moment he looked down into an abyss that was dark and deep and found himself hanging there, his chest held back by the smooth, curved back of a single claw.

The äis moved forward and Eldet pulled him way from the edge. A single, glistening jewel fell from the darkness above them into Eldet's claw. Well, actually, the jewel almost missed his claw and the äis but he saw the Sagitæ in time to stretch out.

The dragon held the Sagitæ up to his eye and the single beam of light reflected through the cosmic jewel from Phigata, opened up his mind and made his heart feel warm. Of all his brothers he had survived to see this and he knew that Opiar and Clevian would have felt as he did right now. As if all the suffering had dropped off his back, all the pain swum away, and somehow all the hurt of his life now meant something more than ever before. He had heard of them of course but he had never seen a Sagitæ. A cosmic jewel so light in the hand he could have been holding a feather. He gave the Sagitæ to Rimfelder and the poet held the warm jewel for a long time staring without speaking.

"Put the Sagitæ in your pocket, poet."

"Where did this come from?"

"The mountain," replied Eldet. "You wanted to know how to put the knowledge of the whole universe into your pocket? Well you've now done so."

"You mean all those towers, the mountain of Losek soil, all became this small jewel?"

"That small jewel is one of the three Sagitæ."

"This is what Crilodach's hunting."

"And still is."

"This is the Sagitæ that Lilah needs to stop Crilodach?"

"To stop It? No. Though finding a Sagitæ makes you and I a prime target for Crilodach. Which is why the jewel was hidden here waiting for us to come at the very last hour, so we could emerge onto the battle ground suddenly and not have to travel any further than necessary to join Lilah."

"She's here?"

"She won't be far away according to the song. It will be coming to Zaqui. Lets hope we meet Lilah first."

"Who'd believe that small jewel was a mountain?"

"A perfect place to hide away," Eldet smiled. "The Sagitæ was secure building up knowledge of this universe while waiting for Zaqui. Never venturing out to the worlds but mirroring their treasures here. Oh, so brilliant. No one would ever have known this was happening. Or why. Until we came by and the Sagitæ knew Zaqui had come. For all Its looking, Crilodach would have seen nothing because there was nothing to see but Xibalba. The very first civilizations of all were built with the help of this Sagitæ. A library being written of everything that ever lived, yet none of us ever knew."

"So that's why the Sagitæ are so important."

"That's the reason this one is important. The others do different work."

"How will we use this jewel?"

"You'll be given the knowledge if the need arises. There's nothing that this Sagitæ doesn't know after all."

The äis turned away and sped from the lava beginning to overflow the very top of the cavern spilling over, spitting and hissing in the empty air.

"Do you think we have to find all the Sagitæ?" asked Rimfelder, finally feeling he was really going to get back to Lilah next and not end up in yet another dark cave or fighting off more creatures in the darkness.

"You're brave poet, and strong, but I don't think the fate of the universe would have been left solely in your hands."

"I'll take that as a no."

"Placing all three where one person could track them down or to make one person track all three would have been dangerously unwise."

"I suppose so," agreed Rimfelder. "I'm sorry. I shouldn't have argued with you about how long things were taking."

"Never be sorry for being who you are. Even Crilodach has never once pretended to be anything but what It is, and neither should we. The atoms in you had to have this experience. Love is driving you and love has changed you."

"Great as that sounds I'll be happier when I'm fighting besides Lilah."

"The Sagitæ's added to the song. Far down in that direction," he pointed, "I think we're coming out at last. This voice is very close. And desperate. Calling for help."

The äis moved forward faster drawing away from the tidal flood of lava that rolled in behind them over the emptiness where the towers had been, pounding the walls like water in a tempest. The äis could not outrun Phigata. Both went faster and faster in the darkness until the äis was surfing on the lava. The wind rushed passed Eldet's ears as there in front of them, they both saw flashes like fireworks and heard shouts. The Gaddia opened up the way back.

Rimfelder recognized the sights and sounds of war. He even recognized some of the voices.

A Child's Sorrow

Demeter, unable to move, looked down at Chloe's dead body. The complete emptiness he felt begged to be filled with tears he had no time to shed. The pain that clawed at his throat was the horror of everything he never wanted to happen, happening. He had not greeted Midrak as the magician escaped the Rounds onto the parapet, or helped with any of the wounded. He just knelt by her broken body, cradled her head in his hands, and tried with every fleeting second to will her back to life. He knew the wish was fruitless. Trecrogo did not have that kind of power. The universe did not have that kind of magic. Life to the universe was an atom not a thinking being. Why create the magic of eternal thoughts, from universe to universe, when atoms are so abundant?

He sat by her body no longer a child. The power which throbbed through his being binding him to Trecrogo and helping him to kill his enemies, had changed him. He could not say the change was for the better. All he knew was that the delight in wielding the power he had inherited, deserted him from the moment Chloe fell. His heart hurt, his eyes smarted as if hot smoke surrounded him, but he could not cry a single tear. He fought not to, for to cry would mean he was convinced she was dead and he did not want to believe she was gone. Or perhaps he really could not cry. Perhaps there was something wrong with him, as with all humans. Something amiss that would not allow him to be like the others on Trecrogo. He looked at her in the fond hope that some magic he did not possess, some magic from the vast store in the cosmos, some spell built into the fortress by the Sangyma for just such an occasion, would encircle her with a sweet fragrance, lift her shattered body up and repair her in a touching desire to ensure no one who is loved, dies.

Rimfelder, who had his own problems at that moment within Phigata, did not see anything light up in the Gaddia that would send his words to Demeter's side. Tegriel, far in the past, would never know of these events. His task was to bring the allies together to fight Crilodach, everything else in these last hours was up to them. Hiesia might have been able to appear, like an unexpected angel, but she could only cure the sick, she could not raise the dead. There were many down the ages and many around him who would have protected her with their lives, but not a one who could give her back her life. She belonged to Zaqui. That gave up no one.

Chloe lay motionless in his arms until the blood stopped flowing from her wounds. He stroked back her hair and clung to the last warmth in her body, as if to his own life and sanity. Others who saw him stood silent. No hero to bring her back, only heroes to mourn her passing.

Demeter would have sat there by her side, like a statue, regardless of the situation, impervious to the dictates of the fight. Crilodach could have stamped upon him and he would not have moved to defend himself. Perhaps that was his way of crying, to act as if he, too, were dead; to fear moving away from this last sight of Chloe in case she should diminish in his thoughts. But he could not sit by her and mourn for he had to battle alongside the living. There was no time to forget. She may have died before him but he knew he would not survive but an hour more, if that. This last of all days. This day that made sense of every day that had ever been or, maybe, would make nonsense of them. Trecrogo was travelling faster than ever now, they would soon be meeting with Crilodach again. The last test of their promises to Tegriel. The moment before oblivion.

Trecrogo made a decision he could never have made, and as with the other dead strewn across the parapet, the fortress slowly enveloped her. She disappeared as if she were sinking quietly into quicksand. Her body dissolved into the fortress, being gently pulled from his arms without fuss or hindrance because he lacked all strength to stop her; because even in his agony of grief he knew this was the right thing to happen. In the voice in his head that came from Trecrogo, like an orchestra of the thoughts of bears and Sangyma, he heard one strain that made him feel he could go on; one small thought that made him realize that perhaps, of all those who had lost their loved ones to Crilodach, he was the most fortunate. His pain would not grow old with him but stay young and fresh because his own death was imminent.

Trecrogo allowed him one last final look at her face, and

then she was gone. A dam of numbness crossed his chest, anger burned in his hands. So hot even his mouth was dry. If anyone had spoken to him now he would have croaked an unintelligible answer, but no one was speaking much. The battle still reverberated around them, and those on the parapet were in shock. The remnant of the cockroach army were just beginning to find out how many of their friends were gone, the Arvernat were so few now they did not stand out amongst the others. Mojolo was sitting looking back straining her eyes to catch if they were being followed. No matter how stunned or fearful any of them were, they had to go on.

With Chloe's body gone a thousand memories flooded the young boy. All the things he had ever said to her or heard her say came to his mind. Her voice vibrated with the flow of his thoughts. He felt as if his bones were crumbling inside him; that his lungs could not find enough air to keep his heart beating; that his heart did not want to beat. For the first time in his short life he hated life. He hated war. He hated being what he was, and doing what he did. He had no friends. Needed no allies. Wanted no part of this place or this war. He had been taught a great deal about his purpose. He knew he had been designed but he also knew no one could design his feelings. He was his own person. Others may have given him birth, named him and chosen his time to live but he would choose his own responses to the torture of loss, to the fire of war and the stench of Crilodach. He would not mourn. Mourning was for others.

Shaking, Demeter rose and turned slowly away from the place where Chloe had fallen. All trace of her was gone. He held his arms as if he could still feel where her head had been and looking down on his knee, he saw a spot of blood. Her precious blood, but that too Trecrogo took until across the parapet you would never know there had just been a battle. Trecrogo's stones were as they had always been. Only the defenders were shattered.

Around him stood those who had just fought for the lives of millions to be born in a new universe who would never know their names, or hear of this fortress, or wonder at the child who could no longer cry. As he looked around him he could barely see three people of the same species in all three hundred that stood waiting for some command, or call to action, or attack. They had their sorrows, their losses, their

Demeter holds Chloe

way of mourning. All these species who had stood against Crilodach, and found themselves here at the last. He knew he should have thought the sight of them magnificent. He knew he should feel their power, their very being and be proud to be amongst them. But he could not. Demeter could barely stand not because he did not have the strength but because he did not have the desire.

Had they expected too much from a child? When the Sangyma planned their strategies had they thought how the effort could break the minds of their own allies, expecting people to do more than any one person could? In hiding their intentions from Crilodach they had left their own friends open to greater pain and greater sorrow, for Its anger had no boundaries.

He wondered where her body had gone. He could not feel her presence in Trecrogo. As the fortress swept towards Zaqui, he saw the same trail of atoms swirling that Lilah and Tethval were watching from Crilodach's armada. And there, ahead of them, similar streams of atoms joined, all heading to one place. The very atoms of the dead had been ripped up and flowed to where they were all going.

He listlessly turned his throbbing head and there in front of him, like a signpost, like an order barked out across the noise and roar of a battlefield that only one soldier hears, like a flashing neon light calling him to enter with an urgency he could not deny, like an invitation he had waited for but never thought would arrive, he glared at the only set of steps still leading down into the fortress.

Down there was the place where he had first learned he had an inborn power. The place where Chloe had opened his eyes to what he was meant to be and meant to do. He saw her standing there, helping him to come to terms with his task. He knew those stairs very well. In the past few days he must have run up and down them a hundred or more times. He had counted them, slipped on them, felt them move beneath him and come to like them. They had opened up his world and his mind. These steps led from the parapet, connecting corridors to rooms, to other steps, that led to the inner regions of the fortress. All over this immense place the steps hurried to rooms he had not even visited, bursting with power and magic. But they also led to the corridors and passages along which thousands of the enemy crawled and crept at this very moment. A lost and bewildered but still lethal invasion force. The soldiers who had, with glee, followed Crilodach into the trap. An infection seeping into the fortress. Enemies that still lived.

Trecrogo was hurtling towards Zaqui, with Crilodach imprisoned within. Demeter focussed upon Its vile, marauding men; well armed, muted, fearfully threading their way across the fortress like a rash creeping along one's skin. They were the friends of the men who had killed Chloe. Had they trained with them? Laughed with them? Eaten with them? Any one of those inside the fortress could have been her murderer.

He felt them. He listened to them. Thousands of soldiers. Thousands of targets. Tens of thousands. All the repulsive trash of a repulsive leader. He smelled them. He saw them in his head. Their armour reeked of the forges of Ghirzanben. Their clad feet did not clatter so exuberantly as when they first entered Trecrogo but they still made a loud noise. Their breathing was more measured now they were not running. Lips that were dry, eyes full of watchfulness, heavy, perspiring hands and even heavier weapons. He could feel how heavy they were. They held themselves as men expecting an attack at any second. They clustered together in the small groups they now found themselves in, so efficiently had Trecrogo pruned them down and kept them apart.

Demeter counted them. All sixty thousand seven hundred and eighteen of them. He did not even consider why they were still alive because he knew the bears had planned for many but had no idea how many would get inside. Certainly high numbers were to be expected but they left the exact details of how to deal with whoever entered with Crilodach, to the defenders of the fortress. If, in fact, they had to deal with them. For the bears did not know where in the battle Crilodach would gain entry to the fortress. They did not know if the trap would even work.

In an instant Demeter knew what he wanted to do.

With a sudden leap, unexpected in someone who had been almost immobile for over an hour, he touched stones with his feet which gave new strength in his legs. He ran to the stairwell, jumping down to the floor below in one go. Gone in a twinkling. The others realized his presence had vanished from the parapet, without seeing him go, with those refined instincts that tell us when someone leaves a dark room, as if they instinctively knew there was one less heartbeat nearby. They looked up from their own silent thoughts. Their own tiredness dissipating with the sudden fear that they were being attacked and needed to be called to arms. But, finding all was quiet, their own sorrows pressed heavily on their minds once more and they settled back into their waiting, into their quietness, into that moment of awareness after a battle when the living know they have survived but as yet do not know why or how. There is no terror in dying or living in war but there is an equal amount of pain in both.

Only one of them moved to the staircase to follow Demeter. Only one of them understood what was in the boy's mind because he had been watching Demeter since he charged out of the Rounds and through the massed ranks of the enemy to be saved by a child whose power seemed incredible. He had seen him fell Rataplan though the general towered above him and swung with the full force of his immense body, such a stroke that had killed hundreds. He had seen the child rip through Rataplan as if he were a polystyrene doll. He had seen the change in Demeter's face as he looked at the stairs. No longer a child fighting for tears and mourning a friend, but an enraged animal. Several of the Brujans Midrak had fought had looked the same. Utterly savage in their determination to carry out their orders. Fulminar was strangely quiet though, as if he already knew what was going to happen. As if he agreed.

Knowing what Demeter was going to do, Midrak followed him at a run all tiredness shaken from his shoulders as he hurried down the steps. The corridors closest to the stairwell were empty but Trecrogo was still changing all the time and once inside he would find following him hard unless the fortress helped him. He thought he could keep up with the boy but he was wrong. Trecrogo was going to help Demeter. The fortress would not harm Midrak nor throw him into a nest of the enemy, but Trecrogo did not want Midrak and Demeter to meet just yet. Fulminar knew why the fortress wanted them kept apart.

Trecrogo was a set of endless gears like a Tetris that played so quickly that within seconds Demeter and Midrak were running along different, parallel corridors, parted from each other by thick stones that themselves changed, making new corridors, new turnings, new stairs, every step they took. Midrak was soon as lost as any of the enemy running forward, listening for the slightest sound, hoping for the merest clue as to where to go but unlike the enemy, Midrak found he never had to make a choice. There was always just one direction to turn, one set of stairs to follow. Unlike Crilodach's armada Demeter and Midrak could see what the fortress was doing. Midrak shouted out Demeter's name. The boy heard him, like a far off, persistent whisper he refused to answer.

Midrak could not stop him but he felt the pain of the boy as he ran. Ceaselessly ran. Angrily ran. Knowing that nothing he did would heal his pain or bring Chloe back. Midrak called out as loudly as he could, stopping every so often to draw enough breath to give a bellow, but his voice, dampened by Trecrogo, did not stop Demeter. Midrak knew that Trecrogo had the power to send Demeter anywhere within these walls, for the boy might have wielded power but he did not decide on all the changes the fortress made. Midrak battled for spells to help him but the spells that held the stones together misdirected him at every turn.

The fortress was angry and getting tired. The fortress wanted to prune down the responsibilities of managing so many enemies. Keeping Midrak away from Demeter was easy. Keeping Midrak away from the enemy was harder. Keeping the enemy away from each other was even harder. Fighting these three things, the fortress, the long–thoughts of the bears and Demeter, Midrak knew he was beaten before he started but he kept on running hoping to be able to do some good and the fortress, knowing the pain in the child was uncontrollable, kept Midrak close enough to handle the crisis that was coming.

The boy found the first group of men, thirty strong, walking in single file towards him. They were terrified to touch the sides of the corridor which burned any one who was foolish enough to lean, fall or stretch out against them. The men half looked behind them as they walked in case of an attack from the rear, some holding the clothes of the men in front to ensure they would stick together. They had rushed in with such delight yet even before they could think, they were down from hundreds to a few. They were heavily armed but hunched over. They did not call out anymore, or scream for blood or even talk. They just walked hoping Crilodach would find them and call them to fight something. Anything. Their heavy lidded eyes picked out shadows in the dark. They stank of sweat. Their grim trudge made them look like men facing execution.

Demeter cleaved his way through their rank as they tried at one and the same time to keep clear of the walls and protect themselves from this lightning strike. They had seen this boy's power on the open battlefield and here, in a confined space, they knew they did not have a chance. He flew at them head first with fierce defiance. Bodies and weapons flew across the corridor hitting the walls and vanishing in wisps of smoke; men screamed and hacked at the air without hitting him once. Whether that was because the attack was too swift for them or their training at the hands of Frin-Ghirzan had never included this kind of fighting was impossible to say. No sooner had the attack started then there were only three men left standing. Demeter looked at them. They knew what was going to happen. Not one of them asked for mercy. Fulminar felt what was happening. Even Sangyma have scores to settle. He said nothing to Midrak.

Midrak came upon the slaughter a few seconds after Demeter had left them behind to carry on his assault. He shouted out for the boy. He touched the walls without fear. He stepped over the vanishing bodies that were so freshly slain they did not even smell of death.

Wherever Demeter found these men, and he found them everywhere, at every turning, on every set of steps, screaming only one name in his head, he hacked and bled them dry with a violence even he found astonishing when he looked back. He was not fighting them, he was harvesting them. Cutting them in half even as their weapons hewed at his body which was impervious to their strikes. Dying men grabbed at his ankles and the light from his fingers sliced their arms away as he strode forward, angry at being slowed down even for a moment. Trecrogo gobbled them all up as they died. No matter how many there were, ten, thirty, even fifty at a time, they did not stand a chance. Now and then some of them found a voice. Tried to surrender to this fearsome enemy. Surrender was not part of their training but they had seen men and women surrender to Rataplan. They had seen that sometimes he let them live. They did not know why. Was Crilodach looking for particular fighters or breeding stock? Did Rataplan have other plans for them or was he feeling generous? All they knew was sometimes, some people lived who lost in battle.

But such hopes were pointless with Demeter. His steps were too assured; the pain ground into his heart by her loss, blotted out all reason; his emptiness was to be seeking one person to be with him who would never be with him again. Her name and her face was all he saw. The helmets and obscured faces of these men were no more than an annoyance. He would not have heard them if they had all shouted out their surrender at the same time. He would not have stopped if he had met them on an open battlefield. He could not stop himself now. He did not want to stop himself. He was doing what he had been born to do. Defeating the enemies of the Sangyma.

Midrak still called out as he tried to follow Demeter, without having the slightest effect. Panting he came upon corridor after corridor of the slaughter. As if Trecrogo were goading him for his inability to stop Demeter. He knew they gave no quarter. They were his enemy too. He hated them with all his heart but he was almost revolted by what was happening. The last men died where they lay even as he passed by. They were taken by the fortress as with all the others. The discarded weapons showed how many they had been. They were like rats caught in a trap. They would have treated him with even less respect yet he still felt sickened. Reliving those violent moments in the tunnels against the Brujans when they had fought with every ounce of their strength. A desperate band of soldiers giving themselves up as dead from the moment they changed back from cockroaches. Fulminar working with him to protect their allies and destroy their enemies with equal measure. Now Midrak's face wore the same look that his sister's had; that of someone who was tired of fighting but could not escape war; who wept for those who had to choose a side not because they wanted to, but because they had to. A destiny only the strongest could ever live.

They should be above this slaughter but could never be. This was one of those events he was glad no one would ever know in the universe to come; that a child could use his immense power to kill so many, so swiftly, without cease. He walked across floor after floor knowing he would find no wounded. Demeter was efficient. Midrak was beginning to slow down not wanting to run into yet more enemy dead. Yet he felt impelled to go on. He wished his sister were here, she would know what to do. Her decisions, taken in a well of sadness, soothed those around her. The Arvernat had been accepting because they, like all those who fought with her, trusted her to death. Trusted that her success made everything important.

Demeter had lost his love of peace. Once dead they were all equal. No longer enemies because to be an enemy you have to be alive. Now they were only a collection of particles that the fortress could send to Zaqui.

"Why do you let him do this?" called out Midrak, but the fortress gave him no answer. "Why do you show me?" he called again. Again no answer.

Fulminar also said nothing but Midrak began to understand. He touched the sides of the corridor and he felt them trembling. For the first time he wondered if Trecrogo had something to fear. Maybe a part of the fortress was alive. Maybe a part did not want to be destroyed. Maybe Trecrogo just wanted to see the enemy wiped from these corridors because like the bears, Trecrogo was tired of them, revolted by their presence, confused by their animosity. Everything, everyone and every bejal was tired. Tiredness diminished them all. Midrak wiped his eyes and moved on through the dead, to find Demeter. Hoping he would be round the next corridor or on the next set of steps. But Demeter was outstripping him in this race. He did not know where he was. Maybe the fortress would never let them meet.

In that imperceptible way in which all creatures communicate, those soldiers who saw him coming but had no idea what had happened to their comrades, still knew they were going to die. Those who had yet to see him felt something terrible was happening, clustered closer and stopped moving, putting up their shields and waiting. The clean walls hid the strength of the terror stalking them. Losing contact with Crilodach had lost them their centre of gravity. They were adrift without orders. The sight of the light from Demeter's hands or that cold look in his eyes that all killers recognize, threw them into a panic. They grouped as close as they could together to stall his assault, but he thrust his small body through their armour and weapons as if he were swimming with the tide, his arms swinging forward and back, the light bouncing off the walls, the floor and ceiling. Power that sliced and cut from every angle. Where he passed nothing living remained. Already he had killed ten thousand. Already the corridors were getting cleaned and parts of Trecrogo ceased moving. When Demeter reached fifty thousand the defenders above knew the fortress was moving faster, humming less and the heaviness in their muscles lifted as Trecrogo concentrated more on helping them.

The way Demeter ran at them without fear, terrified Crilodach's soldiers. Those that saw their comrades in front fall, even though they towered over their attacker, could only see the swiftness of the one-sided battle and that weapons seemed to hit their mark without any apparent effect. They longed for the corridors to change, to hide this enemy from them and them from the enemy. Like rabbits caught by gas in their warrens they ran back and into each other, they did not look to see who was with them, they did not care what corridor they were in, they just concentrated on the sound of their comrades dying and how close the boy was getting. No matter where they ran the fortress gave them no way out. Demeter was Trecrogo's answer to an immediate problem. There were too many men to deal with and the fortress needed to stop changing. Needed the corridors empty. There would never be time to know if Demeter was acting out of his own pain or if the fortress, so closely tied to his being, had planted the idea in his head. Which of them really wanted what was happening?

The soldiers that saw his face saw no rage, no great champion of war, no hatred, but they could tell how detached he was from what he was doing. They had all shared that face in the heat of battle. They, too, had ripped their way through enemy ranks, they too had hacked and killed in numbers uncounted. Here they were, seeing what they were for the first time, and sharing a different face. The face of the victim who knows they have no chance. A face they were not used to having at all, and certainly not used to seeing in their comrades who ran into them in their desperate attempts to retreat. With the face came a sound. A voice. Distant yet insistent. Midrak's voice calling out Demeter's name over and over. They knew that sound, they knew the voice wanted Demeter to stop. One or two of them heard so well they called to Demeter by name as they tried to surrender.

Now there were only three thousand men left and still the boy's pain was unquenchable. Midrak was walking, now sure the fortress was keeping him close to the boy but preventing his seeing him. He was almost too tired to care.

A few of those Demeter fought against had stood as proud and straight as when they had fought outside Trecrogo. They had stared their enemies in the eyes even as they died. Many of Crilodach's enemies had shaken so violently their armour rattled, the sweat pouring off them as Crilodach's strongest destroyed hope, then bodies. Then Crilodach's men had been an armada, then they had some power. They had had a purpose and mission. They dispensed nothing but violence. In these corridors they were the ones who were nothing, Demeter was everything. That mind–breaking sense of being nothing bit deeply into every one of them.

The tragedy that ripped through his small body and then ripped through them was the same tragedy. Their screams and shouts could not overwhelm the screaming inside his own mind. If Midrak had had time to describe the scenes he might have described them as the soldiers willingly dying to atone for the crimes they had committed, but Crilodach's soldiers never consider forgiveness. They did not die willingly. They were neither glad of nor welcoming to, their murderer. They were helpless. Some did not even raise their weapons but stood still, compliant to Demeter's will and such was Demeter's fury that he did not even notice. For these were no longer individuals to Demeter, they were no longer men with names or histories, they were just there and he did not want them there. They were paper, he was engulfing fire. They were drowning, he was the vengeful water.

How long did he take? He did not count the minutes. He did not think if Trecrogo were helping him by throwing more men in his path, or that the fortress might be glad of getting rid of so many soldiers. He did not notice the corridors changing less and less the more men he killed. He did not think about anything but the pain, the sorrow and the injustice that any of them should live whilst Chloe had died. He began to grow arrogant, for he knew there was another prize in these corridors, the leader of these soldiers. He wanted Crilodach Itself and as that desire formed in his mind the fortress knew what he wanted and knew he was not powerful enough for that, and so finally, Trecrogo brought Midrak onto the same path as Demeter. A voice of reason. A voice Demeter might listen to. But right now he might also fight Midrak without any thought. Midrak knew the risk but he was prepared to put his life in danger to help Demeter. Because he had not followed Demeter through some agency of Trecrogo, but because of who he was and who his sister was. They had been born to care about everything that was born. They had been chosen to bear the tragedy of existence because they never lost sight of others.

"We can take no chances when we are so close to success," said Fulminar, finally breaking his silence.

"But to kill so many without hesitation," whispered Midrak.

"Nothing here compares to the numbers that have already died."

"Slaughter is never nothing. And to make a child do this. I do not think this is the Sangyma way."

"Trecrogo was built by the bears not the Sangyma, we just added our spells."

"You expect me to see wisdom in this?"

"No, wisdom never exists in war. We need to succeed as much as It does."

Demeter found the two last men standing near the entrance to a corridor, right beside a set of steps, guarding Crilodach and Nu–An. They had shields marked with the emblem of Frin-Ghirzan's private guards. They did not look scared but defiant, their thick legs set to take the impact of any sudden blow. They did not know how Demeter had found them. The blood that spattered his clothes as he walked closer to them convinced them that many of their comrades had died at the hands of this child. They ground their tough teeth together slightly growling. He was still only a child. They were men. Three times his height. Surely they were a match for him?

Two men were all that were left after so many thousands so why did Demeter hesitate? Just two more and though the pain would not diminish, the killing would be over for a while. He would have cleansed the fortress. There would be nothing left to kill except Crilodach Itself. A hollow beast held captive by Nu–An. Surely an easy target? After all the running and screaming, the pounding of his heart and his indifference to anything that lived in the fortress, why did he not just finish with them?

The sight of Crilodach stopped Demeter. Until now he had been a distant enemy roaring commands from amidst millions of men. The beast figure in a thousand stories; the power behind the thrones of hundreds of planets; the calculation everyone had to take into account in order to live; the challenge many failed. This towering beast whose very name sent shivers down the spines of the strong, who was even prayed to by those in danger in the hope It would be merciful, was imposing to look at even now It was stock still. It was almost mesmerizing. Close up, he saw the muscles in the beast, the heavy jowls and rough, hard teeth. The eyes, which were focussed on Nu-An, also seemed to bore into him at the same time. Those eyes that were everywhere at once. The claws were dug deep into Nu-An and both had their feet set square and pushed against the other until even Crilodach was sweating. Motionless as statues their presence soaked up all the air in the corridor. Draining everyone nearby of their strength. They found thinking hard and concentration impossible. That was why the guards had not attacked him on sight. They could not move quickly. Their bodies were glued to Crilodach's presence.

Crilodach seemed to drain the agony from Demeter as if It were feeding on him. Demeter dropped his hands to his sides his mind empty of any thoughts. He just stood there and the guards just stood there and everyone forgot time was passing and forgot what they were here to do. Like a tableau. The two guards dithered for a moment unsure whether to attack the boy or hang back. They did not feel of much use against Nu-An but they had been contemplating hacking away at the robot to help Crilodach before Demeter appeared. What held them back was Crilodach who remained silent and gave no orders. They did not want to make things worse for their leader. Frin-Ghirzan did not encourage initiative amongst his forces so they did not know how to act without orders.

Midrak came up softly from the shadows. He had no idea how long Demeter had been standing motionless in front of the beast. He alone was not affected by the closeness of Crilodach. Magicians knew well the stories of how Crilodach, snake-like, could mesmerize Its soldiers with Its presence. When Lilah had left his brain after killing the Lazab she had given him a good deal of information he had never known before which had been slowly trickling into his consciousness ever since. As if she had inoculated him against the more subtle magic of their enemies, with her knowledge. He was well prepared to meet Crilodach. He quickly ran to Demeter's side putting a gentle hand on the boy's shoulder,

"At last," he said softly. "I thought I would never catch up."

These were first words Demeter had heard clearly since Chloe had died. The first hand that had touched him which he did not instantly cut off. The voice. Why did he recognize the voice? The boy looked at Midrak breathing no harder than if he had been for a casual walk.

"You're her brother?" Demeter said.

"I am."

"You shouldn't have followed me," he replied.

"I am needed here," Midrak told him.

"Why?"

"Fulminar tells me you cannot fight It."

Demeter, who had saved Midrak's life at the last possible moment, felt that Midrak was returning the favour. Images of what he had just done flooded into his mind but whether they came from Trecrogo, Midrak or Fulminar he did not know.

"I would never let you suffer alone," added Midrak.

"How do you know I suffer?"

"I felt your pain. When you ran down from the parapet. I did not know the girl but I know she meant everything to you."

"She taught me."

"You are very young to be taught to fight like that."

"I'm ancient. A clone from the last human being," Demeter told him.

He turned away from the magician and made his hands into fists. The soldiers heard the soft words from Midrak. The coolness of his voice made them almost wish to have friends who could feel their pain, but the pain they thought about was that which had scarred their skin. Metal and whips. They knew nothing about inner pain, that suffering of the gentle that can only be born with a courage beyond that of Frin-Ghirzan's soldiers.

"Is there anything I can do?" Midrak asked him.

In the simple questions there are sometimes the deepest thoughts. Demeter turned back to Midrak. He looked into his eyes. They were like Lilah's eyes. The face was smooth, with the first lines of age crossing his forehead. The kind of face that made Demeter wish Midrak could live to be an old man with long white hair and a hundred stories of the great days of fighting Crilodach. A face he could trust. A face that struggled out of the pits of the Brujans, walked in Pângil, took chances no one else would take and still came out smiling. The hand had lost none of his gentleness as the palm rested on Demeter's shoulder despite being a hand at war.

Like a son greeting his father, Demeter put his arms around the magician, buried his head in his stomach and finally, as if released from a prison after far too long, he cried.

Midrak cuddled the boy and stroked his damp hair and felt how hot his head had become with all the fighting. A lump was in Midrak's throat. He could not speak. The time and the needs of the Sangyma did this to children.

The soldiers watched Demeter with Midrak. They were trained enough to know they were not dealing with a mere child and his father. They were completely nonplussed by what they saw. These were not the kind of odds they liked with the enemy having chosen the battle ground and their master seemingly immobilized. The certainties of their world had vanished never to return from the moment they had entered the fortress. Trecrogo had been defended by far fewer soldiers than they possessed. They had stormed in from the back, which had been undefended. They should have had mastery of the situation. Yet their side had been vanquished without them meeting with a single defender until now. They were uncertain of their next move so they gripped their shields tighter, stood very close and glared at Midrak and Demeter, daring them to attack.

"What are they doing?" asked Demeter, after a few moments, looking at Crilodach and Nu–An, "Why aren't they moving?"

"What did you expect to see?"

"I ... I'm not sure. It seemed violent and unstoppable on the battlefield. Here Its caught like a fly in honey. Even if It had wings It wouldn't be buzzing."

"They are evenly matched," replied Midrak. "Pitted against each others magic and strength. No, do not go too close. Crilodach is still cunning he would use you in some way to gain advantage. That is why I had to stop you attacking It."

"You knew I wanted to?" asked Demeter.

"We sensed you did."

"You're right, I did, but somehow the fight went out of me when I saw It standing there as if transfixed."

"But still the most dangerous enemy of all," warned Midrak.

The two soldiers heard Midrak's words. Able to understand him by the subtle spells that Crilodach wrapped about Itself even now, they shifted on their feet, then turned and ran at Nu-An hoping to free Crilodach but the few feet they had to run was too far for them to go with Demeter there. The boy reacted without any sense of revenge this time, but only to protect Nu-An.

Their heads rolled onto the floor from one flick of his finger and burned up against the walls before they had taken two strides. The faint hiss of burning hair was all that filled the air and soon that stopped as the bodies vanished. Trecrogo was finally left to concentrate solely upon Crilodach. The fortress now returned to normal and many of those on the parapet, especially the wounded, came down to the lower levels to rest leaving the parapet to the look-outs. The rooms beneath the parapet broadened out to accommodate the numbers and many bedded down for an hour on the floor and instead of feeling stone felt soft, downy pillows and good mattresses. They fell asleep. A good number of them would never wake up again, their dreams in this last sleep were of happier times, before they were lost in Pângil. They slept soundly. Only the remaining Arvernat and a few of Gertis' army would see the final battle. This was Trecrogo's way of giving them some peace in return for their valiance. The bears, who had designed Trecrogo, and with the Sangyma and others built the fortress, built a hard, tough, brutal weapon to defend and destroy. But by nature they were not willingly so harsh. In between the stones, in some deep rooms and etched into walls, were designs that lent a softer tone to Trecrogo's character. Enabling the magic to be at once seek-to-kill with Demeter, as well as seek-to-soften the deaths of his allies.

Demeter finally sat down, cross-legged. He dried his tears. Midrak crouched by his side. They both stared in the dimness at Crilodach as if neither of them could believe they were so close to It. What would any of the Sangyma say now if they were here? Whenever they had met It, they had had to fight for their lives but after their long years of planning

It stood immobile. Midrak wondered if any of them would have regretted not being able to stop It earlier, or wish to have It here even with the high cost that had been paid. Perhaps to talk to It. Persuade It to stop. He knew they could not of course, he knew Crilodach would not have listened but if It had, what a different history would have been theirs. What kind of fate did they have that so many magnificent people had to have their lives dictated by the actions of this one individual? At that moment the pangs that seared his heart made him hold his chest with the pain. 'If only ...' were not questions he should ask.

"Did all that killing help?" Midrak asked Demeter after a moment, feeling the boy shivering even in the warmth of the fortress.

"Nothing helps. I didn't want to believe she was dead."

"Whether your friends' or your enemies', death is never simple."

"I'd kill Crilodach if I thought I could," replied Demeter.

"Even if you could, killing the beast would change nothing."

"I don't possess the power. My task is only to pen It up here and let Zaqui do the rest."

"Do you know how long that will be?" asked Midrak.

"We haven't time to walk all the way back to the parapet."

"Well you did run through almost the entire fortress to get here."

"It may have seemed like that but Trecrogo was funnelling them towards me all the time. In fact we're close to where they found Mojolo."

"Mojolo?"

"Sanjava hid her away down here, waiting for us."

"I wonder what he would say if he were sitting here, looking at the beast so still. You feel you could touch It. Yet even what is left of It here fills me with dread."

"As long as no one tries anything as stupid as I nearly did you don't have to fear It. We'll arrive before Nu–An begins to weaken."

"But he will weaken eventually."

"Don't we all?" replied Demeter.

"You snapped once," said Midrak, understandingly, "Bloody though your action was you actually did not harm the fortress or Nu–An."

"Have I done wrong Midrak?"

379

Midrak looked down at the boy for a moment and then stared back at Crilodach. Here was a creature who never did anything Midrak would have considered to be right, but by Its own rules It was never wrong.

"In killing your enemies you mean?"

"In killing them without seeking their surrender."

"They came to destroy us," said Midrak.

"Some of them tried to surrender. They called my name after they heard you shout for me."

Midrak knew that for Demeter to admit this to him was very difficult. The boy was going over each and every fight he had just fought. Fulminar suggested they could not allow him to despair over his actions.

"You saw them surrendering?" he asked softly.

"I saw some throw away their weapons. I saw some begging on their knees. At least I think they were begging. Some shouted out words I didn't want to hear."

"Such as?"

"'Demeter.' 'No fight.' 'No more.'"

The words hanged between them in the quietness, spoken by Demeter almost exactly as he had heard them in their coarse voices, dry and raw with fear.

"How could you have taken their surrender alone, when you needed to move on and find more of them? You had no support from your allies."

"I could've called to the others. There are some not sleeping. I didn't have to act alone. I could've sent them to other rooms with a flick of a wrist and locked the doors. They had already disarmed themselves."

"I think Trecrogo wanted you to act against them."

"You do?" Demeter asked.

"The fortress kept me away from you though I tried calling out to get you to stop. I couldn't have been far away since I met with you here within minutes of your arriving."

"You may be right. Trecrogo feels much lighter now they have all gone."

"Do you think you did wrong?" asked Midrak.

"I'm tired of thinking, Midrak. I felt so powerful when this fortress gave me knowledge. Did you see what I could do, the armies I could stop? The light at my fingertips could illumine or destroy. I was charged with great responsibility, I was an integral part of Trecrogo. Without me this place could not have worked. Lilah trusted me. Copret looked to me for support. Yet I could not help my friends. I could not protect Copret, I could not save Chloe, I didn't get to you before half your numbers were hacked to pieces. With all my power why couldn't I keep everyone safe?"

"The inevitable loss of friends is terrible but that burden is shared by us all."

"Such loss should not be inevitable."

"Demeter, saving Chloe was not your task. Nor was saving me though you did. Nor would be saving Lilah. We were chosen so that no one person would have to shoulder the whole responsibility. No one person can – not even a spellmaker, not even a Sangyma. Yet together each of us has a crucial role to play though some of us are not fully aware of what that role may be. Look at Gertis who prepared an entire secret army and died in the first minutes of the battle. You cannot say he threw his life away yet I wish he were right here sitting with us."

Demeter rubbed his eyes, sat up straight feeling the wall against his spine, and tapped his knees with his fingers as if tapping out a tune in his head.

"The times are upside down. I found such ease in taking thousands of lives, and yet I could not save one," he said.

"The heat of battle is a place where we have to think faster than we are sometimes able. That is why we train so long, so we can do some things without thinking," said Midrak.

"I certainly killed without thinking."

"Kill or be killed," recited Midrak.

"I was in no danger from those men. They didn't have the power to harm me. Maybe Rataplan or Frin-Ghirzan would have had a surprise or two but not the armada."

"You think I have not killed in my time?"

"I came here unaware of what I was, Midrak. I learned. I learned all that could be taught in a short time. The bears knew they had to teach me the difference between warring and murder, I thought I'd learned their lesson but I was wrong."

"If you have judged yourself, you hardly need me to express an opinion."

"Crilodach didn't bring war to us, he brought madness. Its own madness worked out in Its general and Its armada. We stood against It because we didn't believe in Its madness."

"You are not mad," said Midrak.

"I was. From the moment she died until I stood here and

looked at It and realized that I too, could become like It if I didn't stop."

"Impossible."

"Not impossible if you have lost all you loved," said Demeter.

"All loves will be lost. Our only wish is that those who evolve after us have a chance to love in their turn."

"Maybe the men I killed also loved."

"Crilodach has never loved. If they were ever given the chance I am sure they did, but Frin-Ghirzan's hands stretch far and he takes them young. Their task is always to kill without feeling. They do not marry. They breed only when allowed. If they have a residue of love in them the feeling must pierce them like a poison dart infusing them with regrets that can never heal," said Midrak.

"What would you have done down here if you'd been me?"

"None of us can live another's life."

"I want the truth. I want to know. I have a lot of blood on my hands right now. I want to understand how you feel about that."

"The important thing is how you feel about that."

"I feel you would've made them surrender. However hurt you were you'd not have forgotten we're better than our enemies. Because you felt like that you were impelled to follow me in the first place. To stop me before I destroyed not just the enemy, but myself. Before I became someone Chloe would have loathed."

"I may have taken their surrender but then they may well have attacked me and killed me. Your way is safer."

"There's no 'may' Midrak. You fought the Brujans in the pits below, you've been in the very heart of Damkina, you know they don't surrender without trying to gain some advantage. They wouldn't have surrendered to you for all your asking."

"Why not?"

"Because they'd have felt they had a chance against you and better to fight you than be called cowards. They were nearly all scared of me. Scared of the fortress. Scared of not being in larger groups and not having Crilodach in sight. I knew they didn't have a chance. Trecrogo knew they didn't have a chance. In these corridors we've stopped Crilodach, what chance would any of Its armada have against me?"

"The power to kill is not the strongest power in our

universe."

"Mine might be."

"If you had taken their surrenders, you would have taken longer to deal with them than the time we have left before Zaqui."

"Maybe not all of them. Some would have lived on."

"But all of them would have fought someone else if they had the chance. Their powerlessness before you made them fear for their lives. You cleansed the fortress of our enemies leaving us to deal with Crilodach alone, which makes our task less complicated. Some may say you played out a good strategy since we can be sure Its armada will attack us again before the end. We can concentrate on one battle front. What if those two guards had worked out they could attack Nu–An and you had not been here? What if Nu–An had fallen?"

"We'd have failed," Demeter said.

"And Crilodach would have been free with his thousands to kill us from within. Would It have taken our surrender?"

"No. It would not," said Demeter, feeling his actions were not quite so bad as he had begun to think, "I'm glad they're all gone but I didn't fight for Lilah or the cause, I fought because I wanted revenge."

"I will not judge you for that. Any one of them would have killed any one of us given the chance. Not one of them would have sat down afterwards and thought for a second they had done anything wrong. That is the difference between them and us."

"Not much of a difference."

"A huge difference Demeter. They revel in what they are, we wish only that they could all have been wiser."

"If the only person who will judge my actions is myself and I don't trust myself anymore, how can any of you trust me? I've lost something. Someone. I'm less than I was."

"I trust you," replied Midrak, "And Lilah trusts you and what is more Chloe would trust you to see this through."

"She would," he agreed.

"If you need her to, Lilah will give you a better answer than I."

"We've run out of time for answers," sighed Demeter.

"Perhaps then, there is no right and wrong. The times in which we live dictate to us what we have to do."

"I'm glad you're here," he said touching Midrak's arm, "I'd have sat here without moving if I had had no one to talk to."

The two of them got to their feet and dusted off their trousers. They had grown so used to the dimness they could see everything clearly. The corridor was eerily quiet. No one else had tried to follow them.

Midrak stared at Crilodach and Nu-An. Two giants were fighting to the bitter end a few feet in front of them. They listened to Its breathing. With a frightened start Midrak thought Crilodach's claw moved, but he was mistaken. Just a play of shadow. Who would believe to look at them that they were locked in such a titanic struggle.

"They do look like statues."

"I feel like one," replied Demeter. "How did you understand what I was going through so well?"

"Magicians are taught about every feeling known," explained Midrak, "We have to know what they are and how they change people's motivations for every planet and race. Feelings bubble up in people in much the same way spells do in us but with very different results. Feelings reveal to us what spells are likely to be the most effective."

"I just point and fire."

"You are unique. Whatever a magician does has an effect; whether by inspiring awe or jealousy, wonder or anger, you have to know and plan accordingly. That is why magicians do not always use the obvious spell."

"I didn't know magic had so much to do with psychology," said Demeter.

"All magic is based on how wise the magician is who casts the spell. The bears for instance knew all about you. That is why you mould into the fortress so perfectly."

"Chloe always nagged me to pay more attention."

"Because you are the mind that strikes in Trecrogo's name. You have to be aware and focus," said Midrak.

"I wasn't made to live in peace. I was made to be able to live in a time of war. As a weapon. I forgot that. I was human back there. Like the humans of old who only thought of themselves. Lilah won't be pleased with me. Copret would have been angry."

"I am told in the stories of Earth, human beings were always doing the right thing, for the wrong reason and always persuading themselves of a good reason for doing the wrong thing."

"I'm true to form."

"The human beings I have read about would not have

fought for other people the way you have. In always fighting for themselves they wiped out other species. They were never trustworthy with other life."

Demeter moved away. Midrak felt the warmth of the fortress against his palm as they rounded the end of the corridor and took one last look back at Crilodach. He hoped to keep Demeter's mind focussed on the final task ahead of them. One last effort. He looked up at the ceiling and said, "I wonder how Lilah and Tethval are getting on."

"Lilah hides from me. She says if I could sense her Crilodach could and she needs to be invisible. The Onäis anyway are a special part of Trecrogo. I can't track them if those using them don't want me to."

"I wonder what formations Frin-Ghirzan will use now he has taken over from Rataplan. He is a cunning adversary."

"He's almost as dangerous as Crilodach," agreed Demeter. "But I wouldn't write Rataplan off yet, he had a magic in him I felt as I killed him. Deep and devastating."

"But you killed him."

"There's a huge library of knowledge in the fortress, every battle, every name of every fighter since Tegriel called forth Bofindle. There are lists of the times they have used magic to win victories. No one knows the spells in Rataplan but they say his death brings a copper-coloured ooze from his body that kills on being touched."

"He died in front of you. Nothing happened," said Midrak.

"All the Sangyma who ever fought him sensed this spell. That is why, when once they could have killed him, they didn't. He will fill the air with this thick copper ooze, changing people's perceptions. They will no longer see anything clearly and will drown. And being dead he will not be in control of the spell. We're coming to a time when all armies will be useless and when altering the way we see might be a very useful, final weapon."

"Amongst all the others," Midrak said.

"Don't let down your guard. Crilodach always pulls surprises. If such an ooze managed to seep into this corridor, It might escape."

"Maybe It would have had we not made Nu-An. He has no senses magic can alter. His brain is synthetic and he scans rather than sees," said Midrak.

"They should have made more like him," said Demeter.

"Had they done that Crilodach would have known about

our best weapon. Keeping Nu–An just for this task was one of Tegriel's strategies."

"Had we had more like him fewer would have died."

"Indeed. So even Tegriel sacrificed people for the sake of winning, and he did not just sacrifice Rataplan's men but his own. Do you think that was wrong?"

"Tegriel can't do any wrong."

"There are those who would argue with that, especially those who lost many they loved because we did not use Nu–An sooner."

"You're very clever Midrak."

"I take my arguments as I find them."

"Everything will soon be settled one way or another. I'll not look for answers anymore."

The two of them walked in silence hugging each other round the shoulders, marvelling at what had been achieved, mourning their lost friends and being grateful they were both there together.

But Crilodach had heard almost every word and though It was caught fast and could not communicate with Its other self, It was angrier than It had ever been in Its life.

Trecrogo began to slow down. The fortress had arrived.

"We will be needed above," suggested Midrak.

"This is the fastest way," replied Demeter, opening up the ceiling and rising swiftly through the floor. Taking Midrak with him and opening up each ceiling they passed through gaining the embattled parapet in a second where the darkness of the sky was the most sorrowful thing either of them had ever seen.

With Dalved being prepared by her spell, Lilah turned to Pashtul, a slight smile playing over her face. She laid a hand on the Arvernat's shoulder. Pashtul felt the warm strength in her hand as Lilah felt the aura of Bofindle still emanating from the skin of the Arvernat glistening like water from a swimmer.

Tethval was in a shocked delight. As if he had forgotten how much he missed his daughter. Forgotten how certain he was of her return. Forgotten in his constant wariness of imminent attack by the enemy that he was still a father and still capable of all the emotions that could turn him inside-out with love and respect.

The words poured from her in a rush to be heard, even as at that moment, Crilodach argued with Frin-Ghirzan and began to conclude It was better off without the armada. Its almost silent eradication of Its forces occurred as Pashtul revealed Zananto's secret. Telling them about Yaltha and Freyom and what Dalved had experienced when he had seen the sun, blazing into his eyes after a lifetime of sombre twilight, darkened corridors and mournful shadows. She had a lot to say but she did not take that long. Everything made such perfect sense to Lilah and even though he had only heard about the Sangyma three days before, everything Pashtul divulged made good sense to Tethval. Almost as if they had always known what she was telling them. As if Zananto had discovered the obvious. As if everything they had ever learned was merely preparing them for the fact that Dalved was the only flesh–and–blood bejal.

"Many years ago I was taught by my tutors that not all those who bear arms play the greatest role in a battle. I was told that those who manage to bring messages in time, bring victory with them. Everyone has a part to play and take any one away, all is lost. Those short days ago leaving the Arvernat behind was the hardest thing I have ever had to do. I was gladdened to find Bofindle had better ideas than I but even I did not know you would make the difference between our success or failure."

Tethval took Pashtul's hand, as if to make sure she was real and this was all happening.

"Do you think anyone else is hiding in there?" he asked her, looking at Bofindle.

"I don't know," she replied honestly, "I never saw anyone else after you left. Do you think we need anyone else?"

"From the look on Lilah's face, I'd say no."

"I thank you Pashtul for bringing us this weapon," Lilah told her.

"I didn't have much choice, Matymus made all the decisions," said Pashtul.

"Look," warned Tethval.

They looked behind them as he indicated and they saw the armada moving on the Rounds like a swarm of locusts across a field of maize.

"Something's happening over there," he said.

"It may be getting ready to follow Trecrogo. I must get back to Demeter, his power is what we will need to activate this bejal," Lilah told them.

"Can a dead man really help us?" asked Tethval.

"How much of him is dead?" Lilah asked him.

"Whatever made him a man, whatever made him breath," replied Tethval.

"And what makes him part of this universe? His heart? His brain? His eyes?"

"All of those," said Tethval.

"And more?"

"All the cells in his body," added Pashtul.

"And all the atoms of which those cells are made. Are they dead as well?" Lilah asked.

"Of course not," Tethval responded. "But how can his atoms fight Crilodach without him being in living form?"

"I have seen things that are dead come alive to fight Crilodach," she told him.

"Things are not people," argued Tethval.

"Although Dalved may have been dead a long time Tethval, I will show you when we find Demeter just how alive he is. Hurry. We need to get back to Trecrogo before Crilodach makes Its final assault."

"The tumult over there is already over," said Pashtul.

Lilah looked up. She had not taken a great interest in the fight because she had a good idea of what was going on but she knew she needed to know what was coming to fight them on the last battleground. The armada was gone. They had never left the Rounds.

"The time has arrived to let Crilodach know we have been watching," said Lilah.

She blew on the Onäis and a small glass prism began to grow, stopping only when the base grew to take all the available space on the Onäis. She smartly ordered them onto Bofindle which possessed a gravity and would not to let them slide off. They were the first non-magical people ever to touch the bejal. They were moved away from the Onäis which stopped growing and, though high, cast no shadows in the darkness. Bofindle moved swiftly and silently away from an enemy who had become silent. Tethval couldn't stop staring trying to discern what had happened to make them so quiet.

"Tell me when you cannot see the prism," Lilah asked them. Pashtul fixed her eyes on the prism floating ever further away from them until her eyes began to ache.

"I've lost sight of the Onäis," Pashtul called out.

Lilah stopped Bofindle and moved slowly back towards the Onäis which was now a stationery speck between them and the desolate Rounds. Such a darkness enveloped everything only the engineered Arvernat eyes could see anything at all. She stopped as the Onäis just came into view again.

"When I ask you to, I want you both to light your eyes and shine them at the prism for one millionth of a second, no more. Ready?" They both steadied themselves. They nodded. They knew Crilodach would see them the instant they lit their eyes. Their hearts beat faster.

"Now."

Tethval and Pashtul lit their eyes and the straight, strong beams hit the prism and immediately curved at a right angle to the Onäis. The light hit Crilodach who responded without a moment's hesitation. Its attack blew the Onäis to pieces. It saw the Onäis, and It knew the light was sent from somewhere else onto the prism but It did not see from where the light originated. In that moment of clarity, hidden from It on Bofindle, Lilah and the Arvernat saw It. It had Its new general and lieutenants with It but otherwise the entire area around It was empty. The soldiers were not lying dead, or in heaps. They had simply vanished. Frin-Ghirzan, Ferveiss, Jurveiss who with Hagouti stood by Crilodach, seemed like something of an army in themselves. There was something immovable in them, something of deadliness mixed with ability. For that second of clarity Tethval got the impression he had seen the dead rise and in his mind he thought that the bejal being made from a dead Dalved was a good thing, for who could fight the dead better than the dead?

"Where has the armada gone?" asked Tethval, in a whisper.

"I doubt It needs an armada now. Where we are going the fight will be so close we will be more able to shake hands with each other than trade blow for blow. Ordinary soldier's weapons, Midrats, Radizlain or any of the rest, will have no place."

"Where did It send them all?" Tethval asked.

"I do not think It sent them anywhere," replied Lilah.

"How could It kill that many men in seconds?" said Tethval.

"We might have had more of a struggle and taken longer, but we could have done as much," replied Lilah.

"They were Its creations," suggested Pashtul, "maybe It

had an off-switch."

"Is there such a thing?" asked Tethval, who thought Pashtul, having spent longer in Bofindle, knew more about magic than he did.

"It just has the power to do in the blink of an eye what takes us longer. That's why our plans were laid deep and long to win this fight against It," said Lilah.

"Did you know It had killed them all before you asked us to shine our eyes onto It?" asked Tethval.

"I wanted to see who was left standing."

"Why did you sacrifice the Onäis?" asked Tethval.

"It will see this as my challenge to finish the fight," she said.

"It doesn't need a challenge," he said.

"It wants to kill me now. Whatever else It wants to achieve my death is one of Its chief goals in this universe."

"It doesn't think we were on the Onäis and It just managed to kill us?" asked Pashtul.

"It is not such a fool. But It knows we have seen It. What It does not know is how much of Its talking we have been privy to, but thanks to Hagouti, I know all we need to know."

"That isn't gratitude," muttered Tethval, "to create an armada and have millions slog away at your enemies for generations and then destroy them all in an instant."

"It had no choice, they revolted against It. What interested me was Frin-Ghirzan and the others, did you see?" asked Lilah.

"The ones left standing all looked dead to me," Tethval told her.

"That is because they are," said Lilah, "When I freed my brother from the Lazab I saw that look coming in his face. He was being devoured from within."

"Then of our enemies only Crilodach is really alive," said Pashtul.

"Oh no, Pashtul," explained Lilah, "what is inside them is very much alive. They will fight with every muscle and sinew and more. The Lazab are legions in their brains. I have faced them before. They may even be faster and stronger than before."

"I don't like the sound of that," Tethval said.

"Stop worrying," Pashtul nudged him, "we have Dalved, Trecrogo and Bofindle remember."

Tethval looked down at the changing body of the servant

who had for one invincible moment, reached beyond himself to change history. Here was yet another fighter. Another victim. He shivered. Even the dead were not left alone by either side in this universal war.

Bofindle moved forward rapidly. They looked back now and again to see if It was following them. Lilah knew the conflict would last moments and be fierce and swift as this was Its final, best chance of possessing the Sagitæ. It was so close she could feel Its hunger. Another reason why she had sacrificed the Onäis. Another few seconds that wrong-footed Crilodach. The precious seconds millions had sacrificed everything to give her.

Bofindle came to a stop above an arid, dark plain that was riven through with deep ravines, each higher than Tethval, wide enough for him to touch both sides with outstretched arms. The last battleground was not a broad plain but crowded into a space he could have walked around in a few minutes. He had expected their next stop would be Trecrogo and for a moment he did not know what was happening. Lilah stepped off first, touching the ground which was hot and dusty, as if stepping too early from a train and feeling the slight jolt in her body as she touched down. Tethval jumped onto the ground beside her in unison with Pashtul and they both took in their surroundings with one, long sweep of their eyes. Tethval laid Dalved's body down and stood guard over him.

"Not the best ground for the face-to-face fight but all that is left in this universe," replied Lilah.

The ground quivered, like a train carrying too much weight struggling to pull away. None of the angles of the rocky terrain around them seemed quite right. Everything was reflecting the small amount of light available in an arbitrary manner as if indifferent to their eyes. They felt unbalanced and instantly out of place.

"Is this Zaqui?" asked Pashtul, looking round and sensing an immense power pulsating nearby.

"No," replied Lilah, "that is Zaqui."

She pointed above their heads. Tethval looking at an enormous darkness in the space above them wondering how he could have missed such obvious blackness. He trembled. Even as he stared he thought he could see movement on the surface but he was not sure. Pashtul gazed and then turned away showing an uncharacteristic defeat in the expressionless look on her face. Zaqui was a huge presence, seeming to grind matter imperceptibly, slowly turning, so slowly that Tethval felt the blackness was calling to him. Calling him because Zaqui needed him. Needed him and all the others coming to this place. Looking made his chest ache with sorrow and fear. How can blackness you cannot see, shimmer? This shimmered. He could not tell where the presence began or ended but he had a feeling like the others, that the blackness was growing larger all the time. Stronger all the time. Calling to them like a siren without any song or false promise. Without a drop of beauty. Holding a fatal attraction.

"That," repeated Lilah, "is the end of everything we know and the beginning of everything we shall never know. Into that, flow the particles of the universe along with all that we are. Magic, people, things, places and bejals all end up in Zaqui because we all come from Zaqui."

Tethval could well understand how this was the end of everything but he had to accept Lilah's assurance that anything could be created from this darkness. And yet he knew all about darkness from the mines. All about the longing for light. Maybe even this Zaqui longed for light so much a new universe would explode into being from such a longing. Maybe in the magic he knew was all around him, even Zaqui was magical, creative, a single beat in the heartbeat of all life.

"So this blackness is magical?" Tethval asked.

"Zaqui is a melting pot of the cosmos. Everything is being swirled around in a vast cauldron of intense pressure that will turn to intense heat once the last atom is in place, and the right amount of time passes. Then Zaqui will expand so fast time will not be able to keep up and the explosion will stall. Once time catches up everything will evolve."

"How much time will that take?" asked Pashtul.

"No one knows. A secret hidden in the Sagitæ which never speak to us."

"So strange, almost as if nothing is there and yet you can't deny what's in front of your own eyes," Tethval said.

"Shine your eyes," Lilah suggested, "but briefly and be careful."

Tethval did but he saw nothing more clearly. The light from his eyes soaking into Zaqui, seemed to be pulled from his eyes against his will until they hurt. He had to stop for fear the blackness would pull them out.

"What happened?" he asked, stepping back as if he wanted to get away, knowing there was nowhere to run.

"Zaqui grips everything and never lets go. The presence that is not living. The centre of death and the centre of life. The presence everyone will feel who comes after us, vibrating through their being, from the great to the small, the young to the old, all feeling Zaqui, feeling the life in death, the death in life and never knowing quite why. This presence holds us together and tears us apart, and in between we think, we live, we love, we fight. That is why Zaqui is the only power in the cosmos that can kill Crilodach."

"But this ground is here. Why aren't we sucked into Zaqui?"

"Because the Sagitæ have yet to join with Zaqui and their power still holds onto our existence."

"So if Crilodach won them It would be able to stand here forever?" asked Tethval.

"It would," she said.

"Not much of a victory," said Pashtul.

"The greatest It could wish. It would have the whole of life locked up in Zaqui never to appear again unless It wanted. Unless it controlled everyone."

"We must lure Crilodach into that?" asked Tethval.

"We must make sure Its man and beast selves do not join, and we must make sure Its drawn into Zaqui before we are. It must neither break free nor survive after us."

"We're to fight It on here?"

"You will discover the plain is smaller than you think. The universe has been shrinking all the time we have been fighting, the last stars have vanished. The only light now is what we make ourselves. The only other place left will be Trecrogo."

"How can we fight hand–to–hand with a being that destroyed an armada in seconds without making a sound?" Pashtul asked.

"As best we can," she said.

"We have to face those four men who are fighting by Its side as well," warned Tethval. "Our fellow Arvernat should be here."

"The fortress is just below our right flank. You do not have to worry about facing the enemy alone," said Lilah.

"Facing the enemy doesn't worry us," responded Tethval, "We would face them alone if we had too. Beating them is the problem."

"You said yourself the men with him are strangely changed now, and far more dangerous. We'll need all the help we can get," added his daughter.

"You have not been part of any of the battles we have had Pashtul, yet you are willing to stand with us now, knowing you may die before we achieve anything?" Pashtul looked at Tethval as Lilah asked her this. She took a deep breath,

"We were slaves once," she told Lilah, "we must always fight for others."

Tethval put his arm around his daughter's shoulders and hugged her. Then he added,

"Yet even with Trecrogo and all our allies, this bejal, this Dalved, is the key to defeating It. A dead man who can't even hold a weapon."

"Take him up and hold him carefully," warned Lilah.

"Don't worry I can't drop him. He's lighter than a feather."

"Good to have you back, I was half afraid you wouldn't get here in time," interrupted Mojolo, walking up to them. Lilah smiled and hugged her,

"You couldn't have kept us away," Tethval told her.

"Is Crilodach still penned-up?" Lilah asked.

"Hasn't even twitched since you've been gone. Your brother and Demeter seem to have become close. There was some friction earlier."

"About what?" asked Lilah.

"I'm not too sure they won't tell anyone but Demeter went flying off into the fortress and quick as you like Midrak went after him shouting for Demeter to stop. Then a few minutes ago they came back like father and son. Popping up through the parapet like jack-in-the-boxes. Telling us Crilodach was still imprisoned but nothing else."

"Did they speak of Crilodach's solders?" Lilah asked.

"Not a word. Should they have?"

"Not in particular," Lilah replied, thoughtfully. "How many of us are left?"

"Three hundred of whom a hundred and nine are awake."

"How many Arvernat?" asked Tethval.

"Thirteen, they arrived before you on an Onäis."

"Only thirteen?" said Tethval.

"Not including you two. They kept putting themselves in the most dangerous places remember, you were there," said Mojolo.

"Do you think that will be enough?"asked Pashtul.

"When Lilah, Demeter, Mojolo and Midrak are amongst them, I do," Tethval replied.

"What are you going to do with him?" Mojolo pointed to the body of Dalved.

"He is the hundred and thirteenth. Where is Demeter?" asked Lilah. She pointed behind them,

"Right about there. He sent me to tell you he was ready for Dalved."

"I need to talk to him immediately. I'll take Dalved with me."

She levitated Dalved off the ground and turned to go to Trecrogo, when she saw Midrak, who was hurrying over, taking this last chance to talk to his sister.

"I always seem to get here when you are ready to leave," he said.

"Crilodach will be here soon," she warned them. "We have no more time."

"Then I will float with you for we have never had much chance to be brother and sister."

"You have always been by my side Midrak."

"I have always followed you, that's not quite the same thing."

"You will never know how knowing you were there, somewhere, fighting the same battle I was fighting, helped me."

"Knowing never helped us to be family," he said.

"We sacrifice the little we had to gain everything," she told him.

"You did not sacrifice me to the mind-imps. You lost valuable time, imperilling everything you have lived for, to rescue me."

"I could not let you go. Frin-Ghirzan and the others have been taken by the Lazab. When you meet with them on the battlefield remember, that is what It wanted to do to you."

Trecrogo was quiet, Zaqui soaked up all sounds and no one's voices carried very far. Lilah found Demeter standing with the others looking over the new battleground, suspending the fortress so near Zaqui as any power could ever get without being sucked in. Just close enough to make Trecrogo invisible. Across the fortress just like the battleground, because of the gravity from Zaqui, things seemed to be slightly off centre. The stones were pulled out-of–shape and everyone's hair except Mojolo's and Lilah's was moving slightly to one side of their heads. Lilah knew they could only hold this vantage point for a few more minutes.

Demeter was suggesting to some of those ready to fight that they should hide in the dried up ravines at various points, ready to spring into action as they thought best. His suggestion was terrible not because the idea was wrong but because of what was coming. Lilah had not seen Rataplan resurrected. In those in the narrow ravines they would die faster. Eagerly they left to take up their positions as Demeter directed.

Lilah was concerned about Demeter. She could see the sorrow still etched across his face. The loss of Chloe was heavy on his heart but he fought through the pain all the time to focus on what he had to do. She looked at Midrak who was looking at Demeter the way a concerned father looks at his child. She had an inkling of what he must have done, sensing as much of the truth from her brother as from Demeter but she said nothing. Her words would mean little now. The hours of wisdom were gone. All sorrows ended here, where they began. Fulminar would not even share with her what had happened. When a Sangyma held their counsel from her she knew better than to ask questions.

"None of the enemy who entered found their way up to the parapet," she said.

"Not one of them," replied Demeter.

"Just as well, I think we have enough to handle," she said.

He was silent for a second. Almost wishing he had the time to explain. Then he asked,

"Can you give us an estimate of the numbers left in Its armada?"

"It will attack with a group of four."

"Is that a joke?" asked Demeter.

"It has nothing else left. It has destroyed Its armada."

"Why would It do that?" asked Demeter.

"Because they rebelled and It had no more use for them. And there is no need to smile," she barked at the others, who seemed delighted by the news, "Crilodach is more than enough to handle on this sparse ground from where we have no retreat, but with It comes Hagouti, Frin-Ghirzan, Ferveiss and Jurveiss. On their good days any one of them might defeat all of you."

"And this isn't a good day," pointed out Demeter.

"No suns, no stars in the sky, no sky to speak of just cold eternity beckoning. I can hardly believe what my eyes can see," said Midrak.

"That has been most of my days," his sister told him.

"But if It killed Its armada and we still have Trecrogo and you Bofindle, not to mention Nu–An holds the beast secure, surely we have the upper hand?" said Demeter.

"When you jumped down into the fray and left the fortress for a moment what did you feel?" she asked him.

"Anger, even desperation to save our friends."

"What else?"

Demeter looked quizzical for a moment and then replied,

"Lighter, quicker than when I was on Trecrogo. Just for a few moments."

"Because?" she asked him.

"Because all my power was focussed upon one objective."

"Think of Crilodach as you; now It has no armada to think about, just you. It will not have to sit and watch others do Its fighting. It will be lighter, quicker and more dangerous than ever. Equally Its men are in the sway of the Lazab, and they will have new moves and greater strength. Added to which Hagouti may yet change sides."

"I'd like to deal with him once and for all," said Demeter.

"I need you to spare your strength. I know you do not want to but I need you to do something." She waved him away from the others and added, "Come. I will tell you what you must do."

Demeter and Lilah walked a little apart from the others and talked. Midrak noticed how straight Demeter stood, almost as if he had grown a foot in height in a few hours. The boy nodded and Lilah laid a hand on his shoulder. He raised his own hand and patted her arm and nodded again as if to reassure her he could do exactly as she requested. Then Dalved's body rose into the darkness and vanished. None of them could see him but Demeter knew exactly where he hovered and as he took his place upon Trecrogo, and for the last time slowly rose above the parapet, everyone on Trecrogo heard a voice, his voice, tell them in their minds,

"Be strong. You will not hear my voice again but you'll know I'm here."

Within the ravines almost a hundred fighters had taken up positions. With them Refrit lay in wait, having seen

Lamellen fall to the thrust of a Stagete. Mojolo wondered if she should join them, but something told her to stay on the edge of the plain. She was not feeling well.

"Seems odd hiding our secret weapon," Mojolo told Pashtul, shrugging as she saw Dalved being moved away.

"The longer we keep him secret the better," Pashtul told her. "We'll only have one chance to use him. One moment in the entire history of the universe that will make the difference between us winning or losing."

Mojolo gripped her chest and winced.

"What's wrong?" asked Pashtul, putting out her hand and grabbing Mojolo's arm to steady her.

"I don't know. Feels very uncomfortable as if something wants to get out. I think my bones ache still from all that time lying down. I've had this feeling since I woke up and thought I'd get better, but I've been getting worse. Maybe I've been exerting myself too much."

"Hardly a choice," smiled Pashtul. "Do you need ..."

"Help? No. As long as I can stand, I can fight. I just hope I don't double up in pain in the battle. I'd make an easy target."

"You don't look at all well," Midrak told her, joining them.

"I'm fine. Both of you leave me be."

"You're not fighting on Trecrogo?" Pashtul asked him.

"The fight will be down here. Trecrogo is best left to Demeter and Dalved.

"Do you know what Dalved can do against Crilodach?" asked Mojolo.

"No," replied Midrak. "Neither does Fulminar. However his even being here is nothing short of miraculous."

"Are you all ready?" called Lilah running over.

"We're all too close together," warned her brother.

"There's nothing we can do about that," said his sister.

"I guess Tegriel must have had success in the past," said Midrak. "Since we are still fighting and we are all here."

"I guess he must," agreed Lilah.

"Look," shouted Mojolo.

The fighters lying in wait in the ravine gripped their weapons and lowered their heads to keep out of sight as long as possible. The others stood slightly apart from each other staring at the approaching enemy.

Like some cheerless remnant of a distant star with an unimpeded instinct to destroy, Crilodach hit the ground with a loud thump that, strangely, did not make the plain tremble, adding to Midrak's sense that this was unreal. The Round upon which It had travelled broke up and swirled towards Zaqui mimicking a swarm of bees setting out to start a new hive. From Its sides, as if they had been part of It, Rataplan and Frin-Ghirzan stepped out whilst Jurveiss and Ferveiss strode forward as soon as they landed. Midrak especially noticed their glassy skin, gritted teeth and wild, blinkless eyes. That, but for Lilah, would have been his fate. He did not worry about what would happen to him now, he and Fulminar had escaped the Lazab and that made him feel he was already victorious.

Lilah was shocked to see Rataplan but as she noted within a split second his body was not healed, Crilodach had replaced his spine and infected him with Lazab for their cruel ability to manipulate the dead. His movements were not fluid. Crilodach would never have bothered with him unless he still possessed the weapon that could be used against them. She looked at the fighters in the ravines. She gripped Bofindle with the anger of the ages in every muscle.

Since Ferveiss' and Jurveiss' fathers had been freed and their filial, mental connection had been remade, they had been seeing visions. Much of their dragon selves was being reborn though Jurveiss had lost his visions since the death of his father Clevian. The dragon minds were something which the Lazab were finding difficult to overcome because many of their thoughts had come from another mind outside of their control.

Hagouti was still himself, his own eyes streaming with pain as Crilodach refused to let him change from his solid form as punishment. It guessed his treachery. But even in his pain he had the sense to avoid Lilah. He was confused. He knew he should fight for his master but Lilah had not lied to him. There were Sagitæ here. If he chose the wrong side now he would die. He didn't see any irony in the greatest harbinger of death being afraid to die.

Midrak and the others looked at their enemies, waiting for the first blow. The sides were tightly enclosed, almost able to reach out and touch each other without effort. A few of the men in the ravines eagerly ran at Frin-Ghirzan. He picked them up with his claws one after the other snapping their necks and throwing them down but the dead bodies were not left on the ground. Zaqui was taking everyone without waiting. Magic is energy said Filvani and all the energy was flowing to one place. Yet even as he understood what was happening, Fulminar could not shake his ever increasing conviction that the Sagitæ were instrumental in this process. Guiding the atoms of all those who had made a choice to their destination, like muscles controlling the direction of a limb. For the first time Fulminar thought the Sagitæ were some kind of mind.

Seeing more of their enemies lying in wait in the ravine, the Lazab made Rataplan jump down and fill the ravines with a copper-coloured ooze pouring from his eyes, sending the defenders running before they were caught. The ooze, like a river wandering the ravines, never broke the banks, and sought out any enemies like a hunter of all things living. The ooze had no smell and made no sound as winding around them like a snake they simply ceased to be alive and sank down out of sight into the copper depths, dissolved without thought. Crilodach had created this spell in Rataplan. A spell It gave to both Its generals. A spell that smelled fear and reached down through the pores of the skin pulling the oxygen right out of the victim in a second and then consuming the remains. Only two escaped the sticky drowning. Those two ran straight into Frin-Ghirzan whose claws grew redder.

Lilah faced slightly away from Crilodach as if listening with her acute ears. The heart beats in Its general and lieutenants were silent. She heard the screams of thousands of questions in their heads and remembered that sound from fighting inside Midrak's brain. She turned to face Crilodach so close she could see Its bloodshot eyes and the blotches on Its slightly long front teeth that snarled at her through broken lips. She wondered if the beast were standing in front of her instead of being locked in combat with Nu-An. Its lieutenants roared for It now, as the Lazab discovered their dragon voices.

Her mind was crystal clear. Bofindle rested in the palm of her hands. Her feet were evenly spaced in perfect balance to her body weight and the weight Bofindle was now exerting, for though no more than the length of a staff, the bejal was as dense as a whole planet. She was not fooled by Crilodach's thin body, she knew hitting It would hurt her more than It. The thick, crusted toughness of the being that was born from cold and loneliness. The hard, unyielding flesh. The impenetrability of Its being was barely matched by Bofindle but Bofindle was the only bejal that had brought It to Its knees. Her fingers tapped lightly for in this moment the fastest, smallest spell would find a weakness better than a giant one.

That they were all here at all was a victory of sorts but this was not the victory she wanted. Only one victory would suffice. Only one victory mattered. It saw the claw of her hand and knew she had brought Copret's being to this battleground. It hated their loyalty to each other more now than before. It loathed their love for each other. These Sangyma with their sickly honour, their vile comradeship and their disease ridden honesty. Crilodach struck out at her as if she had been them all.

Mojolo could not bear the pain in her body anymore and to distract herself she attacked Rataplan even as he jumped out of the ravine tottering like a drunk for the spell had seeped into his ears and was affecting the Lazab. Rataplan dived for the ground as Mojolo's lariat lashed at his sword arm but for all his speed the whip cut the back of his hand as he drew his sword up to defend his face. He sliced at the whip's second strike cutting through a weapon heard of in the stories old soldiers told each other of difficult battles and mighty enemies. Mojolo threw the half still in her hand away, and drew from her back one of the arrows she had recovered from Chloe. Without a bow a single arrow is not such a precise weapon but the Lazab knew Mojolo would find his skin if they were not careful. They had the sense to know that she was holding back something. Crilodach thought It could sense that too as he leapt to grab at Lilah. It sensed another fighter who was not standing on this battleground. Brooding. Strong. Endless. It had never sensed such vast strength before inside Its old enemy Mojolo. It did not recognise Its own creation. But It, of all of them, should have known that doorways come in all shapes and sizes.

Rataplan would have held back, walked around her and watched for a weakness in her fighting style but the Lazab were impatient creatures. They could tell she was in pain. They thought she was going to be easy to kill. Rataplan would have been wary of her because she seemed to be so much bigger than she looked, and so much more dangerous. The Lazab threw him at her with all the strategy of a five year old. He rolled on the ground and leapt up as if he had springs for ankles and knees, flaying at her face–to–face avoiding as much of her hair as he could. But in their more cramped battleground he had come up not a foot away from Midrak. Midrak had the advantage of taking in the whole battleground in one go in his mind and with an almost instinctive blow from his left arm, strengthened by Fulminar turning the skin momentarily to metal, he unbalanced Rataplan as he stood up and sent him flying onto his already broken back from where the Lazab struggled to get him to his knees.

Even as he fell Jurveiss took a lucky strike at Midrak with his shield and sent the magician stumbling back with blood pouring from a gash in his forehead that blinded him for a second. As he stumbled to get up he grabbed Tethval's leg who was about to parry a thrust from Ferveiss. As Ferveiss hit out Tethval grabbed at his arms and then with Midrak on his knees, all of them tumbled onto the ground in a heap, cursing but Ferveiss managed to bite into Tethval's hard, green skin. Tethval broke his nose with his fist with such a blow some of the Lazab fell out of Ferveiss' ears.

There was a heaviness that dragged at their muscles. They were not just fighting each other, but also Zaqui. Only Lilah and Crilodach seemed at this moment unaffected by the increase in gravity around them.

Momentarily open to attack Mojolo's hair juggled the arrow then she lunged at Rataplan while still on the ground, thrust the barbed and poisoned arrow into his helmet and caught the general in his temple even as he twisted around finally bringing his sword down onto her head with a cry of agony no one had ever heard from Rataplan before but which came from the Lazab ripped to pieces in his head. Staggering back, blood oozing out of her mouth, Mojolo stood like a statue, her body unable to fall even though she should have been dead. The Lazab cried in pain from the poison in the arrow and could think of nothing but escape but in the open ground they were sucked away into Zaqui still spewing out their questions and cursing their enemies.

When Mojolo stood before Rataplan she had felt both weak and strong. Her body had been bubbling inside herself for hours with a very uncomfortable feeling. Her battered and broken armour did not shine anymore. She felt a strange vastness as if there was a dread encroaching upon her from all sides she could not escape. Building up like nothing she had ever felt before. Beginning to fill her mind with strange sights and sounds. Beyond the swell of her lungs filling with air, beyond the wild beating of her heart enjoying a stiff sea–breeze, as if the sea were inside her. She had been glad to see Lilah arrive and thought preparing for the fight would ease the discomfort, but things just got worse, almost as if she were calling the sea to come to her.

She was aware that Rataplan had cut into her head but she felt nothing. Sanjava's gift to her breathed out one last time and her hair wrapped around her body and then went still. Her eyes welled up as if they would pop out of her head but the blood on her face stopped gushing. Everyone including Crilodach, saw and did not believe. Mojolo standing looking at them all as if from a great distance, as if this fight were already over, as if she had a secret and in death she would reveal all. Rataplan staggered to one knee surrounded by his own ooze curling like a worm towards Mojolo and around the battleground. Using his sword to steady himself he coughed up blood. His eyes dimmed. The ooze stopped flowing. The Lazab in his head were gone. As their hold on him waned he returned to the death Demeter had given him falling onto his face and being ripped to pieces by Zaqui.

Its eyes focussed upon Mojolo, still standing. She was no longer a person. She radiated a great heat. All of them had to turn their heads away as waves of heat came out from her. Even Crilodach stopped in Its assault of Lilah. It did not know what was happening and tried to work out what scheme of Lilah's was now afoot. It looked at Mojolo and saw that she was looking straight back at It. Rataplan dead and gone, Frin-Ghirzan flaying on the ground with the last of the Arvernat repeatedly striking at him and Midrak, on his feet again, following Fulminar's spells that were trying to keep Frin-Ghirzan's new extra arms from doing any damage.

Mojolo looked at and through It, Its armada destroyed, Its champions puppets to Its will, Rataplan, broken and defeated, Frin-Ghirzan willing himself to fight against heavy odds, Ferveiss bleeding and scared at what was coming towards them, Jurveiss surrounded and wounded, Hagouti holding back unable to choose a side. She knew she was dying but she realized before anyone that she was not dying from the wound. She was dying from the magic inside her, the fate Sanjava had prepared her for. Her mind flooded with his secret words to her. The true nature of one so loved of the sea whose peerless will had sacrificed her whole life but for two days to save Sanjava, came to her. Sanjava had given her back the last two days of all to be witness to a triumph longed planned by Zananto.

Like a bolt from the blue there appeared a bear. Landing with all four claws, grasping Hagouti who was trying to move towards Trecrogo with the plodding steps of someone burdened by too much weight. She, who was the only one there to have seen him created in the depths of Ghirzanben, ripped into him with the relish of one who had long planned his death. He had no time to tell Hiesia he had not taken part in the fight. She wounded him deeply and threw him to one side. She was here in fulfillment of the promise made to her by Tegriel when she agreed to carry the Sagitæ. Stealing the cosmic jewel from Crilodach to enable her family to escape Ghirzanben.

Tegriel told her then she would live to see Crilodach fall.

Brought to this small plain by the Sagitæ that sustained her, so that the three cosmic jewels could be together, called at this exact moment because Rimfelder was riding the tide of Phigata to bring his Sagitæ to Zaqui.

Mojolo's feelings crescendoed until she felt as if her blood were boiling. Inside her was a sea ready to spring out. She opened her hands as she had done many times to feel the salt air on her face, only this time the magic in her raised her up from the ground and from her small body, which had been calling the sea onwards for hours and hours, Phigata broke free, flooding the ground and burning everything, eradicating the remnants of Rataplan's spell. Burning into the ravines and flooding over the ground in a display of red-hot power. An endless flood that burned and hissed so much and so fast you would have to have been a spellmaker to see, flying out with the great dragon Eldet, Rimfelder, the man of words and thoughts who never dreamed anyone would be glad to see him or that he would bring a kind of deliverance to the end of the universe, clutching the Gaddia as the äis flew to Lilah's side and lifted up all those still alive, saving them from Phigata as they scrambled aboard. He did not yet see they had arrived by springing out from Mojolo. He did not know who she was. Hiesia saw. Crilodach saw. Midrak saw. Fulminar smiled.

Wise people have often thought there are more beginnings

than endings because few have ever been able to grasp the meaning of everything, or the reason behind all that happens. Here, at the very end, despite the sacrifice and the pain, there were also many answers. In all the spells exchanged by Lilah and Crilodach, in the three Sagitæ coming together, even in rescuing fighters so they could live the bare seconds left to them. Creation herself was the reason. The mother even of Crilodach. Creation that, almost as an after-thought, had given them all minds and by so doing had given them all choices.

The lava poured over everything, taking away their last battleground, swirling into space and flaming into Zaqui like the burning tail of some mythical beast. Crilodach rose out of the way. It did not see the dragon, or the poet or the book or even the äis, none of which could have held Its attention for very long anyway, nor took in the long, sonorous roar of a dragon brother long out of Its mind.

What It did see shone. What It did see was in Rimfelder's pocket. A Sagitæ, not concealed as were Lilah's and Hiesia's. It made a move to grab at him and was thrown back by the Gaddia working once more with Bofindle to protect Rimfelder. Crilodach could not believe Its claws were turned away and It shouted such a shout Its beast self heard and knew.

Rimfelder, who was now having to battle Lilah with the speed and dexterity of an octopus, heard Crilodach scream but whether from his action or from some attack of Lilah's he could not say, because he could not turn his face away from Mojolo whose body floated above them whilst Phigata gushed from her until every last drop had flowed from her. Then she vanished completely. As if she had never been there. He could not believe so small a space could give vent to so much. To see below him the lava which had hounded him for ages, and realize that they were being called the whole time by the song within Mojolo staggered even him who had seen so many strange and wonderful things. Then, as he saw her vanish and Phigata became a waterfall melting everything, swirling madly like a maelstrom making everyone on the battlefield an enemy, he came to his senses.

The last thrust forward had been so fast he barely knew what was happening as Eldet had beaten his wings in long, sweeping flaps that helped to lift them up and propelled the äis forward as fast as a roller-coaster at full speed. Seeing

Lilah made his heart happy. Quickly he started helping desperate hands grabbing at the äis. He lifted strange creatures to be his fellow passengers. His hair was burnt off as he lent over time and again to lift someone new up onto the deck. Some hands and paws he grabbed but the rest of the bodies vanished. Killed by the very weapon he had brought with him.

Crilodach tried to evade Lilah but Lilah followed It knowing what It was after. It wanted to grab at mountains and crush them to dust, blinding her, using the dust storm to sneak up on Rimfelder. But there were no mountains. It wanted to call great giants to Its aid but the giants had all gone. It wanted to reach into a sun and pull out the fiery heart and scald her, but there were no suns. Crilodach was powerful but right now It was alone. It had never been alone before. Not since that day so long ago when It had met Tegriel for the first time. They had played a good hand to get It here before It had won but It knew this was not their victory, this was their end. The Sagitæ were together as they all knew they would be. Lilah and Rimfelder had two and there was that wretched Hiesia with the one she had stolen from It. All three were within Its grasp. Its fear of death would vanish as It held them.

It wanted hoards of living flesh eaters to bite Lilah's body as they twisted and turned struggling with each other, but she floated near Its side, unafraid and determined. It struck at her with Its feet, she slammed them with Bofindle. Scooping up two handfuls of lava It blew upon them and showers of sparks like millions of fireworks filled the space around them. Lilah changed into a small spark herself and was blown clear by Its own magic, and as the sparks dissipated she took her form again. Before It could grab at Rimfelder with Its eager hands several people around It, seeing instantly Its intent, rose to defend the poet. It swept them away in a moment, but in that moment It lost the poet yet again as the äis swept him out of immediate reach. Rimfelder was trying to turn the pages of Gaddia but as Eldet had said the book's time to help them was over. They were on their own now. Several gave their lives for him in the second Lilah took to chase It down, hitting Crilodach upon Its head.

Frin-Ghirzan had grabbed the äis from underneath with his last strength and even as Crilodach was thrown clear he crawled up and hacked at his enemies who were clustered together like a shoal of fish in an evaporating pond.

Crilodach turned in mid air in time to feel the air around It becoming heavy and viscous trying to glue It in place. It was too close to Zaqui. It was angry and hurt, sending out Its fingers like tentacles to grab at the matter still flowing into Zaqui, and taking chunks It hammered them with Its fists, fashioning weapons of molten elements, then used them to strike out at her. Bofindle diverted the strikes but even Bofindle vibrated at the contact. Lilah felt her hands tremble. She gripped Bofindle closer striking the heaving, molten matter, watching the sound waves send Frin-Ghirzan, and the others fighting on the äis, spinning wildly. So brutal was even a wounded Frin-Ghirzan the äis was being weeded of her allies.

From Trecrogo, out of the darkness, an onäis had swept down picking up the quickest of the allies as they jumped out of the way of Phigata gushing out of Mojolo. Hagouti, dying, found himself thrown by Hiesia onto the onäis looking at the eyes of those who came at him in a flock. He found he could be mist again and he wafted away. He had had enough of killing. The creature of death had lost his love of Crilodach and everything It stood for. But a spout of lava caught his heel and though he tried to stay as mist, the spout dragged on him and would not let him wrestle free. Sweeping him along he called out, "You promised ..." to Lilah, so faintly no one heard as he flowed with Phigata to his end. His body breaking up and in some unspoken way giving him the first release from pain he had ever known.

Frin-Ghirzan, well balanced on the äis, looked at Midrak much as a gladiator in ancient Rome would look upon a child. After all he was the master of hundreds of weapons and the two swords he held in his hands were not even the beginnings of his power, since Crilodach had given him two other arms and hands which detached and fought to the commands of the Lazab. The only drawback was that these two arms could not fight at any great distance from his body. Crilodach did not expend gifts that would enable Frin-Ghirzan to attack It from behind for even now Crilodach trusted no one, especially not the Lazab. Midrak watched as the four swords placed themselves around him. Only two of them had a body he could hit. He tightened his coat and the first sword slashed at him and bounced off the coat which was as tough as the forces that hold atoms together. Frin-Ghirzan felt the hardness and realized swords would not do the trick, so he threw them to the ground and armed himself with orbs of gold that cut like lasers swirling above his head.

Two others who had recovered from Crilodach's onslaught ran at Frin-Ghirzan and the orbs cut them in two. Leoprin lost his leg and cursing his luck decided to free up the space on the äis rather than lie where he could be a hazard. He dropped off the äis into the lava which even now was disappearing, so efficiently was Phigata being sucked into Zaqui. There was no one, not even Lilah, to witness Leoprin's sacrifice.

Midrak now felt the heat as the lava bubbled away around them. In the midst of a swirling storm his coat began to fall apart. At that moment Frin-Ghirzan was thrown to the ground by a wounded Pashtul and Midrak who was about to kill the man with Fulminar's help, found himself struggling, held in mid air by Crilodach's spell who was fighting them all one way or another. Frin-Ghirzan laughed as the magician grappled with two strong arms that were now behind him looking for an opening to strike. For a second Midrak did not have a foot hold. For a second he was not in command of his agility and Fulminar spoke softly as Frin-Ghirzan struck out. The weapons missed by a hair. Then Midrak felt the strength of Crilodach's hold weaken as Lilah struck It again, and Its attention was diverted way from the äis.

With the refined instincts of a seasoned magician, Midrak placed himself above Frin-Ghirzan as the two arms threw the orbs at him from behind, dodging them as in a game, they tried to curve round to follow him but struck the äis close to their master's feet where they exploded and sent Frin-Ghirzan flying. Midrak picked up one of the swords and sent the blade after him pinning Frin-Ghirzan's leg to the äis. There the metal of the sword bonded with the äis and the new general, so long a thorn in their side, found he was pinned in place unable to get away. The Lazab screamed in frustration.

Pashtul, before she ran to help Midrak, was by Tethval's side as Ferveiss made his initial attack. With unbounded energy and ceaseless movement Ferveiss came at them. So swiftly neither of them could even see his weapons. They defended themselves but Pashtul fell at the first onslaught her hand severed at the wrist and she was thrown close to

Rataplan's side as he felt the arrow slice into his head. Knowing she was useless in this fight she turned and saw Frin-Ghirzan struggling to get free and with the last of her strength she ran to escape the ooze and leapt onto the äis helped by the last spell from the Gaddia. Tethval, already wounded, and pulled down along with Ferveiss could not help her as his eyes lit up and he caught the flashes of the sword in Ferveiss' hands, too late to defend himself. Ferveiss impaled him on his sword and left him lying on the ground to be burned up by the lava but not before Tethval's own weapons with an unexpected strength, had cut into the dragon son's neck sending Ferveiss falling backwards.

Swinging round from the mad dash to escape before the lava burned them up, Eldet saw Jurveiss and he flew at him with all the power of his mighty wings. Jurveiss' speed was of no consequence now for the eyes of dragons are unbelievably fast, Jurveiss hit out at Eldet but the dragon's tail flicked him into the air like a ball and there in mid air they played their deadly dance, with Jurveiss slashing at Eldet and the dragon parrying with his claws and tail all the time kicking the warrior like a football player playing with a ball he must not let fall to the ground.

"We are the last," said Eldet, "of a tragic family."

"We're enough to kill you," cursed the Lazab. Eldet heard the distance in the boy's voice and knew what had happened. All their sons were dead. That made this easier for him.

"Let's see you win without wings."

Jurveiss struggled to keep his head clear as he was bounced all around the place by Eldet's tail. He knew that his father was going to kill him. The Lazab in his head screamed in fear as they could not fully control the contest and Jurveiss seeing the mighty dragon he could have been, with the last little bit of dragon left in him, wished to lose.

He found a way into the chain mail of skin and cut deep but not before Eldet's claw dug so deep into his throat he lost consciousness. They both dropped together like a stone, one dead and one dying, never hitting the ground but being pulled into Zaqui. Everything was gone. Only Crilodach remained looking madly for the Sagitæ It knew was here. It was frothing at the mouth looking for Its general and lieutenants. Seeing them dead, It cursed. Was this the final betrayal? They were useless soldiers after all and all the victories they had given It were as nothing compared to this failure. But in the mêlée It had a chance to look over the enemy. It was aware Demeter had not been part of the defence. It knew Trecrogo was close by and It believed the fortress would be their escape plan. With the Sagitæ they hoped to take the fortress through to the next universe. A safe enclosure for hundreds of their friends. Inside Its beast–self was a prisoner. They would torture It. They would exact revenge for every loss they had suffered for eternity because that is what It would do to them if It could.

Demeter's fingers felt numb. As if he had been holding onto a thin piece of ledge for hours and hours, or thrust his fingers into ice so that now they were nothing more than a bloodless, heavy weight unbendable at any of the knuckles. In fact he had just been holding the fortress back from Zaqui watching his allies fall one after the other and as each had died he had been filled with pain. He was shaking with anger but Lilah had been specific. She had told him all would be lost if he did not do exactly what she told him to do. He must not waver for a second. She had told him what he would see and sensing what he had done after the death of Chloe she knew he would find this task the hardest of all. If the battle had continued much longer his fingers would have snapped but he probably would have still stayed at his position. He trusted Lilah's commands. Trecrogo was also strong but the onslaught from the enemy, coming from inside and outside, had weakened even the greatest fortress ever built. The beast held by Nu–An sensed the man outside was close and hungered to be free. Demeter's light, that had shone with immense power, was diminishing. He had conserved all the power he could for the last effort.

Crilodach, burning with anger, longed to rip the skin from Lilah's body. But so close had everything come that now Its beast–self, continuously calling out since Its capture from within Trecrogo, was audible to them all. Demeter could not mask the call. It knew the direction the call was coming from so It knew where the fortress lay hidden. It had one last chance to turn this around and join again with Its beast–self, gain mastery over Its enemies and grab the Sagitæ from them. It could see Itself standing upon the parapet, victorious.

"You will never gain what you desire," she told It.

"I will win the Sagitæ so that you die here," It replied.

Crilodach seized Its last chance and jumped upon Trecrogo

but she had waited for Its move, so accurately did she read Its mind. Her single clear voice shouted out,

"Now Demeter!"

Demeter put all his effort and strength into sending out a single beam of turquoise light into the darkness. Not just light. The essence of Trecrogo flowed out of him. Like a feeling in your toes from warm sand. Crilodach saw the light pass him and for a second It thought Demeter had missed him but then It realized that the beam was not aimed at It. Before It landed upon Trecrogo It turned Its head and saw the beam hit a dark, small object It had not seen before, free floating in space. Lilah created a spell that touched Dalved at the same moment as the turquoise light. A spell Zananto had told her had never been made before but would be her greatest achievement. Only in these last hours did Lilah understand why Zananto had talked to her about such a spell. Zananto who had created Dalved. Who had planned in secret and told no one. Who had planted signs in Xibalba and talked long into the night with Vingura.

The object captured the light as Crilodach fell onto Its feet and the crystals in Dalved's cells returned the beam almost perfectly intact directly across Trecrogo, but in between the light broken up like a rainbow, re-tuned to harmonics resonating deep within matter, were perfect lines of black light. Like bars across which no light could pass. No atom could pass. Crilodach was intercepted by this light, this warmth. The light turned as Dalved's body turned. Demeter turned the fortress throwing Crilodach back. He let Trecrogo vanish into Zaqui, which began to spin and swallowed forever half of the power It needed to win the battle. The beast was gone. It hung in space for the first time sensing defeat. Its beast self broke into millions of atoms and after all the ages in which they had been moulded into each other It felt the power escaping from It. It was no stronger than a one armed man fighting Lilah. It was a wounded soldier thrown over the Rounds into space. It was Rataplan with his broken back. It screamed in pain and turned round to find Its enemy. It was still Crilodach. As a man It would have defeated Tegriel but for the fighter they had sent against It. The same fighter whose presence It sensed close by. This unknown enemy who had changed It, would stop It even now. An enemy whose name It did not know, whom It had never seen. Where could such a champion have been born? How could It have never known who he was? Why had Its enemies found him and It had not? Why had Its strategy with Its daughters failed It?

Crilodach was covered in fear. All those years ago when Dalved has leapt upon It just before It felt the man land on Its back Crilodach had heard his breath. Wheezing. A slight cough at the effort the man had put into launching himself from a rock onto the back of his adversary mixed with uncertainty as to what would be the result and the feeling that death awaited him. And there had been a fragrance. The smells of Samphin had hanged upon Dalved's clothes and skin. Crilodach looked around but there was nothing. Not even the beating of a wing. The essence of all that Dalved had become wrapped around Crilodach in the darkness. Crilodach roared and swung in circles. Lilah watched thinking It had gone insane. The fragrance was everywhere, beckoning It. Filling Its lungs until they burned. It swung this way and that fighting phantoms. Lilah stood back as Crilodach twisted and turned and clawed at the emptiness. She and Rimfelder, still clutching the Gaddia, watched their enemy lose Its mind as Zaqui and Dalved sucked at Its power.

"There, Crilodach," called Hiesia her eyes glowering with hate, "See how I stand over you as I promised to stand, watching you die."

Rimfelder did not speak. He had nothing to say. Then the book jumped out of his hands and vanished. Was this the end? He had seen Eldet drown in Phigata. He had seen Tethval fall. He had watched Trecrogo dissolve. He had seen Midrak fall never having been able to become his friend but knowing enough to chance his life by his side. He was still reeling from his sudden release from his own struggle into this close–quarters mayhem. And yet the madness was not over. Not even now. Crilodach still lived.

Crilodach fell, scratching Itself until more blood flowed and boiled from Its wounds than they had ever seen. Still It smelled the perfume of Dalved, the sense of another being inside Its own being. It could not rip him out of Itself, It could not free Itself of this unwanted closeness. Then Rimfelder thought he heard a faint voice on the air, Vingura, speaking words he did not understand and for a moment he could have sworn Lilah answered him. Crilodach was carried kicking out and screaming, pulled cursing and fighting, into the revolving mass like not much more than a broken toy being thrown away by a spoiled child. The only victory It had was to have survived to the last seconds, a scourge until the end.

Rimfelder had broken his shoulder but he did not know when. In the sudden thankfulness that Crilodach was gone he felt a pounding across his back. His left arm was numb. The noise of the battle did not stop reverberating inside his head. His pocket was heavy. He lifted out the Sagitæ. The cosmic jewel seemed to have a deep shine he had missed in the race to get here. Then he saw a reflection and looking up he saw a single, small bright light as the Sagitæ in Lilah's hand responded to his. He was unable to move towards her as he was hanging a little distance from Zaqui with no ground at all to step upon. She came over to him, obviously tired and hurt, almost using Bofindle as a crutch. The anger in her eyes softened. The tension in her muscles waned.

Somehow they sensed nothing was over. All was still in flux, still to do, even though their limbs and hearts were tired and they so very much wanted to cry for their dead friends. For the millions they did not know who had sacrificed so much. For Tegriel who would never know if his plans had been successful. For any of the thousands of names in Lilah's mind all of whom wanted to defeat Crilodach, none of whom were alive when It was finally thrown into Zaqui.

Only Lilah, Hiesia and Rimfelder knew. Three extraordinary beings with very different backgrounds. With the noise lessening in their ears so they could finally talk again, they knew. As they looked at each other, each holding a Sagitæ, they knew. Rimfelder would have put up a stiff argument as to the cost of their knowing, if he could have argued for anything. Lilah would not have argued back. She lived with that cost every second of her life. The loves untouched, the friendships broken, the talent trodden underfoot, the children who never grew up, the fighters who never grew old. When she had fought It their names were in her mind like a mantra that could never be repeated because the list never ended.

Though Lilah knew and had learned at the feet of the wisest, she was not yet ready to die herself. She had to be sure. Utterly sure It was gone. These last seconds were the most precious in Rimfelder's life.

"You are bleeding," Lilah noticed.

"I'm surprised I still have a head on my shoulders," he told her.

"Your shoulder is broken, what happened to your hair?"

"No matter."

"I can mend the break for you," she offered.

"I've no more work to do with my writing hand."

"This story is not written on paper, but held by the stars themselves," she said.

"How will they read about us in the stars?"

"With patience, with spells and a little imagination."

"I've never had enough patience," the poet said, sadly.

For one moment he thought she was going to tell him she was glad he was there with her but she went on,

"You arrived just in time to cement Crilodach's fate."

"I saw Phigata kill many of our friends before we did so."

"Crilodach is in Zaqui without the Sagitæ. That is all that matters," Lilah said.

The bubbling and gurgling suddenly stopped. Phigata curled for the last time, a little like a tail without a dog, and the last drops flowed into Zaqui. So long had Phigata been bearing down on Rimfelder that, though he saw the lava vanish with his own eyes, he still felt the intense heat on his skin. He had been striving only to get to Lilah's side but the events in Xibalba and everything he had seen were burned into his being. He could not bring himself to believe the fight was over.

What struck him most was not Zaqui or the vanished stars. Nor so much the knowledge that all his friends and everyone he knew was now dead, but that Eldet was not by his side. Not remonstrating with him or advising him or with eyes shining, telling him some wondrous fact about a common pebble he had entirely missed. He had been impressed by all the brothers but he found in those precious hours when they had striven to survive together he had grown to love dragons. Eldet should be with them to share their victory.

"I'd never have gotten here without the dragon brothers," he said out loud.

"What was the name of the one who came with you?"

"Eldet, but he had two brothers Opiar and Clevian, who fell fighting on the way, killed by the Irghwol."

"I know of their story," she said softly, looking at Zaqui with the eyes of someone seeing into the future, "one of the many tragedies It created."

"He shaded me with his wings when he thought I was in danger. Advised me. Taught me. Clevian shared his mind with me."

"There are many to miss," she said and then added, "You have learned a great deal since we first met."

"The dragons thought I needed to know more, Vingura told me more than I knew he told me."

"That is Vingura all over."

"The Sagitæ I brought with me knows everything," said the poet.

"Everything in this universe and many others," she told him.

She looked at the poet with Bofindle bruised and quiet by her side. The limping äis had slowly moved beneath them and they crumpled to the deck, Rimfelder staring at the place where Clevian had rolled off the side. Finally coming to terms with all he had been through. Reliving the fear as if for the first time. He was shaking. Lilah, too, was sad but sadder yet was her feeling that he was, even in his unsure way, a man of great thoughts and great heart. Unknowing what he could do, he had done everything people had asked him to do, and though he needed help, he had accomplished much; thinking that her brother had been faithful to the end and struggled through everything to be at their last stand; thinking that Demeter has sent himself into Zaqui denying Crilodach all hope of merging once more with Its beast self, taking with him the great fortress of the mighty bears; thinking about Gertis dying while leading from the front with his hidden army and of Dalved the unknown, the only ally to whom she had never spoken, living a hard and thankless life to be killed by Crilodach but instrumental in stopping Crilodach. Missing Copret. Chloe. So many. So very many.

In olden days each one of them would have had their story told. Each one would have gone down in memory as a great fighter. Sagas would have borne their names. But there was no more time for stories. No more time for women and animals to sit around and trade their versions of the adventures of the Sangyma. Adventures that Lilah had heard a hundred times and never grown bored of hearing. No more ears to hear. No more eyes to see.

In her hand she still held a Sagitæ, descended to her through Kalevala and the planet Earth. The cosmic jewel gave her some comfort. She leaned over and took Rimfelder's hand and placed the two Sagitæ together. The first time they been together in all the ages. No sparks flew. No magic ensued. They were just two interesting jewels, side by side.

"Didn't you say there were three?" he asked, returning her gaze.

"And here is the third," said Hiesia, jumping on the äis almost unscathed. Her claws were broken. Lilah looked at the body she was carrying. Midrak, still barely breathing.

"Fulminar saved his strength in the final hours," said Hiesia, "and has helped your brother to live a while longer." Lilah looked at Midrak. He could not speak and as he was laid on the äis Fulminar wafted out of his body, turned softly in the air and like a shadow waved goodbye to them all. Midrak closed his eyes, took Lilah's hand, squeezed, and died without a whisper.

"Thank you for carrying him here," Lilah said to Hiesia. Hiesia patted Lilah on the back with her heavy, wounded paw. She lifted the Sagitæ out of her fur.

"I stole this Sagitæ back from It. That is why It hated me so much. I escaped Ghirzanben with Its prized Sagitæ, and this has enabled me to bound through all history bringing ruin upon Its best laid plots."

"I am glad you are here," said Lilah.

"I thought you'd forgotten your great–aunt."

She hugged Lilah and in her bear fashion she picked Rimfelder up and hugged him too.

"I'm pleased to meet you. The dragons told me a good deal about you before they died."

"You talked to them?" asked Rimfelder, wondering when and how.

"As only a dragon daughter may. A gift given to me by a very dear friend."

"Hiesia can talk to all living things," said Lilah.

"The living universe is shrunk to just us and the Sagitæ," said Hiesia. "And we cannot linger here. Zaqui requires us."

"Can't you go back in time?" asked the poet.

"Not without my Sagitæ and that must stay here."

"These are what the war was all about?" said Rimfelder. He raised his to his eye. "I could swear this was brighter when we were on the äis," he said.

"Zaqui is taking all light away," said Lilah.

"What do they do?" he asked.

Filvani

"I have never known. Possessing them has given us all the power to stay above Zaqui, but what they do in Zaqui or after is eternally hidden," said Lilah.

"I think they're just there to make us work hard," smiled Hiesia, "but I can tell you both, mine protected me when all other bejals failed."

"We just expended every ounce of energy and the lives of our friends to stop It getting these," said Rimfelder, "and we don't know why."

"Of course we know why. For freedom to choose, for freedom to love, for freedom to live. For the love of life, the discourse of friendship, the free flow of magic. We just do not know how the Sagitæ achieve all that for us," said Lilah.

"Filvani was sure the Sagitæ do more than just survive in

Zaqui. He said everything has a purpose, and survival is merely the mechanism by which they ensure they serve their purpose," explained Hiesia.

"Why don't we know?" he persisted, feeling he was being robbed by not having an explanation.

"Because no one lives to see what they do, not even Crilodach. I doubt It had the slightest idea what surviving Zaqui would be like, or what Sagitæ magic would do for It if It did," said Hiesia.

"We could never take the chance the Sagitæ would not kill It," said Lilah.

"So all we've done is make sure It didn't get the chance to find out?" asked Rimfelder.

"For Crilodach to know that not everything bowed to It, was necessary. To stand against It and show Its reflection in our eyes. Our efforts hurt It because they existed, just as much as because we were sometimes successful. I do not even know if Dalved changed It because Crilodach protected Itself from the magic in him, or whether Dalved's magic protected him from Crilodach," said Lilah.

"You've never been sure?" Rimfelder asked.

"The day they took me and started to train me I was sure they were the people I wanted to stand beside, they were the people I wanted to fight beside, they were the people I loved. I have always been sure. That certainty was what Crilodach always felt when we met. When he met any of the Sangyma or spellmakers. If I had had a slight uncertainty It would have exploited that as my weakness," said Lilah.

"Uncertainty is only a weakness if you fear being unsure. Learn to live with uncertainty and you'll find you are far stronger than other beings," said Hiesia.

"As the only being who dots all over time that's easy for you to say," said Lilah.

"As the only being who's lived in many different times I know what I'm talking about," replied Hiesia.

"You have lived to see It destroyed," said Lilah.

"Indeed I have," replied Hiesia, "and in the process I have lived to see you grow in power and spirit. I'm just sorry not to see Copret here with us."

"He fell defending Trecrogo," Lilah told her. She showed Hiesia her hand "I replaced my hand with his paw so part of him would fight on." Hiesia bent down and kissed the paw of her son.

Rimfelder knew in his hands he held the dreams of all who had ever heard of the Sagitæ or never wanted the freshness of life to end. By his side was the woman he loved. But there were no stars for them. No moons to walk beneath. No life together, no children to be born. Before him the ever shrinking ball of matter swayed between the half life of devouring and the wild expectation of creating. Between what was, and what is to be. Within Zaqui were battles being fought between particles even now that would determine so much. And the concentration of magic in the atoms increased all the time as life fulfilled creation's powerful promise in each universe. Always the magic got bigger. Stronger. Encompassing every dream of every living being.

These moments, however long they lasted, wherever they came from, were given to them as the last drops of water to the dying, the last ray of light before being blinded, the last word ever written by a writer stopped in mid-sentence, never to have a full stop. A strange fate that all living things should strive to survive but they alone of all their friends on Trecrogo, through all the dangers they had all travelled; they alone had to strive to die in one certain way and no other.

"We've lost everything and we seem to have gained nothing for ourselves at all. Not even a chance to say goodbye to our friends," said Rimfelder.

"We never mattered as individuals. Just links in a chain that stretches across time." said Lilah.

"When I was a child I thought happiness was the greatest thing a man could achieve. I spent long hours trying to work out what made me most happy, so I would know happiness. Then I thought happiness was a state of mind and had nothing to do with anything I could touch. Now, I don't even know if breathing is worthwhile. In Xibalba I just wanted to see you again, nothing else mattered."

"Thank you," she said.

"Yet all we achieve is always for someone else. How will the new universe be, tell me that; better than we have known?"

"That will be for others to know and others to fight for. We give them the chance."

"That's the hope?"

"That's the only hope," Hiesia agreed.

"Other people will take on the task, we shall not see what

is going to be but we have made them possible. However small our contribution, however unknown, we have helped them. Just as we inherited the effort and sacrifice of those who came before us," said Lilah.

"This has all happened before?" he asked.

"Not each individual event but the fight happened before, with other people and other magicians. Crilodach is the constant that never goes away." Lilah looked at the poet. "You see in a way Its being always survives but not with memory. It will be born again but something in the Sagitæ we do not understand holds It back while others evolve."

She went to let go of Bofindle thinking her time was over and Rimfelder begged her,

"Not yet."

"I think we have done everything we can do. We are all that is left alive. We cannot remain here much longer," she told him.

"Why not?"

"There is nothing here for us," she said.

"There's us," he whispered.

"That is not enough."

"You're all I have," he told her.

"To love at the end of universe is unwise, Rimfelder. Doubly unwise to love a spellmaker."

"Why? Because you have a destiny greater than I could give you?"

"No, because love suffers, that is how you know what you feel is love. I am not free to love anyone, all I would ever give is suffering."

"I would still wish this moment last a little longer."

"Really Rimfelder? No air to breath. No knowledge to be gained. Kept alive by the Sagitæ. Just balanced here. The potential of the new universe willfully imprisoned by your desires?" She looked at him with her steady black eyes.

"Why should anyone depend upon me to decide who lives and dies? I never wanted any of this," he said.

"Then why did you take to being a poet?"

"That's only words."

"You spoke and things happened. Nothing is more important. Everyone relied upon you at crucial moments. The Gaddia was given to you, you broke out of Xibalba the second ever to do so, you freed the dragon brothers, you imprisoned Hagouti, without you none of this," she gestured with her arms, "would have happened."

"Without many people none of this would have happened," he said.

"But none of them lived this long."

"Why did I?"

"Because you can understand enough to take every pitfall and twist, every cut and bruise, every bit of hurt and still stand up and still try. Because you can never curse no matter how difficult the fight. Because you can never retreat no matter how bitter the enemy. Because though uncertain and unsure you never give up. Because you are a poet."

"I struggled through for you, no other reason," he said.

"There are worse reasons for doing the right thing."

"I'm in pieces at the thought of losing you," he cried.

"Zaqui is not complete until we join our friends. They await us."

"Tell me we'll live again and I'll gladly die."

"Tethval once said he knew he would see the woman he loved again but for all I know this life may well be all we have."

"I'm scared you are right."

She was quiet and so was he. He closed his eyes to stop the tears and he felt her hand gently stroke them away. He looked at her, and he knew at that moment that though everything was going away from him, he still had attained everything he could have wished.

"Doubly unwise to love a poet," he said.

"Love is not a choice," she replied.

"I ask but one more thing of you. Before we vanish from time."

"What in all the universe is there left to give?"

"A kiss."

She closed her eyes and dropped her head. The tension of the struggle was still in her limbs. The noise of battle still reverberated in her head. And though she did not show him, she wanted the pain of the loss of all she had ever known to go from her heart. As long as she remained with Rimfelder the pain would never cease. Hiesia said nothing. She felt she should not even be listening. Her own heart was broken by the poet's words.

"We are too late for our love," she said.

"We can have forever," he replied, pointing to the Sagitæ. "We have the power, here, we can be together you and I."

"No."

"Why not?"

"Because Tegriel said that could not be."

"He knew? How could he? He never met me."

"He forbade me to love, he said love killed Sangyma and spellmakers before me. He told me to be careful and keep my heart closed."

"Is that cause enough to allow our love to die here, at this time?"

"I was faithful to his advice until I met you," she said.

"Surely we could have some time. Not forever that was stupid, but some time." She touched his cheek and smiled,

"He did not tell me my destiny was to love a poet, he obviously never knew. I am content Rimfelder, you must be too."

"I've never felt contentment. I don't feel any now even with the Sagitæ here and our enemies defeated."

"You are the hardest person of all for me to leave."

"You're the reason I found for fighting and never giving up. Is that what magic feels like? To be inspired to never give up."

"In part."

"And we have power here in our hands."

"We have nothing. Zaqui is all powerful."

"The Sagitæ are stopping us from falling."

"No they are not."

"Tell me poet," explained Hiesia, "what stops you from killing anything you have power over?" Rimfelder looked at Hiesia.

"I don't want to," he answered her.

"Why not?"

"I have no need to kill if I'm not hungry."

"So for that moment you respect the life for simply being?"

"I respect any life. All life."

"As does Zaqui. You see poet magic teaches us that everything lives, not just the things that breathe and talk. Everything. Zaqui is alive. We could be taken, we could all now be dead, but Zaqui is allowing us to make our decisions out of the same respect for us you show to those you could kill but don't."

"Respect and love," added Lilah, "are the only reasons we have for not taking advantage of other life."

"They are the only forces that can limit the powerful,"

added Hiesia finally giving Rimfelder her Sagitæ. The three jewels rested peacefully in his hand.

"The universe is the most patient being any of us will ever know. She waits for us to come to her in our own time."

Rimfelder's eyes brimmed with tears. Lilah turned her face to his and like new-found lovers they gently kissed each other on the lips. She was crying. So was he. The tears lasted no more than a second. Hiesia shouted her warning.

Out of the depths of Zaqui a hand reached out, struggling with all Its titanic power to free Itself. Crilodach was struggling in agony to get out. Its hands bubbled up like hot syrup and part of Its face appeared, hissing ancient spells to struggle free. Its body was a mass of cuts, Its eyes looked stripped away from Its face.

Lilah was shocked. Just a few seconds before she had been ready to end her life believing the fight was finally over. But for Rimfelder she would have already joined Zaqui. She knew they could not allow Crilodach to escape. She knew It might yet succeed and would stand as Rimfelder almost wanted, in a universe of emptiness with the Sagitæ for company, emperor of all potential lives captured forever in Zaqui. Making and killing anything It pleased, content to grab from time to time a ball of matter and see what happened in Its perverse attempts to create life, but It would never allow the new Universe to be created unless It was sure It could rule absolutely, and rule every universe to come.

So even as Rimfelder pressed his lips to hers she pulled away from him, as Hiesia grabbed Bofindle with her. As Rimfelder turned to see Hiesia and Lilah swept from him. Lilah still looking into his eyes and the cry of anguish in his voice could not be given, could not be heard. She was telling him he had to let go, that their being was needed to finish the cycle. That all would be lost if he did not follow her. But she did not say a word. All the words were contained in the tears in her eyes.

Bofindle rotated on end a few times and plunged into the core of Zaqui striking the struggling Crilodach and forcing It back, along with Hiesia and Lilah driving with all their might, so deep, they were all ripped to shreds before his eyes.

Rimfelder, his heart broken, his mind empty, still with her kiss on his lips, felt himself falling, turning to see the Sagitæ keeping up with him, like spirits seeing him safely on his way.

His body flew into Zaqui without a second's delay. He no longer felt any pain or had any sorrows.

And all was silence.

THE END

Index

A descriptive index is downloadable from
www.footsteps.co/ruzniel

S

Sagitæ 5, 8, 14, 63, 67, 79, 82 –
83, 85, 87, 95, 107, 110, 113 – 114,
116, 121 – 123, 131, 134 – 135,
137, 151 – 152, 154 – 155, 192 –
193, 199, 206, 211, 218 – 221, 225,
236 – 237, 241 – 242, 252 – 253,
261, 267, 269, 274, 280, 316, 320,
323, 327, 350, 354, 358 – 360,
391 – 393, 399 – 400, 404 – 406,
409 – 410, 413 – 418, 420 – 423

Samphin 49, 53, 58, 71, 105, 196,
204, 225, 233, 236, 244 – 245, 268,
270, 296 – 297, 299, 315, 351, 412

Sangyma 1, 3 – 8, 10, 12 – 13,
15 – 17, 19, 21, 23, 33, 35, 38, 41,
47 – 51, 64, 67 – 68, 71, 73 – 74,
79, 81 – 83, 85 – 87, 90, 94, 96, 98
– 99, 104, 106 – 108, 110, 117, 119,
120 – 121, 125, 127, 136 – 137, 140,
142 – 143, 145 – 147, 157 – 158,
179, 189, 193 – 194, 199, 201 – 202,
209, 213, 220 – 221, 223 – 228,
230 – 232, 237, 243, 246, 260, 269,
274, 283, 291, 294, 296 – 297, 299 –
303, 308, 313, 317, 319, 321 – 324,
327 – 328, 331, 352 – 353, 361 –
362, 365, 369, 370, 374, 377 – 378,
381, 385, 387, 401, 415, 418, 422

Sanjava 66 – 68, 73 – 75, 78 – 82,
93, 121, 125 – 127, 148, 153, 193,
328, 331, 379, 403 – 404, 431

Sewalt 51

Sindal Hills 258

Stagetes 68, 73, 113, 121, 398

Sunpeppers 17

T

talik wood 76, 79

Tatlit 100

Tegriel 2 – 3, 7, 9 – 10, 12, 17 –
23, 41 – 43, 46 – 51, 53 – 55, 57
– 60, 62, 64, 66, 69, 74, 79, 83, 89,
94 – 96, 107, 109, 119, 125, 138,
142 – 143, 148, 154, 163, 195 – 199,
201, 204, 206, 211, 213 – 214, 217
– 232, 234 – 236, 239, 244 – 245,
258, 268 – 270, 277, 280, 283, 294,
296, 297 – 301, 303 – 328, 340,

349, 351 – 352, 361, 362, 385 –
386, 398, 404, 406, 411, 413, 422

Tethval 21, 46, 64 – 65, 71, 79,
82 – 85, 98, 104, 113, 130, 134, 138,
140, 142 – 144, 148, 154 – 157, 159,
263 – 264, 266 – 272, 275, 278, 280,
282 – 284, 288, 292 – 295, 365, 385
– 395, 402, 408 – 409, 412, 421, 431

Tobia 2 – 6, 8 – 11, 15 – 22,
47 – 48, 53 – 54, 57 – 60, 64, 69,
148, 156, 196, 207, 219, 220 –
224, 227 – 230, 232, 234 – 236,
297 – 298, 300 – 301, 303 – 306,
308 – 318, 321 – 324, 326, 328

Trecrogo 45, 48, 64 – 66, 71, 73
– 74, 79, 82 – 83, 85 – 89, 91, 92,
93, 95, 98, 99 – 100, 103, 106, 108,
111 – 113, 115 – 123, 125 – 126,
128, 130 – 131, 133 – 137, 139 –
146, 148 – 154, 156, 222, 237, 239,
241 – 243, 253, 256, 258 – 259,
263, 265, 271, 275, 284 – 285, 295,
331, 349, 361 – 363, 365 – 374,
376 – 380, 382, 384 – 388, 390
– 391, 393, 394 – 395, 397 – 398,
404, 407, 410 – 412, 418, 419

Tsarbo 248

U

Upala 1 – 4, 7 – 10, 15, 17,
22, 38, 43, 46 – 48, 51, 54, 56,
58, 59 – 61, 204 – 205, 225,
226, 232, 235, 236, 297, 310

Uriedi 51

V

Vemadi 76

Voltia 107, 112

W

Waliro 312

X

Xibalba 157 – 158, 160, 168, 174,
178, 184 – 186, 249, 331, 345 – 348,
350 – 352, 359, 411, 414, 419 – 420

Y

Yaltha 24, 26, 28 – 33, 36 – 44,
46 – 53, 55, 58 – 59, 109, 196 –
210, 212 – 219, 230, 236, 244,
289 – 290, 294, 299, 311 – 312,
314 – 315, 317 – 328, 387

Yomiel 299

Z

Zananto 147, 158, 162, 177, 278,
291 – 295, 331, 387, 404, 411

Zandin 129

Zaqui 1, 3 – 5, 8, 10, 45, 65, 82 –
83, 86, 88, 119, 123, 131, 136, 146,
150 – 151, 157 – 158, 169 – 170,
178, 204, 222, 226, 241, 254 – 255,
260, 264, 275, 281, 287, 294, 331,
344, 352, 359, 362, 365 – 366, 371,
379, 383, 391 – 393, 395, 399, 402 –
405, 407 – 418, 419, 421, 423, 424

Books about the Ruzniel Universe

Ruzniel:
Book One – The Laws of Magic
Book Two – The End of the Universe

Other books dealing with stories set around the characters in Ruzniel:

Midrak Earthshaker
ISBN: 978-1-908867-06-3
Midrak's first fight as a magician to save the Tree of Life.
Artwork John-Thomas Pryor.
http://footsteps.co/midrak
Published 2013

Coming Soon:

Mojolo and Sanjava:
The adventures of Mojolo with Sanjava before the events in Ruzniel. ISBN: 978-1-908867-78-0

Fulminar the Good Magician:
Fulminar arrives on Earth, fighting five wizards to save the five pictures of rhyme. ISBN: 978-1-908867-79-7

The Mirror of Flame:
The story of Tethval's people, their rebellion and the part Robin plays in their victory. ISBN: 978-1-908867-80-3

www.footsteps.co

www.ingramcontent.com/pod-product-compliance
Lightning Source LLC
Chambersburg PA
CBHW060807030726

47503CB00002B/382